HOUSEKEEPER IN THE HEADLINES

CHANTELLE SHAW

ONE SCANDALOUS CHRISTMAS EVE

SUSAN STEPHENS

MILLS & BOON

First Published in Great Britain 2020
by Mills & Boon, an imprint of HarperCollins*Publishers*
1 London Bridge Street, London, SE1 9GF

Housekeeper in the Headlines © 2020 Chantelle Shaw

One Scandalous Christmas Eve © 2020 Susan Stephens

ISBN: 978-0-263-27836-1

MIX
Paper from
responsible sources
FSC® C007454

This book is produced from independently certified FSC™ paper
to ensure responsible forest management.
For more information visit www.harpercollins.co.uk/green.

Printed and bound in Spain
by CPI, Barcelona

Chantelle Shaw lives on the Kent coast and thinks up her stories while walking on the beach. She has been married for over thirty years and has six children. Her love affair with reading and writing Mills & Boon stories began as a teenager, and her first book was published in 2006. She likes strong-willed, slightly unusual characters. Chantelle also loves gardening, walking and wine!

Susan Stephens was a professional singer before meeting her husband on the Mediterranean island of Malta. In true Mills & Boon style, they met on Monday, became engaged on Friday and married three months later. Susan enjoys entertaining, travel and going to the theatre. To relax she reads, cooks and plays the piano, and when she's had enough of relaxing she throws herself off mountains on skis or gallops through the countryside, singing loudly.

HOUSEKEEPER IN THE HEADLINES

CHANTELLE SHAW

For Rosie and Lucy,
my amazing, adventurous and inspirational daughters,
who are true Modern heroines.
Love you. Mum xxx

CHAPTER ONE

'Is it true?'

'Of course it's not true.' Carlos Segarra scowled at the newspaper in his hands and swore. He looked at his father and recognised the expression of disappointment on Roderigo's face. *Dios*, he had given his father plenty of reasons to be disappointed with him over the years, Carlos acknowledged grimly. But *this* was something else, and he was innocent of the claim that had been made against him.

'I do not have a secret love child,' he said grittily. 'The story in the tabloids is a complete fabrication.'

Roderigo's breath wheezed in his chest. He had been lucky to survive a stroke a year ago, and a bout of pneumonia had put him back in hospital for the past month. 'So, you don't know this woman, Betsy Miller, who is alleged to be the mother of your son?'

Carlos's gut clenched as memories he should have forgotten after all this time surfaced. Pansy-brown eyes and hair a shade somewhere between caramel and golden honey that fell in silky curls around a pretty, passion-flushed face.

He remembered the moist softness of Betsy's lips and her husky moans of pleasure when he'd made love to her. She had tested his self-control for weeks, and that night two years ago—the night after he had achieved his dream of winning the men's singles title at the world-renown British International Tennis Championships—his control had shattered spectacularly.

'I knew her briefly in London,' he said stiffly. 'But I am not the father of her child.'

Roderigo gave him a close look. 'You are one hundred percent certain?'

'*Si.*' Carlos stared at the photo of Betsy on the front page of the newspaper. Even though she was wearing a shapeless raincoat and her hair was hidden beneath an unflattering woollen hat, he felt a sizzle of heat in his blood. The strength of his reaction was perplexing. He had never had a hang-up about any woman, ever. And he did *not* have one about an unsophisticated, English housekeeper, he assured himself.

'There is virtually zero possibility that the child is mine,' he insisted. The photo showed Betsy holding a child who looked to be a similar age to Carlos's nephew. The toddler's features were obscured by the hood of his coat.

If Betsy *had* fallen pregnant by him, why would she have waited until now to make it public? Carlos brooded. Why wouldn't she have told him first? Surely, a more likely explanation was that she had lied to the newspapers and been paid for her story.

Carlos recalled that circumstances had meant he had left the house where he had been staying in south-west London without seeing Betsy again after they had spent the night together. But he'd been unable to forget her, and a few weeks after he had returned to Spain, he'd sent her a gift of a bracelet, as well as his phone number, and suggested that she could call him if she wanted to meet him again. She had not replied, and he hadn't tried to contact her again. Carlos did not chase women, and usually he did not have to. But if Betsy had conceived his baby, he would have expected her to get in touch with him and at the very least ask for financial support for the child.

'This is simply another form of a kiss-and-tell story that the tabloids love to print,' he told his father as he threw the newspaper down on the bed. 'There are women who deliberately sleep with a well-known figure and then sell the story to the press.'

'If you had not earned a reputation as a playboy, perhaps this woman would not have targeted you.'

The disapproval in Roderigo's voice irritated Carlos. He thought of the annexe that he'd had built onto his house in Toledo to provide his father with private living accommodation. Carlos paid for Roderigo to receive round the clock care from a team of nurses instead of having to move into a nursing home. He had hoped that by offering his father a home, they might be able to re-establish their relationship which had once been close. He did not expect forgiveness. How could he, when he would never forgive himself for the part he had played in his mother's death? But he had sensed a softening in Roderigo's attitude towards him in recent months. Carlos had hoped for a rapprochement between them, but the story in the newspaper was damning, and his father's lack of faith in him felt like a knife in his ribs.

He rose from the chair next to his father's bed and paced restlessly around the hospital room. 'What will you do?' Roderigo asked.

'My jet is being prepared to take me to England immediately after I leave here.' It was sheer coincidence that Carlos had planned a business trip to the UK. Ironically, he had considered getting back in touch with Betsy, reasoning that if they had an affair, his fascination with her would undoubtedly fade. Now he was determined to track her down, and his first priority was to contact a DNA clinic to arrange a paternity test.

He wanted answers, and when he had proof that Betsy Miller was a liar, he would make her regret that she'd made a fool of him, Carlos vowed in silent fury.

The river had burst its banks during the night. June had been unseasonably wet, and a month's worth of rain fell in twenty-four hours, turning the pretty stream that meandered through the Dorset village of Fraddlington into a raging torrent.

Betsy had piled sandbags around the front door of the cottage, but in the morning she discovered that the floors of the downstairs rooms were submerged beneath inches of filthy brown water—although fortunately the kitchen at the back of the house had been built on a slightly higher level and remained dry. The water had gradually drained away but it left behind a thick layer of black silt that stunk.

Sebastian stood behind the child gate that Betsy had fixed across the doorway between the kitchen and the sitting room. He was nearly fifteen months old and utterly adorable. His brown eyes were flecked with gold, just like his father's eyes. But Betsy refused to think about Carlos.

'I'm afraid you will have to stay there while I clear up this mess,' she told her little son as she leaned down and kissed his dark brown curls.

Betsy rented the cottage and had no idea where she and Sebastian could go while the flood damage was repaired. The village had been on high alert to the possibility of the river bursting its banks for several days, and news crews had flocked to Fraddlington to report on the unfolding situation. When she dragged a sodden rug outside and dumped it in the front garden, she saw her neighbour talking to a man holding a microphone.

Betsy went back inside and shut the door, thinking about another journalist who had approached her a few days ago while she had been pushing Sebastian in his buggy. She had suddenly realised where she had seen the journalist before.

Two years ago, he had come to her aunt's house in south-west London to interview Carlos Segarra, that year's winner of the men's singles title at the British International Tennis Championships, widely known as the BITC. Betsy had been working as the housekeeper there, and Carlos had leased the house for several weeks during the tournament while Aunt Alice had gone abroad.

After spending the night with Carlos, Betsy had woken late the next morning and, finding herself alone in his bed, had gone to look for him. She had ached in places she'd never ached before, and the lingering proof of Carlos's intimate caresses had made her long for him to make love to her again.

Memories of that night pushed into her mind. What a naive fool she had been, she thought bitterly as she pushed the mop across the floor and wrung a stream of muddy water into a bucket.

Growing up in the war zone of her parents' toxic marriage and their acrimonious divorce had made her sceptical about the idea of falling in love. She had been on a few dates with guys she'd met at university, but she'd never had a serious romantic relationship because she was fearful of lowering her barriers and risking being hurt. And yet deep down she had still cherished a hope of meeting her prince—and he had arrived in the form of a tall, bronzed and impossibly handsome tennis star.

For the only time in her life Betsy had let her guard

down, with Carlos, believing that there was a special connection between them. But the truth was that she had been just another notch on his crowded bedpost. She had overheard him telling the journalist who had come to the house to interview him about his success that she was 'a casual fling'.

Peeling off her rubber gloves, Betsy felt a surge of despair as she glanced around the cottage. She had enough to worry about without the sense of foreboding that had gripped her since she'd recognised that journalist in the village. She was sure that he remembered her from two years ago, and it made his curiosity about Sebastian unsettling.

A knock on the front door made her jump. It was probably someone from the emergency services, checking on the residents who had been affected by the floods, she told herself. She looked in the kitchen and saw Sebastian sitting on his playmat. There was another loud knock and she moved towards the front door. Through the frosted glass pane she could make out a tall figure, and inexplicably her heart started to thud.

'Hi…' Betsy's voice faltered as she opened the door— and stared at Carlos.

Shock turned the blood in her veins to ice. It *couldn't* be him. He did not know where she lived and there was no reason why he would be looking for her. No reason that he would be interested in anyway.

She had forgotten how gorgeous he was. Not that she'd been able to forget him at all. But Carlos Segarra in the flesh was a thousand times more devastatingly handsome than the man who regularly haunted her dreams.

Her eyes roamed his hard-boned features, taking in his masculine beauty; the razor-edged cheekbones above the hollow planes of his face, the square jaw shadowed with dark stubble, and the mouth that she knew could be sensual or cruel, but right now was drawn into a grim expression that made Betsy's heart sink.

Carlos's stunning looks and his fame as a superstar sporting legend, not to mention his reputation as a prolific playboy, meant that he often featured in celebrity magazines. Betsy hated herself every time she succumbed to her curiosity and bought a magazine that had a picture of Carlos, dubbed 'Spain's sexiest man', on the front cover. But she had been irresistibly attracted to him the moment she'd set eyes on him two years ago, and now she was dismayed to discover that his impact on her had not lessened.

She felt a quiver in the pit of her stomach as her gaze locked with his sherry-gold eyes, gleaming beneath thick, dark lashes.

It wasn't only his eyes that made her think of a jungle cat. She pictured the lean, muscular body, honed to physical perfection, that had made him a superb athlete. On the tennis circuit he had been nicknamed 'The Jaguar', because of his speed around the court and his unpredictability. You could never know what a jaguar was thinking, and the same went for Carlos Segarra.

Swallowing hard, Betsy ran her eyes over Carlos's elegant grey suit. The bottom few inches of his trousers were damp and his brown leather shoes were caked in mud. 'You should have worn boots.' She bit her lip when she realised that that was an odd way to greet him after two years. 'Why are you here?'

His heavy brows snapped together. 'I have only just arrived in England and I was not aware of the floods that have affected this part of the country.'

His accented voice sent a shiver of response across Betsy's skin. She could feel the pulse at the base of her throat hammering and lifted her hand to hide her traitorous body's reaction to him.

Carlos's hard gaze flicked over her shapeless tee shirt and faded sweatpants. She'd dressed in old clothes, knowing that she was bound to get filthy in the clean-up operation. He glanced down at her mud-spattered wellington boots and his mouth flattened. Betsy resisted the temptation to remove the scarf that she'd tied over her hair. She looked a mess, but she did not give a damn what Carlos thought of her, she assured herself.

'The flooding has been a big story in the media. I'm surprised you haven't read about it.' She looked at the newspaper he was carrying under his arm. 'If you had it might have saved your suit.'

'To hell with my suit.' Carlos's tone was blistering. 'Are you trying to be funny?'

She blinked. 'What do you mean?'

He thrust the newspaper into her hand and stepped into the cottage without waiting for her to invite him in.

'Dios...' he muttered as he glanced around the sitting room. There was a brown tidemark halfway up the cream sofa, and an unpleasant smell permeated the room. 'I'm guessing that this flood damage will be expensive to repair. Is that why you did it?' he demanded.

'Did what? I don't understand.' Betsy backed away from the lethal gleam in Carlos's eyes. He was clearly furious. Once again she felt a sense of foreboding.

She looked at the front page of the newspaper. It was one of the more lurid tabloids and her heart slammed against her ribs as the headline leapt out at her.

Tennis Ace Segarra's Secret Son!

There was a photo of Betsy, standing in front of the cottage holding Sebastian. The picture was rather grainy, and her son was wearing a rain suit with the hood up so that his face was mostly obscured.

She immediately thought of the journalist who had carried sandbags up the garden path and helped her pile them against the door.

'You don't mind if I take a photo, do you?' he'd asked. 'I'm writing a piece about the floods for the local rag and the editor likes to include pictures showing the human element of the story.'

Betsy had felt she couldn't refuse, seeing as he had helped her. The journalist had then casually asked Sebastian's age and commented on his olive complexion. But she was sure she hadn't said anything which would have led him to guess that Carlos Segarra was her baby's father.

'I have no idea how this story got into the papers,' she said shakily. 'I've never told anyone that Sebastian is yours.'

Carlos snorted. 'Of course you know. How much did you get paid for this garbage that has been printed which accuses me of abandoning my child?'

'I didn't—' She broke off as Carlos slashed his hand through the air with an impatient gesture.

'Last night I received a tip-off that the story that I had a secret love child was about to break in the British tabloids. I was too late to seek a legal injunction to prevent the story being published,' he said tersely. 'My informant said that the "scoop" had been uncovered by a scumbag journalist called Tom Vane, who believes he has a score to settle with me because he blames me after he was sacked from his job as a sports reporter. He wrote a load of lies about my reasons for retiring from playing competition tennis and I complained to the newspaper he worked for.'

'I don't know the journalist's name,' Betsy muttered. 'He was hanging around the village a couple of days ago and he told me he worked for a local newspaper. He seemed familiar and I remembered that I'd seen him once at my aunt's house in London.'

Carlos's jaw hardened. 'Do you expect me to believe you?' he asked sardonically. 'It's obvious that you and Vane devised this story that I have a secret child. I suppose he promised you that the tabloids would pay you a fortune if you said that I am the father of your baby? But you won't get away with it. I want a paternity test. And when I have proof that the child isn't mine, I will sue you for libel.'

Betsy had often tried to imagine Carlos's reaction if she told him about his son. Sebastian was growing up fast and was already developing a cheeky personality. It had saddened her that his father would never know him. Her conscience had pricked. Maybe she should have given Carlos the chance to decide if he wanted to be involved with Sebastian. But he had just given a TV interview in which he'd stated that he had no desire to settle down and have a family. Betsy had taken that as proof that he would not be interested in his son. And besides, she'd had no way of getting in touch with Carlos after he had returned to Spain.

She supposed that she could have tried to contact him through his management company, but she hadn't because her deepest fear had been that Carlos might decide that he *did* want Sebastian and try to take the little boy from her. Betsy knew what it was like to be at the centre of a custody battle. Her parents had fought over her, and she had felt torn between them. She was determined to spare Sebastian the same ordeal.

Now she felt relief at Carlos's reaction, which confirmed what she'd guessed: fatherhood held no appeal for him. But his accusation that she had sold her story to the newspapers made her furious.

For a moment, she contemplated denying that Sebastian was Carlos's son. Then he might go away and leave her in peace. But if he carried out his threat to sue her for libel the truth was bound to come out.

She lifted her chin and met Carlos's angry glare proudly. 'A paternity test will prove that I am telling the truth. Sebastian *is* your son.'

Carlos was taken aback by Betsy's vehement response, but he reminded himself that she was bound to stick to her claim that she'd had a child by him. Surely she must realise she wouldn't get away with making such a false accusation.

'We spent one night together, and I used protection both times we had sex,' he said curtly. 'Frankly, it would have been a miracle if you had conceived my baby.'

She nodded. 'I don't know how it happened, but I agree that our son is a miracle.' She walked across the room to where a gate was fixed in the door frame and held out her arms. 'Isn't that right, poppet? You are Mama's little miracle.'

Carlos stiffened as he watched a small child walk unsteadily over to the gate and lift his arms to Betsy. She picked him up and balanced him on her hip.

'This is Sebastian.'

There was fierce pride in her voice, and the look of love in her eyes as she smiled at the baby evoked a tug in Carlos's chest. A long time ago his mother had smiled at *him* with the same loving pride.

He pushed the memory away as he stared at the little boy, who had big brown eyes and a halo of dark curls and bore a striking similarity to Carlos's nephew. His sister's son, Miguel, was two, and he guessed that Betsy's child was a few months younger—which meant that she must have fallen pregnant around two years ago.

'He's yours,' Betsy said quietly. 'He's almost fifteen months old. He was born on the seventeenth of April, exactly nine months after you and I slept together. Before you suggest that I could have slept with another man at around the same time—I didn't. I was a virgin and I haven't been with anyone since you.'

It was impossible, Carlos assured himself.

He was conscious that his heart was pounding as hard as if he'd played a five-set tennis match. The fact that this child bore a resemblance to his nephew proved nothing. Sebastian could have inherited his brown eyes from his mother.

But when Betsy walked towards him, carrying her son, Carlos discovered that the little boy's eyes were the tawny colour of light sherry and flecked with gold—exactly like his own.

Something close to panic gripped him. He *couldn't* have a child. He'd spent his entire adult life avoiding responsibility.

His mind flew back to two years ago. He had been at the peak of his career; winner on the international tennis circuit more times than any other player. But the London tournament's coveted gold trophy had eluded him. It was the one victory he'd wanted above all others and his driving ambition had been to win the tournament in his mother's honour.

He had rented a house in London close to the tennis club, where he trained for a few weeks before the start of the tournament. But his determination to avoid distraction and focus on his game had been tested when an attractive young brunette had greeted him.

'I'm the housekeeper, Betsy Miller,' she'd introduced herself with a shy smile. 'Don't worry,' she'd assured him quickly when he had frowned. 'I promise that you won't notice me around the house.'

Her skin was pale cream and the rosy flush that had spread over her cheeks had snagged his attention. His initial opinion that she was simply attractive fell far short of the truth, he'd realised. This housekeeper was pretty in a wholesome, fresh-faced way that he'd found unexpectedly sexy.

She was petite, and her figure was slim rather than fashionably skinny. His eyes had been drawn to the firm swell of her breasts before he'd dropped his gaze to the narrow indent of her waist and the gentle flare of her hips.

Returning his eyes to her face, he had watched her blush deepen and recognised awareness in her expression. It happened to him so often that he was never surprised. He was rarely intrigued by a woman. But something about Betsy had stirred his jaded libido.

'Don't be too confident of that promise,' he'd murmured. 'You are *very* noticeable, Betsy Miller.'

Dios! Carlos forced his mind back to the present in this flood-damaged cottage. The woman standing in front of him looked like a character from a Dickensian novel in her filthy old clothes and with her hair hidden beneath a scarf. But even though Betsy wore no make-up, and lacked the glamour and sophistication of his numerous past mistresses, her natural beauty and innate sensuality lit a flame inside him.

To his astonishment, he felt his body spring to urgent life. Why her? he wondered furiously. He'd gone through a rocky period after he'd won the BITC, and his libido had fallen off a cliff. In fact, he hadn't slept with any other woman since Betsy.

The startling realisation did nothing to improve his temper.

'I have never had a condom fail before,' he said harshly. 'And if by a minuscule chance it did, why didn't you tell me when you found out you were pregnant?'

'I didn't know until a few weeks after you had gone back to Spain.' She bit her lip. 'I saw you being interviewed on television, soon after you had announced your retirement from competition tennis. After there had been rumours in the media that you planned to marry your girlfriend, the model Lorena Lopez, and start a family.'

Carlos gave a snort. 'I had a brief affair with Lorena, but it was over before I went to England to prepare for the championship. I had made it clear that there was never a chance I would marry her, but she wouldn't accept it and told the press that we were engaged.'

Betsy nodded. 'You told the TV chat show host that you were a "lone wolf" and did not intend to ever marry or have children. I realised then that you wouldn't want your baby.'

It could not be true.

Carlos raked his fingers through his hair. When he'd seen that newspaper headline he had been certain the allegation that he had a secret son was untrue. Now he did not know what to think. Betsy was either a very good liar or she was telling the truth, and the child who was struggling to wriggle out of her arms was his flesh and blood.

'Poppet, I can't put you down on the dirty floor,' Betsy

murmured, trying to pacify the little boy, who had started to grizzle.

Sebastian might only be fifteen months old, but he was already showing signs that he was strong-willed. *Had he inherited the trait from* him? Carlos wondered.

'I have arranged for a paternity test to be carried out,' he said abruptly. 'A doctor is waiting at a hotel a few miles from here to take the necessary samples and the DNA testing clinic guarantees the result in twenty-four hours.'

'What do you intend to do when the result is positive?' Betsy challenged him. 'If you plan to regard Sebastian as merely your responsibility, or worse an inconvenience, it might be better not to do the test. You can walk away right now and forget about him.'

'Is your reluctance because you know the test will prove you are a liar?' His jaw hardened. 'You have publicly alleged that I am your child's father and I am determined to clear my name.'

Angry spots of colour flared on her cheeks. 'I swear that the story in the tabloids had nothing to do with me.'

'It couldn't have happened at a worse time.' Carlos could not hide his frustration. 'This evening there is a party in London to launch the UK office of my sports management company. Veloz represents some of the biggest names in the world of sport. But now my integrity is being questioned. I want the truth, and a paternity test is the only way I can be sure to get it.'

'Fine.' Betsy did not drop her gaze from his. 'I'm all for the truth. But how can we go anywhere while the village is flooded? I'm surprised you were able to get here.'

'I came to Fraddlington by helicopter and walked across a field as the main road is impassable.' Carlos strode towards the front door, grimacing as his hand-crafted Italian leather shoes squelched in the layer of mud on the floor. 'Let's go.'

'You obviously know nothing about small children if you think I can simply leave the house.'

Betsy's wry voice stopped him.

'I'll need to pack a change bag for Sebastian and make up a bottle of his formula milk.'

The toddler had stopped squirming in her arms and was staring at Carlos. He was a beautiful child. Carlos was once again struck by Sebastian's resemblance to his nephew.

He walked back to Betsy, compelled by a feeling he could not explain as he studied her son's apple-round cheeks and mop of dark curls. 'I'll hold him while you organise what you need,' he said tersely.

She hesitated. 'He might not want to go to you. He's wary of strangers.'

Carlos held out his hands and took the unresisting little boy from her. He had some experience, having been coerced by his sister to hold his nephew since Miguel had been a tiny baby.

The strong similarity between the two boys *could* simply be coincidence, he assured himself. He was not going to jump to conclusions ahead of the DNA test. Nevertheless, he felt an unnerving sense of recognition when his gaze locked with Sebastian's sherry-gold eyes.

Betsy had asked what he intended to do if he had proof that he was her baby's father. Up until he'd walked into the cottage he had not seriously considered it a possibility. But she sounded so certain that he had to accept it might be true. And if it was…if Sebastian was his…

A host of conflicting emotions surged through Carlos, but the fiercest and most unexpected was protectiveness. Since he was a teenager he had not had the support from his own father that he had desperately wanted, and he had even doubted that Roderigo loved him. If Sebastian *was* his, he would claim his son and love him unconditionally.

CHAPTER TWO

BETSY HELD HER breath as the helicopter took off. After the torrential rain that had caused the floods it was a beautiful sunny day and there was not a cloud in the blue sky.

'Are you nervous about flying?' Carlos was sprawled in a seat opposite her in the luxurious cabin and appeared totally relaxed, unlike Betsy.

'I'm not a fan,' she admitted, and gasped as the helicopter jolted.

'That was just some turbulence.'

His gravelly voice sent a shiver of sexual awareness across Betsy's skin and she knew the knot of tension in her stomach had nothing to do with her nervousness about being in the helicopter.

She couldn't quite believe that Carlos had turned up at the cottage. If only she'd had prior knowledge of his visit she might have been able to erect some defences against his smouldering sensuality, but instead she felt like a teenager on a first date.

'Have you flown in a helicopter before?' he asked.

'Not since I was a child and visited my father. He had a pilot's licence and lived in a remote part of Canada which was only accessible by helicopter.'

'Why didn't you live with him?'

'My parents divorced when I was eight and my mother

was awarded custody of me, but the access arrangement stipulated that I could spend time with my dad.'

Betsy looked away from Carlos and stared out of the window as memories crowded her mind. After the divorce she had lived with her mother in London, but every school holiday she'd been put on a plane to Toronto to visit her father. Towards the end of one visit, Drake Miller had driven her to a small airfield where they had boarded a helicopter.

'We're going to have an adventure,' he'd told her. 'Just you and me, exploring one of the wildest areas of Canada.'

'Is Mum okay with it?' Betsy had felt uneasy. 'I have to go back to England before school starts next week.'

'The truth is, honey, that your mother doesn't want you living with her any more.' Drake had frowned when she'd started to cry. 'Hey, what are your tears for? Don't you want to be with your old dad?'

Of course she did, she had quickly assured him as she'd scrubbed her tears away. She'd loved both her parents. But she thought she must have done something terrible for her mum to have sent her away permanently.

Six months later the Canadian police had arrived at the log cabin in a remote part of British Colombia where Betsy had been living with her father and she'd learned the truth. Drake had kidnapped her. He had lied when he'd said that her mother did not want her. He'd maintained that he had done it because he could not bear to live apart from his only daughter. But Betsy suspected that he'd kept her hidden out of spite, as part of his festering feud with her mother.

Her childhood had left her with a deep mistrust of the concept of romantic love, and she could not understand why she had fallen under Carlos's spell so completely.

What she'd felt had been lust, she reminded herself. And that was certainly all it had been for Carlos.

After she had overheard him telling the journalist that she was a casual fling, she'd written him a note, making the excuse that she'd had sex with him because he was famous and telling him that to avoid any awkwardness it would be better if they did not see each other again. Then she had left the house, and when she'd returned, hours later, he had gone.

Sebastian was growing bored with sitting still and tried to wriggle off Betsy's lap. She was conscious of Carlos's brooding gaze, watching them, and wondered if he was judging her parenting skills.

Motherhood had been a steep learning curve for her, especially as she'd had no help from anyone. Her mother had flown over from LA, where she now lived, when Sebastian was six weeks old, but Stephanie Miller had spent most of the visit telling Betsy that she did not feel old enough to be a grandmother and that it would be the end of her acting career if film producers discovered her real age.

Betsy had refrained from pointing out that her mother hadn't had a big film role for years. And after several glasses of wine Stephanie had admitted that she had money problems.

'I wish I could help you out, darling, but my finances are stretched. I expect your father is raking it in with the royalties from his books,' she said bitterly. 'Apparently, he's the top thriller writer in North America, although I'm surprised that he has the energy to write. His latest wife is only a year or so older than you.'

Betsy had not met her father's third wife. She'd been estranged from him since she'd fallen out with wife number two and Drake had told her it was best if she didn't visit again. She'd phoned him when Sebastian was born, and he'd sent a congratulations card, but he had never met his grandson.

'I don't need money from Drake,' she'd told her mother. 'My pet portrait business is doing quite well, and I supplement what I earn from painting with my job at the village pub.'

Now she doubted that she would be able to resume her job as barmaid. Her friend Sarah, who owned the pub, had said that it been badly damaged in the floods. And she would have to move out of the cottage, where she had a painting studio in the attic.

Sebastian started to grizzle, and Betsy stroked his curls off his brow. 'Not long now, poppet,' she said, trying to soothe him. She glanced at Carlos. 'How far is the hotel?'

He spoke to the pilot over the intercom. 'We'll be there in a couple of minutes.'

Carlos's sunglasses hid his expression and Betsy had no idea what he was thinking. When he had held Sebastian at the cottage she'd hoped for *something*—a sign that he recognised his son. Seeing Sebastian with his father had emphasised their physical likeness, but perhaps Carlos couldn't see it—or more likely he didn't want to accept the baby was his.

She wondered what his reaction would be when he had proof of paternity. His main concern seemed to be damage to his reputation, which might affect his business interests. But the news story would be forgotten in a few days.

And she had no intention of asking Carlos for financial support. Sebastian was her responsibility. She wasn't the first woman to have listened to her heart rather than her head and then had to cope with the consequences, Betsy thought ruefully.

Her stomach muscles clenched as she inhaled the evocative spicy scent of Carlos's cologne. Desire flared sweet and sharp inside her as her mind flew back to the night that she had spent with him.

The velvet sofa had felt sensuous against her skin as Carlos had eased her down onto the cushions. She hadn't been aware of him undressing her, or himself, until she'd felt the roughness of his chest hair on her breasts. His hands had been everywhere, working their magic on her breasts and skimming over her thighs as he'd parted her legs and tested her wet heat with his fingers.

She remembered how big and hard his manhood had felt when she'd touched him, and the nervous flutter of her heart when he'd pressed forward and entered her. He had filled her, completed her. And now the dampness between her legs was shameful proof that she only had to look at him and her body turned to mush.

She blushed when she realised that she was staring at him. She wished she could rip off his sunglasses to see if he was affected by the sexual chemistry that was almost tangible in the confines of the helicopter cabin.

A nerve flickered in his cheek—but perhaps she had imagined it. Carlos had dated some of the world's most beautiful women and he wouldn't be interested in *her*, Betsy reminded herself. He was gorgeous and exotic and so sexy he should come with a health warning.

'We're about to land,' he told her smoothly.

Get a grip, she ordered herself a few minutes later as she followed him across the helipad in the grounds of his hotel. The impressive country house was *the* place to stay in Dorset. Betsy had changed out of her old leggings before leaving the cottage, but when she walked into the elegant foyer of the hotel she was conscious of the receptionist's disapproving glance at her jeans and strap top.

Carlos led her over to the lift, which whisked them up to the penthouse suite. There, a doctor was waiting to take cheek swabs from all three of them.

After carrying out the simple procedure, the doctor left. Carlos's phone rang and he went into the bedroom to take the call.

Sebastian was due for a nap, but he wasn't ready to give in and protested loudly while Betsy changed his nappy. She searched in the change bag for his favourite toy but couldn't find it, and in desperation emptied the bag over the floor.

Carlos walked back into the room as Sebastian's screams reached a crescendo. 'What's the matter with him?'

'He's tired,' Betsy said shortly. 'And I must have left his cuddly toy rabbit at the cottage.'

'Surely if Sebastian is tired he will fall asleep without the toy,' Carlos said, in a dry tone that exacerbated Betsy's frustration and the feeling that she was a useless mother.

Her fierce awareness of Carlos did not help. He had changed out of his suit and muddy shoes into black jeans, a black polo shirt and a matching leather jacket. He quite simply took her breath away.

'What do you know about childcare?' she snapped, raising her voice above Sebastian's yells.

Exhaustion was catching up with her after a sleepless night spent listening to the river flooding into the cottage. It was sinking in that she was homeless, Sebastian was crying because he wanted the familiarity and security of falling asleep in his cot, and Betsy felt close to tears as she wondered what she was going to do.

'Perhaps if you calmed down Sebastian would stop crying?' Carlos murmured. 'He is probably picking up on your tension.'

'It's your fault that I'm tense.' Betsy glared at him. 'I feel violated.'

He frowned. 'How so?'

'I found it humiliating to have a stranger take samples from me and Sebastian for DNA testing,' she said hotly. 'You and I might have only spent one night together, but I was your housekeeper for six weeks and we got to know each other fairly well. I thought we had become friends.' She bit her lip. 'What makes you think I would lie about you being Sebastian's father?'

'Everything I believed I knew about you went up in smoke when I found your note saying that the only reason you'd had sex with me was because I was famous,' Carlos said tersely.

'I wrote that note after I overheard you telling the journalist who had come to interview you that I was a casual fling.' Betsy grimaced. 'Sebastian is the consequence of the night we spent together.'

'So you say,' Carlos drawled. 'The truth will be confirmed in twenty-four hours. I intend to stay in London tonight. You and Sebastian can stay here as you can't sleep at the cottage. There is a cot in the bedroom. I'll be in touch tomorrow.'

'I can't wait,' Betsy muttered sarcastically as she swept past Carlos and carried Sebastian into the bedroom.

He had worn himself out with crying and was asleep almost as soon as she laid him in the cot.

When she returned to the sitting room Carlos had gone, and she was angry with herself for feeling disappointed. He made her feel alive in a way that no other man had ever done, she acknowledged with a sigh. She dragged her thoughts from him, knowing that she needed to make long-term plans.

Her landlord had called to say that he intended to sell the cottage, and a trawl on the internet of estate agents' websites showed there was nothing suitable in the local area that Betsy could afford to rent. She would be lucky to find a place with enough room that she could set up a studio, she realised as she read the details of a poky basement flat.

She thought of the picture that she had worked on recently. The portrait of a golden Labrador had been commissioned by a client as a birthday present for his wife. The painting was finished, and she needed to arrange for it to be delivered to the client. The money she would be paid for the painting was even more vital now, as it would be a while before she could accept any more commissions.

Betsy switched on the television and watched a local news report that told her the floodwater around Fraddlington had receded and the main road was open again. Maybe she would be able to go back to the cottage to collect Sebastian's cuddly toy and pack up the painting.

'We're going to go on a bus,' she told him when he woke up from his nap.

Although he didn't understand, he gave a grin that showed off his two new teeth and Betsy's heart melted. But when she carried him out of the hotel, they were immediately surrounded by press photographers.

A journalist thrust a microphone towards her. 'Miss Miller. Is tennis legend Carlos Segarra really your son's father?'

'How long have you been in a relationship with Carlos?'

'Is it true that you had sex with Segarra on a famous London tennis court?'

'Of course it isn't true,' Betsy denied angrily.

She clutched Sebastian tightly as the press pack swarmed closer. He was whimpering and pushing his face into her neck.

'Please let me pass,' she appealed to the photographers. She felt like a rabbit caught in a car's headlights as camera flashbulbs went off all around her.

'Miss Miller, if you would like to come with me?'

Betsy turned towards the calm voice amid the chaos and saw a smartly dressed man pushing through the crowd of paparazzi.

'I'm Brian Waring, the manager of the hotel,' he introduced himself as he slipped a hand beneath her arm and led her quickly back inside the hotel.

To Betsy's relief, the photographers did not follow.

The manager escorted to the lift. 'Might I suggest that you remain in the hotel and its grounds, where you will not be troubled by the press? Mr Segarra has asked me personally to ensure that you and your son have everything you need.' He gave a kindly smile, perhaps realising that Betsy was still too shocked by what had happened to be able to speak. 'I'll arrange for lunch to be served in your suite.'

She bit her lip. 'I don't know how the press found out I was here.'

'The paparazzi are renowned for using underhand methods in their pursuit of a story,' the manager murmured. 'I believe that the tabloid newspapers are prepared to pay thousands of pounds for a picture of a celebrity or someone close to them, especially if there is a whiff of a scandal.'

So her little son was a scandal!

Perhaps she would wake up and find that this day from hell was simply a nightmare, Betsy thought when she and Sebastian were safely back inside the hotel suite. The incident with the photographers had left her badly shaken and had brought back memories of the intrusive media coverage of her father's trial after he had been accused of abducting her.

She shuddered at the thought that now her name was in the public domain the media might dig up the story of her parents' famously acrimonious divorce. Neither her mother nor her father had seemed to care that their lives had become a soap opera, played out in regular instalments in the tabloids, but Betsy had hated the press attention on her family.

Her phone rang, and she stared at it suspiciously before breathing a sigh of relief when she saw that it was her friend Sarah who was calling.

'Betsy, I've just seen the headlines. We've been so busy clearing up the pub, and I hadn't looked on social media, but Mike popped to the shop and bought a paper...'

'It was the same for me,' Betsy said ruefully. 'The first I knew of the story was when Carlos arrived at the cottage and showed me a newspaper.'

'Oh, my goodness! What did he say about Sebastian?'

'He has demanded proof of paternity.'

'The thing is...' Sarah sounded strained. 'I think it's my fault that the story was published.'

'How do you mean?'

'You know how for the past few days we've been putting up defences in the hope of stopping the pub from being flooded? To be honest, saving the business that Mike and I have worked so hard to establish was all I could think about. Well, a journalist came into the pub and said he was covering the story now that the river was likely to burst its banks. He seemed a nice guy, and he offered to help move the furniture and carpets upstairs.'

Sarah sighed.

'I feel such an idiot for believing him when he said he was a friend of yours from London and he already knew that Carlos Segarra was Sebastian's father. If I'd been thinking straight I might have been more suspicious. Instead I said something along the lines that I thought it was about time Carlos accepted responsibility for his son. But when I saw today's newspapers I remembered that you had said I was the *only* person you had confided in. I'm so sorry, Betsy. Are you all right?'

'Not really.' Betsy explained what had happened when she'd tried to leave the hotel.

'The paparazzi are outside your cottage, too. Me and my big mouth,' Sarah muttered. 'But I'm sure that in a couple of days the press will forget the story and move on to something else,' she said consolingly.

But the damage had been done, Betsy thought heavily. Tomorrow Carlos would have proof that he was Sebastian's father, but he had given no indication that he would welcome the news.

The rest of the day dragged, as she tried to keep Sebastian entertained in the hotel suite that had become a prison. Luckily she'd packed spare clothes for him, as well as pouches of food and cartons of ready-made formula milk.

After she'd settled him in the cot for the night, she ran a bath and tipped a liberal splash of gorgeously scented bubble bath into the water. After a long soak, she wrapped herself in one of the hotel's fluffy robes and rinsed out her knickers in the bathwater.

Dinner was delivered to the room, but she felt too tense to eat. She had been jogging along nicely, but in the past twenty-four hours her life had imploded. She'd lost her home and her painting studio, and Carlos has stormed back on to the scene. But there was nothing she could do tonight, she thought wearily as she curled up on the sofa and tried to concentrate on a political thriller on the television.

Betsy woke with a start and for a moment felt disorientated before she remembered that she was in the hotel suite. Something had disturbed her, and she sprang up from the sofa. The television was still on—perhaps she had been woken by a sound from it. But her skin prickled as she sensed that someone was in the bedroom where Sebastian was sleeping.

Heart pounding, she ran into the bedroom and saw a figure leaning over the cot.

'Carlos?'

She let out a shaky breath and slumped against the door frame as he turned around and the soft light from the bedside lamp illuminated his handsome face.

'You scared me. I thought a photographer had managed to get into the room.'

Carlos frowned. 'Have the paparazzi been here?'

'There was a crowd of them outside the hotel earlier. I wanted to go back to the cottage, but they wouldn't leave me alone and Sebastian was frightened.' Betsy had spoken quietly, but Sebastian stirred. She held her breath and after a moment he settled again. 'What are you doing here?' she whispered to Carlos.

He stared down into the cot before walking across the room. She followed him into the sitting room, pulling the door closed behind them.

'I accept that Sebastian is my son.'

Betsy's heart lurched. 'I thought you wouldn't receive the result of the DNA test until tomorrow.'

'I haven't heard back from the clinic.'

'Oh!' She couldn't hide her shock. She felt as if a weight had lifted from her. But her pleasure that Carlos seemed to trust her was quickly doused.

'I cannot ignore the evidence. Sebastian bears a strong physical resemblance to me. I checked his birth certificate to verify his date of birth.' He gave her a sardonic look. 'You didn't think I would simply take your word, did you? I realise that Sebastian must have been conceived at the time I was in England for the tournament.' Carlos's eyes glittered with fury. 'I will *never* forgive you for keeping him from me. I had a right to know that I am his father.'

His words tugged on emotions that Betsy did not want to feel. Deep in her heart she knew that she should have tried to contact Carlos when she'd discovered she was pregnant. But he had abandoned her after he'd slept with her in London and she had felt foolish because she'd trusted him. He was no better than her father, who had seemed to want her but had abandoned her in favour of his second wife.

'You publicly stated that you didn't want children,' she said to Carlos defensively. 'I was suffering from awful morning sickness when I watched you being interviewed, and I was convinced that you wouldn't want your baby.'

He said something in Spanish that she guessed from his savage tone was not complimentary. 'You should have told me instead of playing judge and jury. Sebastian has two parents, but you have deliberately deprived him of his father.'

A voice from the past slid into Betsy's mind and she recalled the words of the judge who had presided over her father's trial when he'd been charged with abducting her.

'*You deliberately and cruelly deprived your daughter of her mother,*' the judge had told Drake.

But the situation between her and Carlos wasn't the same as her parents, she tried to reassure herself. Her father's behaviour had been driven by a desire to hurt her mother. Betsy had kept Sebastian a secret from Carlos because… Had she subconsciously wanted to punish him for returning to Spain after he'd taken her virginity and crushed her heart?

She swallowed hard, unable to face the uncomfortable thoughts swirling in her head and unwilling to meet Carlos's hard gaze.

'What do you want?' she asked huskily.

'My son.' His tone was grim and uncompromising. 'Sebastian is a Segarra. You have stolen the first fifteen months of his life, but from now on his home will be with me in Spain.'

CHAPTER THREE

'ARE YOU THREATENING to take Sebastian away from me? You have no rights to him.'

Carlos heard fear in Betsy's voice and saw her mouth tremble before she quickly firmed her lips. But the sign of her vulnerability did not lessen his anger. *Dios*—'angry' did not come anywhere near to describing the bitter betrayal he felt. He had a child, a son.

But Betsy hadn't told him.

'I am determined to be fully involved in my son's life,' he said harshly. 'I have already spoken to my lawyer who has advised me that when I have proof of paternity I can apply to the court for a Parental Responsibility Order, which will give me the right to be included in decisions made about Sebastian's upbringing.'

Betsy's shocked expression gave Carlos a stab of satisfaction. *See how she likes having the ground ripped from beneath her feet,* he thought.

His common sense had urged him to wait for the result of the paternity test. But in his heart he had known that Sebastian was his when he'd held the toddler in his arms at the cottage.

It wasn't only their physical similarity, and the fact that Sebastian bore a close resemblance to Carlos's nephew. The connection he felt with Sebastian was on a fundamental level—as if his soul had recognised the blood bond between them.

While he had been at the Veloz party in London his conviction that the little boy was his had intensified. Launching his sports management agency in England had been Carlos's focus for months, but he'd made an excuse to his business partner and left the party early to rush back to Dorset.

'I'm…glad that you believe Sebastian is yours.'

Betsy did not sound glad—she sounded as if she'd swallowed glass.

'I won't object if you want to be part of his life, and maybe when he is older he could spend holidays with you in Spain. But his home is in England, with me.'

'Your home will be uninhabitable for many weeks until the flood damage is repaired.'

Carlos frowned as he pictured the poky cottage where Betsy had been bringing up Sebastian. Had a lack of money driven her to tell the press that she'd had a child by him?

He had retired from the international tennis circuit two years ago. But he had dominated the game for over a decade and still played exhibition matches around the world. The paparazzi's fascination with his private life showed no sign of lessening and the tabloids must have paid thousands of pounds for the story.

'No doubt you were paid well by the tabloids for the revelation that I am Sebastian's father,' he said grimly. 'But I guarantee that what you received was a tiny fraction of my personal fortune. Sebastian is entitled to the lifestyle and benefits that my wealth can provide. I own a beautiful house in Toledo, where he will be able to thrive, and I can give him opportunities far beyond anything you can offer him.'

Betsy stared at him. 'Sebastian is my world. I can give him everything he needs, and his needs are simple. Love, safety and security—not a big house and a bucketload of cash.'

The belt of her robe had loosened, causing the front to gape open slightly, giving Carlos a tantalising view of the pale slopes of her breasts. He was infuriated by his body's instant response as a jolt of electricity arced through him and centred in his groin. He was still at a loss to understand why this woman, pretty but not in the supermodel league, made his skin feel too tight and his pulse quicken.

He wanted to hate Betsy for what she had done. He told himself that he did. But he could not resist stepping closer to her.

She smelled divine. Her hair was loose, tumbling in soft waves around her shoulders, a delicious mix of honey and caramel shades. Her brown eyes were wary, and her mouth was set in a sulky line that tempted him to crush her lips beneath his and kiss her until she made those soft moans in her throat that he still remembered.

Two years ago he had decided that she was too young and unworldly for him—especially while he needed to focus on preparing for the tennis tournament in London. His inconvenient attraction to a star-struck ingénue who seemed refreshingly unaware of her allure had been something Carlos had been determined to ignore. He'd almost succeeded.

But it had been impossible to ignore Betsy completely when she made his breakfast every morning and prepared dinner for him every evening.

It was ridiculous for them to eat separately, he'd told her after the first week, and he'd insisted that they dined together. With sex off the table—although he'd had several erotic fantasies in which he made love to her on the polished walnut surface of the dining table—he'd had to fall back on conversation. And not the kind of small talk he usually made with women as a prelude to taking them to bed.

His discussions with Betsy had covered a wide range of subjects, although he hadn't talked about his family and nor had she, except to tell him that the house belonged to her aunt and she combined her housekeeping duties with studying for an art degree.

In the tournament's final he'd played the best tennis of his life. And when he'd held the trophy aloft it had felt like a dream. But his euphoria had been tinged with guilt, because he had known his ferocious ambition had destroyed his family. His father's absence from the supporters' box had hurt.

Carlos had smiled for the photographers and kissed the trophy, but in his heart he would have gladly exchanged his success for his mother's life.

That evening he'd left the competitors' ball early and had felt dangerously out of control as he'd raced back to Betsy. He'd needed an outlet for the wild emotions that he hadn't been able to deal with.

Sexual chemistry had simmered between them for weeks, and when he'd pulled her into his arms that chemistry had ignited as fast as a Bunsen burner.

Carlos swore beneath his breath as he forced his mind from the past. Jaw tense, he strode across the hotel room to the minibar. The whisky was a blended variety, not his preferred single malt, but it would do.

He glanced at Betsy. 'Would you like a drink?'

'Why not? I could do with some Dutch courage,' she said, in a wry voice that tugged on something deep inside Carlos. Despite his fury, he disliked the idea that she might be afraid of him.

He half-filled two glasses and sensed without turning around that she had walked over to him. Her bare feet made no sound on the plush carpet, but his senses were assailed by her scent: something lightly floral, mixed with the vanilla fragrance of her skin, that made his gut clench.

He handed her a drink and led the way over to a sofa and chairs which were grouped around a coffee table. Lowering himself onto the sofa, he gave her a sardonic look when she made for the armchair furthest away from him. She took a sip of whisky and spluttered.

Two years ago Carlos had found her lack of sophistication refreshing, but now he could not decide if her unworldly air was real or if she had ruthlessly manipulated the media.

As if she had read his thoughts, she said quietly, 'The journalist who came to the village must have remembered that he had seen me with you at my aunt's house. It was a long shot that he guessed that Sebastian is your son. He found out that I worked at the pub and told the landlady there that he and I were friends in London and that he knew you are Sebastian's father. Sarah unthinkingly confirmed it because she was distracted by the threat of the flood.'

It was possible that Betsy was telling the truth, Carlos conceded. The antipathy between him and Tom Vane after he'd been instrumental in the journalist being sacked from his job had escalated further when Vane had threatened to make public some details he'd discovered about Carlos's mother's death. But the blackmail attempt failed when Carlos had informed the police.

'Even if what you say is true, how could the pub landlady have confirmed to Vane that I am Sebastian's father?' he asked coldly.

A scarlet stain spread over Betsy's face. 'Sarah is my closest friend…and I confided in her.'

Carlos swore. 'When I showed you that tabloid headline you assured me that you hadn't told *anyone.* Clearly that was another lie. Did you not think I had the right to be informed that I have a son?' he gritted. 'I should have been the first to know, instead of discovering from a goddamned newspaper that I am a father.'

'*How* could I have told you? Either when I found out I was pregnant or after Sebastian was born? You went back to Spain the day after we had slept together and I had no way of contacting you.'

'That's not true. I included my phone number and an invitation to visit me in Spain with the bracelet I sent you.'

Betsy stared at him. 'What invitation? What bracelet?'

He frowned. 'Are you saying that you did not receive a package? It was addressed to you, and I received notification from the courier that it had been delivered to your aunt's house.'

'I never heard from you again after you left and, frankly, I don't believe you sent me anything. You're making it up so that it doesn't look like you abandoned me.'

'*You* are accusing *me* of lying?' Carlos couldn't believe what he was hearing, and his temper simmered.

'It doesn't feel good, does it?' Betsy said coolly.

His jaw clenched at her belligerence, but he felt a reluctant respect for her. Two years ago Betsy had been star-struck and in awe of him, but motherhood had turned her into a lioness determined to protect her cub.

Was she lying when she insisted that she hadn't received the bracelet? Carlos raked a hand through his hair, frustrated by this unexpected turn of events. Betsy's surprise seemed genuine. Her accusation that he had abandoned her would make more sense if she had not received his gift.

He had been piqued by her lack of response, and hadn't tried to contact her again. But that did not excuse her failure to tell him he had a child.

He welcomed the resurgence of his anger. It was safer to feel furious than to admit to himself that he longed to open her robe and trace his hands over her delectable curves. The idea that she was naked beneath the robe was a distraction he was struggling to ignore.

'I am willing to believe that you did not sell out to the tabloids,' he said curtly. 'In some ways I suppose I should be grateful that the story has broken. Would you have *ever* told me about my son?'

She bit her lip. 'I don't know. I wanted to, but I didn't know how you would feel. When you came to the cottage this morning your reaction was exactly as I feared.'

It had not been his finest moment, Carlos acknowledged. His shock when he'd seen Sebastian had been mixed with something close to fear. He knew his failings. His first thought had been that he wasn't up to the task of being a father. More importantly, that he did not deserve to have a child. Panic had gripped him, and he'd rejected the idea of such a huge responsibility.

But Sebastian was his. And maybe, Carlos brooded, this was his chance to atone for the past and his mother's untimely death.

Inside his head, Carlos heard his father's voice. *'You killed her. Mi querida Marta.'* Tears had streamed down Roderigo Segarra's face.

The horror of that day would never leave Carlos, nor would his father's condemnation of him. It was the reason he had isolated his emotions from everyone—even his sister, who had been just a child when she had been made motherless. By him.

Panic seized Carlos once again. He did not deserve to be part of his baby son's life. What if he destroyed Sebastian like he had destroyed everything else that was good and pure? It would be better—safer—if he bought Betsy a house in England and gave her a generous allowance so that she could be a full-time mother to Sebastian.

His conscience pricked at the idea that she struggled financially. 'Who looks after Sebastian while you work at the pub?'

'When he was a small baby I used to leave him asleep in his pram in a room behind the bar. He was perfectly safe,' Betsy said when Carlos frowned. 'But he's too big to do that now. Luckily Sarah's sister offered to babysit on the evenings I worked. Polly can get on with her homework because Sebastian usually sleeps soundly. Unless he's teething,' she added ruefully.

'*Homework?* How old is this babysitter?'

'She's fifteen, and very responsible.' Betsy glared at him. 'I have always done the best I can to keep a roof over our heads and Sebastian clothed and fed. And working behind the bar in the evenings means that I have a couple of hours during the day when Sebastian has a nap to build up my pet portrait business.'

'Your—*what*?'

'I paint portraits of people's pets. Dogs and cats, mainly, but I've done a few rabbits—and a bearded dragon. Admittedly, I don't earn a fortune, but the business is starting to grow.' She sighed. 'The flooding means that I won't be able to accept any new commissions. My studio is in the attic, but I'll have to move out of the cottage and I don't know where or when I'll be able to paint again.'

Betsy sipped her whisky and wrinkled her nose. She looked very young, wrapped in the too-big towelling robe. But she must be in her mid-twenties, Carlos thought, and she possessed an inherent sensuality that he found irresistible. He could not prevent his gaze from straying to that enticing glimpse of her cleavage and he swore silently as his body tightened and his blood pulsed hot in his veins. Desiring the mother of his child was a complication he did not need when there was something far more important to be resolved.

Hearing how Betsy had struggled to bring up Sebastian on her own, leaving him in the care of a schoolgirl while she went to work, had filled Carlos with horror. As for painting pets—it might be a nice hobby, but Betsy couldn't seriously expect to make a living from it.

'I can solve all your problems,' he said coolly.

She looked at him warily. 'How?'

Carlos was aware of the powerful beat of his heart. Since his mother had died, he'd avoided all responsibility and commitment. He had lived up to his public persona of a playboy because that way no one expected anything of him, and no one got hurt. But this was too big and too important for him to run away from.

He had a son, and he would not allow Sebastian to grow up feeling rejected by his father the way Carlos had felt rejected by his own father.

'Marry me.'

He ignored Betsy's shocked gasp.

'If you agree to be my wife, I will take care of you and our son and your worries will be over.'

'Of…of course I'm not going to marry you,' Betsy stammered when the shock that had seized her released its stranglehold on her vocal cords.

Carlos's proposal had sounded more like an order, and she was in no doubt that he did not want *her*. Astonishingly, he *did* want his son.

'In the twenty-first century people don't get married because they have a baby.'

'I do. I *will*.' His voice was hard, implacable, and Betsy's heart collided with her ribs when she realised that he was only controlling his temper with ferocious will power.

'I won't allow my son to be illegitimate,' he told her. 'And before you say that it doesn't matter—it does. Sebastian should have *my* name on his birth certificate, and he should not be denied the name Segarra or his Spanish heritage.'

'You're crazy.'

Fear churned in the pit of her stomach. Carlos sounded as if he meant it. As if he actually expected her to marry him.

'I don't want to get married. I have no objection if you want to have a relationship with Sebastian—'

Carlos cut her off. 'How can I trust that you won't disappear with him? Once we are married and my name is included on Sebastian's birth certificate we will share equal parental rights.'

'Have I hurt your pride? Is that what this is about? You can't simply waltz into Sebastian's life when you feel like it and disappear again when you find that fatherhood doesn't suit your playboy lifestyle. Details of which are documented in unedifying detail in all the gossip magazines,' she added caustically.

'I'm flattered that you obviously take a close interest in my personal life.'

Beneath his mockery, the sting in his voice warned Betsy that he was furious.

'I don't want access rights to my son, or occasional visits. I want to see him every day and tuck him into bed every night.' His voice deepened. 'It is important to me that as Sebastian grows up he knows I'll always be there for him and will support him whatever happens.'

Despite herself Betsy felt a tug on her emotions in response to Carlos's statement, which sounded like a holy vow. She was stunned that he was prepared to go to such extreme lengths—even marry her—to claim Sebastian. But his talk of marriage brought back memories of her parents screaming abuse at each other. She would not risk her little boy having the kind of fractured childhood that she'd had.

The sound of crying from the bedroom gave her an excuse to drop her gaze from Carlos's and she put her drink down and sped across the room.

Sebastian's flushed cheek was a sure sign that he was cutting another tooth. Betsy picked him up and tried to soothe him.

'There's some teething gel in his change bag,' she told Carlos when he followed her into the bedroom.

He found the gel and she rubbed some onto Sebastian's gums, but his cries did not abate.

'Let me take him.' Carlos stretched out his arms and, after a moment's hesitation, Betsy handed the baby to him. 'Shh, *conejito*...' Carlos murmured, tucking Sebastian against his shoulder.

A lump formed in Betsy's throat at the sight of her little boy being comforted by his father. She realised that she could not deny Sebastian his daddy, nor Carlos his son. But she wouldn't marry him. No way.

'We'll talk in the morning,' Carlos told her when Sebastian had eventually fallen asleep and he'd laid him in the cot. 'You can sleep in the bed and I'll take the sofa in the sitting room.'

He left the room without glancing at her again, and Betsy let out a shaky sigh when he closed the door behind him. She felt physically and mentally exhausted and simply slipped off her bathrobe before she climbed into bed and sank into oblivion.

Sunlight was poking through the gap in the curtains when Betsy opened her eyes. For a few seconds she wondered where she was, but then memories crowded her mind: finding Carlos in the hotel suite, his acceptance that Sebastian was his, and his shocking marriage proposal.

Her watch showed nine o'clock. It was unusual for Sebastian to sleep so late. She looked over at the cot and her heart juddered to a standstill when she saw that it was empty. For a few seconds her brain struggled to comprehend the unthinkable.

Her baby had disappeared.

In sheer panic she leapt out of bed and ran across the room. As she wrenched open the door she told herself that Sebastian must have woken and Carlos had picked him up and taken him out of the cot.

But they weren't in the sitting room.

Terror swept through her as she remembered how Carlos had said that from now on his son would live with him in Spain. What if he had abducted Sebastian? How would she get her baby back? It had taken months for the Canadian authorities to find her when she had been kidnapped by her father.

Betsy choked back a sob. She could not bear to be parted from Sebastian for one day.

Her handbag was on the coffee table—and it was open.

Before the cottage had flooded she had put her and Sebastian's passports, his birth certificate and other important documents in her bag for safekeeping. With mounting dread, Betsy rifled through the bag and discovered that the passports were missing.

She remembered that Carlos had said he had checked Sebastian's date of birth. She'd assumed he had looked online. Birth certificates were a matter of public record and available for anyone to see. But he must have opened her bag, found the birth certificate and removed the passports—which meant he could already have taken Sebastian abroad.

Fear cramped in Betsy's stomach.

When the door at the far end of suite opened and Carlos emerged from the bathroom, holding Sebastian, her knees sagged as relief swept through her.

'I woke up and...and Sebastian was missing.' Her voice shook. 'I thought you had taken him to Spain.' Anger replaced her fear and she glared at Carlos. 'Where are our passports?'

'I locked them in the safety deposit box,' he said calmly. 'You had left your handbag open and I noticed the passports and moved them. You shouldn't leave them lying around. All kinds of hotel staff have access to the suite.'

Carlos set Sebastian down on his feet and he toddled across the room and picked up a fluffy toy. 'You said that you had forgotten his favourite toy rabbit, so I bought him a replacement while I was in London.'

Betsy exhaled slowly as some of the tension drained from her body. 'That was kind of you.'

'Sebastian needed his nappy changed, but I thought you might be disturbed if I took him into the en suite bathroom.'

She became aware that Carlos was staring at her, and

her heart skipped a beat as she belatedly remembered that she had slept naked because she hadn't brought any nightwear with her to the hotel. When she'd leapt out of bed she'd been frantic to find Sebastian and hadn't thought to pull on the bathrobe.

Carlos looked as though he had been chiselled from marble, so still was he. His skin was drawn as tight as a drum over the sharp edges of his cheekbones and there was tension in the unforgiving line of his jaw. Beneath his heavy brows his eyes glittered, and Betsy's pulse quickened in response.

She remembered the one and only other time she had been naked in front of a man. This man.

Two years ago, Carlos had laid her down on the sofa and knelt over her, supporting his weight on his elbows while his gaze roamed over her body. When his eyes had returned to her face there had been a fierce hunger in his expression that had filled her with nervous excitement. She had been a virgin, and unprepared for the intensity of his unbridled passion.

He had marked her for ever when he'd made her his. She understood that now, and it made the ache in the pit of her stomach more intense, heavier, *needier.*

There was no mistaking the feral hunger in Carlos's eyes as he subjected her to a leisurely inspection, allowing his gaze to linger on her breasts before moving down to the slight curve of her stomach, the flare of her hips, and finally to the dusting of honey-brown curls between her thighs.

Heat scorched Betsy and a red stain spread over her cheeks. Her entire body felt on fire, and she burned hotter still when her nipples tingled and tightened, jutting forward as if begging for his touch, his mouth.

A lifetime passed, or so it felt, and the air between

them throbbed with sexual tension. Betsy could not control the wild restlessness inside her, the fire that consumed her. She was transfixed by the golden gleam in Carlos's eyes, the hunger he could not hide.

Until he had turned up at the cottage she'd never expected to see him again. And since then he had been so angry that it hadn't occurred to her that he might find her attractive. But desire was stamped on his hard features and on his full, sensual lips, which for once were not curled in an expression of cynical contempt.

Moments ago she had been terrified that he had taken Sebastian to Spain. Now she was terrified that if Carlos kissed her she would be unable to resist him.

She crossed her arms over her breasts and blushed again when he gave her a sardonic look that said it was too late for modesty.

'I have to…' Her voice trailed away. She couldn't think straight while Carlos continued to stare at her as if she were prey and he was preparing to devour her.

But the spell was broken. He blinked, and when his thick black lashes lifted again his eyes were coolly dismissive.

'Hurry up and put some clothes on. We'll go to your cottage so that you can pack everything you and Sebastian might need before we fly to Spain today.'

CHAPTER FOUR

CARLOS RAKED HIS hands through his hair as Betsy spun round and raced back into the bedroom. His eyes followed the gorgeous rounded curves of her bottom and he did not know how he stopped himself from going after her.

When he'd walked into the sitting room and she had been standing there, completely and beautifully naked, he'd felt stunned. She was every bit as lovely as he remembered and then some. Motherhood had softened the angles of her body and given her a sensual allure that made him catch his breath. With her hair rippling in silky waves on her bare shoulders she'd reminded Carlos of a painting by one of the Old Masters.

She had been Aphrodite, or a Siren, and he'd wanted to worship her with his mouth pressed against her creamy skin. As he'd watched a flush of rose-pink spread down her throat and across her décolletage and lushly perfect breasts he had wanted to reacquaint himself with her tantalising contours. He could not remember wanting anything so badly in his life.

His mind flew back to two years ago. Betsy had been in the lounge at the house in London when he'd hurried back from the competitors' ball.

'Did you wait up for me?' he'd asked her.

'Of course I waited up for you.'

Her shy smile had floored him. He had wanted her for weeks, but he'd made himself wait for her to give him a sign. She'd walked over to him and wound her arms around his neck. When she'd drawn his head down and pressed her lips against his, the wolf inside him had howled.

He had been too impatient to take her upstairs to the bedroom and had tugged her clothes off before tumbling her down onto the sofa. The moonlight slanting through the blinds had cast a pearly shimmer over her nakedness so that she had seemed ethereal. He remembered the soft gasp she'd given as he'd cupped her breasts and licked her nipples. And when he'd slipped his hand between her thighs and touched her intimately she'd made a choked sound that he had thought was pleasure.

Could it have been surprise? Surely he would have known if she had been a virgin? But he had been so hungry for her, and intent on satisfying his desire, Carlos thought uncomfortably as he pulled his mind back to the present.

The previous day, when he had been tipped off about the story in the British tabloids that said he had a secret child, he hadn't believed it for a minute. He knew he could have instructed his lawyers to investigate. But for two years he'd been unable to get Betsy out of his mind and, if he was honest, he'd seized the excuse to meet her again. He had felt confident that his inexplicable fascination with her would end once he saw her and realised that she was nothing out of the ordinary. And when he had proof from a paternity test that she was a liar he would be able to dismiss her as a mistake from his past.

But she was the mother of his son. He had received the confirmation email from the DNA clinic an hour ago, and it had reinforced his determination that Sebastian would not be illegitimate. To claim his son, he knew he must marry Betsy. But it was disturbing to realise how close he had come to losing his self-control simply by looking at her.

Since he had lost his temper with devastating results when he was a teenager, Carlos had kept a tight hold on his emotions, and he never made rash decisions. But in the past thirty-six hours all that had changed—and Betsy was to blame, he acknowledged grimly.

Two years ago she had gotten under his skin in a way that no other woman had ever done, and she was having the same effect on him now. But, just because she made him feel like a callow youth with an overload of hormones, it did not mean that he was in danger of succumbing to his inconvenient desire for her, he assured himself.

He *could* handle her, and he *would* marry her for his son's sake. Sebastian was the innocent one in this messy situation that his parents had made.

It occurred to him that Sebastian was being unusually quiet. The reason became clear when he looked across the room and saw that the toddler had found the baby wipes in the change bag and was pulling them out of the packet. All around him the carpet was littered with wipes.

'Hey, *conejito*! That means little rabbit in Spanish,' he told his son as he hunkered down next to Sebastian and shoved the wipes back into the packet. 'We had better not tell your mama what you've done or we'll both be in trouble.'

No doubt Betsy would accuse him of failing to keep a close eye on the baby, Carlos thought ruefully.

Sebastian's lower lip wobbled ominously when he realised he could no longer play with the wipes. Carlos quickly handed him the new toy rabbit. Sebastian grabbed it and his rosebud mouth curved into a smile that would melt the steeliest heart.

Carlos sucked in a breath. He still couldn't quite comprehend that this angelic little boy was his son. His fingers shook as he brushed them over Sebastian's silky brown curls. He was utterly perfect and enchanting.

Carlos stood up and scooped the baby into his arms. The skin on Sebastian's cheeks was as soft and downy as a peach, and his black eyelashes were impossibly long and curling. He was unmistakably a Segarra—although Sebastian had his mother's button nose, Carlos thought, running his finger along his own nose, which had been described as 'aquiline' by a female fashion editor who had written gushingly about him in a magazine when he'd modelled a brand of sportswear.

Since he'd retired from playing tennis he'd felt adrift. Sure, he'd established his sports management agency, and was actively involved in running Veloz, but he had a superb team of executives and the reality, Carlos knew, was that he was just the figurehead of the company. His charity, the Segarra Foundation, was important to him, but in truth he had been struggling to find purpose in his life. What better purpose could he have than being a father to his son?

Sebastian's face was so close to his that Carlos could count his long eyelashes. He wondered if his own father had felt this overwhelming urge to protect him when *he* was a child. Carlos had been closer to his mother, but he'd had a good relationship with his father—until that fateful day—the day when he had destroyed his family. His father had never forgiven him.

A small finger poked into his eye made Carlos wince. 'Steady there, *conejito*,' he said softly as Sebastian continued to explore his face with chubby little hands. And then, quite unexpectedly, Sebastian pressed his mouth against Carlos's cheek and gave him a dribbly kiss.

Carlos had noticed that Betsy was demonstrative with the baby, and often kissed his cheeks, and there was no doubt that Sebastian was copying the affectionate gesture.

Dios! His heart clenched. *'Tu es mi hijo,'* he told Sebastian huskily. 'You are my son. I will take care of you and love you always.'

Betsy could not put off facing Carlos any longer. She had taken her time dressing, but she only had to put on her jeans and top and tie the laces on her trainers. Bundling her hair into a loose knot on top of her head had wasted another couple of minutes. Her reflection in the mirror revealed a hectic flush on her cheeks. She wished that instead of a skimpy strap top she could cover up with a baggy sweatshirt to disguise the betraying peaks of her nipples.

Her stomach muscles clenched as she recalled how Carlos's eyes had roamed over her naked body with a shocking possessiveness that had infuriated her. She wasn't *his*. But the hunger in his gaze had warned her that if Sebastian had not been in the room Carlos would have tumbled her down on the sofa and trapped her beneath him with a muscular thigh, just as he had done two years ago.

She was appalled by how excited she felt at the idea of him making love to her.

Taking a deep breath, she opened the door and sidled into the sitting room. While she had been hiding in the bedroom a breakfast trolley had been delivered to the suite. The aroma of ground coffee and freshly cooked toast assailed her, and she discovered that she was starving. Sebastian was sitting in a high chair and Carlos was feeding him yoghurt.

'Stop hovering,' he drawled when he glanced over at her. 'It wasn't the first time I've seen you naked.'

She might have guessed that he wouldn't be tactful and refrain from mentioning the embarrassing incident.

Flushing hotly, she marched across the room and sat down at the table. 'It's lucky the paparazzi can't see you now. It wouldn't do your playboy reputation any good if word got out that you are adept at nappy-changing and feeding a baby.' She gave him a puzzled look. 'I didn't expect you to be so at ease with Sebastian.'

'I've had plenty of practice with my nephew. My sister has a two-year-old son,' Carlos explained as he fed Sebastian a spoonful of yoghurt. 'Graciela gave birth the night after I'd won the championship. She said that the tension of watching my match on TV brought on her labour.'

He grimaced.

'Miguel was born with a heart defect that required emergency surgery a few hours after his birth. My sister was in pieces when she called me. Her husband is a naval officer, and his ship was on a tour of Antarctica, and our father is mostly confined to bed or wheelchair-bound after he suffered a stroke a year ago. I rushed back to Spain the morning after you and I had spent the night together to be with Graciela.'

Betsy believed him. It wasn't likely that he'd make up a story about his nephew needing life-saving surgery.

'It must have been so frightening for your sister.'

She remembered how overwhelmed she'd felt when the midwife had placed Sebastian in her arms moments after he'd been born. He had seemed fragile, even though he'd been a strong, healthy baby.

'You mentioned your father, but not your mother,' she said carefully. Perhaps Carlos's family was as splintered as hers.

'She's dead.' His voice was emotionless. 'She died when I was fourteen and Graciela was ten. My sister grew up without her mother, and it was hard for her—especially when Miguel was ill, and she was so worried about him. She needed support from her family.'

Something about Carlos's closed expression stopped Betsy from prying into his mother's death. 'Was Miguel's surgery successful?' she asked.

'Thankfully, yes. He is a normal, active two-year-old.'

Carlos watched Sebastian munch on a finger of toast that Betsy had given him.

'The first time I saw my nephew he was in a neonatal unit and attached to various tubes and wires that were keeping him alive.' A muscle in his jaw clenched. 'It put my victory into perspective. I had won the trophy I'd coveted, but it seemed meaningless when my sister's baby's life hung in the balance.'

'Did it have anything to do with your decision to retire from playing professional tennis?'

Betsy had been as shocked as Carlos's legions of fans when he'd announced that he would not be defending his BITC title nor playing any more tournaments.

He nodded. 'I'd achieved everything I had set out to do playing tennis.'

Once again his voice was expressionless, but Betsy had the feeling that he was keeping something back and exerting fierce control over his emotions.

The media portrayed Carlos as a shallow playboy who preferred to party with his jet-set friends and surrounded himself with a bevy of beautiful women. But the man she had got to know during those few weeks when she'd worked as his housekeeper had been unexpectedly insightful. Carlos had even told her about the Segarra Foundation, a charity he had set up with the aim of giving children from deprived backgrounds access to all sports and in particular tennis.

Betsy had been charmed by him once before, and it would be easy to fall under his spell again, she thought as she sipped her coffee. But she was no longer a naïve young woman with a head full of dreams. Becoming a single mother had made her grow up fast.

'I can't marry you,' she said abruptly.

Her hand was unsteady when she placed her cup back on the saucer and the delicate china rattled.

'Why not?'

She glanced at him, surprised that he sounded calm rather than confrontational, which he had been up until now.

'Isn't it obvious?'

Carlos frowned. 'Is there a boyfriend on the scene?'

'No. Bringing up a child alone doesn't leave much time for dating,' Betsy told him drily.

Silently she acknowledged that she compared every man to Carlos, and she had never been as fiercely attracted to anyone else.

'Then what are your objections? Every child needs a mother and a father.' There was an odd note in Carlos's voice that made Betsy curious. 'It would be better for our son to grow up with both his parents.'

'Would it?' She sighed. 'We don't even like each other, so how could we create a happy family for Sebastian? What if it didn't work out and we divorced? I won't risk putting Sebastian through a vicious custody battle like my parents did to me.'

Carlos gave her an intent look. 'You said you were

eight when your parents' marriage ended. It sounds like it was a difficult time.'

'It was. I loved my mum and dad equally, but their divorce was acrimonious and I was torn between them. My loyalties were divided. I lost who *I* was because I tried so hard to make each of them happy.'

Betsy hated talking about her childhood. Even before her parents had split up there had been arguments and sulking, tears and tantrums on both sides. She had felt as if she was walking a tightrope. One wrong step and everything would come crashing down.

'The truth is that I was just something else my parents fought over—like money and who got the dog,' she told Carlos. 'But as their fights got louder and more vicious, the quieter I became. Sometimes I even considered running away. I thought that if I wasn't around they would stop arguing.'

'*Dios*. You actually thought that?'

'After the divorce I lived with my mother and I hoped that things would settle down...' She hesitated, reluctant to reveal how dysfunctional her family had been. But she needed to make him understand why she was so against marriage. 'It all blew up when my dad kidnapped me.'

She could not bring herself to look at Carlos, but she sensed from his silence that she had shocked him.

He swore softly. 'No wonder you were terrified when you woke up and found Sebastian missing from his cot.'

Had there been sympathy in his voice? She felt the press of tears behind her eyelids and quickly brushed her hand over her eyes. 'I was scared you had taken my baby.'

Carlos exhaled slowly. 'Of course I don't want to separate you and Sebastian.' His tone hardened. 'But he is my son and I won't walk away from him. Marriage will allow us to both be part of his life.'

'The idea of getting married fills me with dread,' Betsy admitted in a low voice. 'My parents were feted as a golden couple on both sides of the Atlantic. The beautiful actress and the brilliant writer. My mother kept newspaper clippings of their fairy-tale wedding. She told me that she and my father had been madly in love. I have a few early memories of the three of us being a happy family. But when things started to go wrong I believed that their rows were my fault.'

She forced herself to meet Carlos's gaze.

'The point I'm trying to make is that my parents married because they were in love, but they ended up hating each other and their divorce destroyed my childhood. You and I barely know each other, and we are certainly not in love. If we married it would be a disaster—for us and more importantly for Sebastian.'

'I disagree,' he said coolly. 'Our marriage will work precisely because it *won't* be founded on a romantic ideal. Your parents fell out of love and you suffered as a consequence. What I am suggesting is an alliance built on the shared goal of giving our son the stable family life that you wish you'd had and I was lucky enough to experience until my mother died.'

Carlos's voice was still carefully controlled, but Betsy sensed pain behind his words.

'Sebastian deserves to grow up feeling secure and loved by *both* his parents,' he continued. 'It is our responsibility to put his needs first.'

Betsy tried not to let his words invade her heart. She needed to think calmly and rationally. But when he'd mentioned family she'd remembered how she had envied her schoolfriends, whose parents did not throw things at each other, or slash their partners' clothes with a pair of scissors, as her mother had once done to her father's suits.

'It wouldn't work,' she muttered.

'It will be up to us to *make* it work,' Carlos said implacably. 'What is the alternative? That we share custody of Sebastian but live separate lives and date other people? You're single now, but you might meet someone in the future. I'll admit that I hate the idea of another man being a stepfather to my son. And it could happen the other way around. How would you feel if I had a relationship with a woman who would be Sebastian's stepmother?'

Betsy had no intention of handing Sebastian over to another woman. She did not have good memories of her first stepmother, who had been her father's second wife. Her relationship with Drake had been strained after he had been released from prison. Betsy hadn't wanted him to be sent to prison, even though she'd understood that he had committed a crime by abducting her. She had hoped for a reconciliation, but when she'd visited him in Canada she'd discovered that Drake had remarried. His new wife had made it plain that she resented having a prepubescent stepdaughter foisted on her.

'I'm sure we can work out a way that will allow us to co-parent Sebastian without having to get married,' she insisted.

Carlos's steely expression made her heart sink.

'You might be willing for him to be teased by his classmates for being a bastard when he's old enough to understand, but I am not,' he said curtly.

'No one cares about that sort of thing any more.'

'My son will bear *my* name.'

The quiet determination in Carlos's voice exacerbated Betsy's tension.

Her shoulders slumped. 'I wish you hadn't found out

about Sebastian.' She had not meant to utter the words out loud, but they seemed to ricochet off the walls.

'I'm not simply going to disappear out of the picture because it suits you,' he said harshly.

'I didn't mean...' But it had been a terrible thing to say and she felt ashamed.

'I am a well-known figure and the paparazzi will continue to be interested in you and Sebastian. How could you ensure his protection?'

'Protection from what?'

'It's not a secret that I became a multi-millionaire from my tennis career and sponsorship deals. My investment portfolio and my sports management agency are also highly lucrative. There are people who would try to snatch my son and demand a ransom for his safe return.'

Carlos frowned when Betsy gave a low cry of distress.

'I'm not trying to scare you. I'm simply stating facts. But you don't need to worry. I will never allow any harm to come to Sebastian or to you. My security team are ex-marines and my house in Toledo was once a fortress.'

She could feel her heart thudding painfully hard in her chest. Maybe Carlos hadn't set out to frighten her, but he'd succeeded. She would never put her baby in danger.

'Would you deny Sebastian everything that should be his by right of birth?' Carlos pressed her. 'My name, the privileges and the security I can give him? A family?'

Betsy stood up and walked over to the window. The room overlooked the hotel's driveway and she saw a group of photographers standing by the front gates with their cameras mounted on tripods. Everything had changed. She and Sebastian would never be able to go back to living in obscurity in a sleepy Dorset village. And Carlos had said he would not walk away from his son and she believed him.

She turned away from the window and watched him lift Sebastian out of the highchair. Their physical likeness was startling, and Betsy felt a tug on her heart as she saw in Carlos the man her son would one day become. The prospect of marrying Carlos was terrifying, but her conscience would not allow her to deny him a relationship with Sebastian.

'*If* we were to marry, you say it will be an alliance?' She felt her way cautiously along a path that her instincts were screaming at her not to take.

He nodded. 'I want us to have an equal partnership in which we will discuss everything concerning our son's upbringing.'

'What if we disagree about something?' She remembered how, as a child, she would lie in bed and pull the duvet over her head to try and block out the sound of her parents rowing.

'We'll find a solution, make compromises…but Sebastian's best interests will always be our objective.'

A marriage proposal where love wasn't mentioned might seem odd to most people, but Betsy felt reassured that Carlos wanted a partnership. And if deep in her heart she still yearned for romance, and the promise of everlasting love, she quashed the feeling. Although when Carlos set Sebastian down on the rug with his toys and walked towards her, she couldn't control her racing pulse.

He stopped in front of her and his eyes narrowed to gleaming gold slits. Jaguar's eyes that gave no clue to his thoughts.

'What is your answer, Betsy? Are you going to marry me for the sake of our son?'

She had no choice. For Sebastian she would do anything, even marry the devil. Betsy tilted her chin and met Carlos's hard gaze. 'I'll marry you on one condition.'

His dark brows lifted. The unexpected gentleness in his face made her want to cry. She had assumed he would be triumphant in victory. Was she crazy to believe they could actually make this work?

'I want us both to sign a prenuptial agreement, setting out how we will share caring for Sebastian if we divorce. I'll marry you so that he is legitimate and he can take your name. But if we separate in the future I don't want him to be the subject of a custody battle or feel that he has to choose between us.'

Her voice thickened with tears. Memories of her childhood were intensely painful, but she was sure that neither of her parents had understood how lonely and scared she'd felt, caught in the midst of their hatred of each other.

'And we will never argue in front of him. Whatever happens between us, Sebastian will only know love.'

Carlos looked startled for a moment, before he nodded. 'I'll have my legal team work out the details. You will only sign the prenuptial agreement when you are happy with it.'

'Thank you.'

Some of Betsy's tension drained away. Their marriage would not be made in heaven, but in a lawyer's office. It was the best way to protect Sebastian.

She could only hope that her heart would survive unscathed with her decision to marry her baby's dangerously fascinating father.

CHAPTER FIVE

'IT DOESN'T LOOK much like a fortress,' Betsy commented as she followed Carlos into the modern open-plan living space of his penthouse apartment in a fashionable area of Madrid.

He saw her catch her bottom lip between her teeth as she glanced around at the décor, pale grey sofas and white rugs on black marble floors. Perhaps she was thinking that the tinted glass cabinets lining one wall would be a magnet for an inquisitive toddler.

'I was referring to my house in Toledo,' he explained. 'Fortaleza Aguila was originally a fortress when it was built in the sixteenth century. I keep this apartment for when I stay in Madrid. There are security cameras in the lobby, and no one can enter the building who shouldn't,' he assured her, aware that she was concerned for Sebastian's safety.

He watched his son, wriggling in Betsy's arms.

'Why don't you put him down? He must want to stretch his legs after being confined in his child seat in the plane and then the car from the airport.'

'I'm worried he'll put sticky fingers on the cushions or slip over on the hard floor and bang his head. It's not exactly a child-friendly environment.'

She shifted Sebastian to her other hip. Carlos had the

feeling that she was holding on to the baby because she felt unsure of herself now that they were in Spain.

Before leaving England they'd gone back to Fraddlington. Photographers had been waiting outside the gates of the hotel and there had been more of them in front of Betsy's cottage. She had directed the driver down a narrow alleyway at the rear of the property and they'd entered the cottage through the back door, without the paparazzi seeing them. Betsy had run upstairs and reappeared a short while later carrying just one suitcase.

'I'll arrange for the rest of your things to be packed up and sent out to Spain,' he'd told her.

She'd looked surprised. 'I don't own anything else. All my belongings and Sebastian's are in this case. I rented the cottage fully furnished, and everything, even the cushions, belongs to the landlord.'

Now the suitcase that held Betsy's entire worldly possessions looked forlorn against the backdrop of his luxurious penthouse. Guilt swirled inside Carlos. He would have provided for her and Sebastian if she had turned to him for help. Instead she had made a meagre living, working behind the bar of the village pub.

While they had been at the cottage she had changed into a black skirt and white blouse. Both items looked cheaply made, and her low-heeled black shoes were scuffed. The outfit was only marginally smarter than the ripped jeans and old trainers she'd worn the previous day.

Carlos's mouth tightened as it occurred to him that the skirt and blouse were probably her smartest clothes, and that she probably wore them when she worked as a barmaid. But the badly fitting clothes did not detract from her beauty. He could not explain why the curve of her cheek and the slight pout of her lips made his mouth run dry.

She was a natural English rose, with porcelain skin and doe eyes that could darken with temper. But right now they were regarding him with a wariness that irritated him. Did she not realise that her life was going to improve vastly when she became his wife? He had plenty of money, several beautiful homes, and she would never have to work again. Many women would jump at the chance to marry him.

But Betsy had good reason to view marriage with trepidation, Carlos reminded himself. She had clearly been affected by her parents' behaviour. Some of the newspapers had already raked up old reports of her parents' public and very nasty divorce, and Betsy had been visibly upset when she'd seen them. Her vulnerability tugged on Carlos's emotions, even though only a day ago he would have sworn that was impossible.

His eyes were drawn to the swell of her breasts outlined beneath her thin cotton blouse and he acknowledged that he had thought about her more often than he'd liked in the past two years.

'Do you *have* to look at me as if I'm a dog's dinner?' she muttered. 'I realise that I'm not sophisticated and glamorous, like the women you are usually photographed with.'

'There will have to be some changes to your wardrobe,' Carlos told her bluntly. 'With that in mind, I have arranged for you to meet a stylist who will take you shopping this afternoon.' Before Betsy could argue, he continued, 'We have come to Madrid to attend a charity fundraising ball for the Segarra Foundation. The paparazzi will be out in full to take pictures of the celebrity guests, and I intend to make a press statement announcing our forthcoming marriage.'

She frowned. 'What about Sebastian? His bedtime is

seven o'clock and I'd like to keep him to his routine. I'm guessing the party will finish much later.'

'We will leave him behind. Not on his own, obviously.' Carlos forestalled the objection he sensed Betsy was about to make. 'He will be with a nanny. Once we are married we'll attend many social functions together, and it will be necessary to employ nursery staff to look after our son.'

Betsy glared at him. 'I can't believe you've hired a nanny without discussing it with me first. You promised that our marriage would be a partnership and that we would jointly make decisions about Sebastian. Now you have steamrollered ahead without asking my opinion. That's not an alliance, that's bullying, and I won't stand for it.'

Her voice had risen during her angry tirade and Sebastian's little face crumpled as he gave a whimper.

Betsy made a choked sound. 'Now we're arguing in front of him. I must have been mad to agree to marry you.'

Her voice wobbled, and Carlos stiffened when he saw a tear slip down her cheek.

'I haven't hired anyone,' he assured her, feeling guilty that he was the cause of Betsy's distress—it was a reminder of why he never made attachments. He was no good at it, and he let people down. 'My sister owns the apartment next door to this one and she has offered to have Sebastian for the night. He can sleep in the nursery with her son, and Miguel's nanny will be on hand to help Graciela with both boys.'

He'd hoped that his explanation would be enough to halt Betsy's tears, but her shoulders shook harder. 'I'm sorry,' she said in a choked voice. 'I'm just so *scared* that once we're married you'll try to take Sebastian away from me.'

'I swear that I will never do that.' Carlos wondered with a flash of anger if her parents had any idea how their behaviour had affected their daughter. 'Betsy, let me hold Sebastian while you pull yourself together.' He held out his hands and after a moment's hesitation she allowed him to take the baby. 'We'll advertise for a nanny once we are in Toledo. We will interview the applicants together, but ultimately the decision of who we employ will be yours, okay?'

'O-okay.' She swallowed and gave him something approaching a smile. 'Sebastian is my world and I love him more than anything.'

He lifted his hand and brushed away a tear from Betsy's cheek. Her skin felt like satin and her eyes were soft, her expression a little stunned. Carlos had the feeling she did not allow herself to cry very often. He had intended to comfort her, but he was conscious of the rapid thud of his pulse as he inhaled the lemony scent of her hair. Barely aware of what he was doing, he lowered his head towards her, drawn to the lush temptation of her mouth.

He was abruptly brought to his senses when Sebastian chose that moment to voice his frustration at being held and gave a loud yell. Carlos stepped back from Betsy at the same time as she jerked away from him. And as he watched a pink stain run under her skin he realised that she felt the simmering sexual awareness between them as fiercely as he did.

'Come and let me introduce you to my sister and her little boy,' he said, moving away from the tempting package of this woman he was determined to marry and just as determined to keep at arm's length. Betsy tested his self-control, but he would not allow her to break it. 'Graciela is keen to meet Sebastian.'

* * *

Betsy stared out of the car window at the blaze of street-lights and car headlamps that lit up Madrid's most famous street at night. Earlier in the day an elegant stylist called Sanchia had taken her shopping on Gran Via. Betsy had lost count of the number of exclusive boutiques and designer stores they had visited. The clothes she'd tried on had received a nod of approval or a shake of the head from Sanchia, and the purchased items had been paid for with Carlos's credit card.

'You are going to be my wife. Like it or not I am a well-known public figure, and I want our marriage to appear genuine. I won't have you dressing like a waitress in a downtown diner,' he'd told her brutally when she had protested about the shopping trip.

By then everything about her new life had felt surreal, and Betsy had simply accepted the stylist's advice on clothes, shoes and accessories. After the shopping there had been a visit to a beauty salon, where glorious-smelling products had been applied to her hair and her skin.

But she had barely glanced at her reflection to see the new and improved version of herself because she had been anxious to get back to Sebastian. Although she need not have worried about him. When she'd returned to Carlos's sister's child-friendly apartment, Sebastian had been in the nursery with his cousin Miguel. Carlos, Graciela and the nanny had been playing with both children.

Betsy had halted outside the room, overwhelmed by a mix of emotions as she heard Sebastian laughing and watched him clamber onto Carlos's knee. Her little boy looked so happy with his new family. And Carlos's sister had been so welcoming when they had been introduced. Graciela had tactfully not asked why Betsy had kept Sebastian a secret.

She pulled her mind back to the present. The car was crawling along in heavy traffic, but she did not mind if their arrival at the party was delayed. Carlos had warned her that there was likely to be a large media presence at the hotel where the event was being held. When Betsy had been a child, the paparazzi had been obsessed with her celebrity parents during their hostile divorce.

Memories of intrusive photographers and their camera flashbulbs going off, plus the knowledge that she would have to face the paparazzi tonight, when she and Carlos stepped out of the car, were partly to blame for her tension. But the main reason why her nerves felt strung out was sprawled next to her on the back seat of the limousine.

She glanced at Carlos's austere profile and butterflies leapt in her stomach when he turned his head towards her. He was so impossibly handsome. The perfect symmetry of his features, those gleaming golden eyes beneath heavy brows and that mouth all promised sensual heaven. And delivered. The memory of his kiss had stayed with her for two long years.

She caught her bottom lip between her teeth. Carlos's eyes narrowed and he lifted his hand and brushed his thumb lightly over the place where she had bitten.

'Are you still worrying about Sebastian? He was fast asleep when we left him at my sister's apartment, and even if he does wake up Graciela and the nanny will take good care of him.'

'I know he will be fine.'

She ran her tongue over her lip, where it tingled from Carlos's touch. His gaze sharpened on her face and Betsy saw a glint of gold beneath his thick lashes. Awareness of his male potency caused the tiny hairs on her body to stand on end.

'I'm sorry I was an idiot earlier today,' she mumbled, embarrassment flaring because she had broken down in front of him.

They had flown to Spain on Carlos's private jet. When Betsy had seen his luxurious penthouse apartment it had been another sign that he was hugely wealthy. But she had grown up with money—although the only winners in her parents' divorce had been the lawyers—and she knew that affluence did not guarantee happiness.

She looked down at the exquisite pear-shaped diamond ring that Carlos had slid onto her finger before they had left his penthouse. The streetlights shining through the window glinted on the diamond so that it sparkled with a fiery brilliance. But the ring, like the designer dress she was wearing, was only to convince the paparazzi that her romance with Carlos was genuine.

Her heart gave a jolt when he captured her hand and lifted it to his mouth. The brush of his lips across her fingers sent a shiver of sensation through her.

'We will both need a period of adjustment,' he murmured. 'I accept that the trauma you experienced as a child when your parents divorced amid such acrimony led to your decision not to tell me about Sebastian. But our marriage will be different. I will do everything possible to make it work.'

Carlos sounded sincere. Betsy tried to remind herself that he was only marrying her to claim his son, but she did want Sebastian to grow up with parents who did not despise each other.

'I will do my best to make our marriage work, too,' she promised.

Her eyes locked with his and she could not look away from him. The atmosphere inside the car was suddenly thick with sexual awareness. Hers. His.

The privacy screen was up, separating them from the driver. Betsy's stomach dipped when Carlos took hold of her chin. She watched his dark head descend and held her breath. Her pulse was thudding and she was transfixed by the feral gleam in his eyes. His gaze was on her lips and she moistened them with the tip of her tongue.

'Perhaps we should seal the deal with a kiss?'

His deep voice was like velvet caressing her skin. She had secretly longed for him to kiss her from the moment he'd stormed into her cottage, Betsy admitted to herself. Her common sense told her to resist her attraction to him. He had the power to hurt her—as he had done once before, and as her father had done when he had dropped out of her life. But her body refused to listen to her brain, and she felt her breasts tighten and her thighs soften. The truth was that she was desperately attracted to Carlos and her lips parted in invitation.

'I agree,' she whispered, casting caution aside.

Anticipation ran like quicksilver through her veins when he dipped his head lower and closed the tiny gap between them. He grazed his lips across hers and she felt him smile before he covered her mouth with his own and kissed her with bone-shaking sensuality.

She caught fire instantly, unable to resist his bold mastery as he coaxed her lips apart with the tip of his tongue and then plundered deep inside her mouth. He released her chin and slid his hand round to her nape. She tipped her head back, twisting in her seat so that she could press her body against him. His fingers tangled in her hair and he skimmed his other hand from her waist to the curve of her breast.

His kiss was even better than she remembered…even more potent than her dreams of being in his arms. The reality was heat and flame and she was powerless to resist his mastery.

'You look incredible,' Carlos whispered against her mouth. 'When I first saw you in that dress you took my breath away.'

Pleasure swept through her at this husky compliment. The dress that the stylist had picked out was a floor-length forget-me-knot-blue silk sheath overlaid with lace and embellished with tiny sparkling crystals. The plunging neckline was more daring than anything Betsy had ever worn before, and the side split in the skirt went up to her mid-thigh. Strappy silver stilettos and a silver clutch bag were the perfect accessories. Her make-up had been kept discreet and the stylist had left her hair loose.

When she'd walked into the sitting room at the apartment the look of admiration on Carlos's face had for a moment helped to ease her nerves about making her first public appearance with him. He looked mouthwatering in a black dinner suit, white silk shirt and black bow tie. The formal clothes emphasised his athletic physique, and his thick, dark hair curled rebelliously over his collar.

Betsy had drawn a sharp breath when he'd pulled a velvet box out of the pocket of his tuxedo and opened it to reveal the diamond engagement ring. 'Is that really necessary?' she'd muttered.

The ring had made her situation real. She had agreed to marry a man who did not love her. But at least Carlos had not made false promises—unlike her father, who had used her as a pawn in his battle of one-upmanship with her mother. In truth, both her parents had put their own selfish aims above her happiness, Betsy thought ruefully.

Now Carlos deepened the kiss, and the firm pressure of his lips on hers decimated the last vestiges of her defences. The world ceased to exist and there was only him.

His arms felt like iron bands around her and his evocative scent—spicy cologne mingled with male pheromones—filled her senses. It had been the same two years ago. One kiss and she had been lost to the intoxicating pleasure that he'd wrought with his mouth and hands.

Right now one of his hands was on her back, tracing along her spine, and the other was splayed over her breast. His thumb stroked her peaked nipple through her dress, sending shockwaves of sensation through her. Desire pooled low in her pelvis and she curled her arms around his neck, so that her breasts were pressed hard against his chest. She could feel the beat of his heart echo the erratic thud of her own.

Outside the window there was a bright flash, then another, and another. Betsy blinked, suddenly aware that the car was no longer moving. Carlos lifted his mouth from hers and growled something in Spanish as he moved along the seat away from her.

Still dazed from their passion, she gave a soft moan of protest which turned into a choked sound of dismay as her brain clicked into gear and she realised they had arrived at the hotel. The blinding flashes had been from the paparazzi's cameras.

Carlos raked his fingers through his hair, and Betsy fancied that his hand was a little unsteady. But when he spoke his voice held its usual blend of cynicism and faint amusement, as if he took nothing in life too seriously. 'Are you ready for showtime?'

The door was opened by the chauffeur and Carlos climbed out of the car and offered his hand to help Betsy step onto the pavement. She was blinded by bright white light and heard the popping sound of more flashbulbs exploding. The press pack surged forward and she was glad of Carlos's solid presence beside her as he slid his arm around her waist. She was still stunned by that passionate kiss in the back of the car, but she told herself that her legs felt wobbly because she was unused to walking in high heels.

'Carlos—is it true that you and Miss Miller have a child?' a photographer called out.

'Why was your baby kept a secret?' someone else shouted.

'You are on record saying that you never wanted children, Carlos. Do you regret the birth of your son?'

Betsy felt Carlos tense as he led her up the steps of the hotel, but when he turned to face the baying press his bland expression revealed nothing of his thoughts.

'It is absolutely true that Miss Miller is the mother of my son,' he said calmly. 'And, far from regretting Sebastian's birth, I am delighted to be a father. Betsy and I had hoped to keep our son out of the spotlight, but now I am very happy to reveal that we intend to marry as soon as possible.'

A babble of voices rose from the crowd of paparazzi.

A photographer pushed closer to Betsy. 'Miss Miller, your high-profile parents went through a notoriously acrimonious divorce and fought for custody of you when you were a child. Your father even kidnapped you at one point. Has that had an effect on how you view marriage?'

She stiffened. The question was intrusive, and it brought back memories she wished she could forget. But she would deal with her demons in private—not in the pages of the tabloids. Ignoring a strong urge to run into the hotel, away from the camera lenses, she forced a smile for the paparazzi.

'My view of marriage is that it is a wonderful institution and I am looking forward to becoming Carlos's wife.' She held out her left hand to show off the engagement ring. 'Diamonds really are a girl's best friend,' she quipped. 'I'm extremely happy.'

To her relief, Carlos ignored further questions from the press and escorted her inside the hotel. As they walked through the opulent foyer Betsy's stiletto heels clicked on the marble floor.

Carlos glanced at her. 'You handled that well.'

The admiration in his voice made her foolish heart leap. She halted and turned to face him.

'Some people sympathised with my father when he kept me hidden in Canada. He was seen as a champion of the rights of fathers. He said he kidnapped me because he loved me, and I felt terrible when he was sent to prison. When he was released I hoped I could rebuild my relationship with him. But I was a teenager by then, and Drake lost interest in me when he realised that he couldn't use me as a way to hurt my mother any more.'

She sighed.

'I'm telling you this because I don't want you to make a public show of claiming your son only to become bored with fatherhood when Sebastian reaches the tantrums stage or when he is no longer a cute toddler.'

An indefinable expression flickered in Carlos's eyes. 'My commitment to my son will be total and for ever.'

She nodded, feeling reassured.

Ahead of them, the double doors leading to the ballroom stood open and guests were already filling the room.

'I'd like to use the bathroom.' She needed a few moments to steel her nerves before she put on a show as Carlos's fiancée.

Thankfully the cloakroom was empty, and there was no one to hear Betsy's groan of dismay when she saw her reflection in the mirror. Her hair was mussed and the neckline of her dress was askew. She ran her finger over lips that were still puffy from Carlos's kisses.

Her stomach swooped as she wondered if he had kissed her deliberately, knowing that the photographers would snap pictures of her looking suitably love-struck. He had warned her that the paparazzi would be waiting for them, but she had forgotten, or simply not cared, because when Carlos had put his mouth on hers she had been instantly lost in the beauty of his kiss.

After reapplying a pale pink gloss to her lips, and taking several deep breaths, she went to find him.

The hotel foyer was crowded now, as more guests arrived. Carlos was standing by the entrance to the ballroom and, Betsy noticed that all the beautiful women gravitated towards him like bees drawn to honey. He looked over in her direction and the lazy smile on his face turned into something far more predatory. The heat of his gaze burned through her and she felt an ache in her womb.

He was the father of her child, and soon she would be his wife, but what did Carlos expect from their marriage—from her? She bit her lip. They'd had sex once, and the next morning he'd left. Those facts were unarguable. If she hadn't had Sebastian she would not be wearing Carlos's ring now. But he had said he wanted their marriage to work—did that mean he wanted to have sex with her?

Shockingly explicit memories flooded her mind of his powerful body looming above her, his thick erection pushing deeper and deeper inside her. Between her legs she felt the sticky heat of desire...

He could not possibly know what she was thinking, she assured herself as she walked towards him. But the golden gleam in his eyes sent her pulse racing and she could not look away from him.

His dark brows quirked. 'Ready?'

Betsy felt a betraying blush spread across her face. She might as well have 'ready for sex' tattooed on her forehead, she thought ruefully. Carlos made her forget her natural caution and behave in a way she had never done with any other man.

But two years ago she had given him her virginity and, although she hadn't expected the night they had spent together to lead to everlasting love, she had felt such a fool when he'd gone back to Spain without a word. She would enter this marriage with no expectations, she vowed silently, and she would guard her heart against Carlos.

Giving him a cool smile, she slipped her hand through the arm that he held out to her and walked beside him into the ballroom.

CHAPTER SIX

THE CHARITY BALL was a spectacular event that would be talked about for weeks afterwards. Carlos had expected nothing less. He employed the best party planners and had funded the event personally. The food was sublime, the champagne flowed, the guests were clearly enjoying themselves—and, most importantly, a substantial amount of money was being raised for the Segarra Foundation.

Since he'd retired from playing tennis competitively, Carlos's passion had been his charity, which aimed to enable kids from deprived backgrounds to access sports which were too often elitist. As a child he had been lucky, because his mother had once been a professional tennis player and had not only encouraged his talent but managed to secure funding for his training. The foundation was his way of putting something back into the world of sport that had made him a household name and a multimillionaire.

The evening was drawing to an end and he should be feeling satisfied. But Carlos grimaced as he acknowledged that *satisfied* was the opposite of how he felt.

Frustration surged through him as he moved around the dance floor with Betsy in his arms. Holding her close like this was pure torture. He was fiercely aware of her soft breasts pressed against his chest, and when the side split in her ballgown parted and he felt the brush of a stocking-clad leg against his thigh, it took all his will-power not to haul her closer still. But if he did she would be bound to realise that he was aroused.

It infuriated him that she made him feel dangerously out of control when no other woman had ever done more than spark his temporary interest. He shouldn't have kissed her in the car. That was when everything had gone wrong. He'd tasted her sweet breath in his mouth and a madness had come over him.

Carlos tried to blame his obsession with Betsy on his libido, which had inconveniently reawakened after the longest period of celibacy he'd had since his first sexual experience when he was sixteen.

He looked down at the top of Betsy's head as she rested it on his chest. The silky caramel curls invited him to spear his fingers in her hair and angle her head so that he could taste her again and plunder the moist lips that she'd parted beneath his during those stolen moments in the back of the limousine.

Maybe she'd sensed his scrutiny, for she looked up at him and he saw her brown eyes darken as the pupils dilated. He could not fault her performance. Why, she had almost convinced *him*, along with the guests and invited members of the press, that she was his adoring fiancée.

For a moment he imagined that this was real. That they were two people who had connected on a fundamental level and were eagerly anticipating spending the rest of their lives together...

Dios. He cursed silently as he reminded himself that the only reason he was marrying Betsy was so that he could be a full-time father to his son.

There was a lull in the music and Betsy gave him a

rueful smile as she pulled out of his arms, leaving him with a sense of regret that added to his fury with himself.

'I'll have to sit this one out,' she said. 'My feet are killing me.'

'The ball is due to finish soon—I was about to suggest that we should leave.'

He was aware that he sounded curt, and caught the look of surprise she darted at him, but he felt marginally more in control now that her delectable body wasn't pressed up against him.

He took out his phone and instructed his driver to bring the car to the front of the hotel.

Five minutes later Betsy blew out a breath as she leaned against the plush leather seat in the back of the car. 'Sorry, but I can't wear my shoes for a second longer.'

'Put your seat belt back on,' Carlos ordered as she released the belt and leaned down to fiddle with her shoes.

'I will in a minute…'

He swore as the car turned a sharp corner and she was flung against him. The sensation of her voluptuous curves pressed against him rattled his hard-won composure and, after securing the seat belt around her once more, he lifted her legs across his lap. His fingers brushed across her slender ankles as he unfastened the tiny buckles on her shoes.

Betsy gave a deep sigh as she kicked off her shoes and wriggled her toes. '*Oh…that's better.*'

Her smile lit up her lovely face and Carlos's heart kicked in his chest.

'The ball seemed to go well. Not that I have much experience of grand parties. The most popular social event at the pub was darts night, when Fraddlington's team played against teams from other villages.'

'Why did you move to Dorset?' he asked, needing to

distract his mind from her slender legs lying across his lap. The split in her skirt had parted to reveal a toned thigh…

'My aunt died and the house in London was sold. Sarah is an old school friend and she offered me a job at the pub that she and Mike had bought in Fraddlington. The landlord of the cottage I rented is a friend of Mike's.'

'What about your parents? Didn't they help you after Sebastian was born?'

'Mum came to visit, but she only stayed for a week. She has lived in LA for a few years now, and she has a new husband. As for my dad…' A look of sadness crossed Betsy's face. 'We keep in contact sporadically, but he's married again too—to his third wife. After he kidnapped me our relationship was never as close as it had been before,' she said flatly.

Carlos turned his gaze away from her and stared out of the window. Betsy's vulnerability tugged on something inside him and he felt surprisingly protective of her. Neither of her parents had been good role models and they had never prioritised their daughter's need for security. But, in contrast, Betsy was a devoted mother to Sebastian and, despite her reservations, she had accepted that marriage to him would allow the little boy to grow up in a safe family environment.

The car pulled into the underground car park and Betsy carried her shoes to the lift, which whisked them up to the top floor of the apartment block. The mirrored walls inside the lift gave Carlos a view of her gorgeous figure from every angle.

She was a pocket Venus, standing there in her stockinged feet, with her long skirt gathered in one hand and her shoes dangling by their straps from the other. He fancied that her mouth was still slightly swollen from where he'd kissed her earlier, and the memory of her lips parting beneath his made his body clench hard.

He ushered her into the penthouse, which had been designed as his bachelor pad but hadn't seen a lot of action in the past two years. In fact he couldn't remember the last time he'd invited a woman back for the night.

Carlos had put his lack of interest in sex down to his change of lifestyle after he'd retired from playing tennis professionally. Achieving the pinnacle of his ambition by winning the tournament in London had left him feeling unsettled and directionless. Grief for his mother, which he'd managed to supress for nearly two decades, had suddenly hit him hard, and guilt had consumed him.

It still did.

Betsy had headed down the corridor towards the guest bedroom. Carlos told himself he was relieved that there would be no further chance for her to flirt with him tonight. Because that was what she'd been doing at the ball—with a shy hesitancy that had affected him much more than if she'd come on to him with the boldness of a *femme fatale*.

As he strode across the lounge he pulled off his bow tie and unfastened the top buttons on his shirt. He extracted a bottle of single malt Scotch from the drinks cabinet, poured a measure into a glass—and stiffened when he sensed that he wasn't alone.

Betsy—minus shoes and evening purse—stood in the doorway.

'I thought you had gone to bed.' Good manners compelled him to ask, 'Is there anything I can get you?'

'I wouldn't mind a nightcap.'

Her husky voice tugged low in his gut. Carlos poured whisky into a second glass and reminded himself that women had thrown themselves at him since he was sixteen. He could handle this unremarkable, unsophisticated woman. No problem.

He carried their drinks over to the coffee table and lowered himself down onto the sofa. An alarm bell rang in his head when Betsy sat next to him. She leaned forward to pick up her glass, and lust speared him in the groin as his gaze was drawn to the front of her dress and the creamy upper slopes of her breasts.

She took a sip of her drink, and Carlos had an idea that she needed the kick of alcohol.

'I would like to clarify a point about our marriage,' she murmured, fixing her big brown eyes on his face.

'Go on.' His gaze narrowed on the pink flush that spread across her cheeks.

'I'm not sure what you will want in…in the bedroom. What I mean is…will we share a bed?'

She caught her lower lip between her teeth, and it was all Carlos could do to restrain himself from demonstrating exactly what he wanted. Her—naked and willing beneath him.

'You say that your commitment to Sebastian will be total, but what about your commitment to our marriage?' Betsy was becoming visibly more embarrassed, but she ploughed on. 'What I'm asking is, will you want me to be a proper wife, or do you intend to keep a mistress discreetly in the background?'

Carlos stretched out his long legs and hooked one ankle over the other. He took a swig of whisky before he answered. 'Would you object if I kept a mistress?' he asked.

'Would it matter if I objected?' She put her head on one side and studied him. 'You've made it clear that you're calling all the shots.'

That vulnerability was there again in her voice. Carlos

told himself that if he was a better man her words might
have stirred his conscience. But his gaze was drawn to the
rise and fall of Betsy's breasts as she took a deep breath.

'I'm simply trying to determine if you will…seek grat-
ification outside of our marriage,' she murmured. 'And,
if so, then it will only be fair for me to enjoy the same
freedom.'

Over his dead body, Carlos thought violently.

He knew he should be appalled by the jealousy that
surged like molten lava through his veins at the idea of
Betsy warming another man's bed. Possessiveness was
not one of his faults, though God knew he had enough of
them. But the proprietorial feeling remained.

'The thing is…' she said softly.

She put her glass on the table and inched along the sofa
towards him. Carlos breathed in her perfume, sweetly
floral with underlying notes of something musky and
deeply sensual that called to the wolf in him.

'You kissed me and…well…'

Her blush spread down her throat and over the slopes
of her breasts, giving them the appearance of rose-flushed
peaches, plump and firm and infinitely inviting. Carlos
could see the outline of her nipples through her dress,
and recalled how they had bloomed beneath his touch
when he'd cupped her breasts in his hands during those
crazy moments in the back of the car.

'Well… I liked it when you kissed me…'

Her honesty felt like a knife in his ribs.

'And I got the impression that you are still attracted to
me. So I'm wondering what you want from our relationship when we marry…or…or even before the wedding.'

So much for his belief that he could handle her! Carlos
mocked himself. She tied him in knots, and he resented it.

He stood up abruptly and paced across the room to

stand by the window. Before him Madrid was a mass of glittering lights against the backdrop of an inky sky. He was sorely tempted to respond to Betsy's sweetly clumsy invitation by carrying her into the bedroom so that he could make love to her. It was what they both wanted.

But something in her eyes told him that she might hope for more than sex—if not immediately then in the future, after they were married. And she would be disappointed. Because he had no intention of falling in love with her. Love meant responsibility, commitment and pain. Carlos had spent the past twenty years avoiding all three, and he was determined to maintain the status quo.

'I will commit to our marriage and I will expect you to do the same,' he growled as he swung round to face her. 'As you pointed out, there is an attraction between us. I foresee that in the future we will have a sexual relationship—especially when you are my wife and we sleep in the same bedroom at my house in Toledo.'

Betsy frowned. 'You want us to share a room?'

'It's customary for married couples to do so,' he said drily. 'But I advise you not to get carried away, nor to forget that we are marrying for the sake of our son. This is not a fairy-tale romance.'

'I'm well aware that you are not Prince Charming,' Betsy snapped.

Carlos watched her turn pale and then flush scarlet once more. Her eyes had darkened with anger, or maybe it was hurt. His conscience pricked again, but he reminded himself that her antipathy was safer than her sweetly clumsy attempt to seduce him.

'You are so *unbelievably* arrogant.'

She jumped to her feet and marched across the room to stand in front of him. But he noticed that she kept a distance between them, and he was glad. The temptation to reach out and pull her into his arms, lose whatever remained of his sanity in her glorious curves, still beat hard in him.

'Two years ago you must have realised I was a virgin, but you went back to Spain without a word—without checking if I was okay.'

'Was it really your first time?' he asked gruffly.

He had not forgotten anything about that night. Her eagerness to make love had delighted him. He had been surprised that she'd seemed to lack experience, but he'd been so hungry for her that he hadn't cared when her hands had fumbled with the zip on his trousers, or when she'd curled her fingers around his erection and squeezed him so enthusiastically that he'd almost come there and then.

'Yes. I wouldn't lie about it.'

His gaze narrowed on her flushed face. 'Why me? You must have had boyfriends before we met—yet you were still a virgin. In your note you said you had slept with me because I was famous. Was that true?'

She dropped her gaze and suddenly seemed to be fascinated with the rug beneath her feet. 'I felt like an idiot when I overheard you telling that journalist that I was a casual fling. The truth is I had sex with you because I fancied you more than any of the guys I dated at university. Although, to be honest, there weren't many. My parents' volatile relationship wasn't a great advertisement for love,' she said wryly. 'But I liked you, and I thought you liked me. I should have known that the sexiest man in Spain would only want a one-night stand with someone like me.'

He frowned. 'Someone like you?'

'Ordinary. You only noticed me because we'd shared a house and I'd cooked your meals. I've seen photos in magazines of the women you date. They're always beautiful and glamorous.'

And shallow, Carlos thought. He could not remember individual faces, let alone the names of his past lovers. Only Betsy Miller had lodged like a burr beneath his skin.

'You shouldn't believe everything you read in the gossip columns,' he said drily. 'For what it's worth, I believe in being truthful as much as you. And I told you, I *did* try to contact you a few weeks after I'd left your aunt's house.'

A tiny frown appeared between her brows. 'I moved from there soon after you had left. My aunt died unexpectedly and her son Lee was her sole heir. He told me that I had to leave because he wanted to sell the house. A removals firm came and took all the furniture and Aunt Alice's personal belongings to a storage unit. I had just found out that I was pregnant, and I asked Lee if I could stay at the house while I looked for somewhere else to live, but he insisted that I had no legal right to stay there and I had to leave immediately.'

'Dios!' Carlos was enraged. 'What kind of man would make a pregnant young woman homeless?'

But he was hardly in a position to judge, he thought grimly. He should have stayed and spoken to Betsy the morning after he'd slept with her. It was true that he'd rushed back to Spain to be with his sister, but he'd received the call from Graciela saying that her baby needed heart surgery when he'd already been in the car on his way to the airport.

If he was honest, he'd felt shaken by his spectacular loss of control with Betsy. That first time with her had been the most satisfying sexual experience he'd ever had. Almost immediately after they'd both climaxed, while he was still inside her, he'd felt himself harden again. He'd quickly changed the condom, but his carelessness was a possible explanation for how she'd fallen pregnant, Carlos realised.

He took a gulp of whisky. 'Even then, when you had nowhere to live and had just found out that you were pregnant with my baby, you didn't ask for my help. Did you believe that I was a man like your aunt's son and I would turn my back on you?'

She had not given him a chance to accept responsibility for his child—perhaps because she had believed in his playboy reputation and the scurrilous gossip written about him to feed a celebrity-obsessed audience.

Guilt ripped through him and he turned away from her. From now on he would give Betsy and their son his protection, Carlos vowed to himself. But that was all he could give her. He had locked his emotions away twenty years ago, when his mother had died and he'd blamed himself.

'Earlier this evening we both agreed to do everything possible to make this a successful marriage,' Betsy said quietly. 'Why did you kiss me?'

Carlos remained where he stood in front of the window and narrowed his eyes until the bright city lights splintered. 'I am a red-blooded male and you made it clear that you wanted to be kissed.'

Behind him he heard her draw a sharp breath. He watched her reflection in the window as she spun round and marched out of the room.

He continued to stand there for a long time afterwards, alone with his demons. Spain's most famous sportsman, an international celebrity, and he was the loneliest man in the world.

CHAPTER SEVEN

BETSY'S PHONE PINGED and her stomach swooped when she saw Carlos's name flash on the screen. It was three weeks since she had woken in the guest bedroom at his penthouse the morning after the charity ball. As soon as she'd opened her eyes she had cringed with embarrassment as she'd recalled how she had propositioned him. She might not have actually *asked* him to have sex with her, but she had dropped unsubtle hints and he had rejected her.

She couldn't understand why she had behaved so out of character. Usually she was so reticent about her feelings.

She had no intention of falling in love with him, Betsy assured herself, but when Carlos had kissed her in the car they had both gone up in flames. His mouth had been hot and demanding as he'd deepened the kiss so that it had become something *more*—something wilder and needier. She had felt the proof of his desire when she'd laid her hand on his chest and felt the thunderous beat of his heart. And when they had danced together at the ball her wayward body had melted against him and she'd been very aware of the hard ridge of his arousal beneath his trousers.

Two years ago passion had exploded between them

with their first kiss, and the same thing had happened here in Madrid.

Betsy knew she hadn't imagined the feral gleam in Carlos's eyes. She had thought of nothing else for the past three weeks. But that morning she had been in an agony of embarrassment, and he'd been coolly aloof in the car when he'd driven them to Toledo, an hour south of the capital.

She had opted to sit in the back with Sebastian, who had been strapped into his baby seat.

Carlos's house stood on a hill overlooking the historical city which had been immortalised by Spain's most famous artist El Greco in his painting *View of Toledo*. And Betsy had been pleasantly surprised to find that although Fortaleza Aguila still bore the evidence that it had once been a fortress, it was now an attractive house built of mellow brick, with terracotta roof tiles which had faded to a dusky pink in the blazing summer sun.

'The English translation of the house's name is Eagle Fortress,' Carlos had told her, when she'd forgotten her awkwardness with him for a few moments and looked with interest at the home that would now be hers and Sebastian's too.

She had felt daunted by all the huge changes to her life—not least when Carlos had lifted Sebastian out of the car and carried him into the house, leaving her to follow him.

The décor was traditionally Spanish, with dark wood panelling, ornate wall tiles and stone floors that were worn smooth with age. Betsy had recognised several original pieces of art that must be worth a fortune. It was all very beautiful, and something of a surprise after the modern penthouse in Madrid, but she felt like a visitor to a stately mansion.

'I arranged for an interior designer to create a nursery for Sebastian, and the decorators have just finished,' Carlos had told her as he'd opened a door on the second floor and ushered her into a large, sun-filled room.

Painted in tones of pale blue, white and yellow, and filled with toys, with a magnificent wooden cot in the centre, it was the kind of nursery Betsy had imagined planning for Sebastian if she won the Lottery. Carlos had set Sebastian on his feet and he'd toddled across the floor towards another oversized fluffy toy rabbit.

'Bun,' he'd said happily, before going off to investigate a pile of colourful plastic bricks.

The nursery was at least four times the size of the box room at the cottage, where Sebastian had slept in a travel cot that had belonged to the landlord. Guilt had been like a lead weight in the pit of Betsy's stomach as she'd acknowledged that Carlos could provide Sebastian with the kind of affluent lifestyle that would have been impossible for her to do on her income from her bar job and her paintings.

'This is your room,' Carlos had told her, and he'd opened a door from the nursery into an adjoining bedroom.

Betsy hadn't known whether she felt relieved or disappointed that he clearly did not expect her to sleep in his room straight away.

She pulled her mind back to the present and added a few more brushstrokes of white paint around the muzzle on the portrait she was working on. This commission had been a welcome surprise. The owners of the Labrador she'd painted while she had been at the cottage had been delighted with the portrait, which she'd had taken to the framers just before she'd left Fraddlington with Carlos.

They had recommended her to a friend of theirs, and her new client had emailed photos of his beautiful chocolate and white Springer Spaniel.

It felt good to be painting again. Betsy had brought her brushes from England, but she'd needed more paints and canvases, and had been pleased when she'd discovered there was an art supplies shop in Toledo. She did not have a driving licence, but Carlos had arranged for his driver to take her into the city whenever she wanted to go.

When she'd walked into the art shop for the first time she'd carried her Spanish phrasebook, but to her relief the young assistant there spoke fluent English, albeit with a distinctive Brummie accent.

Hector's arms were covered in artistic tattoos and he had long black hair and wore big silver earrings. He looked like one of the art students Betsy had known at university.

'My dad is Spanish and I lived in Spain until I was twelve, when my parents split up and I moved to Birmingham with my mum,' he'd explained.

Hector was friendly—and *ordinary*, compared to Carlos's friends, who were all wealthy high-fliers. Betsy had become a regular visitor to his art shop, and found Hector was the only person she could really talk to. There was Carlos, of course, but her awareness of him was stronger than ever. And her fear of making a fool of herself, like she'd done at the penthouse, meant that she avoided being alone with him whenever possible.

With a faint sigh, she put down her brush and wiped her hands on a rag before she picked up her phone to read Carlos's message.

Come to my study so that we can discuss the wedding.

She grimaced as she pictured his autocratic features and rashly messaged back.

Yes, sir!

Her old jeans were covered in paint stains. She quickly changed out of them and put on one of her new dresses—a pale lemon silk wrap style, with a pretty floral pattern. She pulled the elastic tie from her hair and slicked pink gloss over her lips, assuring herself that as Carlos's future wife she couldn't run around the house in her old jeans. She hadn't changed her clothes in the hope of pleasing him, she told her reflection.

She went through the door from her bedroom that led directly into the nursery. Sebastian had been having his morning nap while she painted, but when she stepped into the room he wasn't in his cot. The nanny was there, folding some of Sebastian's new clothes.

Betsy had liked Ginette the moment she'd met her. English by birth, she had moved to Spain some twenty years ago, when she'd married her Spanish husband, and she spoke both languages fluently.

'My husband and I were not blessed with children of our own,' Ginette had explained at her interview. 'But I have loved looking after the children of the families I worked for. Now that Ernesto has passed away, I'm looking for a live-in position.'

Ginette smiled now, when she saw Betsy. 'Sebastian woke up about ten minutes ago, and Carlos took him downstairs.'

We will need a period of adjustment.

Carlos's words came back to Betsy and she acknowledged the truth of them. She had been her son's sole carer since he was born, and she was finding it hard to share the responsibility for him.

Her heart gave a jolt when she walked down the stairs and watched Sebastian toddling across the stone-flagged entrance hall, chasing after a plastic football. Carlos was crouched at one end of the hall and holding his arms out to his son.

'*Bueno, chico!* Kick the ball, *conejito.*'

'I think he might be a bit young to learn how to play football,' Betsy said drily, trying to hide her emotional response to seeing Sebastian so happy with his father. She wanted to scoop her baby into her arms and breathe in the delicious scent of him, but it was Carlos's arms that Sebastian ran to. She couldn't pretend to herself that it didn't hurt. 'You're already speaking to him in Spanish? Don't you think it will be confusing for him? He doesn't know many English words yet.'

Carlos lifted Sebastian up and strolled over to her. 'We agreed to bring him up to be bilingual,' he reminded her. 'And the best way for him to learn will be for him to hear words in both languages.'

That was fine for Carlos, who spoke English as fluently as his native tongue. But she would have to learn to speak Spanish quickly, otherwise she would be excluded from the relationship that Carlos and Sebastian would share when they talked in Spanish.

Maybe Carlos *wanted* to exclude her, Betsy brooded.

His gaze narrowed on her face. 'Is something the matter?'

She wasn't going to admit how vulnerable she felt. 'I was just thinking that Sebastian has adapted well to living here.'

'This is his home—and yours. Are you not adapting well, *querida*?'

Betsy made a mental note to ask Ginette what *querida* meant. She bit her lip. 'It's just very different to the life I had in England.'

Carlos stretched out his hand and ran his thumb lightly across her lower lip, where she had bitten the skin. 'I realise that everything here is new for you, and I appreciate it that you have allowed me to bring Sebastian to Spain.'

The warmth in his sherry-gold eyes curled around Betsy's heart. She refrained from pointing out that he hadn't given her much choice about where Sebastian would grow up. Since they had arrived in Toledo she'd gained a better understanding of how important it was to Carlos that Sebastian should bear his name. He was proud of his Spanish heritage and proud of his son. She saw it in the way his features softened every time he looked at the toddler who bore such a striking resemblance to him.

Betsy did not doubt that Carlos loved Sebastian, and that was why she had agreed to marry him. But she still felt like a fish out of water in this new country where the language, culture and customs were so different from the way of life she was used to in England.

Carlos seemed to have an uncanny knack of being able to read her thoughts. 'You will feel more settled once you are my wife,' he said softly.

The golden glint in his eyes caused Betsy's heart to miss a beat, and she could not look away from him. Time seemed to slow, and the air quivered with their mutual awareness. But then he blinked, and the connection she had sensed between them vanished. He looked across the hall and, following his gaze, she saw Ginette walking towards them.

'I thought I'd put Sebastian in his pushchair and take him for a walk in the garden,' Ginette said as she took him from Carlos.

'He will need to wear sunscreen.' Betsy was immediately a mother hen, determined to protect her chick. The temperature in Toledo in July was much hotter than the soggy English summer they had left behind. 'And don't forget to put the parasol up.'

'Ginette is highly experienced in childcare and has excellent references,' Carlos murmured when the nanny had carried Sebastian away.

'I know. But it's a mother's instinct to take care of her child and put his welfare above everything else.'

An odd expression flickered on his face, but it was gone before Betsy could decipher it. He said no more as he opened the door to his study and ushered her into the room.

'Have you heard from your parents?' he asked, waving her to a chair before he walked around the desk and sat down.

'I invited both of them to the wedding, as you suggested. But I warned you it would be pointless. My mother says she won't attend if my father brings "the trollop he is married to now", and Drake refuses to come without his third wife.' She shrugged. 'It was the same when I invited my parents to my graduation ceremony after university. They wanted me to choose between them, which I refused to do. The result was that neither of them came. I can't please one without upsetting the other.'

It was her childhood all over again, Betsy thought dismally. Her parents were the reason why she had never wanted to marry. Her chest felt tight with panic at the idea of being trapped in an unhappy relationship.

'I'm not sure I can do this,' she told Carlos.

Once again he seemed to read her mind. 'Our marriage won't be like theirs.'

'How do you know? We might fight all the time, and
Sebastian will be caught in the middle like I was when
I was a child.'

'The whole reason we are marrying is to give him a
family. We are putting our child's needs first—which,
from the sound of it, your parents failed to do with you.'

Carlos stood up and walked around to where she was
sitting. He leaned his hip against the desk, much too
close for Betsy's comfort. His fitted black trousers emphasised his rangy frame, and his white shirt was open
at the throat, giving her a glimpse of his tanned skin and
black chest hair.

She sighed. If only he wasn't so beautiful. She wished
she could control her body's unbidden response to his
potent masculinity, but when she lifted her hand to her
throat she could feel the betraying thud of her pulse.

'You said that you would put Sebastian's welfare above
everything else,' Carlos reminded her. 'And that means
marrying me.'

She nodded. Sebastian adored his *papà*, and it had become increasingly clear to her that she did not have the
right to separate her son from his father, nor deny Sebastian his Spanish heritage.

'I do want him to be legitimate. I expect all brides
have pre-wedding jitters,' she forced herself to say lightly.

Carlos released his breath slowly. 'Is it important to
you that your parents attend the wedding?'

'I *would* like my father to give me away, and my
mother to be at the church wearing an outrageous mother-
of-the-bride hat.' Betsy's sigh was unconsciously wistful.
'But it will be easier if they're not there. At least Sarah
and Mike are coming, and a few of my friends from university. Although my side of the church is going to look

very empty when the three hundred guests you have invited fill the pews on the other side.'

She dropped her gaze from Carlos's and stared at the huge diamond sparkling like a teardrop on her finger.

'Why do we have to have such a big wedding in full view of the media? It's going to be a circus, and I'll be the clown,' she muttered.

Carlos frowned. 'Would you prefer it if we sneaked off to the local town hall and married in secret? There have been too many secrets,' he said grimly. 'My tennis career gave me international fame, and being a public figure allows me to promote the Segarra Foundation. It is important to me that in the eyes of the world I am seen to be doing the right thing by marrying the mother of my son. When Sebastian is old enough to understand he will know that I wanted him, and that I do not regret his birth as some of the tabloids have speculated.'

His fiercely spoken words dispelled the last of Betsy's doubts. Her conscience pricked. She should tell him how much she regretted the way she'd handled the situation two years ago, when she'd discovered that she was pregnant. For the first time she really tried to imagine how he must have felt when he read in a newspaper that he was a father, and his sense of betrayal when the paternity test had proved that Sebastian was his son.

'Fine—we'll do the wedding your way,' she mumbled.

'I understand that the stylist has helped you choose a bridal gown?'

'Yes. I'm having a fitting later today.'

She felt a thrill of guilty pleasure as she pictured the dress. The stylist had picked out an elegant, understated gown in ivory silk, but Betsy had been drawn to a confection of pure white tulle. Reasoning that she was only going to get married once—unlike her parents, who had so far clocked up five weddings between them—she had decided she wanted her dress to be a fairy tale even if her marriage was not.

With a sweetheart neckline, exquisite lace detail on the bodice and a sweeping train, the wedding dress was worthy of a princess. Betsy hoped it would disguise the fact that she was an ordinary girl who had captured the attention but not the heart of the man dubbed Spain's sexiest sporting legend.

'My father wants to meet his grandson,' Carlos told her. 'He was discharged from hospital yesterday, and has been resting this morning, but I've had a message from his nurse to say that he is awake now.'

Betsy knew that Roderigo Segarra lived in an annexe off the main house. Carlos had told her that his father was partially paralysed after he'd suffered a stroke a year ago. He had been forced to move here from his home in the centre of Toledo and to sell the bakery which had been a family business for four generations.

'Why was your father in hospital?' she asked, as Carlos opened the door and she preceded him out of the study.

'He has been ill with pneumonia. His health is not good. But he hates being inactive and he misses the bakery. He started working there when he was fifteen, and took over running the business when my grandfather retired.'

'Was he disappointed that you didn't go into the family business?'

'I have been a constant disappointment to my father throughout my life.'

Carlos's voice was devoid of emotion, and when Betsy glanced at him she saw his sculpted features were expressionless.

'I bet he's proud of you.' She tried to lighten the atmosphere that suddenly swirled with dark undercurrents. 'After all, you're regarded as the finest sportsman Spain has ever produced and you're a national hero.'

He laughed, but it was not a happy sound, and it hurt Betsy although she couldn't explain why.

'I am no hero,' he said harshly. 'My father would tell you that.'

Ginette came in from the garden with Sebastian just then, and there was no time for Betsy to ask Carlos any more questions. But she sensed his tension as he knocked on the door of his father's private apartment. It surprised her, because Carlos always seemed in complete control of his emotions—*except for that one occasion when he took you to bed and made love to you with a wild passion that spoiled you for any other man*, whispered a voice in her head.

His control had shattered when he had been thrusting inside her, and he'd cursed and told her she had cast a spell on him. And then he'd groaned and slumped on top of her, and she had gloried in her newfound power.

Hastily banishing the erotic images from her mind, Betsy lifted Sebastian out of the pushchair and checked that his face was clean. He looked adorable, in new shorts and a tee shirt, and although she was careful to keep him out of the sun as much as possible his chubby arms and legs were golden-brown.

A nurse came to the door and they followed her into Roderigo's bedroom. The grey-haired man who was propped against the pillows bore little resemblance to Carlos.

Betsy balanced Sebastian on her hip and stepped closer to the bed.

'*Papà*, this is Betsy, and my little boy, Sebastian.'

There was fierce pride in Carlos's voice as he introduced his son.

The elderly man stared at Sebastian. *'Se parece a tu madre.'*

'Betsy doesn't speak Spanish,' Carlos told the older man. 'My father said that Sebastian looks like my mother,' he explained to Betsy.

Roderigo stretched out a bony hand and picked up a framed photograph from the bedside table. 'Carlos's mother—my wife Marta. *Dios la bendiga,*' he said thickly, and kissed the photo before he held it out to Betsy.

The woman in the picture was strikingly beautiful, with masses of dark curling hair and sherry-gold eyes. It was easy to see which of his parents Carlos had inherited his good looks from, Betsy thought as she studied the photo.

'Your wife was very pretty,' she said.

Tears filled Roderigo's eyes. 'She died before her time and did not have the chance to see her children become adults or to meet her grandchildren.'

A heavy silence filled the room. *'Papà...'* Carlos murmured.

Roderigo frowned. 'I understand that Sebastian was born over a year ago? Why has it taken you until now to acknowledge your child, Carlos? The story of your secret son is in all the newspapers. Yet again you have brought shame on our family with your playboy reputation and lack of responsibility.'

Beside her, Betsy felt Carlos stiffen. She was startled by his father's accusations and the animosity in Roderigo's voice.

An image flashed into her mind of Carlos kneeling on the stone-flagged floor with his arms wide open to catch Sebastian if he fell, and she remembered the pride in Carlos's voice when he'd introduced his son.

From the minute he'd realised that Sebastian was his, he had offered to support and protect both of them. His father's criticism was unjust, and she was partly to blame, she thought guiltily. She *should* have told Carlos about Sebastian.

'It was my fault that Carlos was unaware he had a child,' she told Roderigo. 'Don't blame your son. There was a misunderstanding which led to us being apart, but now we are going to get married and we are both determined to make a family for Sebastian.'

CHAPTER EIGHT

CARLOS WONDERED IF he had heard correctly. Impossibly, it had sounded as though Betsy was defending him when she'd told his father that *she* had been to blame for keeping Sebastian's birth a secret.

Betsy had wanted to protect him!

Carlos did not know what to make of that, nor of the warmth that curled around his frozen heart. She had no idea how little he deserved her to champion him, he thought bleakly. But his father knew. And Roderigo's tears for his beloved wife had the same impact on Carlos that they always did.

A familiar sense of guilt ripped through him. And now there was new guilt—because he should have stayed and spoken to Betsy after he'd slept with her, instead of rushing back to Spain like a goddamned coward. But he'd been shaken by how she'd made him feel. Scared that she'd made him feel at all when he'd blocked out his emotions for his entire adult life.

How had he thought that this woman was unremarkable? Carlos thought wryly. Betsy never ceased to amaze him. She looked like a ray of sunshine in her yellow dress. The caramel streaks in her hair had lightened to blonde in the sun, and her lush mouth tempted him to claim her lips with his. He had ached to kiss her since he had brought her and his son to Toledo.

But right now Betsy was sitting on the edge of his father's bed, and had Sebastian balanced on her knees. 'He's a good baby, and mostly he sleeps well at night—except when he's cutting a tooth,' she told Roderigo. 'During the day he has so much energy. As soon as he learned to walk, he wanted to run.'

'Carlos was the same when he was young. His mother used to say she could not keep up with him.'

Roderigo chuckled, and Carlos decided that he must have stepped into a parallel universe. He couldn't remember the last time he'd heard his father laugh, but he guessed it had been twenty years ago—before his teenage emotions and hot temper had ruined everything.

Nothing good ever came from making an emotional response to a situation, Carlos brooded. But that wasn't entirely true, he realised as he looked at his beautiful son. Two years ago he had recognised that Betsy was a threat to his peace of mind, but he'd ignored the alarm bells in his head, driven by something more than simply lust when he'd taken her to bed. The result was this unplanned child who had captured his heart.

They stayed for a while longer, until Sebastian started to become fractious and his grandfather looked tired.

'Will you bring *el nene* to visit me tomorrow?' Roderigo asked as Carlos scooped his son off Betsy's lap.

'I'm flying to South Africa later today, to play in an exhibition match, and I'll be away for the rest of the week. When I return, I'll bring Sebastian to see you.'

His father lay back on the pillows. 'So you are still putting tennis first, Carlos. You have brought Betsy and Sebastian to Spain, but now you are about to leave them and travel halfway around the world. Family is precious. You, of all people, should know that.'

'The exhibition match was arranged months ago and the revenue from the ticket sales will go to the Segarra Foundation.'

Carlos's jaw clenched. He did not need his father to remind him that the price of his ruthless ambition had been his mother's life. She had been the lynchpin of the family and the person he'd loved most in the world.

'Carlos's charity does important work for underprivileged children, and I wouldn't want him to cancel a fundraising match,' Betsy told Roderigo. 'But I can bring Sebastian to visit you.'

They left his father's apartment and Carlos carried a by now very fretful Sebastian back to the main part of the house.

'He's hungry—I need to give him his lunch,' Betsy said.

Carlos's suitcase and tennis rackets were by the front door. 'I'll have to go to the airport soon,' he told her. He tightened his arms around his son, hating the prospect of leaving him behind. Ginette came down the stairs. 'Let Ginette give Sebastian his lunch. I want to talk to you,' he told Betsy.

'I thought we'd finished discussing the wedding.' She gave him a puzzled look after the nanny had taken Sebastian to the kitchen.

'In future, when I play exhibition matches abroad, I'll take you and Sebastian with me.' He grimaced. 'I don't want you to think I am abandoning you.'

'I don't think that.' She met his gaze. 'I know how much you care about Sebastian.'

'I care about your feelings too.'

Carlos did not know if he or Betsy was more surprised

by his statement. He had spoken unthinkingly, but it was the truth, he realised.

'I want you to be happy here.' He released his breath slowly. 'Why did you tell my father that you had kept Sebastian a secret from me?'

'Because it's true. He blamed you unfairly and it was only right that I explained the situation.' She hesitated before saying in a low voice, 'I'm sorry I didn't tell you that you had a child. You had a right to know.'

The ice around Carlos's heart thawed a little. Betsy's apology meant a lot. But an unanswered question still remained. Would she *ever* have told him that she'd given birth to his son? If fate hadn't sent that journalist to report on the floods in a Dorset village, would Betsy have kept Sebastian a secret for ever?

Since that night at the penthouse, when he had quite literally turned his back on Betsy to stop himself from pulling her into his arms, he had struggled to control his hunger for her. He'd resorted to keeping his distance from her unless they were both spending time with Sebastian.

The evenings when there were just the two of them at dinner had tested his self-control, so he arranged dinner parties or accepted social engagements, telling Betsy that it was a chance for her to meet his friends.

But they were alone now, and it was impossible to ignore the sexual chemistry simmering between them.

Carlos had spent his whole adult life pretending to be someone else, and he'd hidden behind his image of careless playboy for so long that it was a shock to realise that he wasn't really an empty shell. There was hot blood in his veins and a fire in his heart—and this woman was the cause.

'I made a mistake when I kissed you,' he muttered.

Colour ran along her cheekbones, but she said drily,

'It's all right, Carlos. I got the message when we went back to your apartment after the party. I'm not likely to forget how I made a fool of myself.'

He moved closer to her, his eyes on the pulse jerking erratically at the base of her throat. 'It was a mistake because one kiss wasn't enough. Not for me, and not for you. Am I right, *querida*?'

This close, he could see the pale blue veins beneath her creamy skin. He thought again that she was an English rose with a heady fragrance that intoxicated his senses.

She swallowed, and her tongue darted across her lower lip. 'What does *querida* mean?'

'In English I suppose it translates to "darling", or "lover".'

'I'm neither of those things to you.'

'We were lovers once.'

Carlos knew that his driver was waiting outside in the car, to take him to the airport, but he could not tear himself away from Betsy. Her eyes were huge in her face.

'We spent one night together. I'm not sure that qualifies us as lovers,' she whispered.

'I haven't forgotten a single second of that night.' Memories of her lush body and her sweet ardency had haunted him for two goddamned years. He slid his hand beneath her silky hair and clasped her nape as he lowered his head towards hers. 'Have you?'

Her reply was muffled against his lips as he brought his mouth down on hers and kissed her as he'd imagined doing every night for the past three weeks, when he'd tossed and turned in his enormous bed and fought the urge to stride down the hallway to Betsy's room.

He kissed her as if he couldn't have enough of her. And she kissed him back with a fervour that made him so much hungrier, so much more desperate to feel her soft curves beneath him. He pressed his mouth to the sweet hollow at the base of her throat before moving up her neck to explore a delicate ear. She gave a little gasp when he nipped her velvety earlobe, and he laughed and kissed her lips again, revelling in their moist softness.

Carlos forgot that Betsy was the only woman who had ever slipped under his guard, and by the time he remembered he didn't care that she had done so again. He was only aware of the taste of her on his tongue, of the lemon-fresh scent of her hair that spilled around them, and the hard points of her nipples pressed against his chest. He skimmed his hand down her spine and spread his fingers over her bottom, hauling her against the throbbing hardness of his erection.

His brain was entirely focused on how quickly he could get her to a bed, or any flat surface. He doubted they'd make it upstairs to the bedroom, but there was a sitting room across the hallway.

Vaguely, Carlos remembered again that his jet had been fuelled, ready to fly him to South Africa, and that he had a number of business commitments besides the exhibition match in Cape Town.

He pushed his tongue into the heat of Betsy's mouth. To hell with the trip. He would pull out of the exhibition match. Nothing was more vital than satisfying the ravenous beast of his desire for this woman who rocked him to his core.

Carlos froze.

What the hell was he doing? he asked himself as sanity made a belated appearance. Why had he forgotten how easily Betsy could dismantle the barriers that he had put in place when he'd been a traumatised teenager?

Dios! If he hadn't come to his senses he would have had sex with her in a room where any of the household staff might have walked in and seen them. It would have been embarrassing, but worse was the realisation that he'd been prepared to cancel an important trip so that he could stay here with Betsy.

He dropped his arms down to his sides and stepped back from her. She looked as stunned as he felt, and there was still a part of him that wanted to draw her against his chest and simply hold her.

He shoved the thought away, appalled by his loss of control, and made a show of checking the time on his watch. 'I must go,' he murmured, thankful that his voice was level even though his heart was thundering. 'I'll be back in a week.'

An expression that might have been disappointment crossed Betsy's face.

'I'm thinking of taking Sebastian to England while you're away. We left Fraddlington in such a hurry and I'd like to catch up with my friends in the village.'

He frowned. 'I doubt the cottage will be habitable yet.'

'Sarah says that we can stay at the pub.'

'Our wedding is in a week. You will see your friends then. Anyway, I'm using the jet to fly to South Africa,' Carlos said dismissively.

'I don't expect to travel by private jet. There are regular flights to England from Madrid. Why are you objecting?' Betsy looked mutinous. 'You're leaving Sebastian—it doesn't matter if he's here or in Dorset. I miss my old life…the regular customers at the pub and the other mothers at the baby group I used to take Sebastian to. I feel cut off here,' she muttered. 'You can't stop me from taking him home.'

'*This* is his home.'

Carlos raked his hair off his brow, feeling frustration

surge through him—and something else that knotted in the pit of his stomach and felt a lot like fear.

'If you disappear with my son there is nowhere in the world you can hide where I won't find you.'

The implied threat in his statement was clearly not lost on Betsy. She bit her lip. 'Do you really think I would abduct Sebastian like my father did to me?' She sighed. 'If our marriage is going to work, you will have to trust me.'

'Trust has to be earned,' he told her curtly. 'I checked with the courier company and their records show that the package I sent to your aunt's house was signed for by "B. Miller". I have proof that you could have called me before Sebastian was born.'

Betsy stared at the mirror and a fairy-tale princess stared back at her. There was an air of unreality about seeing herself in a wedding dress, having vowed since she was eight years old that she never wanted to get married. It did not help that in this particular story the handsome prince had awoken her desire with a kiss before he'd abandoned her—again.

Carlos had arrived back from his trip to South Africa late the previous night, but Betsy had already been in bed and so hadn't seen him. When she'd woken this morning she had heard him in the nursery, talking to Sebastian in Spanish.

Shyness, or bridal nerves—probably a mixture of both—had stopped her from opening the connecting door between her room and the nursery. It was supposed to be unlucky for the groom to see the bride before the wedding. Betsy wasn't superstitious, but her marriage had enough bad omens without tempting fate.

For the past week she had spoken to Carlos on the phone every day. They had mostly talked about Sebastian, but Carlos had also told her about the series of exhibition matches he'd played. Betsy had found it easier to chat to him on the phone, when she was not physically aware of him. Without the sexual tension that simmered between them when they were together she was able to relax, and she'd found herself looking forward to his calls.

She had decided against taking Sebastian to England to visit her old friends in the village. It was understandable that Carlos did not trust her, she acknowledged. But she was determined to prove to him that she genuinely regretted not telling him about Sebastian when he had been born.

Her sense of isolation had increased while Carlos had been away. None of the household staff spoke more than a few words of English, and Betsy felt that she did not belong in a grand house that was served by a butler, a housekeeper, a cook and several maids. Her only friend in the whole of Spain was Hector, at the art supplies shop, and she had found excuses to visit the shop often, so that she could chat to him and ease her loneliness.

The grandfather clock on the landing chimed twice and Betsy's heart missed a beat. Carlos, Sebastian and Ginette the nanny had gone ahead to the church. Now it was time for her to go to her wedding.

She made a last check that her chignon was secure and tucked an escapee curl behind her ear before she picked up her bouquet of palest pink roses. She wished that her parents could be there to see her marry, but yet again they had put their acrimony before her happiness, she thought sadly.

Thinking about their bitter divorce added to her tension. Was she doing the right thing by marrying for convenience rather than love? She thought of the love that

Carlos clearly felt for Sebastian, and knew she had no choice.

Carlos had told her that their wedding was to be held in a church in the centre of Toledo, but to Betsy's surprise the driver turned the car in the opposite direction from the city. Soon they were travelling along narrow roads surrounded by wide open plains and vast vineyards and dotted with squat white windmills, beneath a cloudless, blue sky. She knew this landscape of the Castile La Mancha area of Spain was often called the heartland of the country.

After a while they came to a small village, and went through some gates into what seemed to be a private estate. A driveway led to a house that looked like a castle, complete with turrets. Further along the driveway was a whitewashed chapel. The driver brought the car to a halt.

'Are you sure this is the right place?' Betsy asked him when he held the door open for her to climb out of the car.

'*Si, señorita.*'

She had been expecting a horde of paparazzi, and was surprised to see that there was just one photographer.

A man stepped out of the church and she stared at him in disbelief.

'*Dad?* I didn't think you were coming. Where's Tiffany?'

Betsy knew she would never hear the last of it if her father and his wife attended the wedding, but her mother was left out.

'Hello, honey. You make a beautiful bride.' Drake Miller smiled as he offered her his arm. 'Tiffany is in Paris.' He rolled his eyes. 'She's probably flexing my credit card in the designer stores. Your mother is in the church,' he said casually.

Betsy stopped walking. 'Are you and Mum…okay together? It doesn't look like a very big church.' She tensed, imagining her parents arguing in front of the other wedding guests.

'Carlos told us that we had to put aside our differences at our daughter's wedding, and he's right. Stephanie and I both want to be here for you on your big day,' Drake reassured her as they stepped into the church porch, where it was cool and dark after the bright sunshine outside. 'Your fiancé is an amazing guy and it's obvious that he is madly in love with you.'

Betsy's steps faltered. Carlos did not love her, nor she him, she reminded herself. Who needed love, anyway? They were marrying for sensible, practical reasons, so that they could both be full-time parents to their son.

Through the doorway she could see the pretty chapel was filled with flowers. In the front pew there was an enormous cerise pink hat which must belong to her mother. She saw Sarah and Mike and other close friends who had flown over from England. On the other side of the nave she recognised some of Carlos's friends, whom she'd met at dinner parties, and she noticed his father in a wheelchair and his sister Graciela, with a man who must be her husband, holding their little boy Miguel. But to Betsy's relief there were certainly not three hundred guests, and not a celebrity in sight.

Finally she turned her gaze to Carlos. He was standing by the altar, his back ramrod-straight, and every few seconds he glanced over his shoulder. He couldn't possibly be feeling nervous, she told herself. His supreme self-confidence was what had helped to make him a world-class tennis champion. He looked devastatingly handsome in a pale grey three-piece suit…the most beautiful man she'd ever seen.

Betsy could not explain the pang her heart gave, nor the tears that pricked her eyes.

At one side of the church a group of musicians were gathered next to the organ. The organist began to play, and the violinists and a cellist picked up their bows. The exquisite notes of Pachelbel's *Canon in D* soared to the rafters as Betsy walked with her father down the aisle.

Carlos had turned his head towards the back of the church when the music had started. His eyes locked on Betsy and he did not look away from her as she made her way towards him. She couldn't fathom the expression that crossed his face, but when she reached his side he said in a hoarse undertone, 'You take my breath away, *mi belleza.*'

The ceremony was simple, but unexpectedly moving. It would be easy to be swept up in the romance of the occasion, thought Betsy, but she knew better than to believe in fairy tales.

Carlos took her hand in his and slid a gold band onto her finger. The priest pronounced them man and wife and her new husband bent his dark head and kissed her while a collective sigh came from the congregation.

It was all a show, Betsy reminded herself. Carlos had been made to look a fool and, worse, callous when the media had discovered he had a secret child. This wedding was to restore his image—but therein was a puzzle.

'Where are the paparazzi you said were bound to be outside the church?' she asked as she and Carlos posed on the steps for the one photographer who was there, taking pictures. 'I thought you wanted a big wedding in the glare of the world's press?'

'But you didn't,' he said softly. 'You were worried that our wedding would be a circus, so I changed the venue and only invited close family and friends to this private chapel, which is owned by a friend of mine. We will have lunch in Sergio's castle, and this evening we will be joined by a couple of hundred other guests for a bigger reception. The paparazzi are banned from entering the estate. We'll choose a few pictures from the photographer and issue them to the press.'

Betsy glanced over at her parents, who were chatting amiably and apparently best friends. 'I can't believe they haven't killed each other,' she murmured. 'What did you do?'

'I reminded them that they had both let you down in the past and warned them that if they upset you today I'd have them forcibly evicted from the wedding.'

'Seriously?'

She stared at him, and her heart flipped when he gave one of his sexy smiles that turned her insides to mush. Sweet heaven! How was she going to survive this? she wondered with a flash of despair. She was touched that he had altered the wedding arrangements to make her happy, and he'd worked a miracle with her parents after she'd admitted that she wished they would attend the wedding.

By the time they returned to Fortaleza Aguila, much later that night, Betsy felt confused. A week ago Carlos had said he could not trust her. But, thanks to him, their wedding day had been a beautiful and memorable event. He had acted the role of loving husband so convincingly that it was difficult to believe he was the same man who had vowed to hunt her to the ends of the earth if she disappeared with Sebastian. The fact that he could even think she would do such a thing reminded her of why she must not fall head over heels in love with him.

'I believe that in England it is traditional for the groom to carry his bride over the threshold,' Carlos said when they alighted from the car and walked towards the house.

'Apparently the ritual goes back to Roman times and was meant to protect the bride from demons that might be in her new home.'

'Luckily we're in Spain.'

Betsy gathered her long skirt in her hands and ran up the steps to the front door. Obscure demons were the least of her concerns. She was far more worried that if Carlos held her in his arms she would be unable to resist pressing her face into his neck and breathing in his evocative male scent.

The door was unlocked, and she pushed it open and sped across the hall as if the devil himself was chasing after her. 'I'm tired and I'm going to bed. Goodnight.'

Upstairs, she stepped quietly into the nursery to check on Sebastian. Ginette had brought him home earlier in the evening, so that he could go to sleep at his usual time. He looked adorable, lying in the cot with his arms above his head, and as usual he had kicked the covers off. Betsy tucked the blanket around him and kissed his cheek.

It had meant a lot to her when she'd watched her parents make a fuss of her baby, especially as it had been the first time her father had met Sebastian. She was stunned that Carlos had gone to such a lot of effort to arrange for her parents to attend the wedding. But family was important, and now, through their marriage, Sebastian was Carlos's legitimate son and heir.

In her bedroom, she kicked off her shoes and pulled the pins from her chignon before raking her fingers through her hair. It had been a long and emotionally draining day. She frowned as she noticed that the sheets had been stripped from the bed. She would have to remake it, but she had no idea where the bedding was kept and was reluctant to disturb the staff so late at night.

Walking into the en suite bathroom, she discovered

that all her toiletries were missing, and back in the bedroom she opened a wardrobe and found it empty.

Betsy was tired, her nerves were frayed, and her temper simmered as she marched down the corridor to Carlos's room. She had never been inside the master bedroom before, and after she'd given a peremptory knock on the door before opening it, her eyes were immediately drawn to the huge four-poster bed in the centre of the room. A gold canopy was draped above the bed, and the gold and black decor gave the room the appearance of a sultan's tent.

Carlos was stretched out on the bed with his arms folded behind his head. He had removed his tie and his shirt was undone to the waist, revealing his impressive abs and that glorious chest, darkly tanned and liberally sprinkled with black body hair. He did not seem surprised to see her, and lifted one dark brow when she walked closer to the bed and glared at him.

'Where are my clothes? Why have all my things been taken out of my room?'

'I asked one of the maids to transfer your belongings here, to the master suite.' Carlos propped himself up on an elbow and waved his hand towards a door. 'Through there is your own bathroom and dressing room. Now that you are my wife you will share my bedroom with me.'

His wolfish smile caused Betsy's womb to contract, and she realised that the biggest threat she faced was not her too-hot-to-handle husband but her irresistible attraction to him when he patted the mattress and murmured, 'Come to bed, *querida.*'

CHAPTER NINE

'YOU SAID THAT our marriage would be a partnership and we would make decisions together.'

Betsy grabbed hold of the nearest bedpost for support as a terrible weakness invaded her body. In her traitorous imagination she pictured herself and Carlos lying on the bed, their naked limbs entwined.

'I have no intention of sleeping in your bedroom with you,' she told him—and herself—firmly. 'In the morning you can ask the staff to return my clothes to my room and remake my bed. But for tonight I'll use this as a cover.'

She snatched up the black velvet throw that was draped across the bottom of Carlos's bed. Her temper fizzed when he said nothing, just lay sprawled on the gold satin bedspread like a demigod—too handsome to be a mere mortal.

'We *will* discuss issues as they arise. But I did previously mention that we would share a bedroom after we married,' he reminded her.

'I didn't realise that you meant on our actual wedding night,' she muttered. 'You also "mentioned" that we would have a sexual relationship at some point. Are you going to demand that I have sex with you tonight?'

'Of course not.' An expression of horror crossed his face. '*Dios*, you can't really believe I would try to force myself on you?' He sounded as though he was struggling to control some violent emotion.

Betsy sighed. 'No, I don't believe that.' Her shock was fading, and she knew with complete certainty that she was safe with Carlos. 'But why is it so important for us to share a room?'

'Can you imagine how the paparazzi would react if they found out that we slept apart?' he demanded. 'The tabloids would speculate that our marriage is already over or that our wedding was a stunt.'

She frowned. 'How would the tabloids find out details about our personal lives?'

'I believe that my household staff are trustworthy,' Carlos told her, 'but it only takes a careless remark to spark a rumour. The maids will know if we are sleeping in separate rooms. I won't risk details of our private lives being aired by the gutter press.'

Betsy was about to say that it was a fanciful idea. But then she remembered that when she was a child an au pair had leaked information to the media about her parents' explosive arguments. Every gory detail of her father's infidelity and her mother's out-of-control spending had been documented and sold to a newspaper. The au pair had only been discovered when she'd left her notebook open in the kitchen and Betsy's mother had seen it.

'I wouldn't care what the press printed about us,' she insisted. But it wasn't true. She hated the thought of her personal life being made public again.

'I don't think you would enjoy being constantly harassed by the paparazzi about the state of our marriage. And it's not just the newspapers. My father lives in the house, and he would soon find out if our relationship was not the happy marriage that we have led him and other members of our families to believe. He adores Sebastian, and if he has reason to think there is a rift between us he'll worry that you might leave and take his grandson away.'

'I've told you I will never do that.' Betsy hesitated, then said, 'I've gained the impression that your relationship with Roderigo is strained. Why is that?'

Carlos stiffened. 'It is a private matter between my father and me.'

'It might help to talk,' she murmured. 'I am part of your family now, and—'

'Leave it,' he ordered curtly. 'There are things that you don't understand.'

Betsy felt a pang of hurt that he was shutting her out. She moved her gaze from the huge bed and glanced at a high-backed armchair. She did not relish trying to sleep on that.

'I didn't expect that we would share a bedroom immediately we were married.'

He stood up and curved his fingers over Betsy's hand, where it was clinging to the bedpost. 'I won't expect anything from you that you are not willing to give. But I know you want me, *querida*.' His voice deepened and his eyes gleamed like molten gold as he lifted his other hand and smoothed her hair back from her flushed face. 'And I want you, my beautiful wife. Two years ago, neither of us could ignore the attraction we felt for each other. That chemistry is still there, hotter and more potent than ever.'

She shook her head, but the faintly sardonic expression in his eyes said that he did not believe her denial. His gaze lowered to the hard peaks of her nipples, outlined beneath the silk bodice of her wedding dress.

'Your body betrays you, *mi belleza*.'

He stepped closer, and his warm breath grazed her

cheek. His mouth was mere centimetres away from hers, but he did not kiss her as she longed for him to do. He captured her free hand in his and lifted it up so that he could press his lips to the gold band sitting next to the exquisite diamond on her finger.

Sensation shot through her as he turned her palm over and kissed her wrist, where her pulse was beating erratically. He feathered kisses along her arm to the crook of her elbow and nipped the delicate skin there very gently with his teeth, sending sparks of fire through her veins. When he lifted his head she released her breath on a soft sigh that turned to a gasp as he licked his way along her collarbone and trailed his lips up her throat and over the sensitive underside of her jaw.

Surely he would kiss her mouth now? He was so close, so tempting. She wanted to spear her fingers into the dark silk of his hair and tug his head closer until his lips were on hers. The ache inside her was sharpest between her legs, and she was conscious of the damp heat of her feminine arousal.

Carlos released her hand and she hovered it over his naked chest. She wanted to touch his warm skin. He smelled of spicy cologne and raw male, and her womanly body responded instinctively to his potency.

'Touch me.'

His voice was thick with desire. Betsy swayed towards him and skimmed her fingers over his chest, feeling the abrasion of his body hair beneath her fingertips. He was the most beautiful man in the world. He could have any woman he wanted, but he wanted *her*. She recognised the hunger in the feral glitter in his eyes and heard it in the raggedness of his breath.

'Come to bed and let me make love to you,' he said roughly. 'We are married now.'

So they might as well have sex?

Was that what Carlos thought?

Cold reality replaced the sensual heat that had fogged Betsy's brain and she snatched her hand away from him. 'But you don't trust me.'

He had made that clear before he'd gone to South Africa, when he'd accused her of lying about not receiving the bracelet that he insisted he had sent her.

Betsy had tried to contact Aunt Alice's son, to ask him if a package had arrived at the house in London after she'd moved out. But, frustratingly, Lee's wife had told her that he was away on a fishing trip in a remote part of Scotland where he couldn't use his phone.

Carlos raked a hand through his hair. *'Querida...'*

'Don't!' she choked. 'I'm not your darling.'

He had the power to destroy her, and the realisation terrified her. If she gave herself to him he would know how much he affected her. She did not trust herself to be able to hide her feelings. She wasn't in love with him, but what she felt was deeper than lust and that made her vulnerable.

'I'm not going to have sex with you.'

His gaze narrowed on her face and she sensed his frustration. But after a few seconds he moved away from her and she released her breath slowly.

'I need to get changed,' she told him. 'I can't sleep in my wedding dress.' She hoped he wouldn't hear the wobble in her voice.

Why not just accept the wedding night Carlos is offering? whispered a voice in her head. Sex without strings would set the tone for their marriage and satisfy her physical craving for him.

But an instinct for self-preservation held her back. He made her feel as defenceless now as she'd felt two years ago. She'd cried into her pillow every night for weeks after he'd returned to Spain. But then she'd found out she was pregnant, and she'd ditched her romantic dreams for the reality of being a single mother.

Carlos crossed the room and opened the door that he'd indicated a few minutes ago. Betsy stepped into a walk-in wardrobe, beyond which was another door to her own bathroom. The new clothes she'd bought since she'd arrived in Spain were on hangers or folded on shelves. She searched the room and eventually found the few possessions she'd brought from England. After taking off her wedding dress she went into the bathroom to wash her face and brush her teeth.

Five minutes later she returned to the bedroom, and her heart lurched when she saw Carlos already in bed, leaning against the pillows. His chest was bare and the sheet was draped across his hips. The thought that he might be completely naked tested her resolve. How would she get to sleep, knowing that all that testosterone was a few feet away from her?

'Madre de Dios!' He sat up straighter when he saw her. 'What the hell are you wearing?'

'My pyjamas. I bought them last winter, to keep out the cold.' Made of thick flannelette, in a violent purple check pattern, they were hideous, but they had been very practical when she'd had to get up to Sebastian in the middle of the night. She would probably boil, wearing them now in the heat of a Spanish summer, but it was worth the risk, she decided. From Carlos's expression it seemed the unflattering pyjamas had cooled his desire, and Betsy told herself she was relieved.

'Your choice of nightwear is not quite what I'd imagined my bride would wear on our wedding night,' he said drily.

Taking a deep breath, Betsy pulled back the sheet on the other side of the bed and slid beneath it. She couldn't get it out of her mind that he might be stark naked. There was a long bolster pillow behind her head, and she placed it down the centre of the bed before she switched off her bedside lamp.

Carlos muttered something in Spanish and turned off his own lamp.

Betsy blinked as her eyes adjusted to the darkness. 'I don't suppose you even imagined your wedding night, as you are on record stating that you never wanted to get married.' She sighed. 'Nor did I. We had a one-night stand, and that's all it should have been. But, unbeknown to either of us, when you returned to Spain I had conceived your baby.'

The mattress dipped as Carlos moved and his face appeared above the bolster. 'Do you regret having Sebastian? I've never asked how you felt about becoming a mother, but I assume you wanted him?'

'Of course I don't regret having him. He's the best thing that has ever happened in my life. I can't begin to explain how much I love him.' Her voice thickened with emotions that she couldn't supress. 'I agreed to this ridiculous marriage for Sebastian's sake.'

Betsy's eyes brimmed with tears and she was glad of the dark as they slipped unchecked down her cheeks. She swallowed hard, but a sob escaped her.

Carlos leaned closer and his gold-flecked eyes glittered in his shadowed face. 'Are you *crying*?'

'N...no.' Her voice cracked on the lie. He swore, and she sensed he was shocked. Embarrassment added to her misery. She couldn't explain why she felt so overwhelmed, but it was a combination of things: seeing her parents behaving civilly to each other, watching Sebastian playing with his cousin Miguel and realising that he already seemed more Spanish than English...

But the main reason why her emotions felt like a wrung-out dishcloth was the memory of Carlos being so attentive to her throughout their wedding day, and holding her close when they'd danced the first dance at the evening reception. She'd almost been fooled into thinking that he cared about her.

More tears filled her eyes and she covered her face with her forearm, feeling exposed and stupid.

For a heartbeat Carlos did not move, but then he grabbed the bolster and hurled it off the bed. 'Come,' he murmured, reaching for her and drawing her across the mattress.

The warmth of his body was irresistible, and Betsy succumbed without a struggle. She wasn't sure if she was relieved or disappointed when her hand brushed against the silk boxers he was wearing.

'Don't cry, *pequeña*.'

He spoke softly, as if she was a small child needing to be comforted, and stroked his hand over her hair. She had seen his gentleness with Sebastian, but now he was being kind to her, and she cried harder.

'Why is our marriage ridiculous?' he asked.

'You...hate me.'

'I don't hate you.' He exhaled heavily. 'I admit I was angry at first, but I have never hated you.'

She sniffed. 'You can't forgive me for keeping your son a secret.'

Once again Carlos hesitated for a heartbeat before he said gruffly, 'I understand why you were afraid to tell me. Your childhood experiences when your parents wanted you to choose between them made you determined to protect Sebastian.' He slid his finger beneath her chin and tilted her face to his. 'We may not have married for conventional reasons, but I believe we can make it work, *querida*.' He rolled onto his back, taking her with him, and tucked her head on his shoulder. Go to sleep now. Things will seem better in the morning.'

Carlos meant, of course, that they had not married for love—and she was fine with that, Betsy assured herself. Her parents had proved that love could be a destructive emotion. And it seemed as though he had forgiven her for keeping Sebastian a secret, but she still felt guilty. Somehow, they had to make a success of their marriage for their son's sake.

Her thoughts blurred as she slipped into sleep. She didn't wish that Carlos would fall in love with her. Really, she didn't.

'Have you seen my wife?' Carlos asked the nanny, who had just emerged from the nursery.

'I believe she has gone into the city. She often goes shopping for a couple of hours in the afternoon. Sebastian has dropped his morning nap, but he still sleeps after he's had his lunch,' Ginette explained. 'If I'd known you were back I would have kept him up so that you could see him,' she said apologetically. 'Betsy thought you wouldn't return from your business trip until later this evening.'

'I'll spend time with him when he wakes up.'

Carlos stepped quietly into the nursery and leaned over the cot to kiss his son's downy cheek. His heart swelled with love for Sebastian and he gave a rueful sigh. In his careless bachelor days he had been adamant that he did not want children. But now he had a child and would willingly give his life for his precious little boy.

Leaving Sebastian to nap, Carlos walked down the

corridor and into the master bedroom. Betsy's scent was everywhere in the house, but it was strongest here, in the bedroom they shared, and his gut clenched. He slung his jacket on the chair and tugged off his tie. Picking up his phone, he logged on to internet banking and checked the account that Betsy withdrew money and made payments from. The balance had not changed in the two weeks since he'd given her a bank card in her married name.

Carlos was fairly sure that Betsy did not have any savings of her own, so how did she pay for whatever she was buying on her shopping trips?

He sat on the edge of the bed, wondering how much longer their marriage could continue to be a Cold War, with both of them entrenched on either side of a goddamned bolster. Cursing, he grabbed the bolster off the bed and threw it out into the corridor. He'd tell the maid to get rid of it.

But the barrier between him and Betsy was more than just the pillow that she placed down the centre of the bed every night. Her tears on their wedding night had made him feel uncomfortable. The evidence of her vulnerability had exacerbated his guilt that he'd forced her into a marriage which she had openly admitted she did not want.

But what other choice had either of them had? Carlos brooded. He had been utterly determined that his son would be legitimate. For Sebastian's sake, he and Betsy must try to make a success of their marriage, but so far it was a disaster for which he must accept most of the blame.

His plan had been that they would have a short period of time while they adjusted to living together, and that this would lead naturally to them beginning a sexual relationship. But Carlos was being hampered by two things. The first was his rampant desire for Betsy, that made it impossible for him to be near her without wanting to haul her off to bed and make love to her until they were both sated. The second but greater problem was his discovery on their wedding night that she could easily be hurt—by him.

He wanted to have sex with her, but he did not want emotional sex. It wasn't his thing. And Carlos sensed that Betsy would want more than he was prepared to give her. Wasn't that always the way with women? he thought frustratedly. He had given Betsy his name, his home and his promise of commitment. But when she'd cried, he'd felt as if his insides had been ripped out. He'd wanted to protect her.

Por Dios! His track record was not good in that department. And so he had kept his distance from his new wife. He'd gone away on business trips and spent several nights at the penthouse in Madrid, so that he didn't have to lie beside Betsy, fantasising about unbuttoning the pyjamas that she wore like a suit of armour. She seemed equally keen to avoid him, and when he was at home he spent a lot of time in her old bedroom.

Carlos decided that he needed to try a new approach. They had done everything the wrong way around. They'd had a baby, then they'd got married, but they had never had a chance to get to know each other. He remembered that Betsy had mentioned she would like to visit the El Greco museum in Toledo. He would meet her and take her there, he thought as he picked up his phone and called her.

She did not answer, nor reply to his text. But Carlos was a man on a mission as he went downstairs and found his driver in the kitchen.

'Do you know which shops Señora Segarra intended to go to?' he asked Pablo.

'*Sí. La señora* always visits the art supplies shop on Calle Santa Tomé.' For some reason the driver looked uncomfortable.

Carlos remembered that Betsy had painted pets' portraits when she'd lived in Dorset. He was puzzled that Pablo avoided his gaze. 'Does she go to the art shop often?'

'Very often. And only to that place. She has asked me to collect her in one hour.'

'Give me directions to the art shop,' Carlos requested. 'I'll drive myself there to meet my wife.'

It did not take him long to reach the city walls, and he parked in a car park that most tourists hadn't discovered. The narrow, cobbled streets of Toledo were thronged with visitors in the summer, but the art shop was tucked down an alleyway where few people ventured.

Carlos walked through the door and glanced at the artists' materials displayed rather haphazardly around the shop. There was no one behind the serving counter, but there was a bell that had a sign next to it saying *Presiona*.

At the rear of the shop was a door which opened on to a courtyard. Carlos felt an odd sensation, as if his heart had performed a somersault, when he saw Betsy through the doorway. Her hair was loose on her shoulders and shone like raw silk in the sunshine. She'd gained a light golden tan since coming to Spain, and she seemed to grow sexier and more beautiful every day.

She was standing by a small fountain in the courtyard, and with her was a long-haired young man whose arms were covered in tattoos and a couple of other arty types. Someone was strumming on a guitar and there was a low hum of easy conversation.

Betsy suddenly gave a shriek as Tattoo Guy splashed

her with water. 'That's not fair!' She laughed and shook
her hair back from her face. Her wet shirt clung to her
breasts—a fact that had not gone unnoticed by Tattoo
Guy.

Something hot and rancid flared in Carlos's gut. Possessiveness ran like wildfire through his veins as the
sound of Betsy's laughter drifted into the shop. She had
never laughed or been so carefree with *him*, he thought
darkly. The sense of betrayal felt like a knife through his
heart. She was his *wife*, goddammit, and the mother of
his son. They were meant to be a family.

It struck him then how badly he wanted a family to
replace the one he had destroyed. But his guilt had made
him think that he did not deserve one, and he acknowledged that he had kept Betsy at a distance because she
was the only woman who threatened to dismantle the
barriers he had erected around his emotions.

Betsy looked at her watch. Pablo would come to collect
her soon, and her heart sank at the prospect of returning to Fortaleza Aguila. Of course she loved being with
Sebastian, but she wished she could meet some other
mothers with toddlers, so that he could mix with children of his age. She thought wistfully of the baby group
in Fraddlington, where she'd made some good friends.

Coming to see Hector at the art shop made a welcome
change, though, from the stiff formality of the dinner parties she attended with Carlos. None of his close friends
had children, and the women were all incredibly glamourous. Betsy found them intimidating.

Her skin prickled and a sixth sense made her turn her
head in the direction of the shop. Her heart gave a jolt
when she saw Carlos step into the courtyard. To anyone
who did not know him he'd appear to be relaxed. But

the hard gleam in his eyes and the tense line of his jaw warned her that he was furious.

She was conscious that her wet shirt was clinging to her breasts. Hector had just been fooling around, but she had a feeling that Carlos would not see it that way. His eyes roamed over her short denim skirt before returning to her breasts. Predictably, she felt her nipples jerk to attention. This inability to control her reaction to her husband was one reason why she spent as little time alone with him as possible.

Hector and his friends Antonio and Sofia were staring at Carlos with awed expressions. Even though he had retired from playing tennis professionally, he was still a national hero in Spain.

'*Holà!* Can I help you?' Hector said in Spanish.

'I'm here to take my wife home.' The Jaguar smiled, baring his teeth.

Hector shot Betsy a rueful look. 'You forgot to mention that your husband is the great Carlos Segarra.'

She bit her lip, unable to explain that she had wanted to make friends on her own merits, rather than impress people by revealing who she was married to.

'Come, *querida*,' Carlos ordered.

Betsy bristled at his arrogance, but his slashing frown warned her against making a scene. 'See you soon,' she told Hector, and swept past Carlos without looking at him.

When they emerged into the street he caught hold of her arm and steered her to where he'd parked his car. Betsy's temper fizzed.

'There's no need to manhandle me,' she muttered, glancing at his scowling face. 'What's biting you?' she demanded when he opened the door of his sports car and she slid into the passenger seat.

'This discussion will wait until we are home,' he growled.

Betsy felt like a naughty schoolgirl, and when they reached the house she half expected Carlos to march her into his study.

She walked quickly ahead of him towards the stairs. 'I'm going to get changed.'

She stopped at the nursery to check on Sebastian and found he was still asleep. Ginette looked up from her book. 'I'll pick him up when he stirs,' the nanny whispered.

In the master bedroom, Betsy stripped off her damp shirt and dropped it in the laundry basket. Carlos's voice sounded from the doorway and she spun round to face him. Her pink lacy bra was no more revealing that the bikini top he'd seen her wearing in the pool, she told herself, but she still felt self-conscious that she was half undressed, and crossed her arms over her chest.

He stepped into the room and shut the door with suppressed violence. 'You are not to see him again.'

She blinked. 'Who?'

'Your boyfriend with the body art.'

'Hector is a friend—he's not my *boyfriend*. I can't believe you're accusing me...'

'I saw the way he looked at you.' Carlos's jaw clenched. 'You were flirting with him and laughing.'

'I wasn't *flirting*. Hector has a girlfriend.' She threw her hands up in exasperation. 'And laughing isn't a crime. The only time I *feel* like laughing is when I'm with the friends I've made at the art shop. Hector lived in England for a while, and it's such a relief to be able to talk to him without a Spanish phrasebook.'

Betsy's shoulders slumped.

'I've been so lonely since I came to live in Spain...

The staff keep themselves to themselves. We socialise with your friends and I have nothing in common with them.' She could not hide the tremor in her voice. 'I'm trying to learn Spanish, but it's hard speaking a new language and living in a new country where I'm an outsider. The staff run the house and we have a nanny to look after Sebastian. It feels like I don't have a role here.'

'Your role is as my wife,' Carlos said tersely.

'You never wanted a wife and our marriage is a…a farce. You're hardly ever at home.' Betsy had opened the floodgates now, and her unhappiness and dissatisfaction poured out. 'How dare you accuse me of flirting with Hector when *you* have spent more nights at your penthouse than here with me in the bedroom you insisted we share? I don't suppose you sleep alone at your bachelor pad in Madrid.'

Carlos swore. 'Do you think I have a mistress?'

'I don't know *what* to think.' It crucified her to imagine him making love to another woman. 'You said you wanted to make our marriage work, but we don't spend time together or have any kind of relationship. At least Hector is interested in me. And he's supportive of my pet portrait business, which happens to be doing very well—as I would have told you if you ever paid me any attention.'

Carlos strode across the room and halted in front of her. He was so close that Betsy felt the warmth of his body through his black silk shirt. His male scent evoked a molten heat low in her pelvis.

'I don't have a mistress,' he ground out. 'I haven't slept with any woman since you.'

Her eyes widened and he gave her a sardonic look.

'It's the truth. I couldn't get you out of my mind for two years.'

He lowered his head and she felt his breath graze her cheek.

'If you want my attention you only have to ask, *mi belleza*,' he said roughly, before he claimed her mouth and kissed her with fierce possession.

CHAPTER TEN

THERE WAS FURY in his kiss and Betsy's temper blazed. Anger and desire were an explosive mix. She welcomed the thrust of his tongue inside her mouth as she parted her lips beneath his and kissed him with all the pent-up frustration that had simmered inside her for weeks.

Every night, when she'd kept to her side of the mattress and Carlos had stayed on the opposite side, she had lacked the nerve to move the wretched bolster from the centre of the bed. She had been responsible for putting the barrier between them and she understood that he would not remove it.

Carlos was proud, but he was also a virile male, and his hunger for her was evident when she pressed herself against him and felt the hard length of his arousal nudge her thigh. A shudder of longing ran through her and she tugged open the buttons on his shirt and skimmed her hands over his bare chest. His olive skin was warm, and she loved the springy feel of his dark chest hair against her palms as she explored the ridges of his powerful muscles.

He muttered something in Spanish, and then the world tilted as he lifted her off her feet and dumped her unceremoniously on the bed. Betsy thought she should care that he was the most arrogant man she'd ever met. But he was Carlos, and she could not fool herself any longer that she had any control where this man was concerned.

He was her husband, and yet not her husband. Not in any way that counted. She had turned him down on their wedding night because she had been afraid that he would destroy her if she had sex with him. Now she knew he would destroy her if he did *not* make love to her.

He knelt on the bed and loomed over her. 'Am I paying you enough attention now, *querida*?'

His eyes glittered as Betsy traced her fingers over his hard jaw. She was so weak for him. But instead of seeing desire as a weakness, perhaps there was strength in admitting what she wanted.

'Not enough attention,' she said huskily. 'I want more.'

'You will be the death of me,' he muttered as he slipped his hands beneath her back and unclipped her bra. He tossed it aside and captured her wrists in one of his hands, holding them above her head. Dull colour winged along his cheekbones as he studied her bare breasts. Betsy felt her nipples grow tight beneath his intent gaze. His features sharpened with a predatory hunger that made the ache in her pelvis so much worse—or better?

She made a choked sound when he bent his head to one breast and flicked his tongue across its rosy peak. Sensation spiralled through her and she arched towards him as he tormented her with delicate licks across her nipple. She tried to tug her hands free, but he held her pinioned against the mattress while he drew her nipple into his mouth.

Why fight him when this was what she craved?

His mouth was creating havoc on her body. He released her hands and she sank them into his hair as he moved across to her other breast and sucked the hot, tight peak. Pleasure arced down to her feminine core and she felt the slippery wetness of her arousal.

Carlos trailed his lips over her abdomen and at the same time shoved her denim skirt up to her waist. He drew lazy patterns on her inner thighs with his fingers, but to her frustration he held back from touching her where she longed to feel him.

His eyes gleamed hard and bright as he trapped her gaze. 'Have you had enough of my attention yet, *mi bella esposa*?'

'Not nearly enough.' The words burst from her, urgent and needy. But she didn't care. She couldn't pretend that he did not affect her. The fire inside her only burned this hot for him.

His mouth twisted, but there was no triumph in his smile, rather a tenderness that she understood would be her downfall. Her thoughts scattered as he stared at the scrap of pink lace that covered her femininity. His smile became wicked as he ran his finger over the damp panel between her legs. And then he simply pulled her panties off and pushed her legs apart.

There was something shockingly intimate about lying splayed open to his hungry gaze. But she did not feel vulnerable. She felt empowered when Carlos groaned, and she knew—*she knew*—that he was at the mercy of their tumultuous desire just as she was.

He moved down the bed so that his shoulders were between her thighs, and she gave a start as she realised what he intended to do. Her protest died on her lips when he ran his tongue along her inner thigh, higher and higher, until he was *there* where she was hottest and neediest. Betsy gave a low cry when he put his mouth on her and bestowed upon her the most intimate caress of all.

It was too much...not enough. She wanted more.

Her hips bucked and she gasped as he explored her with his tongue and simultaneously pressed his thumb against the tight nub of her clitoris.

The effect was cataclysmic. Pleasure that was indescribable, so intense she could hardly bear it, rolled through her in wave after rippling wave as her internal muscles clenched and released in the sweetest rhythm.

She remembered that first time two years ago, when he had brought her to orgasm with his fingers. While she had still been in the throes of her climax he'd pressed forward and eased his erection into her.

Now, as then, the beauty of his lovemaking brought tears to her eyes. She tried to blink them away as Carlos sat back on his haunches and surveyed the evidence of her complete capitulation: her skirt rucked up around her waist and her thighs spread wide open.

Betsy quickly brushed her hand over her eyes before she reached for Carlos's belt buckle. She could tell from the rigid set of his jaw that he was holding himself back, but she wanted everything he could give her and she wanted to give him pleasure in return.

He caught the errant tear on her cheek with his thumb and swore. 'I lost my temper.' His voice was harsh with self-recrimination.

She recalled their argument after he'd followed her into the bedroom. They had both been angry, but it had been an anger born of frustration that had quickly turned into desire.

'Carlos...'

But her hands dropped away from him as he leapt off the bed and stared at her. He swore again, and tugged her skirt into place so that it covered her nakedness.

'I never, *ever* allow myself to lose my temper,' he said tightly. 'But when I watched you laughing with another man I saw red. I wanted to kill him.' Carlos raked both his hands through his hair. 'I was furious. I couldn't control my anger.'

'If I had seen you with another woman I would probably have reacted the same way,' Betsy murmured. 'Nothing happened just now that I didn't want to happen. I wanted you.' She flushed. 'I still do.'

He finished buttoning his shirt. 'Don't make excuses for me. That makes it worse,' he grated. 'When I'm with you I lose control.'

He said it as if it was a bad thing. As if he bitterly regretted the passion that had exploded between them.

He strode over to the door and paused on his way out of the room to look back at Betsy. 'It won't happen again,' he told her savagely, and then he was gone.

Carlos could not forget Betsy's stricken expression, nor forgive himself. The shimmer of tears in her eyes and her attempt to hide her distress as she'd brushed her hand over her face had jolted him to his senses. He knew he should not have followed her up to the bedroom. It would have been safer if he'd gone to his study and brought his anger under control before going to find her. Perhaps if he had they would have had a calm discussion about the problems with their marriage.

But a wild fury had overwhelmed him as he'd remembered how happy and relaxed Betsy had been with that guy at the art shop. If he hadn't known better he might have thought the corrosive sensation in his gut was jealousy. But nothing excused the fact that he had kissed her in anger. Had he learned nothing from the past, when his temper had caused such devastation?

He had promised himself that he would wait until Betsy was ready to consummate their marriage. Yes, she had asked for his attention, but instead of talking to her he had seduced her.

Full of self-loathing, he strode down to the gym in the basement of the house, changed into sports gear and jumped onto the treadmill. Since he was fourteen, physical exercise had been his method of temporarily blocking out the voices of his demons, who never allowed him to forget his guilt. His superb athleticism had made him a tennis world champion, but training for hours and pushing his body to its limits also gave him control over his emotions.

For two hours he ran, lifted weights and slammed his fists into a punchbag. But nothing silenced the recriminations in his head when he remembered that Betsy had said she'd felt lonely since he had brought her to Spain.

Before leaving Dorset they had gone to the pub in Fraddlington, so that she could say goodbye to her friend Sarah. The pub had been damaged in the flood, but many of the villagers had come to help clean up the mess and everyone there had known Betsy by name. Carlos realised that she missed the close-knit community she had left behind.

He had done little to help her settle into her new home, he thought guiltily. He'd introduced her to his friends, but Betsy was shy and there was the language barrier. It was no wonder that she had become friendly with this tattooed guy who spoke English and shared her interest in art.

Breathing hard from physical exertion, he threw off his boxing gloves and picked up his phone to look on the internet. Betsy had said that her pet portrait business was doing well, and when he typed in her name he was directed to her website.

Carlos knew a little about art, and nothing about domestic pets, but it was apparent from Betsy's online portfolio and her many glowing reviews that she was a talented artist and her clientele list was growing.

She hadn't told him about her work—but he'd never asked her about it, he thought guiltily. He had been so intent on fighting his desire for her that he'd missed his chances to understand the fascinating woman he had married.

After he'd showered, Carlos went to the nursery and found Betsy playing with Sebastian. She blushed when he walked into the room, and avoided his gaze as she scooped the toddler up.

'Look, poppet, your *papà* has come to play with you,' she said to Sebastian in a fiercely bright voice. 'You can take over for a while,' she told Carlos as she handed him his son. 'He might be persuaded to sit in his buggy— you could take him for a walk in the olive groves, where there's some shade under the trees.'

'We need to talk,' he murmured as she walked over to the door.

She rolled her eyes. 'Because that went *so* well the last time we tried it.'

His jaw clenched. 'Betsy…'

'Did I do something wrong?' she asked huskily. 'Is that why you had a face like thunder when you walked out? You are the only man I've been with…maybe you find my lack of experience a turn-off?'

'*Dios*, no.' Once again he realised how vulnerable she was. 'It wasn't you. It's me.'

She gave him a wry look. 'Those words are usually a prelude to "We'll be better off apart".'

'I don't think that.' His stomach hollowed. 'Do you?'

'The truth is, I don't know,' she choked.

* * *

Later, after Carlos had taken Sebastian for a walk and fed him his tea, Ginette offered to give the little boy his bath. Carlos knocked on the door of the room adjoining the nursery, which had been Betsy's bedroom before their marriage.

Her smile faded when she saw him. 'I thought you were Ginette.' She glanced down at her paint-spattered shirt. 'I'll just get cleaned up before I come and see to Sebastian's bedtime routine.'

'Ginette is bathing him. Can I come in?'

She shrugged and stepped aside for him to enter the room. 'It's a bit of a mess. I'm trying to finish a portrait that a client commissioned as a wedding anniversary present for her husband.'

Carlos saw the canvas propped against the back of a chair next to the window. The dressing table was covered with paints and brushes. To his inexpert eye, the painting of a German Shepherd looked to be completed.

'The light is no good in here in the afternoon.' Betsy frowned as she stared at the painting. 'I can't get Ludo's eyes right...' She sifted through several photos of the dog.

'I've wondered how you persuade your subjects to sit still while you paint them,' Carlos said, aware of Betsy's surprise that he was showing an interest in her work. 'I checked out your website. Your paintings are amazing.'

She flushed. 'Thank you. I ask clients to take high-resolution photos of their pet so that I can create the best likeness.' She picked up a brush and focused her attention back on the German Shepherd.

'Why do you paint animal portraits? Do you never have people as your subjects?'

'I prefer to paint animals—especially dogs—because

they're so honest and uncomplicated. When you look into a dog's eyes you can see its soul, and the love they can give is unconditional.' She sighed. 'When I was a child, we had a dog. He was a miniature white poodle that my father had bought for my mother. She named him The-odore and made a huge fuss of him for a week. But he went out of favour after he chewed one of her shoes and I was allowed to have his basket in my bedroom. I called him Teddy and I adored him.'

Carlos frowned. 'I sense that this story doesn't have a happy ending?'

'In the divorce my father insisted that he had paid for the dog and so should be allowed to keep him. He didn't really want Teddy—he did it to annoy my mother. Then Dad moved to Canada and took the dog with him. When I went there to visit, I couldn't wait to see Teddy, but my father said he had escaped from the garden and been killed. He ran into the road and was hit by a car.'

Betsy's voice was carefully controlled as she re-counted this story from her childhood. Her parents had no idea how much damage they had done to their daugh-ter, Carlos brooded as he watched her pick up a brush and continue to work on the painting.

She stepped back and surveyed what she had done. 'That's better. He looks like Ludo now.'

Carlos studied the portrait. With a few brushstrokes Betsy had captured the German Shepherd's expression perfectly.

'Your parents' relationship has understandably made you wary,' he said. 'But our marriage is not the same as theirs.'

'At least they liked each other to start with...'

He heard the catch in her voice and his heart clenched. 'I like you, *querida*.'

'That's not the impression you gave this afternoon.'

He looked at her stiff shoulders and sensed her hurt pride. 'I would like us to go away together—just the two of us. It's traditional for newlyweds to have a honeymoon,' he murmured when she stared at him.

'What about Sebastian?'

'Ginette is happy to look after him. And my sister has agreed to bring Miguel and come and stay at the house while we are away. Graciela loves Sebastian, and the two boys enjoy each other's company.'

Betsy stared at him. 'You really want us to have a honeymoon? When would we go?'

Carlos discovered that he had been holding his breath while he waited for her response. He exhaled slowly. 'We're leaving in ten minutes. A maid has packed a bag for you.' He forestalled the protest he could see she was about to make. 'It's only a short flight to Palma and we'll arrive before sunset.'

The sun was sliding into the sea when Carlos drove into a small fishing village on Mallorca. Betsy glanced at him and her heart gave a familiar pang. He'd opened the sunroof and his dark hair was tousled by the breeze. His aviator sunglasses were the epitome of style, and his pale denim shirt was open at the throat. He was so sexy it hurt her to look at him, so she turned her attention to the island's stunning scenery.

They passed through the village and a few minutes later he drove up a narrow lane and stopped the car outside a pretty stone cottage with cream shutters at the windows and ivy growing over the walls.

'Our honeymoon destination: Casita Viola,' he said.

He sounded relaxed and his wide smile stole Betsy's breath.

'I was expecting a glamorous five-star hotel,' she murmured.

He tensed and looked away from her. 'You're disappointed? We can go to a hotel if you like.'

'No, it's beautiful here.' She climbed out of the car and turned to admire the view of a crystal-clear sea beyond the white cliffs.

'Those steps lead down to a private beach,' Carlos told her, pointing to some steps carved into the cliff.

The sky was streaked with pink and gold from the setting sun, and the air was filled with the scents of lavender and frangipani which she could see grew in the garden. There was a sense of peace here, Betsy thought as she followed Carlos into the cottage.

Inside, it was full of rustic charm, with exposed stone walls and tiled floors.

'My mother grew up here,' he told her. 'She moved to Toledo when she married my father, but we used to visit my grandparents and spend holidays here.'

Carlos rarely spoke about his mother. Betsy found she was holding her breath, hoping he would open up more. 'What happened to her?'

A shadow crossed his face. 'She died suddenly from an undiagnosed medical condition. Both my grandparents outlived their daughter. Then the cottage was put up for sale by my uncle, who had inherited it, and I bought it to use as a bolthole.'

'Another bachelor pad like your penthouse in Madrid?' Betsy suggested.

'Apart from my sister, you are the only woman I've ever brought here.'

Carlos took off his sunglasses, and the gleam in his gold-flecked gaze made Betsy's heart-rate quicken.

'There's just us here. No staff. A woman from the

village keeps an eye on the place and stocks the fridge when I tell her I'm coming.' He gave a disarming grin. 'I'll admit I can't cook, but there are several good restaurants locally.'

'I'm happy to cook. You used to like the meals I prepared for you when I was your housekeeper.'

'It wasn't just the meals you served that I liked, *querida*.'

She felt herself blush. Carlos's voice was like molten honey. 'Are you flirting with me?' she asked.

'Absolutely. I'm flirting with my wife on our honeymoon.' He picked up their bags, which he'd brought in from the car, and made for the stairs. 'I'll show you the rest of the house.'

Upstairs there were three smallish bedrooms and a couple of bathrooms. Carlos pushed open the door to the larger room. 'This is the master suite, where I usually sleep.' He set her bag down on the landing. 'Like I said, we're completely alone, and it's not necessary for us to share a bedroom. You can decide which room you want,' he said casually.

She bit her lip. 'This is our honeymoon…but you seem to be saying that we should sleep separately.' Frustration and hurt made her voice ragged. 'You blow hot and cold, and I don't know what you want from me.'

'I want you to feel you have choices, because so far I have given you none.' His jaw clenched. 'I forced you into marriage *and* into my bed.' He held his finger lightly against her lips when she tried to say something. 'I scared you. Why else would you have put that damn bolster between us? I would like you to be my wife in every sense. The truth is that I've kept away from you because I can't trust myself. You are beautiful, and sexy, and you drive me insane,' he said thickly. 'But I will respect your wishes if you choose a separate room.'

The band that had lashed around Betsy's heart when Carlos had returned to Spain two years ago unravelled. If sex was all he would give her then she would accept. Passion without emotion was not perfect, but it was better than nothing. And Carlos wanted her as badly as she wanted him. She could see the restraint he was imposing on himself in the tense line of his jaw.

She picked up her holdall and walked through the door he had opened. 'I choose this room.' There was a hint of challenge in the tilt of her chin, and she held his brilliant gaze when he followed her into the master bedroom and closed the door, leaning his back against it. 'I choose you, Carlos.'

'Come here and take me, then, *mi belleza*,' he growled, in a voice so deep and dark it rolled through her.

Gone was the careless playboy—a reputation he had deliberately cultivated, Betsy realised. Now hunger sharpened his features, so that his skin was drawn tightly over his sculpted cheekbones. She took a step towards him and he levered himself away from the door and moved to stand in front of her. He was so close that she could see the faint grooves on either side of his mouth and hear the unevenness of his breaths.

Outside, dusk was falling, and the room was filled with soft shadows. Time slowed as he lowered his head and angled his mouth over hers. The first brush of his lips was gently evocative…a kiss of sweet delight as he eased her lips apart and sipped from her. His tenderness was unexpected, and she felt the press of tears behind her eyes.

Then he increased the pressure a fraction, and the kiss became a sensual feast, exquisitely erotic. He tasted her, coaxing a response from her, until suddenly his restraint snapped and he groaned and hauled her into his arms, deepening the kiss with the fierce passion that Betsy craved.

When at last he lifted his head, she stared into eyes that were molten gold and glazed with desire. 'I have a confession to make,' he said thickly. 'I instructed the maid not to pack your pyjamas.'

She smiled against his lips. 'How will I keep warm in the night?'

'I'll warm you with my body.' He trailed kisses down her throat, and then lower to the swell of her breasts. 'Shall I demonstrate?'

His hands were busy untying the straps of her sundress. He tugged the dress down to her waist and made an approving sound when he discovered that she was braless.

Her breasts felt heavy, the nipples taut and expectant as he kissed his way down her body and closed his mouth around one peak while he rolled its twin between his fingers. The pleasure he evoked with his simultaneous caresses sent an arrow of need to the core of her femininity.

Somehow her dress was on the floor, and his hand roamed over her bottom before he eased the panel of her knickers aside and rubbed his finger over her moist opening.

Her body was ready for him and her hands moved feverishly, tugging the buttons on his shirt open and pushing the material over his broad shoulders. He was a work of art, and she gloried in the firmness of his abdominal muscles. When she laid her palms flat on his chest she felt the uneven thud of his heart, and when she followed the arrowing of black hair down to the waistband of his jeans and slid his zip down he muttered something in Spanish.

'I need you now.'

The admission was raw, ravenous, and the feral gleam in his eyes sent a shiver of anticipation through her. He shrugged out of the rest of his clothes with haste rather than grace, and his impatience snagged her emotions. She cupped his rough jaw between her palms and pulled his mouth down onto hers, kissing him with joy in her heart.

She *hadn't* imagined that their passion two years ago had been out of the ordinary. Afterwards, she had been ashamed of herself for falling into bed with him so easily. But he was as irresistible now as he had been then, and their mutual desire was blazing out of control.

He lifted her up and she wrapped her legs around his hips as he carried her over to the bed. When he laid her down and stretched out on top of her, she felt the powerful muscles and sinews of his thighs, and the hard length of his arousal jabbing her belly. He tugged her panties off and skimmed his hand over the dusting of caramel curls between her legs, parting her so that he could slide one finger, two, into her molten heat.

She caught her breath as he began to move his hand. 'I want you…'

'*Sí*, I know, *querida*.'

'No, I want *you*.' Nothing but his full possession would ease the ache inside her.

He cursed softly. 'The condoms are in my jeans.' He started to move away from her, but she curled her arms around his neck.

'I asked the doctor who sees Sebastian when he's ill to give me a prescription for the pill.' She flushed. 'It seemed a good idea at the time.'

Carlos gave her a sexy smile and pulled her beneath him. 'So there is no reason not to do this?' he murmured, and he positioned himself over her so that the blunt tip of his erection nudged her opening. His eyes locked with hers as he pressed forward and eased his hard length into her slowly, so slowly, claiming her inch by exquisite inch.

It was better than she remembered. When she had given her virginity to him there had been slight discomfort, but now there was pure bliss as he pushed deeper and her internal muscles stretched to accommodate him. She lifted her hips towards him and splayed her fingers over his taut buttocks, drawing him deeper still so that he filled her.

'Ah, *querida*…' he said roughly, his lips against her throat.

And then his kissed her mouth, slow and sweet, and then hot and hungry as his body began to move within her. Each thrust was more satisfying than the one before, harder, faster, creating an erotic friction that drove her higher.

He supported his weight on his elbows and lengthened each rhythmic stroke. Dimly, Betsy was aware of the sound of her panting breaths…*his*. They moved together as one in the dance of lovers. She heard her blood pounding in her ears as it coursed through her veins, hotter, wilder. In his arms she became a wanton creature, tracing her hands boldly over his body so that he groaned.

'Now, *mi belleza*.'

'Yes.'

She quivered as he held her at the edge. His jaw was rigid, his eyes narrowed, and she felt the tension that gripped his big body. And then he thrust again, and she shattered around him, her internal muscles clenching and releasing and sending ripples of pleasure radiating from her core. He climaxed seconds after her, and his hoarse cry wrapped around her heart and lingered there long after their breathing had slowed.

He kissed the tears that clung to her eyelashes and rolled off her, drawing her against his side. *'Dios!'* His big chest rose and fell. 'I meant to take things slowly.' His voice was harsh with self-recrimination. 'Did I hurt you?'

'No. That was…' She was lost for words to describe the rapture of making love with him.

'Amazing,' he finished for her.

Betsy felt him smile against her brow as he kissed her hair, and it was that little affectionate gesture which delighted her the most. But she reminded herself to guard her foolish heart against falling for her enigmatic husband…

CHAPTER ELEVEN

'I SEEM TO remember you promised me a sightseeing trip today,' Betsy said lightly.

Carlos was propped on an elbow, lying on the blanket that they had spread out on the sand. His eyes roamed over her tiny silver bikini top. Since they had come to Casita Viola ten days ago he had tested the weight of her firm breasts countless times and felt the thrust of her nipples against his tongue. But, however many times he had her, he wanted her again and again.

'I am enjoying the sight of you, *querida*. Although the view would be even better if you took your top off,' he murmured, stretching out his hand and tugging at the ties.

She laughed and evaded his fingers. 'You're insatiable.'

'Is that a complaint?'

Beneath his teasing, he was serious. He was sure that Betsy enjoyed their lovemaking as much as he did, but he found his desire for her was limitless. In a distant corner of his mind an alarm bell rang, but he ignored it and bent his head to claim her mouth in a lingering kiss.

He was in control, he assured himself. But he was at Casita Viola, the place he loved more than anywhere in the world, with his beautiful, sexy wife, and there was no harm in letting his guard down a little.

When he slipped his hand between Betsy's soft thighs, she pushed against his chest. 'Food,' she muttered. 'I'm going to make lunch, and afterwards we will have a siesta.'

'I'll hold you to that promise, *querida*. And later I'll keep mine and take you to Palma. It's a beautiful city to explore. We won't have any time for sightseeing after Sebastian arrives tomorrow.'

'I can't wait to see him. I've missed him.' Betsy grinned and jumped up from the blanket. 'Although you *have* kept me entertained.'

Carlos watched her walk up the cliff steps to the house, admiring her pert derriere, barely covered by tiny denim shorts. The idea of a honeymoon had been a stroke of genius, he congratulated himself. These past days had been a revelation, and he and Betsy had both been more relaxed without the strain that their relationship had been under before.

Carlos acknowledged that the main reason for his good mood was the fact that he was getting great sex regularly. As he'd suspected, he and Betsy were highly sexually compatible. Not only that, he liked being with her. She was good company, witty and funny, and he was genuinely interested in her.

He was aware that while he'd expected Betsy to leave her old life and her friends in Dorset and move to Spain, he had not had to make *any* sacrifices. Of course he'd had to give up his freedom, but he didn't miss his playboy lifestyle when he had a far more meaningful life as a father. And besides, he hadn't looked at another woman for longer than he cared to recall. Making Betsy happy had become his mission. Having a contented wife made life a lot easier than having her unhappy with their marriage arrangement, he reasoned.

After a swim in the sea, Carlos made his way back to the house and found Betsy carrying a bowl of salad outside to the terrace, where she had set the table for lunch.

'Can you bring the wine from the kitchen?' she called to him.

He uncorked the bottle of red wine that had been produced at a local vineyard before he followed her outside.

'While I was looking for a clean tablecloth I found some photo albums with pictures of you when you were younger,' Betsy said, indicating the albums on the table. 'Do you mind if I look through them after lunch?'

'Help yourself.'

They ate fresh prawns that Carlos had bought from a local fisherman, and then carried their wine glasses over to a corner of the garden shaded by a pergola, where vivid pink bougainvillea grew in abundance.

'Is that you?' Betsy asked, pointing to a photo of a small boy holding a tennis racket that was almost as big as him.

'I must have been about three years old then. My mother introduced me to tennis at an early age.' Carlos pointed to another photo. 'I was eight in this one, and I'd just won an under-twelves regional championship. My mother realised that I had talent, and she hired José Vidal, who had been her tennis coach when she played professionally, to work with me.'

'I didn't realise that your mother was a tennis player.'

'She was runner-up in the Spanish and French championships, and she played in London on a wild card and got to the quarter-finals. It was her dream to win the BITC, but she retired from the game to focus on her family.'

'You must have been close to her with your shared love of tennis,' Betsy said softly. She looked at a photo of Carlos laughing with his father. 'It looks as though you had a strong bond with your dad, too.'

'We were close once.' Guilt snaked through Carlos. 'Everything changed when my mother died.'

He could see that Betsy was curious, but he wasn't about to tell her that he had his mother's blood on his hands, and that was why his father had turned against him. If he admitted what he had done he was certain he would see disgust in Betsy's eyes.

With a jolt of shock, Carlos realised that her opinion of him mattered.

'Who is this?' she asked, indicating a picture of a man standing next to a teenage Carlos.

'That's my coach, José. When I was fifteen, I was offered funding on the condition that I moved to Barcelona to train. My father ran a business in Toledo, and couldn't uproot my sister, so I left home and lodged with José and his wife.'

'You had recently lost your mother, hadn't you? It must have been hard to leave your father and sister, and they must have missed you.'

'My father wanted me to go.'

In his mind, Carlos heard Roderigo Segarra's voice. *Don't let your mother's death be in vain. Go and learn to be a champion for her sake. It's the least you can do to honour her memory.'*

But Carlos had been prepared to give up his pursuit of the dream that had torn his family apart. *'I'll stay, Papà, and learn to be a baker so that I can take over the shop, like you hoped I would.'*

Roderigo had actually looked horrified at the prospect. *'My hopes died with your mother,'* he'd said bitterly. *'I don't want you to stay here.'*

They had been devastating words to a fifteen-year-old boy, and twenty years later his father's rejection still scraped a raw place on Carlos's heart.

'José Vidal was my coach for ten years,' he told Betsy. 'He became a father figure to me, and I trusted him. I was certain that with his support I would become the greatest tennis champion. By my early twenties I was ranked number three in the world and had already won four world titles.'

He lifted his glass to his lips and drank some wine.

'I'll admit that fame and glory went to my head.' His laugh was self-derisive. 'I endorsed several big sports brands and got paid a fortune for using a certain tennis racket or modelling a particular range of sportswear. I had money, and beautiful women flocked around me. Training took second place to living the good life. But everything changed when I got very drunk one night and fell down a flight of steps. My shoulder was broken in three places and there was significant muscle and ligament damage. The surgeon was doubtful that I would play tennis at competition level again.'

Betsy looked shocked. 'I had no idea. You must have felt devastated, believing that your career could be over.'

It had been a bleak time in his life, and Carlos rarely allowed himself to dwell on it. Like other dark events in his past, he compartmentalised the memories and buried them deep inside him. He had no idea why he was spilling his guts to Betsy.

'More devastating than my injuries was the attitude of my coach. José came to visit me in hospital and told me that he would no longer oversee my training. He'd read the medical reports and didn't believe I would ever recover properly and regain my tennis ranking. As far as he was concerned I wouldn't be a champion and earn the big money, so he dropped me in favour of another rising tennis star.'

'That's awful.'

There was a sympathy in Betsy's voice that Carlos told himself he neither wanted nor deserved.

'That's life,' he said harshly. 'When I watched José walk out of that hospital room, I vowed two things. The first was that I would be a champion without his help, and the second was that I would never trust anyone again.'

Carlos stared at another photo. It was of him, his parents and his sister, who had been only ten at the time. It was the last picture of his family before his mother had died. Thinking about her made his heart grow heavy. His *madre* would have loved Sebastian, and her other grandson Miguel. But her life had been cruelly cut short—by *him*.

Carlos's jaw clenched. He did not deserve a family after he'd destroyed the one he had been born into. He hadn't planned to have a child, but fate had intervened and given him a son he adored. He had a wife too, although he hadn't expected to marry.

He had married Betsy so that he could claim his son, he reminded himself. But deep down he knew that hadn't been the only reason.

He forced his mind away from the past, aware that Betsy was looking at him with a concerned expression on her face. 'You mentioned a siesta,' he murmured.

'Carlos…' She lifted a hand and let it fall helplessly. 'You told me that there are things I don't understand. But how *can* I understand, or try to help you, if you don't talk to me?'

'Help me?' He shook his head. 'All the talking in the world won't make any difference. There is nothing you can do.'

She tilted her chin. 'Try me.'

He remembered how she had defended him against his father's criticism, and was almost tempted to reveal the dark secret that festered inside him. But shame stopped him.

The silence stretched between them until Betsy gave a soft sigh and stood up. 'I need a shower before we go to Palma.'

Carlos told himself he wouldn't follow her. But when Betsy walked into the house he felt as if she had taken the sunshine with her and coldness seeped into his bones.

He did not need her. That was a ridiculous idea, he assured himself. But somehow he was standing in the bedroom and staring at her silver bikini that she'd left on the floor outside the bathroom door.

Carlos stripped off his swim shorts and stepped into the steamy shower cubicle. He paused for a moment, watching the water cascade over Betsy's gorgeous curves, and then moved to stand behind her. He slid his arms around her and cupped her breasts in his hands, pulling her against him so that her bottom was pressing on his erection.

'I have a surprise for you when we go back to Fortaleza Aguila,' he murmured in her ear.

She wriggled out of his arms and turned to face him. 'What is it?'

'It won't be a surprise if I tell you.'

He inhaled sharply when she dropped to her knees in front of him. Water streamed over her face and hair as she looked up at him, and her smile was like a sunbeam lighting the darkness in his heart.

'Maybe I can persuade you to tell me,' she said softly.

And then she put her mouth on him, and he could not

control the shudders that racked him when she moved her tongue along his hard length.

That alarm bell in his mind rang again. Control was everything to Carlos, and losing control was a weakness he could not contemplate. For twenty years he had not allowed anything to touch him deeply enough so that he cared.

He told himself that he did not care about Betsy, beyond the fact that she was the mother of his son. The passion they shared was just a bonus in their marriage, and he had no doubt that in time his physical infatuation with her would settle to something less needy that he could control.

But in the meantime he threaded his fingers into her hair as he fell back against the wall of the shower cubicle and lost control spectacularly.

'Do you want to see your surprise?' Carlos asked Betsy as she walked down the stairs at Fortaleza Aguila. They had arrived at the house twenty minutes ago and she'd just carried Sebastian up to the nursery.

'I'm sure he has grown taller,' Ginette had said fondly as she'd watched the toddler charge over to his toy box. 'Did you and Carlos have a relaxing holiday?'

Betsy had felt herself blush as she'd thought of the amount of mind-blowing sex they'd had. Their honeymoon had been the most exhilarating few weeks of her life. But it wasn't only physically that her relationship with Carlos had developed. They had grown closer in so many other ways and had talked for hours.

The time they had spent together in Mallorca had reminded her of when she had been his housekeeper in London and cooked dinner for them every evening. Carlos had needed to unwind after his heavy training sessions or playing matches when the tournament had begun. Often they had watched a film together, or read, and they'd both tried to ignore the sexual chemistry that had simmered between them until that last night, when it had exploded into passion.

At Casita Viola, Betsy had cooked Carlos's favourite meals and taken pleasure in his enjoyment of the food she'd prepared. When Ginette had brought Sebastian to Mallorca and then returned to Toledo, Betsy had loved the fact that they were a little family. She'd been happy, pottering about the cottage or taking Sebastian to the beach. And at night, when their son had been tucked up in his cot, Carlos had brought her body to quivering life with his caresses and she had acknowledged that she was halfway to being in love with him.

Her heart gave a familiar flip as she walked across the hall towards him. Sun-bleached jeans hugged his lean hips, and a black tee shirt moulded his magnificent chest.

'Is my surprise in your study?' she asked.

She was puzzled when he opened the door and ushered her into the room.

'Oh!'

She stopped dead and looked around in amazement. The study had been transformed into an art studio. An easel stood next to the window, and there was a long workbench and storage drawers beneath it, a table with her sketchbook and pencils, and at one end of the room a big leather sofa.

'The sofa is for me, when I come and visit you in your studio,' Carlos told her with a grin.

'But you need your study. You often work from home.'

'I've relocated to another room. Your friend Hector said that this was the best room for natural light coming through the window.'

She stared at him. 'You asked Hector?'

'While we were in Mallorca I phoned the art supplies shop and spoke to him. He was very helpful, advising me on what equipment you would need. I thought you might like to invite Hector and his girlfriend to dinner one evening. You have met my friends—it's about time I got to know yours,' Carlos said.

She swallowed the lump in her throat. 'I can't believe you've done such a lovely thing for me. I've always wanted a proper studio.'

'I'm glad you like it. It's important to me that we make a success of our marriage, *querida*.'

'It is?' Tremulous hope filled her.

'Of course. Sebastian deserves to have parents who are united.'

Betsy could not fault his reasoning. And her parents' love had turned to hatred. So why did she yearn for Carlos to see her as more than the mother of his child? Her pleasure in the studio was dimmed slightly, knowing that he believed it was his *duty* to keep her happy. When she was a child her parents had competed for who could buy her the most expensive birthday and Christmas presents, but all she'd really wanted was for them to love her instead of using her to argue over.

Carlos captured her chin and tilted her face up to his. 'You look sad. Did I forget something for the studio?'

'No, it's perfect.' She sternly told herself to stop wishing for the moon and smiled at him. 'Thank you.'

'I think we should try out the sofa.' He drew her into his arms and nuzzled the sensitive spot behind her ear. 'I had a lock fitted on the door so that you won't be disturbed when you are working.'

'I'm not working now...'

Her breath hitched in her throat when he slipped his

hand beneath her tee shirt and cupped a breast, dragging his thumb across its tender peak.

'That's why I locked the door,' he said thickly, and he dropped down on the sofa and pulled her onto his lap.

Desire gleamed golden bright in his eyes and Betsy melted instantly, as she always did when her handsome husband made love to her. But she could not ignore the whispered warning in her head.

If his passion for her faded in the future, would he still be committed to their marriage?

But Carlos threaded his fingers through her hair with a tenderness that lit a spark of hope inside her, and when he claimed her mouth she pushed her doubts away and sank into his kiss.

The days slipped into weeks, and the fiercely hot temperature so characteristic of Toledo in midsummer dropped a few degrees to become pleasantly warm in early autumn.

Betsy put down her brush and stepped back from the easel to study her latest animal portrait with a critical eye. The horse she was painting was owned by Carlos's close friend Sergio and his wife Martina. The couple often came to dinner and Betsy had discovered that she and Martina, who owned a riding stables, shared a love of animals. Also, Martina's sister Mia had a daughter the same age as Sebastian, and had invited Betsy to a mother and baby group.

It helped that she was picking up more Spanish words, so that she was able to chat to the other mothers in the group, and Sebastian loved playing with other children.

She and Carlos had also met Hector and his girlfriend for dinner and the two men had got on well. Now that she had a social life with new friends, and her pet portrait business was doing so well that she had a waiting list of clients, Betsy felt more settled.

She moved closer to the window overlooking the garden and watched Carlos playing with their son. He had already introduced Sebastian to a child-sized tennis racket and spongy balls. At nearly eighteen months old, the toddler showed amazing hand-eye coordination.

'Do you hope Sebastian will be a tennis champion?' Betsy had asked Carlos once.

'I'll support him in whatever he chooses to do,' Carlos had replied, with an odd note in his voice.

She remembered he'd said that his father had not been proud of his sporting success, but her attempts to get Carlos to open up about his strained relationship with Roderigo had been politely but firmly rebuffed.

Betsy gave a soft sigh. To other people her marriage must seem perfect. And it almost was. She and Carlos got on brilliantly, and they spent a lot of time together because he was often at home now. He'd cut down on his business trips, saying that he wanted to be with Sebastian as much as possible.

She would always feel guilty that she'd stolen the first fifteen months of his son's life from him, but Carlos had said that they had both made mistakes and it was time to put the past behind them and move on.

As for the physical side of their marriage—it got better and better. There was no longer a bolster down the centre of the bed, and they made love most nights. The sofa in her art studio had proved to be very useful too… Heat stained Betsy's face as she recalled how Carlos had bent her over the leather arm while he stood behind her and eased his erection between her thighs.

He took her apart every time he made love to her, but he never lost control with complete abandon the way he'd done at the cottage. She longed to shatter his restraint, but he seemed determined not to allow it to happen, and sex had become something of a battle of wills which Betsy always lost.

Yes, her life was very nearly perfect—especially now there was a new member of their family. She looked over at the fluffy bundle of mischief who was curled up in a dog basket.

'He's half miniature poodle and the other half is anyone's guess,' Carlos had said a few weeks ago when he'd carried the small, apricot-coloured dog into the house and placed him in Betsy's arms. 'The staff at the dog rescue centre think he's about a year old, and he's good around children. His previous owner died, which is why he is up for adoption.' Carlos had hesitated when Betsy had looked stunned. 'I thought you would like him.'

'He's the most beautiful dog in the world,' she'd said in a choked voice when she'd been able to speak. 'Are you sure we can keep him?' She'd been afraid to get her hopes up.

'He's yours, *querida*,' Carlos had told her gruffly. 'The name on his collar is Chico, but I guess you can choose a different name for him.'

Now, Betsy walked across her studio and opened the door. 'Come, Chico!' The little dog was instantly at her feet, tail wagging.

Chico's unconditional love helped to ease the ache in her heart but did not erase it. She told herself she was greedy to want more than she had. A healthy son, a beautiful home and an attentive and charming husband. Her marriage exceeded all her expectations.

But she was in love with Carlos—deeply, desperately in love with him.

It wasn't the gifts he'd given her—although her studio and her dog brought her so much joy, and she appreciated the jewellery and flowers he often surprised her with. She loved him because he was a wonderful father to Sebastian. And he took an interest in her art and treated her as if she mattered to him.

But she knew he only did those things because she was the mother of his child, and the stark truth was that if she hadn't fallen pregnant two years ago, Carlos would never have returned to England to find her.

The butler met Betsy in the entrance hall when she stepped out of her studio. '*Un paquete* is here for you,' Eduardo said haltingly as he handed her a padded envelope.

It had an English postmark and Betsy was curious as she opened the envelope and found another parcel. Inside this was a slim box, and when she lifted the lid she gasped at the sight of a row of diamonds sparkling on a black velvet cushion. It was known as a tennis bracelet—a single row of diamonds on a gold chain.

Also in the box was a card with her name on, and a message scrawled in a bold hand.

Mi querida Betsy,
Perhaps you will wear this bracelet and think of me.
  Call me if you would like to meet me again.
I hope to hear from you soon.
Carlos.

At the bottom of the card was a phone number.

Carlos *hadn't* abandoned her after they'd spent the night together. He *had* wanted to see her again.

Betsy's hands shook as she read the note which had been inside the envelope. It was from her Aunt Alice's son, the one who had inherited the house in London when Alice died.

Betsy,
I recently found this parcel addressed to you while
I was clearing out the unit where my mother's per-
sonal belongings were stored when the house was
sold. I remembered that it arrived after you moved
away.
Hope it wasn't important.
Lee

On the back of the envelope was the sender's name
and address. *Bradley Miller.* Of course! Betsy remembered that Alice's son's full name was Bradley, but he
always used the abbreviation Lee. He must have signed
for the delivery as B. Miller, exactly as the courier had
reported to Carlos.

The parcel containing the bracelet *was* important.

It changed everything.

CHAPTER TWELVE

WAS SHE CRAZY? Probably, Betsy answered herself. She hugged her arms around herself as nerves threatened to overwhelm her. She was about to take the biggest gamble of her life, and if it failed she would be looking into the abyss.

But it wouldn't fail, she tried to assure herself. When she'd opened the parcel earlier in the day and discovered the bracelet Carlos had sent her two years ago, she had been convinced it was proof that he had felt something for her. She hadn't been just a casual fling as he'd told the journalist.

If only she had been at the house in London and read his note when it had been delivered. She would have called him and told him she was pregnant. It was bittersweet to realise that things could have been so different. Carlos would have met his son when he was born instead of fifteen months later.

She couldn't give him back the time he'd missed with Sebastian. But at least he would know now that she hadn't lied when she'd denied receiving the parcel. She had always been honest with him, and it was only right that she should be honest about her feelings for him now.

'Are we celebrating something?'

Carlo's deep voice was indulgent as he strolled across

the terrace. Betsy had asked the staff to set up a table and two chairs beside the pool. She gave a tense glance at the snowy white cloth, silver cutlery and long-stemmed glasses to check that everything was perfect. An arrangement of white roses in the centre of the table gave off a heady perfume. Her fingers were unsteady as she lit the candles before she turned to face him. She smoothed her hand nervously down the black silk sheath dress that fitted her like a second skin.

'I thought it would be nice to dress up for dinner,' she said huskily. Carlos looked mouthwatering in fitted black trousers and a soft cream shirt unbuttoned at the throat. 'I've been wearing my painting shirt all day while I finished Sergio and Martina's picture.'

'You look amazing in that dress,' he murmured as he stood in front of her. The dress had a halter neck and Carlos brushed his lips over one bare shoulder. 'I hope you haven't planned a dinner with many courses, because I'm ready for dessert now, *mi belleza*.'

Her heart lurched as her awareness of him, as always, collided with her nerves. He smelled divine. The evocative scent of his sandalwood cologne teased her senses and suddenly she felt shy—which was ridiculous when he had seen every inch of her body, and stared into her eyes and glimpsed her soul each time she'd climaxed beneath him.

'Let's sit down,' she said jerkily.

His gaze sharpened on her hot face, but he said nothing as he pulled out her chair and waited for her to be seated before he moved around the table and sat down. The first course of gazpacho, a traditional Spanish cold soup, was already in bowls in front of them.

Betsy lifted the cover from her bowl and reached for the bottle of red wine that she'd asked the butler to uncork and leave open to breathe. As she filled Carlos's glass the diamond bracelet on her wrist sparkled in the candlelight. He stared at the bracelet and then at her.

'My aunt's son found the package that you sent to the house in London and posted it on to me. I remember I asked you once what a tennis bracelet was. Now I know.' She turned her wrist and the diamonds glittered. 'I'm two years too late, but it's beautiful. Thank you.'

He leaned back in his chair. 'So you really didn't receive the gift I sent you when I returned to Spain?'

She shook her head. 'If I'd had your phone number I would have called you. Fate is capricious,' she murmured. 'Things would have been different if I had known that you wanted to see me again.'

'In what way different?'

'I assume we would have been together when Sebastian was born, and there would not have been all these misunderstandings between us.'

He nodded. 'It's true. I would have married you when I learned of your pregnancy to ensure that my child was legitimate at his birth.'

Carlos's matter-of-fact statement sent a ripple of unease through Betsy. 'But my pregnancy wouldn't have been the only reason you'd have married me, would it?'

His brows drew together. 'What do you mean?'

She put down her spoon, her soup untouched, and lifted her arm to look at the diamond bracelet. 'You sent me a beautiful gift and said you wanted to see me again. That means a lot to me.' Her voice shook. 'I love the bracelet...and I love you, Carlos. I fell in love with you two years ago, and I think... I hope...you feel the same way about me.'

Something flared in his eyes, but was gone before she could assimilate what it was she had seen. And maybe she'd imagined it. His face was a beautiful sculpted mask that revealed no emotion, and his silence seemed faintly stunned, pressing against Betsy's ears. Her stomach cramped with nervous tension at the creeping realisation that she might have gotten things horribly wrong.

'I don't share your feelings,' he said abruptly.

She bit down on her lip hard and tasted blood in her mouth. 'So if I hadn't fallen pregnant, if we hadn't had Sebastian, where would our relationship have been?' Ice formed around her heart. 'Or are you saying that we wouldn't have had a relationship? Even though you must have felt *something* for me to have sent the bracelet?'

He dropped his gaze from hers. 'That wasn't the first time I'd given a bracelet as a gift.'

Understanding dawned, and she would have sworn she actually heard her heart shatter. 'You used to send bracelets to women when you wanted to have an affair with them. It was your calling card, and I was just one in a long line of casual flings like you told that journalist, wasn't I?'

'You didn't want high emotion and drama,' Carlos reminded her, almost aggressively. 'Your parents' volatile relationship ruined your childhood. You don't want that for Sebastian, and nor do I.' He raked his hair off his brow. 'What we have is good—solid. A marriage based on reason and common sense and a desire to do the best for our son.'

'Is that really all our marriage is to you?' She had built castles in the air and now they were tumbling down. 'Our honeymoon felt like more than common sense.'

He looked away from her. 'I needed to break the deadlock between us.'

'And so you seduced me?'

'If you remember, *querida*, you seduced *me*,' he said softly.

She had made it so easy for him, Betsy thought bleakly. He had spun his sensual web and she'd walked straight into it.

'The passion we share is unique,' he said. 'I have never wanted any woman the way I want you.'

'Is that supposed to make me feel better? That I'm a good lay?'

'You know that's not what I meant.' He picked up his wine glass and drained it in a couple of gulps. 'I have never wanted to fall in love. I told you when I asked you to marry me that we wouldn't have a fairy tale romance.' He gave her a frustrated look. 'I'm not cut out for love.'

'You love Sebastian.'

He lifted his shoulders. 'That's different. I had no choice. The moment I held my son I was overwhelmed with love for him.'

'But you don't love me,' she said quietly.

She seemed to have spent most of her life being quiet, not making a fuss so that then maybe everything would be all right and the shouting would stop. She wanted to curl up in a ball and pull the duvet over her head, like she'd done as a child to block out her parents' angry voices. Now she wanted to block out the pity she'd heard in Carlos's voice. *Pity.*

She felt sick. Her throat burned with the tears that she was trying to swallow because she couldn't let herself break down in front of him.

He scraped back his chair and stood up. 'You don't want me to love you. Really you don't, *querida*. I am no good at it.'

Beneath his savage voice there was a rawness that startled Betsy.

'*I'm* no good,' Carlos told her grimly.

And then he walked away, leaving her alone with her heart in a thousand pieces.

How long she sat there she did not know. The butler came with the main course and she sent him back to the kitchen with her apologies to the cook. Betsy did not think she would ever want to eat again, or smile, or paint. Life had been drained of joy.

If only she had been content with what she had instead of wanting more. She had put Carlos under pressure to admit how he felt about her and his answer had ripped her heart out. Now that she had revealed her emotions they would not be able to return to how they had been.

The thought of facing him again made her insides squirm. She couldn't share a bed with him and make love with him, knowing that for him it was just sex. How could she stay with him now she knew that he would never love her as she loved him?

She stood up and blew out the flames on the candles that had burnt down almost to nothing. A muscle in her leg twinged and she realised that she had been sitting in the same position for too long. Sleep would be impossible, and she didn't even know where she would go to bed.

Filled with restlessness, she walked into the pool house and changed into her one-piece costume before she headed back to the pool. The underwater lights had come on and she dived into the water and started to swim, length after length, punishing herself for wanting the one thing she could not have. Her husband's heart.

He had hurt her. He'd seen the evidence in the way her mouth had crumpled and her eyes had shimmered overbright in the candlelight.

But what else could he have done? Carlos asked himself as guilt jagged through him. He couldn't have lied and made false promises. Betsy deserved better than that. She deserved his honesty. She was so honest herself, and fierce and brave and loving. He saw her generous nature every day as she showered their son with love. Betsy had a big heart and a deep well of kindness. She cared for her friends and she adored the little dog which was utterly devoted to her. She was charming to the staff and she took Sebastian to visit his grandfather daily.

And she loved him.

Carlos cursed as he strode through the house with no idea of where he was headed. The bottom of a whisky bottle was tempting. But he couldn't hide from his demons any longer. He couldn't keep running. Betsy *loved* him. But she wouldn't if she knew what he had done. He didn't deserve her love.

But he wanted it.

His breath left him on a groan and he stumbled and leaned against the wall, feeling as if he'd been winded. Feeling as if his heart was being squeezed in a vice. This was why he had spent his adult life burying his emotions. Love hurt. It was killing him to know that he had hurt Betsy.

This was the truth of him, Carlos thought savagely. He destroyed everything that was good.

A memory that he had spent twenty years trying to eradicate by pushing his body to the extreme of its physical capability slid like a poisonous serpent into his mind. His mother lying slumped on the tennis court while he cradled her in his arms, feeling helpless as the life left her body on a shuddering final breath. He'd sprinted over to where he'd left his bag and grabbed his phone, but even as he'd called the emergency services he'd known it was too late.

He remembered how tears had streamed down his father's face. 'You knew your mother felt unwell with a headache, but still you nagged her to be your practice partner. All you care about is tennis and the glory of winning. Now your mother has paid the price for your ambition with her life. Never forget that, Carlos.'

He looked around and discovered that his feet had brought him to the annexe of the house. He hammered on the door of his father's suite and the nurse let him in. He strode into his father's bedroom. Roderigo rarely left his bed these days, and his bony hand pressed the control to bring him up into a sitting position.

'Why didn't you come to watch me play in the London final? I wanted you to be there.' The words burst out of Carlos. 'I won it for *her*. I thought you would be proud of me at last.' The ache in his chest expanded. 'I hoped you would forgive me, Papà.'

'I couldn't bring myself to go,' his father rasped. 'It had been your mother's dream to win the ladies' tournament there.' He sighed. 'She could have done it. She was a great player, and her coach said she had the potential to be a world champion. But I stopped her from pursuing her dream. I resented the hours of training she put in, and the weeks and months she spent away on the tennis tours. I put pressure on her to start a family. I told her I wanted a child—a son who would one day take over the bakery from me as I had done when my father retired. But motherhood meant the end of her tennis career.'

Carlos stared at his father. 'Are you saying that Mamà did not want me?'

'She wanted you,' Roderigo said softly. 'Your mother adored you and Graciela. She never regretted choosing to be a mother. But as you grew up, and it became apparent that you had inherited her talent for tennis, I realised how much she had missed playing competitively. She lived her dream through you, and I resented you because your success reminded me of the career she might have had if my selfishness hadn't denied her the chance to chase her dream.'

Carlos swallowed. 'You sent me away to live in Barcelona. You blamed me for her death and you were right. I killed her.'

'I regret what I said. I was in shock. I didn't really blame you. I didn't realise that you had remembered it for all these years.'

'It wasn't something I was likely to forget,' Carlos said curtly.

'Forgive me.' A tear slid down Roderigo's papery cheek. 'Your mother had died and it was too late for me tell her that I was sorry, that I wished I'd encouraged her tennis career. I couldn't go to watch you in London because *she* should have played there and I felt so guilty. I sent you to live with your coach because I was determined to give you the chance that I had taken away from you mother. You are a great champion and she would have been proud of you…as I am proud of you, *mi hijo*.'

'Papà…' Carlos sat on the bed and clasped his father's hand.

'You have a beautiful wife and son. Don't make the mistakes I made.' Roderigo squeezed Carlos's fingers. 'Don't leave things unsaid and spend the rest of your life regretting it.'

Carlos's mind was reeling as he left the annexe and returned to the main house. The glass doors were open in the sitting room, and he frowned when he heard someone shouting. The room overlooked the pool terrace, and he saw the butler running across the tiles.

'La señora—se ha ahogada!'

Drowned!

Carlos tore down the steps from the house. As he raced across the terrace he saw a shape lying motionless next to the pool. His heart slammed against his ribs. In his mind he saw his mother, slumped on the tennis court.

'*Betsy!*'

His roar was that of a wounded animal. He dropped onto his knees beside her, relief pouring through him when she half sat up and coughed up water.

She groaned and clutched her leg. 'Cramp in my calf muscle,' she muttered. 'I was swimming and my leg seized up. I couldn't move. Luckily Eduardo saw me and managed to pull me out of the water.'

'It's all right, *querida*.' Carlos's hands were shaking as he gathered her close.

She tensed and pulled away from him. 'It's not all right,' she choked, 'and it never will be. I've ruined everything.'

Betsy would rather have walked over hot coals than for Carlos to lift her into his arms. But the pain in her calf muscle was so excruciating that walking was impossible, and she had no choice but to suffer him carrying her back to the house.

'You can put me down on the sofa. I'll be fine in a few minutes,' she muttered, her gaze fixed on his shirt collar rather than on his face.

He ignored her and strode across the hall and up the stairs, heading along the corridor towards their bedroom. They had separate bathrooms, but hers only had a shower. He carried her into his and sat her on a chair while he turned on the taps to fill the bath, adding a handful of bath crystals.

'Hot water will help the muscle to relax. Cramp in

the gastrocnemius—that's the big muscle in your calf—is agony,' he explained. 'I was once carried off a tennis court halfway through a match that I was winning because of cramp.'

She suspected he was chatting normally to make her feel less embarrassed. *Some hope*, Betsy thought bleakly. His kindness made things so much worse.

She stared down at her feet so that he would not see the tears brimming in her eyes. 'The pain is going off a bit. I can manage now. Will you go and check on Sebastian?'

'Don't lock the door in case you need my help.'

When he had gone, she peeled off her swimsuit and climbed into the bath. It was deep and she sank into the water, flexing the calf muscle that now ached dully. Her mind replayed those terrifying minutes in the pool, when she'd literally been unable to move her leg. The pain had been so intense that she had panicked and swallowed a mouthful of pool water.

Tears slipped down her cheeks. She told herself they were a reaction to shock but knew she was lying to herself. There was a movement by the door, and through her tears she saw Carlos's blurred figure leaning against the frame.

'When I was fourteen I had the chance to become the youngest player to win an international boys' tournament, but I lost the final match,' he said heavily. 'I was furious and I lost my temper. I had a complete meltdown on the court and smashed my racket. I received an official reprimand from the umpire. In the car afterwards, my father told me that my behaviour had brought shame on the family. My mother was upset. When we got home, she said she had a headache. But I nagged her to come to the practice court and be my hitting partner.'

He pushed his hands into his pockets and kicked the door frame with his toe.

'I served a ball hard and it caught her on her shoulder. She fell to the ground. I was annoyed because I thought she was making a fuss. But she didn't move.'

Betsy held her breath as Carlos continued.

'I ran across to her and supported her head in my arms. I still thought she had been hurt by the tennis ball and she would get up in a minute. But she died. Right there in my arms, my mother died.'

'Oh, Carlos, I'm so sorry.'

His face twisted. 'It wasn't the tennis ball. She died of a brain aneurysm. The headache had been a warning sign. Someone called my father and he came to the tennis court, but he was too late. He sobbed like a child over my mother's body—and then he told me that I had killed her.'

'I don't believe that,' Betsy said urgently. 'The aneurysm could have ruptured at any time.'

He nodded. 'But I was convinced that my hot temper had resulted in my mother's death, and I vowed never to lose control of my emotions ever again. *Any* of my emotions,' he said roughly. 'For twenty years I never got angry, or sad, or wildly happy. I didn't allow myself to feel anything too deeply.'

The pain in his voice tore on her heart. 'Carlos...'

'And then I met you, Betsy Miller. You were my housekeeper and you assured me that I wouldn't notice you.'

He smiled ruefully, but the expression in his eyes made her heart lurch.

'I wanted you from that moment.'

'And after I had fallen into your bed like a ripe plum, you decided you would have an affair with me.' The bubbles were rapidly disappearing, and she sank lower in the bathwater. 'If I had seen your note and met you in Spain I

suppose you would have invited me to stay at your bachelor penthouse in Madrid, until you grew bored with a
shy housekeeper and ditched me for a glamorous model.'

'That bathwater must be getting cold.'

He levered himself away from the door and, before
Betsy realised his intention, leaned down and scooped
her out of the bath.

'I'm making you wet,' she muttered as he held her
against his chest and carried her into the bedroom. Being
in his arms was torture, and she longed to press her lips
to his rough jaw. When he sat her on the bed, she grabbed
the towel he offered and wrapped it around herself.

'I planned to take you to Mallorca, to Casita Viola,'
he said.

She stared at him. 'I thought you never invited your
lovers to the cottage?'

'I didn't.'

He hesitated for a heartbeat, and Betsy had the crazy
idea that he was unsure of himself.

'But you were different.'

Yet more tears filled her eyes. She wanted to believe
him so badly, but he'd warned her not to believe in fairy
tales. 'Carlos, please don't feel sorry for me. I shouldn't
have said what I did at dinner.'

'You told me that you loved me.'

His voice was velvet-soft and she tried to steel herself
against his tenderness. He was a nice guy, and he was
trying to let her down gently.

'Do we have to have a post-mortem on how I made a
fool of myself again?'

The mattress dipped as Carlos sat beside her and captured her chin, tilting her face up to his. Gold-flecked
eyes searched her gaze. 'Did you mean it?'

She gave a little sigh. He was her world, and now she

understood how he had been affected by his mother's death. He was afraid of strong emotions, and wary of love, but perhaps in time he would grow to care for her.

'I have never lied to you,' she said softly.

'*Santa Madre!*'

He closed his eyes briefly, and when he opened them again his expression stopped Betsy's heart in its tracks.

'I love you, *mi corazón...mi amor.*'

A tear slid down her cheek and he caught it on his thumb. 'Why are you shaking your head, *querida?* Don't you want me to love you?'

His voice was rough, uncertain, and her tears fell faster. 'I want your love so much, but I'm scared to believe you.'

'Why would I lie?'

His smile stole her breath and, impossibly, she saw that his lashes were damp.

'How could I not love you, Betsy? You stole my heart two years ago. But I had got used to feeling nothing. It was easier...safer. I couldn't hurt anyone if I didn't care about them.' His mouth twisted. 'And I couldn't be hurt if I didn't fall in love. I tried to deny how I felt about you, but when I saw you next to the pool tonight I thought—' he swallowed hard '—I feared I had lost you. And I had to face the fact that without you the world is grey, because you are my sunshine and I will love you for eternity.'

She fell into his arms, because it was the only place she wanted to be. His heart thundered beneath her hands as she tugged open his shirt buttons and pressed her face against his warm olive skin.

She could not quite believe that he was hers, but when she lifted her head the golden gleam in his eyes was love—pure and precious and all for her. With a soft cry of joy she curled her arms around his neck and pulled his head down. He claimed her mouth and kissed her fiercely, but with an innate tenderness that told her without words that his love was the lasting kind.

'I love you. And it will last, won't it?' she whispered as he unwrapped the towel from around her body and stripped off his clothes before stretching out on the bed beside her. She bit her lip. 'It's not just sex?'

'Every time we made love I told you with my body what my brain was too stubborn to accept,' Carlos said deeply. He held her hand over his heart. 'Feel what you do to me, *mi corazón*. My heart beats for you.'

His hands shook as he traced them over every dip and curve of her body. He feathered kisses over her breasts and his breath grazed her inner thighs as his caresses became ever more erotic. And when he lifted himself over her and possessed her, with a bone-shaking tenderness and a possessiveness that thrilled her, Carlos told her in the language of lovers that he would worship her always and for ever.

EPILOGUE

'YOU ARE A miracle-worker,' Betsy told her husband of two years.

They had recently celebrated their second wedding anniversary with a romantic weekend in Mallorca.

'We can go anywhere in the world,' Carlos had said when he'd suggested the trip. 'The best hotel or a luxury cruise ship. You choose.'

'I choose Casita Viola. We never did get around to making love on the beach.'

Carlos had taken care of that, and had made love to her with such dedication that she had felt she loved him even more, if that was possible.

'What miracle have I performed?' he murmured now, as he came over to where she was standing by the window in her art studio. He slid his arms around her waist and pulled her against his chest, his lips nuzzling her ear.

She pointed to the garden, where her parents were each pushing a pram up and down the lawn. 'Mum and Dad have been here for three days and they haven't argued once. They even get on with each other's new partners. What did you do?'

'I very cleverly made you pregnant with twins, so that they had a granddaughter each to coo over.' Carlos winced as they watched Sebastian charge across the grass and kick a football, which sailed over the pram where six-month-old Ana-Marta was sleeping. Betsy's mother was pushing the other pram, with baby Alicia inside. 'I don't know where our son gets his energy from.'

'I wonder...' Betsy said drily. 'I can't decide if he is going to be a famous footballer or a tennis champion, but all that matters is that he is happy.' She turned in Carlos's arms and captured his beloved face in her hands. 'Have you any idea how happy you make *me*?'

'I love you.' He kissed her lingeringly. 'I never believed I could be this happy. A beautiful wife and three gorgeous children—what more could I want?'

'How about four gorgeous children?' Betsy grinned at his startled expression. 'All that sex on the beach in Mallorca has given us a lovely surprise.'

Carlos laughed and hugged her tight before he scooped her up and carried her over to the sofa. 'I'm delighted by your news. But how do you feel about falling pregnant so soon after having the twins?'

'I feel that I am the luckiest woman in the world. You are my world, Carlos. You and our children. My parents, your father, Graciela and Miguel, Chico... It's my dream come true. Family.'

'For ever,' he said softly, before he kissed her. 'By the way, I have locked the door, *querida,* and you will have my undivided attention.'

* * * * *

ONE
SCANDALOUS
CHRISTMAS EVE

SUSAN STEPHENS

For Pippa Roscoe, Mother of Wolves,
amazing author of Mills & Boon Modern,
and whipper-upper of enthusiasm for more Acostas.
If we hadn't been chatting over tapas in a
Spanish restaurant called Lobos (Wolves),
Team Lobos might never have taken to the saddle.

Thank you to all involved for bringing back
the dangerous glamour of the Acostas clan!

CHAPTER ONE

THE SHADOW OF a helicopter briefly dimmed the sunshine of a crisp November day. Jess Slatehome's breath hitched. The logo on the side, a shield of gold on a ground of black, stated boldly, Acosta España.

The Acostas were *back*!

It had been a long ten years since Jess had last met up with the Spanish Acosta family—four handsome brothers with an elegant sister at home—when they had come to trial some ponies on her family farm in Yorkshire.

When she had kissed one of them.

Closing her eyes briefly on that embarrassing thought, Jess knew she had to focus on today, and an idea born of desperation. Sell the stock, save the farm had become her mantra. A seal of approval from the Acostas would assure the success of the big family event Jess had arranged to showcase her father's prize-winning polo ponies, in the hope of selling at least some of them, in an attempt to stave off the bank and bail her father out of financial trouble.

Jess's father, Jim Slatehome, was a much-loved local character and everyone from the village had pitched in to help. Using every penny of her savings, as well as a small bequest from her mother, with the invaluable assistance of an army of volunteers, Jess had been able to plan big. Sending out dozens of invitations in the hope of attracting the glitterati of the polo circuit, she had made it her goal to return her father to the spotlight he deserved. Before her mother's death Jim Slatehome had been the go-to trainer and breeder of world-class ponies. Felled by grief, he had retreated from the world and it had taken all Jess's persuasion to persuade him that five years was long enough to shut himself away, and that today marked his return.

Success hovered tantalisingly within their grasp now. Gazing up as the helicopter prepared to land, she knew that if a member of the Acosta family bought some ponies her father would be back on top. But who would step out of that aircraft?

Jess's mouth dried as she thought back ten years to when the gleam of wealth and success blazing from the Acosta brothers had almost blinded her when they arrived on the farm to buy horses. Finding herself alone with Dante Acosta in the stable, some fan girl craziness had prompted her to launch herself at him and plant a kiss on his mouth. He'd stepped away with a huff of disbelief. The scorch of humiliation felt as keen today as it had done then. But she'd never forgotten the kiss. Or that for a moment—and she was never quite sure if she imagined this or not— Dante Acosta had responded.

Jess tensed as the aircraft door swung open. This was madness, she told herself firmly. And yet she waited, breath held, to see if the fiery superstar of the polo world would descend the steps. She'd followed his career keenly since that first memorable encounter between a naïve seventeen-year-old country girl with a head full of daydreams and a mouth full of cheek and a youth who already boasted the dazzling glamour for which he had since become famous. Dante Acosta's intuition where horses were concerned was said to be second to none, like his success with women. With an army of glamorous female admirers, would he even remember the first time they'd met? Jess's idea of glamour was a night down the pub with her dad, jingling the change in her pocket as she tried to work out if she had enough money to buy him a lemonade.

'Jess—'

She almost jumped out of her skin as she spun around. 'Yes?' It was one of the helpers from the village.

'Your father needs you in the house. I think he's nervous about his welcoming speech.'

'Don't worry. I'll come now and go through it with him.'

It was a relief to drag her attention from the helicopter. Ten years was a long time. These days, she was a fully qualified physiotherapist with a blossoming career, specialising in treating athletes, a fact that would soon bring her face to face with Dante Acosta, whether he appeared today or not. Because of her recent successes in restoring injured athletes to full strength, the Acosta family had chosen Jess to treat their brother's damaged leg, which meant travelling to Spain to Dante's fabulous *estancia*. How he'd feel about the identity of the therapist they'd chosen for him remained to be seen.

She couldn't think about that now. There was today to get though first. Whoever climbed out of the helicopter, it was more likely to be a foreman from one of the Acosta ranches rather than a member of such a wealthy and successful family. Jess's focus was saving the farm, so her father could recover in his own time without upheaval. There were plenty of helpers around to direct the latest arrival to the hospitality marquee where her father was soon to give what Jess passionately hoped would be the sales pitch of his life.

Dante's expression darkened as the cane he was forced to use sank into the claggy mire of a churned-up field. With a vicious curse, he accepted the regrettable conditions. This was no state-of-the-art facility but a beat-up farm in the middle of nowhere.

A farm that boasted some of the best horses in the world, he reminded himself as he ploughed on, which was why he was here. He'd be a fool to miss an opportunity like this. He was always on the lookout for exciting new bloodlines to improve his stock. Aside from playing polo, breeding ponies was his passion, and was the only lure that could drag him out of hibernation after his accident on the polo field. That and the fact that his people had told him the farm was in trouble, and that now would be a good time to buy. He was receiving a constant stream of information from his team to keep him up to speed with any likely competition, as well as likely downsides to a potential purchase. As of now, he was only interested in buying stock.

Another colourful curse heralded a pause as he eased the cramp in his damaged leg. Glancing around, he surveyed the motley throng of farmers, local families and the elite of the horse world, jostling happily alongside each other. They all had one thing in common, which was a deep love of the animals they had come to see, and the sport they provided. A local band added to the upbeat atmosphere. Only Dante's scowl was out of place.

Someone had done a good job of arranging entertainment for the assembled guests, he conceded, taking in the food stalls and all the gaudy trappings of a fairground. This posed a disadvantage for him. He hadn't expected quite so many people. Briefly, he considered the humiliation of the great *El Lobo*, or The Wolf as Dante was known in polo circles, showing himself to the world, staggering along with a cane.

He brushed this off with a snarling curse. Everyone was paparazzo these days. He stood as much chance of being photographed on his *estancia* as he did here.

Dante's stubble-blackened chin lifted at the sound of a young colt neighing. He studied the ponies running free in a field. Young, hard-muscled and spirited, they were perfect. *That* was why he was here.

Really?

Shrugging off the attention of a marshal who had raced to his aid with the offer of a lift in a service vehicle, he asked for Jim Slatehome, the owner of the farm.

'Jim's still in the farmhouse,' the man told him with a shrug. 'Probably running through his speech—'

Dante was already on his way. He hadn't travelled from Spain to indulge in fairground sport or well meaning but ultimately dull parochial chitchat. Nor had he the slightest intention of being last in line when it came to nailing the best stock. A deal would be arranged within the next hour or so, and then he was out of here.

Was he? Was buying new stock the only reason he was here?

The monotony of life since the accident was wearing him down. He needed a distraction. Any distraction. An unsophisticated young country girl stood a chance of taking his mind off the fact that his brothers and sister had gone over his head to arrange a physiotherapist to treat him back in Spain. Dante had discharged himself from hospital prematurely, so his siblings had decided to bring the hospital to him. They knew he wouldn't refuse family. The Acostas were tight and stood by each other always.

Dante's hard mouth tugged with faint amusement as he approached the ramshackle farmhouse with its peeling paint and crooked roof. It was ten years since he'd been here. Was it likely he'd find the little vixen he'd first encountered in the stable? Would she be married now? Engaged? Would he find a significant other by her side? Maybe he should have put his team to work on these details too. The worst he could imagine was that Jim Slatehome's daughter had mellowed to the point of boring, though with her abundance of fiery auburn hair and those flashing emerald eyes he thought it unlikely. One thing was certain. He and Jess Slatehome had unfinished business between them. With this in mind, he planted his cane and lurched on.

'I can't stay long. I have to get back to the marquee to keep people happy until you're ready to give your speech,' Jess explained when her father looked at her with anxiety glistening in his eyes.

He shouldn't be here in the kitchen, nursing a mug of tea, when there were potential buyers for the ponies outside, waiting to meet him. 'Everyone's looking forward to your speech,' she enthused, kneeling by his side at the kitchen table. 'You can do this,' she stated firmly as she got up, wishing she felt as confident as she sounded.

Her father had aged since her mother's death, which was years ago now. It was as if he'd lost hope. He hadn't even shaved today, and his outfit for such a big occasion comprised a random mix of ancient tweed, a greasy flat cap and worn corduroy trousers.

But that was his charm, Jess reminded herself. Jim Slatehome had used to be the go-to trainer and breeder of the best polo ponies in the world, and she was determined to see him back on top again. Her father was every bit as special and unique as the glossiest billionaire newly arrived in his state-of-the-art helicopter, and she loved him to bits.

Yes. Dante was a billionaire. The Acostas were a massively wealthy family, thanks to land holdings, an international tech company, and their skill on a world stage with horses. But this small farm was equally precious to Jess. It had been in her family for generations and she would defend it to the end.

Leaning down to give her father a hug, she was shocked to see tears in his eyes.

'Those ponies mean everything to me, Jess. I can't bear to let them go.'

'But you have to, if you want to keep the farm,' she explained gently. 'Come on; you can do this,' she coaxed.

He gave her a heartbreaking look. 'If you say so. I suppose I'd better go and clean up. I won't let you down, Jess.'

'I know that,' she whispered.

Her father was up and down the stairs in double-quick time and nothing about his appearance had changed, as far as Jess could tell. Apart from his determination, she was relieved to see. 'You're right. I can do this,' he stated firmly. 'I'll go ahead. You stay here. I don't want our guests thinking I need you to prop me up because I've lost confidence in my ponies.'

'Good idea,' Jess agreed.

She was just clearing up their tea things when the kitchen door swung open. She froze on the spot. Breath hitched in her throat. She must have turned ashen, though heat was surging through her veins. Dante Acosta, looking grimmer and tougher than she remembered, was standing in the doorway.

'Dante!'

'Jess…'

Those eyes…that voice…that powerful, compelling presence.

His deep, sonorous voice with its seductive Spanish sibilance rolled across her senses like black velvet brushed lightly, yet so effectively across every sensitive zone she had. His eyes were black pools of experience, while his mouth was a straight, hard line. There was nothing soft or yielding about Dante Acosta—there never had been, she remembered.

Everything in the room disappeared except him. Dante Acosta was the essence of masculinity, the living embodiment of sex. New scars—she guessed they must have been gained on the polo field at the same time as the damage to his leg—cut livid stripes from the upswept tip of one ebony brow to the corner of his firm, cruel mouth. Wind had whipped his thick black hair into such disarray that it had caught on his stubble. A gold hoop glittered in his right ear, adding to a barbaric appearance that seemed at odds with his aura of wealth. But this was no effete billionaire. This was a man of fierce passion and resolve. Beneath his rugged jacket, she knew from the popular press that Dante, like the other members of his polo team, bore a tattoo of a snarling wolf over his heart. This was the insignia of his polo team, Lobos. The team name alone was enough to strike terror in the hearts of their opponents. Lobos was the Spanish word for wolves—a pack of merciless wolves. On the back of Dante's neck, beneath copious glossy whorls of pitch-black hair, he had another tattoo of a skull and crossed mallets, a warning that Team Lobos took no prisoners, and confidently expected to win every match.

A clatter distracted her. The cane he'd discarded by the door had fallen. Jess frowned. He should be cured by now, with no need for a cane. No wonder his siblings were concerned. Fortunately, they'd sent on his medical records, so she knew the extent of his injury. If Dante hadn't discharged himself from the hospital prematurely, he'd be done with that cane by now.

'Dante,' she said politely, reaching out to shake his hand when he shifted position impatiently. 'How nice to see you again.'

Taking both her hands in a firm grip, he drew her towards him and proceeded to inspect her as if she were a potential purchase like the ponies.

Would you like to examine my teeth? ran through her mind, though she knew that for the sake of any potential purchase she had to mind her manners and remain calm. That wasn't easy when she was practically drowning in charisma, so she closed her eyes.

'Let me look at you...'

That voice again. She jerked her hands free. Dante Acosta was a exciting force of nature but he knew it and had no shame when it came to wielding his power. It was up to Jess to resist him. *If she could.* She hadn't made too good a job of resisting him ten years ago and, seeing him again, she was inclined to forgive her teenage self.

Her hands had felt so small and safe in his—which was all part of the illusion. This was no time to be seduced by a man with more money than Croesus and the morals of an alley cat. How would that help her father? If there was one thing she'd learned since returning home to take care of her father, it was that vultures were always circling. Everyone was out for a deal. Why should Dante Acosta be any different?

'Jess?'

'Apologies. Sorry. I'm forgetting my manners. Welcome—welcome to Bell Farm. Would you like a drink? I expect you've had a long journey.'

'From Spain?' A casual shrug of his massive shoulders hinted at executive travel in the most luxurious of circumstances. 'Not so bad.'

Why did everything about Dante Acosta make her feel like this? She was always blasé about men. Because none could compare with Dante Acosta, as she had discovered ten years ago when she kissed him.

'Tea, surely?' she said to distract herself from the insistent throb between her legs.

'Can't stand the stuff.'

'Oh.' That took her by surprise. 'Something else, perhaps?'

'What have you got?'

From any other lips those words could be taken as an innocent request for a verbal menu. When they came from Dante Acosta the prompt was laden with deadly charm.

'Whatever you like,' she said brightly. 'The stalls outside sell pretty much everything.'

As one corner of his mouth tugged slightly as if to say *Touché*, she knew he'd feel like velvet steel beneath her hands.

Had nothing changed in ten years? Was she still as reckless?

Far from it, Jess told herself firmly. She was no longer a reckless teen but a medical professional who had left a successful career at a leading London teaching hospital to come home to help her father.

'I'm sure you want to see my father, not me,' she said pleasantly. 'Would you like me to take you to him?'

'There's no need,' Dante said with a narrow-eyed look. 'I'll find my own way.'

As he turned, Jess felt as if she'd been appraised and discarded. That was fine. This wasn't about her. She'd arranged the event with the specific intention of attracting an Acosta or the like, someone with a deep love of horses and plenty of money to bail her father out of trouble by buying up his stock. If Dante didn't bite she'd have to find someone who would.

So, Dante mused as he wove his way through the crowd to reach the show ring—if a hastily tidied up paddock with a rickety fence could be described as such a thing—the little vixen he remembered had matured into a beautiful, understated, though rather too serious woman. He missed the mischief in Jess's eyes, as well as the excessively impulsive nature that had prompted her, at the tender age of seventeen, to stand on tiptoe to plant a kiss on his lips.

His senses surged, remembering. He had reined in those senses then and would do so again. He wasn't here to waste time on a serious-minded woman. He wasn't ready to take any woman seriously. Why restrict his diet when the menu was so varied?

Leaning on the hated cane, he paused to greet some fellow polo players. Jess had attracted a motley crowd, from locals to minor royals and celebrities as well as sightseers from far and wide. Towering men in black suits with earpieces and suspicious bulges beneath their jackets followed hot on the heels of a well-known sheikh. Dante had never relied on security personnel for his safety, preferring to rely on his own skills to protect him.

One career had foundered while the other had soared, he mused, moving on when he spotted Jess walking arm in arm with her father. His team had informed him that the farm was in serious financial trouble. They were already working on the ins and outs and would advise him on the questions he'd pose before the day was out.

One thing was certain. Jess had left her job and risked her career to come here to save her father and the farm. She was unusually determined, and he admired that.

He also detested loose ends. If Jess hadn't been seventeen ten years ago, who knew what might have happened between them?

The marquee was already crowded by the time he entered. He recognised more horse breeders, trainers and players like himself jostling to get to the front under Jim Slatehome's nose. He wouldn't have it all his own way today. There would be stiff competition for the better horses.

So he'd go one better.

He could offer double—triple—what anyone else could without feeling a pinch. He could easily afford it. Jim had sold him some good stock in the past, and what he'd seen of the ponies in the field so far suggested Jim had never really gone away, but had made himself invisible so he could nurse his grief.

The urge to help Jim Slatehome overwhelmed him suddenly. To fend off the competition meant putting something else in the pot. After the most recent text from his team an idea was already brewing. How would Jess take his idea, if he went ahead and bought the farm? Not well, he suspected as watched her standing like a protection officer at her father's side. It had cost her everything to be here, financially, career-wise, every which way. His team had filled him in on the details. She'd qualified top of her class as a physiotherapist specialising in sports injuries. Her first job was at a prestigious teaching hospital in London, but she'd given that up to go freelance, which could be tricky. Rumour said she was successful. If she was as good as her reputation suggested, she could guarantee an endless stream of patients from the battleground of polo alone. The thought of those soft hands tracking right up his legs was—

Out of bounds, Dante told himself sternly. He was here for business and nothing else. He'd seen the vixen and satisfied his curiosity, and that had to be enough.

Thankfully, the Sheikh sidled up to him at that moment and as they got talking about horses Dante grew more determined than ever to win the day. He'd handle Jess's objections. As her father mounted the podium and began his speech, Dante stared at Jess.

CHAPTER TWO

HER FATHER'S SPEECH went well. He seemed buoyed up. Maybe the brief chats he'd managed to snatch with Dante had served as a reminder that Jim Slatehome had once been great and would be so again. That was Jess's dearest hope as she congratulated her father, and prompted him to start discussing specific ponies with potential buyers.

'Be patient,' he implored. 'I'm going to speak to Dante while you circulate amongst our guests. Keep them happy while I'm away. This talk is important, Jess,' he added with a significant look.

'I'd rather stay with you.' She glanced at Dante, standing waiting for her father to join him, and felt the same punch to her senses, added to which was the fear that they were cooking something up between them. Dante's expression betrayed nothing beyond a cool stare in her direction.

'This is still my farm, Jess.'

The reminder struck home. Anything she could do to see her father back on top had to be all right with Jess. 'Promise me you won't do anything silly before you and I have talked it through.'

'Like fortune-telling in a tent under the name of Skylar?' her father suggested, lifting one bushy brow.

'You've got me there,' Jess admitted wryly as she checked her watch to make sure she had time to chat to the guests before she was due to inhabit the small gaudy tent that would house the mysterious Skylar.

'Go,' her father prompted urgently.

With a last suspicious glance at the tall, dark man in the shadows who made her heart pound like crazy, she planted a kiss on her father's cheek and did as he said.

The day had turned cold Jess discovered when she stepped out of the marquee. Or maybe apprehension was chilling her. The sky was blue. There wasn't a cloud to be seen and if the air wasn't exactly tropical it was still warm for the time of year in this part of England. In honour of the heatwave Jess had dressed in a thick sweater, a down gilet and a padded coat. Even in summer it could be frigid on the moors.

It would have been a great time to appreciate how well the event was going, had it not been for the turmoil in her head. Seeing Dante again had affected her more than she could ever have imagined, bringing back those few moments in the stable ten years ago, when just for a moment Dante had responded, spoiling her for all other men. There had been men—of course there had, she was almost twenty-seven—serious men, driven by the need to educate; nerdy men obsessed with their phones; *bon viveurs* whose sole aim in life appeared to be preserving their bodies by pickling them in alcohol; gym bunnies and those she would have been wiser to swerve. But none compared to the brigand with attitude, known to one and all as The Wolf.

And now he was even more attractive. And more elusive. With homes across the world, Dante Acosta could pitch up anywhere.

Face it, the gulf between them was a mile wide.

Jess threw herself back into chatting with as many of their visitors as she could. Her reaction to seeing Dante again was an overreaction.

Tell that to her heart. Tell that to her body. Tell her stubborn mind, that doggedly refused to accept it. Making her excuses to the smiling guests, she moved on. What better way to take her mind off Dante Acosta than to get stuck into some fortune-telling, Jess concluded wryly as she headed back to the house to change into Skylar's costume.

Perhaps she could tell her own fortune. Although surely that could easily be predicted. Dante Acosta could, and probably would, disappear from her life again as swiftly as he had recently appeared.

The ground was hard with frost and the views between the field and the farmhouse far-reaching and mesmerising. Jess stopped briefly to admire them, and to chat silently to her mother, as she so often did. Her mother had been dead for more than five years but her presence remained constant in Jess's heart.

She reviewed the promises she'd made—to complete her studies, to look after her father and make sure he kept the farm. Generations of farming ran through her father's blood. He'd have no purpose in life and nowhere to live, her mother had impressed upon her, so these were sacred vows as far as Jess was concerned.

She had never cried at the loss of her mother, Jess realised as the wind whipped her face, prompting her to move on. Her father had cried enough for both of them, but Jess had bottled up her grief deep inside because her father's tears had solved nothing. They hadn't brought her mother back or sent the bank packing. She had to save him, as she'd promised, and so she mourned silently and dealt firmly with the bank. So far she'd managed to stave off repossession of the farm, but for how long? A good sale today might postpone the inevitable, but it wouldn't solve the problem, which meant there was a possibility they might have to sell off some of the land.

Jess's mood lifted when she turned to see how many people were grouped around her father. He looked as happy as she'd ever seen him, dispensing advice and answering questions. Jim Slatehome was back! People in the horse world who mattered were hanging on his every word.

But there was no sign of Dante. Had he lost interest? There was no time to dwell. She had to prepare to tell fortunes.

When Jess came downstairs after changing into Skylar's colourful costume of voluminous, ankle-length skirt strewn with bells and a heavy fringed shawl to wrap around her shoulders, Dante and her father were sitting in the kitchen. The way the two men fell silent the moment she walked in made her instantly suspicious. What were they up to?

Dante's incredulous stare made her self-conscious. She doubted he'd seen many women with scarves and bells tied around their hair, dressed in shapeless clothes that looked as if they belonged in a jumble sale—which was actually where she'd found them. Even in jeans and workmanlike boots, he managed to look like a king amongst men. But her father seemed happy enough and what else mattered?

'I'm doubly glad I came,' Dante murmured, tongue firmly planted in his cheek.

'And we're extremely glad you could find time to come to our event, aren't we, Dad?' she responded politely through gritted teeth.

Her father was definitely hiding something. She knew that guilty look. And she had only succeeded in sounding ridiculous, like Eliza Doolittle trying to please Professor Higgins, when Dante deserved no such consideration with that smirk on his face. 'It's nice to see you again,' she added, aiming for casual.

'*Nice?*' Dante queried in a deep, husky tone that ran tremors through every part of her. Why wasn't her father helping out? Why must she deal with this man on her own?

'Is the apron to protect you from the kittens?' Dante asked straight-faced.

His comment launched her back to the past and the first time they'd met, when Jess had been caring for a litter of kittens. One of them had chosen the precise moment Dante walked into the stables to pee down her front.

'It's part of my costume,' she said primly.

When she'd almost lost hope that her father might find some way to ease the tension between Jess and Dante he sprang back to life. 'Come on,' he urged, standing up. 'I'll escort you to the fortune-telling tent. I might even be one of your first clients.'

'Do you read tea leaves?' Dante enquired, still holding back on that laugh.

'Jess is a dab hand with a crystal ball,' her father explained, oblivious to the war of hard stares currently being exchanged between Jess and Dante. 'She's great at telling fortunes. You should try her.'

'I might do that,' Dante murmured with a long look at Jess.

He infuriated her but melted her from the inside out too, which was inconvenient. Dante Acosta was a storming force of nature that commanded her attention whether she wanted him to or not.

Jess stalked ahead of her father to the fortune-telling tent. She was annoyed with her wilful body for responding so enthusiastically to Dante. Her nipples had tightened into taut, cheeky buds, while her lips felt swollen and her breasts felt heavy. And that was the least of it.

The sky was clouding over but in spite of the rapidly worsening weather there was a long line waiting for Jess outside Skylar's tent. There was nothing like a bit of supernatural hocus pocus to put the seal of success on a day out like this. Jess's father really believed she'd got a gift, while her mother had dubbed her Skylar years ago, saying Jess should have a magic name to go with her gift. Jess had always suspected that this was just her mother's way of putting steel in the spine of a painfully shy child.

It must have worked, she concluded, thinking back ten years to when she'd launched herself at the most eligible bachelor on the planet.

Ten years on, was she running away from him?

She glanced over her shoulder before ducking inside the tent. No one was following. Dante was as disinterested in her now as he had been then. It was time to forget him and get on with the job.

For the first time ever he was having trouble concentrating as he struck a deal with Jess's father. Jess remained on his mind as he wove his way through the crowd to discover what his future held.

Okay, he was a cynic when it came to telling fortunes, but that didn't stop him wanting to see Jess. Ten years back, he'd been twenty-two and dismissive of potential mates unless they satisfied his demanding criteria. Jess with her paint-free face, scraped-back hair and clothes smelling of cat pee, not to mention the mouth on her like a paint-stripper, had been as far from his ideal as it was possible to get.

Until she kissed him.

That had been one big surprise, and a kick to his senses, reminding him not to overlook something when it was right under his nose.

The long line in front of Skylar's tent stopped him in his tracks. He wasn't a man to queue.

With that kiss he'd had the good sense to curtail ten years ago nagging at his mind, he wasn't a man to wait either. No longer a naïve teen, Jess was a beautiful and intriguing woman. Shapely and soft on the outside, the intrigue came from the will of steel that blazed from her eyes.

That same determination had enabled her to save the farm. According to his team, Jess had no funds other than her meagre savings. She'd stripped these bare to put on this show and save her father. Using persuasion, and bartering her physiotherapy services where necessary, she had managed to recruit practically every member of the village to ensure today's success. The result was this confidence-boosting exercise for Jim Slatehome that should put him firmly back on the map.

He stopped in front of the small, gaudily decorated tent. A large banner hung from the turret, declaring boldly: *Skylar Slates—fortune-teller to the stars!* His cynical smile was back. He guessed he qualified. Now his only problem was how to crash the line.

Retracing his steps, he bought a pack of water from a stall. 'I can handle it,' he snapped at the woman behind the counter when she gazed at his stick. Clamping the unwieldy bundle beneath one arm, he stabbed his stick into the ground and set his sights on his goal.

'Water for the fortune-teller,' he announced as he approached the ever-lengthening line in front of Skylar's tent. 'To keep her voice running smoothly,' he explained, mustering every bit of his rusty charm. The throng parted like the Red Sea to allow the unfortunate man with his lurching gait to move through them with his awkward burden. He vowed on the spot that this would be the one and only time that he viewed his injury as a benefit.

Having arrived at his destination, he rested his cane against the canvas wall and, drawing the flap aside, he ducked his head and walked in.

'Excuse me,' Jess rapped with the paint-stripping look he remembered so well. 'I'll call you in when I'm free.'

'Oh, no, no, please,' the woman seated at the table opposite Jess insisted, getting up to make way for him.

'What do you think you're doing?' Jess demanded, shooting emerald fire his way.

He would have known those flashing eyes anywhere, and those lips that formed a perfect Cupid's bow of possibility. The urge to taste the creamy perfection of Jess's rain-washed skin and rasp his stubble against its soft perfection was overwhelming right now. But he had business to transact. 'I'm here to cross your palm with silver and your lips with a bottle of water,' he explained.

'You're asking me to tell your fortune?' she asked with surprise.

Having put the bottles down, he delved in his pocket for some coins to toss on the table, but his casual air was halted by a bolt of pain.

'You'd better sit down,' she said. 'Where's your cane?'

'Thank you for reminding me.'

The look she gave him told him she understood what it must have cost him to come here today with his cane, in front of all these people. And yet what was pride when there was a deal to be done? They measured each other for a few moments and then she reached out to take his hand. Full marks to Jess, he conceded, for retaining her composure, and remembering that he might save the farm. She had guts, and to spare, he reflected.

'Are you sure you want this?' she asked.

'I wouldn't be here if I didn't,' he assured her, while his senses prompted him to take her somewhere where they could be alone. 'Why does that surprise you?'

'I can't believe Señor Acosta is incapable of predicting his own future.'

'Oh, but I can.' He held Jess's gaze locked in his and was rewarded when she blushed deeply.

'You crashed the line,' she scolded.

'I did,' he agreed with a shrug. How beautiful she was, even with what looked like a piece of Christmas tinsel wrapped around her head. Her hair glowed like fire in the soft light of a lamp, over which she'd draped a piece of red chiffon, while her eyes were deep pools of unfathomable green.

'Stop staring at me. I'm supposed to be reading you, not the other way around.'

'Then get on with it,' he suggested.

She reached across and rattled an old biscuit tin that had an opening cut in the top. 'Put your money in here—those pieces of silver,' she reminded him.

'Of course…'

He added a few more coins to those he'd already tossed down on the table. She still held out the tin. 'A twenty should do it,' she prompted bluntly.

'Twenty?' He pulled his head back with surprise.

'Can't you afford it?'

Her lips curved in the first real smile he'd seen and her eyes danced with laughter. That was the Jess he remembered from the stable ten years ago—feisty and free to speak her mind, rather than constrained by the fact that he might be her father's last hope when it came to saving the farm. He preferred this Jess.

'Every penny goes directly to charity,' she explained. 'Nothing I take in this tent will be kept for the farm.'

'Then you can have all my cash.' Levering himself to his feet, he reached into his back pocket to bring out a wad of notes. He fed them into her tin. 'This had better be worth it,' he warned.

But fortune-telling wasn't on Jess's mind now. 'Your leg,' she said with concern. 'You really must agree to treatment. Please don't be stubborn if the appropriate therapy is offered to you, or you could be left with a permanent limp.'

'Did you see that in your crystal ball?' he demanded edgily as he sat down again.

'I don't need a crystal ball to see that. I'm a fully qualified physiotherapist, more than used to dealing with injuries like yours. Which is why I can tell you with authority that you can't afford to leave this any longer,' she added before he could get a word in.

'Well, thank you for your advice, *Skylar*,' he gritted out, 'but that's not what I'm paying you for. What *can* you see in that crystal ball...if anything?'

'A very difficult man,' she fired back.

They glared at each other, and for a good few moments fire flashed between them. Just like ten years ago, it seemed they were destined to strike sparks off each other whenever they met.

'You'll have to be quiet or I can't concentrate,' she said.

'That's the best line I've heard yet,' he muttered as he settled back in his seat.

But Jess did appear to compose herself, before dipping her head and cupping her hands around the ball. His groin tightened at the sight of slender fingers caressing the inanimate object. This was ridiculous. He'd never reacted like this.

Then Jess looked up and made things ten times worse. Her green eyes flayed him before she even spoke, and then she exploded, 'No way!' Pushing the crystal ball away, she snapped, 'This session is at an end.'

'I'm sorry?' he queried dryly. 'Did I miss something, only you don't seem to have told me anything yet.'

Standing up, she stared pointedly at the exit. 'There are people waiting outside. Thank you for your contribution, but—'

'But get lost?' he suggested. 'Is that any way to treat a prospective buyer?'

'If you'd seen what I've seen, you'd be begging to go.'

'All that money and I don't get a second chance?'

'Believe me. You don't want a second chance,' Jess assured him.

He felt a frisson of something as he stared at her, but dismissed it out of hand. No one could foretell the future. This was all an act.

'I can tell you one thing,' she said. 'Like your namesake The Wolf, you should shed your old winter coat, to be ready for spring and changes.'

'Claptrap.'

'Is it?' she challenged, eyes flashing fire as they refocused on his face. 'Or are you afraid to face what lies ahead?'

'Frightened?' he queried with a short, humourless laugh. 'Are we talking about therapy for my leg?'

'Might be. You must accept treatment before it's too late.'

'Is that what you do?' He gestured around the tent. 'Offer advice under the guise of fortune-telling?'

Jess sighed softly. 'Is that so terrible? Sometimes it's the only way people will hear and take in what they need to. I don't mean any harm.'

'I'm sure you don't,' he agreed grimly. 'But, thank you very much, my siblings have arranged something for me, so you don't need to worry about my leg.'

'That's good news,' she said.

He grunted. 'Don't keep your other mugs waiting.'

'Let's hope they're politer than you.'

But Jess said this with a smile and a genuinely concerned look, which made it hard to remain angry for long. The most annoying teen had grown into a most annoying, hot as hell woman.

CHAPTER THREE

So JESS WAS unmarried and unattached. Why that should please him, he couldn't say. After all, it wasn't as though he was interested in a relationship with her. Still, his conversation with her father when he returned to the farmhouse hadn't been solely confined to business, and Jim Slatehome had confided that Jess was single. Jim was proud of his daughter, and eager to talk about what she'd achieved. 'Without anyone's help,' he told Dante. 'I just feel sometimes that I'm holding her back. Jess has a big heart. She should share it with a family of her own.'

He fell silent, and the pause was only broken by the crackle of the fire and an old clock ticking on the mantelpiece. And then Jess walked in.

Her father visibly brightened. 'Come and join us,' he said, pulling out a chair.

'When I've showered and changed,' she promised.

Without sparing him a glance, she gathered up the mud-soaked hem of her skirt and dashed upstairs.

She didn't take long to return. Still glowing from the shower, she radiated energy and purpose, and even in a pair of old jeans, scrappy slippers and a nondescript top she was beautiful. She'd made no attempt to impress, which was probably what impressed him most of all.

'Talks between you two go well?' she prompted with

seeming unconcern, but there was an edge of tension in her voice.

'Extremely well,' her father enthused, which only succeeded in making Jess pale.

'Well?' she pressed. 'Aren't you going to tell me what you've decided? Are you buying the horses, Dante?'

'All in good time,' her father promised, thwarting Jess's attempt to turn the spotlight on him. 'Deal or no deal, Dante's still our guest, and he doesn't want to go over the details time and time again. We'll have plenty of chance to discuss it when he's gone.'

Jess's jaw worked as if she disagreed, but she sensibly remained silent. The chance of a deal could not be risked, and she was wise enough to know this.

'Did Skylar do well in the end?' he asked to break the ice when she sat with them in silence.

'You tell me,' she said, fixing him with a look. 'Did you find me convincing?'

'I mean financially,' he explained, matching her no-nonsense look and raising it with serious concern of his own. 'You said it was for charity, so I hope you raked in lots of money.'

'Your generous donation helped,' she admitted. 'I don't think we've ever raised so much.'

'You'll have to come back every year,' her father put in.

Jess drew in a settling breath. 'Yes, why don't you?'

'I intend to.'

'That's good,' her father exclaimed, thumping the table in his enthusiasm. 'Now we'll never lose contact again. The day's been a huge success, and that's all down to you, Jess.'

'And your wonderful ponies, and our helpers from the village,' she insisted, shaking off her father's praise as if she didn't deserve it.

'Sometimes, just say thank you,' he advised good-humouredly.

She shot him a narrow-eyed look, and now her father looked guilty as hell.

'What's going on?' Jess challenged.

'Going on?' her father echoed in a splutter. 'Absolutely nothing,' he protested. 'We've struck a wonderful deal.'

As if to confirm this, the sound of helicopters roaring overhead prevented conversation for a while.

'So all the other potential purchasers are leaving,' Jess commented, staring skywards. She stabbed a look into his eyes. 'So, it's all down to you.'

'Stop fretting, Jess,' her father insisted. 'Dante bought all the horses.'

'All of them?' she murmured, frowning. 'Why do I get the feeling there's something more?'

'Shake his hand, Jess. The farm is saved. The deal is done.'

If looks could kill, the Acostas would be short one member of the family. Jess could afford to show her true feelings now. Standing up, she extended her hand for him to shake. As he captured the tiny fist in his giant paw he was surprised to discover how strong she was. This was no soft, vulnerable individual, but a worthy opponent. That pleased him. He was tired of sycophants and creeps. Extreme wealth came with disadvantages, not least of which was its effect on other people. He couldn't count the times he'd been fawned over, when all he required was to be tested and judged on his merits as a man.

'You can let me go now,' she said.

Realising they were still hand-clasping, he released her. 'Skylar was right about one thing,' he admitted.

'Oh?' Jess's green stare pierced his.

'The deal I struck with your father marks the start of a new chapter in my life.'

'Does that happen every time you buy a few horses?' she demanded suspiciously.

'These aren't just any horses,' her father interrupted, clearly keen to bring Jess's line of questioning to an end. 'These are Slatehome ponies.'

Jess hummed, her suspicion by no means satisfied.

'How did you come by the name Skylar?' he enquired, to break the tension between them when, at her father's insistence, Jess sat down again.

'It was a nickname my mother dreamed up for me when I was heading into my shell and she wanted me to shine. She said Skylar was a witchy name for people with The Sight and it would give me special powers. We laughed about it, and I never felt shy again, because I had this other person inside me: Skylar Slates, fortune-teller extraordinaire. Even now the name reminds me of my mother and the many ways she had to make people feel good about themselves. That was her gift. Skylar's predictions try to encourage hopes and dreams and soothe worries. It seems to help,' she added with a self-deprecating shrug, 'but that's all thanks to my mother.'

'You must miss her terribly.'

'I do.'

For a second he saw that, in one area at least, Jess was vulnerable. The raw wound of loss had never healed. It had been some time since her mother's death. He didn't know exactly. He was guilty of losing touch with anything outside his privileged cocoon and had become even more isolated since the accident.

'My ancestors on my mother's side were *gitanos*,' he revealed. 'Mountain people. Some would call them gypsies. Many of them have The Sight.'

'Jess is shrewd and intuitive, but her magic is confined to making the best cup of tea in Yorkshire,' her father interrupted with his broadest hint yet.

'Make mine coffee,' he reminded Jess.

Having arranged three mugs on the range, she absentmindedly filled them all with tea from the pot. 'Oh, look at me!' she exclaimed with impatience.

He was having difficulty doing anything else.

After making a coffee for Dante she left the two men in the kitchen. She didn't mean to listen in on her return. Who ever did? Her father was telling Dante it was time for him to say goodbye to the last of his guests, and the moment the kitchen door closed behind him Dante was on the phone. 'It's all done,' he said. 'Everything wrapped up to my satisfaction. Notify the lawyers and have the contract drawn up ASAP.'

The covering certificate for each individual pony was already to hand, Jess reasoned with a frown, together with all the requirements for any valuable pedigree horse changing hands. This included a DNA hair sample from both the Sire and Dam to confirm the pony's parentage. The deed of sale was a straightforward matter that would be handled by her father's lawyer. So why was more paperwork necessary?

She barely had chance to reason this through when there was a crash in the kitchen, followed by an earth-shattering curse. Bursting in, she rushed to Dante's side. 'Let me help you up.' Crossing the kitchen without his cane, he'd tripped over a chair leg.

When he snapped tersely, 'My cane, please,' she let it go. The loss of face on a daily basis for a man like Dante Acosta had to be monumental. If he refused treatment, nothing would change.

Handing him the cane, she stood back.

'And no bloody lectures about accepting treatment,' he warned.

'Just do it,' she suggested mildly.

This was rewarded by a grunt. 'Let me look at that leg,' she insisted. 'You might have caused more damage when you fell. Please,' she added when Dante looked at her in silence.

'Very well,' he agreed reluctantly.

She knelt on the floor in front of him, while Dante sat down on the chair. Rolling up the leg of his jeans, she quickly reassured herself that no further damage had been done.

'*Gracias*,' he grated out when she told him this, and got up.

'It's my job,' she said with a shrug. 'Here,' she said when he began to rise. 'Don't forget your cane.'

He took hold of it, and for some reason she didn't let go. For a few potent seconds they were connected by a length of polished wood. Then, to her horror, he began to reel her in. She could let go but she didn't, and Dante only stopped when their faces were almost touching. Closing her eyes, she wondered if she'd have the strength to resist him, or if she would follow the urges of a body that had been denied release and satisfaction for far too long.

'You like playing with fire, don't you, Skylar?' Dante murmured,

She dropped the cane like a red-hot poker. 'I'm trying to help.'

'Yourself?' Dante suggested.

'I don't know what you mean.'

'I think you do,' he argued. 'And if you play with my fire you will definitely get burned. Is that what you want?'

She gave a short huff of incredulity. 'My interest in you is purely professional.'

Furious with herself for succumbing to the notorious Acosta charm, she crossed the room and reached for her coat. Ramming her feet into boots, she went to join her father in saying goodbye to their guests, leaving the mighty Dante Acosta to sort himself out.

He refused to go unless Jess came with him. She plagued his mind and tormented his body, and until she agreed to accompany him to Spain he wasn't going anywhere.

How was that supposed to happen when they weren't on speaking terms?

He'd find a way.

Confined to the house long enough, he gritted out a curse and heaved himself to his feet.

He found Jess riding in the outside arena. From the look of concentration on her face he guessed she found solace as he did, by twinning her soul with a horse. Animal and human moving as one, with scarcely a visible adjustment on Jess's part to suggest she was directing the intricate moves, was the most healing activity he could think of. She was a master equestrian. He should have expected that. He was impressed.

Worthy sentiments were soon surpassed by a flash of triumph as he reflected that all this belonged to him now. Jess didn't know the extent of his deal with her father. Jim Slatehome had asked that they keep it between themselves for the time being that Dante had bought the farm and everything on it. 'She can be difficult, our Jess,' her father had explained. 'She's had a tough time. I'll know when it's the right time to tell her. Until then, say nothing. I don't want her upset after all she's done.'

Triumph yielded to lust as Jess brought her pony alongside him at the fence. 'This is our best horse. Her name is Moon,' she informed him.

'You handle her well.'

She smiled. 'High praise indeed.'

'I mean it.'

This was possibly the first relaxed conversation they'd had, and it allowed him to press forward with his plan; rather than alienating Jess, he had to form a connection with a woman who could be useful to him. There were always vacancies for top-class riders in one of his teams. 'Show me what she can do,' he encouraged.

'I just did.'

'Please,' he coaxed, dialling up the charm.

'As it's you…' But she was smiling.

He leaned on a fencepost as Jess put the promising mare through her paces. The pony could be difficult and liked to show off. Sensing he was watching her, Moon kicked out her back legs and bucked. Jess remained perfectly balanced throughout.

'Good job,' he said when she returned to his side.

'I love the challenge of a spirited pony,' she enthused as she reined in.

'I love a challenge full stop.'

She blushed.

'You've got a good seat.' She had a great seat. It would fit his hands perfectly. 'Do you play?'

'I take it you're referring to polo?'

'What else?' he asked, throwing her a surprised look.

'I used to play,' she admitted, 'but I'm usually too tired by the end of each day, so I read instead, play the piano, or crash out in front of a soap.'

'Everyone needs fresh air. You should get out more.'

'Says you?' she jibed.

Humour drained from his eyes. It was common knowledge that Dante Acosta had been housebound since discharging himself from hospital, and that this was his first appearance in public. 'Don't make me regret accepting the invitation to come here today.'

Jess had the good sense to say nothing. She didn't need to. Her eyes spoke eloquently, telling him, *I'm not sure yet what's in it for you, but you would have left by now if the answer was nothing.*

'What are you doing?' she asked as he opened the gate to join her in the paddock.

'I want to see Moon close up for myself.'

'Take care; she bites.'

'You or the horse?'

'She won't like your cane.'

'Then may I suggest you dismount and hand her over to a groom?'

'A groom?' Jess intoned. 'Where do you think you are? This is a working farm, not some billionaire's playground.'

His hackles lifted. 'I live on a working ranch. My business life and home life are very different. Do you want me to trial her or not?'

'You already own her.'

'I do.'

'Then she's all yours,' Jess said with a shrug, but as she turned he saw that accepting the inevitable wasn't easy for Jess. She loved these animals and couldn't bear the thought of never seeing them again.

'Be careful,' she said as he vaulted into the saddle using only the strength of his arms. 'Moon can be tricky.'

'You care?' he asked as he soothed the horse.

'I care about Moon,' she told him.

'Hey, *querida*, let's see what you can do,' he whispered, adding soothing words in Spanish. The pony's flattened ears pricked up at the sound of his warm, encouraging tone and she didn't disappoint, though each swerve and bounce jangled his damaged nerve-endings.

'A good enough reason to accept treatment?' Jess suggested as he made sure not to stumble as he dismounted, by taking the weight on his one good leg.

'She'll make the first team,' he said, ignoring her question.

'Your reputation is well deserved,' she commented as he handed over the reins.

'Do you mean I can ride?' he suggested with a grin.

'Like a master,' she said frankly.

'Your father has lost nothing when it comes to his gift for breeding and training some of the best horses in the world, and some of it's rubbed off on you.'

'Only some of it?' she said, smiling.

'All right…' With a conciliatory gesture, he smiled too. That connection he'd wanted was on the rise.

'Do you want to trial any more ponies?' Jess asked.

'I'll leave that to my grooms. I trust a practised eye and intuition.' And his leg couldn't take any more today.

'How will you transport the ponies to Spain?' Jess asked with concern, glancing at his helicopter in the next field.

'The same way my grooms arrived today. In a specially adapted jet,' he revealed.

'You haven't wasted much time,' she observed suspiciously.

'I never do.' He let the silence hang for a few seconds before adding, 'You should come with me when I go back to Spain—to settle the horses,' he went on before she could argue.

'Can't your grooms do that?'

'I thought you'd like to do it. The ponies know you. They don't know my grooms yet.'

She couldn't argue with that, but she did raise one objection. 'I have work commitments.'

So it wasn't a flat no, he registered with satisfaction.

'And luckily they dovetail nicely.'

Well, that was a surprise. 'So you're saying yes?'

'I believe I am,' Jess confirmed, as if all the advantage in coming to Spain with him was on her side.

CHAPTER FOUR

JESS HAD NEVER seen her father looking so relaxed. He looked ten years younger, as if all his worries were behind him. She'd just sat down when Dante entered the kitchen.

'It was good of you to judge the children's pony race,' her father exclaimed as Dante sat next to her.

Tingling apart, she was surprised to learn that the great Dante Acosta had joined in to such an extent. 'I didn't know you'd been so busy,' she admitted.

'I enjoyed it,' Dante confessed with a sideways look that heated her up from the inside out. 'We'll have to make it an annual event. You were busy being Skylar,' he reminded her.

'It must have been a bit different to your usual afternoon,' her father ventured with a laugh.

'I enjoyed every moment,' Dante assured him with a look at Jess.

'Dante picked prize winners in each different age group,' her father revealed, 'and spent extra time with a little girl who forfeited her race to go back and help her younger brother.'

Saint Dante? Jess reflected, amused in a good way. What Dante had done today had put him in the spotlight, which couldn't have been easy for him, but the children would have loved having one of polo's biggest stars taking an interest in them.

'That was very good of you,' she said frankly.

'So. Transport tomorrow,' he said.

'*Tomorrow?*' Jess hadn't expected to be leaving the farm quite so soon.

'I don't waste time. Remember?' Dante prompted.

Only an Acosta could make things work as fast as this. Jess's spine prickled. What was she getting into?

'You'll find my jet comfortable, and the ponies will have the best care possible.' Dante was continuing as if there was nothing unusual in making a decision one minute, a plan the next, and executing that plan the following day. 'A vet and her assistant will be on duty throughout, while my grooms will be in constant attendance. You'll have very little to do, other than to keep a watchful eye on the animals and inform my grooms if they have any quirks or preferences.'

'But I must be home for Christmas.' Dry-mouthed and backtracking fast as the extent of her commitment to a man she hardly knew, who lived in a country she wasn't used to, hit home, Jess added, 'I won't leave my father on his own.'

'How old do you think I am, Jess?' her father protested. 'You have to stay in Spain until you're sure those animals are happily settled. You know how much they mean to me.'

And there was that contract she'd signed for the Acostas, which could keep her in Spain a lot longer than that. 'I'll be back for Christmas,' she stated firmly.

Jess managed to convince herself that this trip made good sense. She was going to reassure herself and her father that the horses were properly settled. That was important. She also had to find the right opportunity to break the news to Dante that she was his new therapist. He wouldn't thank her. The regime she'd mapped out would be punishing. He'd left it so long—too long—that only the most intense therapy would stand a chance of effecting change. Even then, there was no guarantee of a full recovery.

With that situation unresolved, she turned her thoughts to something she could influence, which was care of the horses. 'I have no idea how the ponies will react until we're in the air,' she admitted honestly. 'I'll feel more confident when we land, especially if your facilities are as good as I hear they are—'

'They are,' Dante assured her.

'Then I don't foresee any problems.'

'And I'm happy to welcome you on board.'

He was proud of his jet. He owned a couple of smaller aircraft as well as several helicopters, one of which was kept on his yacht, but this huge aircraft with its custom fittings and long-range capabilities was his particular pride and joy. It enabled him to be anywhere in the world on a whim—with or without his horses. There were stalls rivalling any in the world on the lower level, and a fully staffed veterinary surgery in case of emergency. The upper level was more like a super-luxe apartment than anything resembling a plane. One of the foremost interior designers had kitted it out to Dante's specific instructions to include bedrooms, a galley manned by a Michelin starred chef, as well as a couple of luxurious bathrooms. In addition to this, he had a full working office and a spacious lounge where he could relax.

'Wow,' Jess gasped when they had boarded and she could look around. 'This isn't so much an aircraft as a flying palace. And you need all this…why?'

'Because I'm a very busy man.'

'I can see that,' she agreed, viewing the tech in his office as he took her on the tour.

'Would you have my horses walk home?'

'Of course not, but it does seem…how can I put this?… very big for one man.'

'How kind of you to highlight my regrettable bachelor status,' he mocked lightly.

'Don't mention it,' Jess returned, matching his tone and adding a grin.

At least she was relaxed. 'Make yourself at home,' he invited. Cabin attendants were standing by with trays of the finest Cristal champagne, as well as delicious canapés designed to tempt a flagging appetite.

'I'd rather see the horses settled, if you don't mind,' Jess told him matter-of-factly, managing a warm smile for the attendants at the same time. 'Could you show me the way, please?' she added.

'Of course.' There were many things he'd like to show Jess, and not with stabling as his first stop. He wanted to introduce her to his world, to show her that it was as purposeful as hers, and that it just had more trimmings. No woman had ever made him feel the need to justify his wealth. Because they took it for granted, he concluded as he led the way to the lower deck. Jess took nothing for granted.

'This is incredible,' she breathed as she stared with interest at his state-of-the-art equine facility. 'I'm even more impressed than I was on the upper deck. 'You've thought of absolutely everything.'

'Horses are my life,' he confessed, dragging deep on the familiar and much-loved scent of warm horse and clean leather.

'Do you mind if I stay down here while we take off? I'm concerned that the noise might spook Moon.'

'The pilot won't allow you to wander around at will. You'll have to be strapped in for take-off. The grooms have their own drop-down seats, much like the cabin attendants on a regular flight.'

'So long as Moon knows I'm here,' she agreed. 'Why don't you go back upstairs and relax? There's no reason for both of us to be here. I'm sure the grooms and I can handle everything. Why don't you take the chance to rest that leg?'

'I'm not an invalid,' he retorted sharply.

'No. You're anything you choose to be,' Jess agreed with a pointed look at his cane.

'I hope you're not suggesting that it's my choice to use this?'

'You don't have much alternative at the moment,' she pointed out. 'Nor will you until you accept treatment.'

'I'll be staying down here too,' he gritted out, keen to change the subject. 'These ponies represent a huge financial outlay—'

'Don't give me that,' she flashed back. 'You love them as much as I do.'

'I care for all my animals,' he conceded, 'and I've noticed, as you must have done, that Moon is particularly edgy, so I'll be staying with her when we take off.'

'One rule for you and another for me?' Jess challenged. 'Don't *you* have to be strapped in?'

'It's my jet and I do what the hell I like.'

'Regardless of safety?'

'Don't make me send you upstairs.'

'Why don't we both stay with Moon to reassure her?' she suggested mildly, refusing to rise to his threat.

'Because spending time with a woman who appears to take pleasure in sticking sharp words into my leg and shattering glances at my cane holds zero appeal.'

'Oh, I think you can take it,' she said. 'As you must shortly take some painful treatment.'

'You know a lot about me. Or think you do.'

Jess ignored this too and as she slipped into Moon's stall he followed her.

Moon became agitated when the jet engines screamed, eyes rolling back in her head.

They stood either side of the anxious mare to soothe

her. Perhaps the combination of two people who cared got through to the spooked animal. Moon settled and allowed him to scratch a favoured spot beneath her chin. By the time the jet had levelled out everything was calm again. Which was why Jess's tense expression surprised him.

'You okay?' he asked.

'Of course.'

He was going home, but Jess was taking a step into the unknown, he reasoned as she worried her bottom lip.

'You've been standing long enough,' she said, switching the spotlight to him.

Who was in charge here? His concern for Jess evaporated. 'You don't give orders on my flight.'

'Agreed,' she said without objection.

'But?'

She braced herself as if preparing to drop a bombshell.

'Spit it out,' he advised.

'You're in my care.'

'I'm sorry?' he queried, frowning.

'This is as good a time as any to explain that your siblings hired me to treat your leg. Which means obeying my instructions,' she went on before he could answer. 'The alternative is to throw their care and love for you back in their faces.'

'How long have you known this?' he asked in an ominously measured tone.

'I swear I haven't had chance to tell you before now. Yesterday flew by—'

'And you could not have made time?' he queried, controlling everything in his manner and voice to avoid upsetting the skittish mare.

'I didn't want anything to worry my father.'

'And how would this news have done that? Surely he'd be glad you've got another high-profile client?'

'All right,' she admitted. 'I anticipated your reaction,

and I'm worried about you. You need this treatment badly, so please don't be angry. I'm very good at what I do. Your brothers and sister wouldn't have hired me otherwise.'

He shook his head. 'You should have told me at the first opportunity.'

'And I have.' She held his stare without blinking. 'You can always refuse treatment, but for your sake I hope you don't.'

Truth might be blazing from Jess's eyes, but that wasn't enough to stop him feeling deceived and wrong-footed. 'We'll pick this up another time.'

'This is surely not a complete shock. You knew you would be undergoing treatment.'

'Not with you. I was expecting a physiotherapist, yes.'

'And you've got one,' Jess pointed out. 'One with three years' experience at a prestigious London teaching hospital before I went into private practice to allow for more flexibility.'

So she could take care of her father, he presumed Jess meant by that. He couldn't knock her for something he would have done. Family meant everything to both of them.

'I'm known for my good results if people listen to me,' she went on. 'That's why your family contacted me. Word of mouth is the most effective marketing tool.'

He didn't trust himself to discuss this yet, and Moon, sensing discord between them, was fast becoming restless.

'You're unsettling her,' Jess murmured as if he needed this pointing out.

'Is that why you chose to tell me here? Because I couldn't make a fuss.'

'I think you'd better leave,' Jess told him in the same calm tone.

'No one tells me to leave.'

'It's best for the horse.'

'And you,' he pointed out with a sceptical huff. 'You go.

I'll take care of Moon. She should know me. You can't cling to her for ever. It isn't fair to the horse. Go,' he instructed Jess as the pony grew increasingly agitated. 'If you love her, you'll entrust her to me.'

Jess's eyes were wide, and threatened tears. 'You'll take good care of her, won't you?'

'The well-being of my animals is paramount.'

'Just one more thing,' she said, and Dante paused for a moment. 'What would you have said if I had introduced myself as your therapist in the first place?'

Based on ten-year-old memories? He would have laughed her out of the room.

'Don't be angry with your family for caring about you,' she said as if reading his mind. 'I'm the best chance of recovery you've got.'

'We'll see, won't we?'

Swinging around, he turned his attention to the horse. The mare was soon quiet again. Moon trusted him instinctively. What she didn't like was friction between him and Jess. 'We'll have to do something about that, won't we?' he murmured in one silken ear.

Moon rewarded him immediately by calmly resting her head on his shoulder and whickering softly, as if to say yes.

CHAPTER FIVE

PERCHED TENSELY ON the edge of a deeply upholstered seat in the lounge area of Dante's super-jet, Jess brooded on whether she should have blurted out sooner, *I'm your therapist. I've been booked by your brothers and sister. Suck it up.* Well, maybe not that last—

'Are you sure you won't have another sparkling water, *señorita*?'

'No, thank you.' Suddenly aware of the empty glass she was nursing, Jess handed it over with a smile. The cabin attendants couldn't have been more helpful. Her surroundings were beyond impressive, from the plush leather and polished wood to the space. There was just so much space. She definitely wasn't used to that in the cheap seats. The interior of Dante's jet was more impressive than a mansion in a magazine. All light and bright and pristine, everything was of the highest quality.

Dante's expression could be described as anything but light and bright when she'd left him on the lower deck; trust was crucial between a therapist and their patient. Had she sacrificed that? Heaving a sigh, she wondered when she could have told him. Things had moved so fast, because that was what her father wanted.

She could have made time.

Maybe, but that might have spoiled yesterday for her

father. And, selfishly, she had wanted time to get to know Dante, and hadn't wanted to put a spike in that either.

And now? What did she want now?

To get through this, and for Dante to accept treatment.

He was perfectly entitled to send her home.

What would be the point in that? Why delay his recovery when he had a therapist on hand? She would be on the *estancia* to see the horses settled, so he might as well accept treatment. Even Dante Acosta wasn't superhuman.

He just looked that way...smelled that way...acted that way—

'Excuse me, *señorita*...?'

It was the cabin attendant again. Jess looked up and smiled. 'Yes?'

'Señor Acosta is waiting in the dining room.'

'I'll be right there.'

Jess's mouth dried. Did Dante's summons herald a reprieve, or was she about to receive her marching orders? Pausing only to smooth her hair and firm her jaw, she set off to confront the wolf in his lair.

Dante had seated himself at the head of a full-sized dining table, where he was ravenously devouring a baguette and cheese. When Jess walked in he looked up briefly. Indicating 'Sit' with a jerk of his chin, he swiped a linen napkin across his mouth. 'Are you hungry?'

'A little,' she admitted.

The look Jess was giving him suggested she couldn't deal with so much charm. Tough. He wasn't about to sugarcoat his manner for someone who had kept vital information from him.

'Eat,' he rapped, 'and then we'll talk.'

'That sounds ominous.'

Ignoring her comment, he finished his food and swilled it down with a large glass of water.

Jess made no attempt to take anything from the laden platters in front of her. 'Do you want something else?' he probed, frowning. 'If you do, ask.'

She looked uncomfortable. 'I don't want to put anyone to any trouble.'

'Really?' he said, sitting back. Keeping his stare fixed on Jess, he waved the attendants away and reached for some fruit.

'I'm not here to eat,' she insisted. 'You wanted to talk to me.'

He shrugged.

'You think I've taken advantage,' she stated tensely.

'That's exactly what I think,' he agreed.

'I'm sorry you feel that way.'

He held up a hand. 'Don't be. We're not so different, you and I. Why shouldn't you seize an opportunity? I would have done exactly the same thing.'

Her frown deepened. 'So…?'

'So we're complicated.' Easing his shoulders, he stared at her. 'Do I have to put something on a plate and feed you myself?'

Her eyes darkened. 'No, I'm—'

'Fine?' he suggested.

'Yes.'

'Relax, Jess. I have the greatest admiration for the caring profession. You should have told me from the start, but it's done. You're here. Now you have to put your manner of telling me behind you, as I do.'

'I didn't mean to deceive you. I just want to help.'

'My leg's aching,' he admitted. 'Why shouldn't you help? Grapes and cheese?'

She looked bemused for a moment, but then she relaxed. 'Thank you. I am hungry, and that would be good. I know I haven't made the best of starts, but I will make up for it.'

She certainly would, he thought.

* * *

The cheese was delicious and Dante was too. He was such a distraction she had trouble remembering important things, like why she was here and what she had come to do. He'd showered and his hair was still damp. It curled in thick black whorls that caught on his stubble. His earring glinted in the overhead lights, while the scent of lemons and something woody surrounded him. On home territory Dante was relaxed, wearing just a loosely belted robe after his shower. When he moved she caught glimpses of his tattoos…an edge of the snarling wolf across his heart and, when he turned to pour another glass of water, a glimpse of the skull and cross mallets tattooed across the back of his neck. How was she supposed to make easy conversation with all that going on?

'Eat up—take more,' he insisted. 'From what you've told me, I'll be working you hard.'

Jess's throat tightened. Shouldn't it be the other way around?

'If my treatment can't wait, I'm sure you're eager to begin,' he suggested dryly, with a long amused yet challenging look.

'Yes, of course,' she agreed in a voice turned dry.

'You have access to my medical history?'

'Scans, X-rays and a full set of notes,' she confirmed.

'Then there's no reason why you can't start right away. We're not going anywhere until this aircraft lands, so you might as well make a start. As you can see,' he added lazily, playing her like a minnow on the end of his rod, 'I dressed with that in mind.'

The thought of laying hands on Dante's body sent Jess's heart into a spin. Would she ever be ready to do that? She was a professional, with a job to do. Of course she could do it.

'I'm happy to start your treatment right now,' she said evenly.

It wasn't just Dante's sporting future she was holding in the palm of her hand, Jess realised. She wasn't so naïve that she didn't understand the boost her CV would receive if Dante's treatment resulted in him returning to world class polo.

'Second thoughts?' he suggested.

'None.'

'Then…' Dante was viewing her with amused eyes, as if he knew every thought in her head. 'You'll need a firm surface to work on, I presume?'

'Correct,' she confirmed.

'I'll make sure you have one. We will begin in half an hour.'

'That's good timing,' she agreed. 'You should digest your food first.'

'It will also give you chance to examine all the reasons you chose to come to Spain.'

'I have a contract,' she countered swiftly. 'And the lower deck of your aircraft is full of ponies that mean the world to me and my father.'

One of Dante's sweeping ebony brows lifted. 'You have an answer for everything, señorita. We will soon see if you have a solution for my damaged leg.'

Get over yourself, Dante mused as the minutes ticked slowly away. He shouldn't have allowed the situation to reach a point where his brothers and sister had been forced to intervene. But that was how the Acostas were. If one needed help and refused it, the others stepped in. Jess was stuck in the middle of a forceful, powerful family. He shouldn't be taking out his frustration on her. He'd been difficult since the polo accident. Hell, he'd always been difficult. He'd been the wayward son before his parents' death. It was only after the tragedy that he realised how much grief he'd given them. Now that grief was his. Verbal jousting with Jess had lifted him. He liked a challenge, and Jess was full of it. Without polo there was no conflict in his life. Jess gave him all he needed. Feeling her hands on his body was something he anticipated with interest.

'My bedroom?' he stated when she appeared at the appointed time.

'Perfect,' she agreed without batting an eyelid. 'We'll have privacy there.'

'So no one will hear me scream?' he suggested dryly.

'The treatment will be painful,' she admitted evenly, 'but I don't imagine you show your feelings as easily as that.'

They stared at each other for a moment. *Pot, kettle, black*, he thought, but at least Jess didn't shy away from her obligations. 'Lead the way,' she said pleasantly instead.

'I'm going to put a towel over you to preserve your modesty,' she told Dante in the reassuring tone she used with all her patients.

'What modesty?' he growled.

She blinked as she turned back to her patient and was confronted by an iron butt. Her heart thundered like crazy at the sight of something that would normally pass her by. A butt was a butt. They came in all shapes and sizes, and she had never judged anyone yet. Before now. In her defence, Dante had an exceptional butt. And the sooner she covered it with a towel the better.

His body was all over magnificent. Dante Acosta was as close to male perfection as it got.

'I'm ready,' he announced.

Are you? she felt like saying, but at least he'd bounced her out of the self-indulgent stare. Members of his crew had arranged a board on top of the bed and she'd added a cover on top so it was comfortable.

'Well?' he prompted. 'What are you waiting for?'

She would have to be made of stone not to appreciate the sight in front of her. 'I'll be starting on your calf and working up.'

'Great.'

'Don't get too excited. According to your notes, there's nothing wrong with your groin.'

'Very witty. I rather thought I would be staying here on my front anyway.'

'You will; don't worry,' she replied as she hauled his legs into a position to suit the upcoming therapy. 'Now lie still and don't move again. And please don't talk. We have less than an hour for this treatment, if you want to take a shower when I've finished.'

'What are you using?' Dante asked suspiciously as she slicked her hands with oil.

'Horse liniment. My bag's in the hold—'

'You're doing *what*?' he roared.

'Joke?' she said mildly, chalking one up for the therapist. 'This is straight out of your bathroom.'

'No more jokes,' Dante growled, which was her signal to dig deep into the muscles on his injured calf.

Applying her skill, she soon discovered the seat of the problem. Starting gently, she built up the pressure until Dante let rip with a violent curse.

'You're supposed to be curing me, not torturing me!'

'If you'd started treatment sooner your muscles wouldn't be in such a knot.'

'Then make allowances for that knot.'

'Stop deafening me. Stay still. Keep quiet,' she instructed. 'This will hurt if you don't submit—'

'*Submit?*' he roared, almost exploding off the bed.

She pressed her weight against his back...his warm, tanned, hard-muscled back. 'Lie back down,' she insisted.

'I could shake you off in an instant,' he warned.

'You could,' she agreed. 'But what good would that do? Meanwhile, I'm hearing your treatment time ticking away.'

'You're cool; I'll give you that,' he conceded.

Thank goodness that was how she appeared. It wasn't how she felt.

'Continue,' Dante instructed as he rested back on the bed. 'Though I imagine you're going to make me pay.'

An unseen smile hovered on her lips. 'Whatever makes you think that?'

'My infamous intuition,' Dante informed her.

He bit back a curse as Jess—or Skylar, as he preferred to think of her in this merciless mood—dug her fingers deep into a nerve.

'This is the price you pay for neglecting follow-up treatment,' she informed him when he snarled a complaint.

He didn't care for the tone of her voice.

'What do you think you're doing?' Jess demanded when he rolled off the bed.

'Getting a few things straight.'

'Like what?' she demanded, lifting her chin to confront him. But her glance dipped to his lips before it returned to his eyes.

They continued to stare at each other until her eyes sparkled and she couldn't hold back a laugh. He laughed too because this was real, this was Jess. She wouldn't have known how to flatter him if she'd tried.

'Down,' she instructed, pointing to the bed. 'I haven't finished with you yet. Take your treatment like a man.'

'With pleasure,' he agreed, smiling.

'There won't be too much of that,' she assured him.

'Pleasure?'

That one word was all he could get out before the torture began, but he had to confess that she was good by the end of the session. 'My leg feels a little easier,' he remarked with surprise.

'You'll pay for it tomorrow,' she predicted. 'One session isn't a cure. It's only the first step in a very long treatment.'

'Excellent.'

'Excellent? I can't promise to be gentle with you.'

'Please,' he said, staring into her eyes, 'don't hold back.' Jess was blushing deeply as he added, 'At least my siblings haven't wasted their money.'

'Wait—I want to check something before you go,' she said as he straightened up. With that, she knelt at his feet.

'You don't have to bow to me— *Mujer!*' he exclaimed as she dug her fingers into an area he had so far treated with the care he might show an eggshell.

'There you go,' she announced with satisfaction. 'It is that muscle at the root of your problem.'

He had more muscles with more problems than she knew.

'And you had to prove it,' he observed as Jess stood up.

'Yes, of course I did. I know what I'm doing, you know.'

There was no doubt in his mind of that.

Something incredible had happened while all this was going on. The anger that had dogged him since the accident—an accident caused by his recklessness, as well as that of his opponent—evaporated and was replaced by good humour. Jess had released something in him. It was the same knack she'd had ten years ago when he was an over-confident youth of twenty-two. She could burst a bubble of entitlement with a flash of her emerald eyes. Maybe she had been in awe of the Acosta brothers when they strode into her father's stable, but she'd hidden it beneath a mix of teenage attitude—and one surprisingly bold action. She hadn't even been fazed by the little fluff-ball disgracing it-self all over her clothes, or if she had, she hadn't shown it.

'Don't you see the funny side of this?' he enquired with

interest. 'Teenage Jess turned regimental sergeant major where my treatment's concerned?'

'No, I don't,' she said flatly. 'Treating patients is a serious occupation for me. I don't find any of this amusing.'

'Liar,' he reprimanded her softly. 'You must be gloating deep down.'

Jess's expression remained unchanged.

Now the session had ended they went their separate ways, Jess to check on the horses, while he went to take a shower and get changed. Had he met his match? The thought that he might have done pleased him as he stared into the glass above the basin. Would she get the better of him? No. That would never happen and it was something Jess still had to learn.

But… As he eased his leg, and for the first time in a long time felt no pain, he thought his accusation of Jess gloating over her control of him had gone too far. Yes, she was in charge of his treatment; that was what she'd been hired to do. Early signs pointed to her therapy being effective. Instead of trying to wind her up, he should be thanking her. Jess was alone on new territory, where he controlled everything outside Jess's treatment plan. A little humility on his part wouldn't go amiss.

CHAPTER SIX

'THANK YOU,' Jess whispered as she stroked Moon's ears. She loved the contrast between sharp-edged cartilage and sleek, velvety hair and, even more than that, she loved the communion between them. The healing power of animals could never be overestimated in Jess's opinion. She only had to be in the stall with Moon to know that this closeness between them was a gift, a space, a special place to be— it was a place where she could always see things clearly. Except for Dante.

All those years she'd dreamed about him, without making allowances for the man he would become. In her mind, Dante had remained the dangerously attractive youth who hovered unseen, and yet so forcibly present, over every relationship she'd ever had. How was she supposed to have a successful love life with Dante Acosta as her template?

That kiss hadn't stopped him when it came to relationships.

No. Far from it. Following Dante's career meant following a great many stories of his private life, which ran alongside his success, both in polo and the tech world. While she applauded his many triumphs, she was forced to see him dating, and that cut deep.

It still did.

It hadn't damaged the connection between them. That was real and strong, at least on Jess's part, but did Dante feel it too? He was impossible to read. Even blazingly alive in front of her rather than haunting her mind, Dante was as intangible as he had ever been.

Could there ever be anything between them?

'Look at the state of me,' she murmured as Moon nuzzled her neck. 'Does that seem likely when women across the world are hammering on Dante's door? Why waste my life on pointless dreaming?'

'So here you are—'

She jumped at the sound of Dante's voice.

'I knew I'd find you with the ponies.'

Her swift intake of breath must have betrayed the fact she'd been thinking about him. If that wasn't enough, her cheeks were blazing and her lips felt swollen, while her breasts were aching for his touch.

Dante appeared totally unaffected. Ditching his cane to come into the stall, he lounged back against the wall to inform her, 'Look, no stick. I'm cured. You can go home now.'

'By parachute?' she suggested.

He laughed, a flash of strong white teeth against his dark, swarthy face, which was the cue for heat to rush through her. If there was one thing more dangerous than a grim-faced Dante Acosta, it was this version. She couldn't resist this one at all.

She must, Jess reminded herself. Professionalism was paramount. 'It's too soon to discard your stick,' she observed. 'I've already warned you that you'll suffer tomorrow if you put too much stress on that leg. You could pay the price with a setback.'

Dante's answer was an easy shrug. 'Relax. I left my cane outside to avoid spooking Moon.'

'And you delight in teasing me. Don't forget that.'

Dante almost turned serious. 'I delight in the improvement I can feel in my leg. You can claim a miracle if you like.'

'I prefer to work steadily until I'm sure that any improvement is lasting. I don't throw up my hands and cheer at the first sign of change.'

'Tell me, how do you remain so controlled?'

'It counters your teasing,' she said honestly. 'As for miracles? All I see in your future is more therapy, hard work and pain.'

'Sounds irresistible.'

'I thought you'd prefer to hear the truth.'

'Did you?'

The look he gave her now made Jess's cheeks flare bright red, while her body responded with far too much enthusiasm. 'I take it you're here to see Moon?' she said in an attempt to distract both of them from the mounting tension.

'I'm here to see you also.'

'Oh?'

'There's something I forgot to say to you.'

'You're fired?' she suggested dryly.

'Now, why would I do that when I think we're making progress?' Dante viewed her steadily. 'Small steps,' he explained.

Was he still referring to his leg? 'Small steps,' she agreed. 'Truce?'

She tensed as he pulled away from the wall. As he came closer and his heat wrapped around her, Dante's energy pervaded the atmosphere.

'I just want to say thank you,' he soothed.

He dipped forward to brush a kiss against her cheek, but she turned her head at entirely the wrong moment and their lips met. It seemed like for ever, though it could have been no more than a heartbeat, that she didn't move, breathe or register anything apart from the fact that Dante was kissing her and seemed in no hurry to move away.

'You okay?' he prompted, pulling back.

The penny dropped. No wonder he was frowning. In

Dante's sophisticated world kisses were exchanged as easily
as handshakes. 'Of course I'm okay.' She shrugged as if men
like Dante Acosta kissed her every day of the week, when
what she really wanted was for him to kiss her as if he really,
really meant it. 'There's no need to thank me. It's my job.'

'You're very good at your job,' he observed in a tone that
bore out every thought she had about the meaning of that
kiss. There was no meaning beyond *Thank you.*

'And now it's time to strap in for landing,' he added
briskly.

You can say that again, Jess thought, curbing misplaced
amusement as Dante's dark stare lingered on her face.

'Now?' he prompted. 'We'll be touching down in a few
minutes.'

His wake-up call was badly needed. She wasn't his type.
If his perfunctory kiss hadn't proved it, any magazine in the
world would show that Dante went for glamorous women,
more at home on the front row of a high fashion show than
the back row of the stalls.

Heading off to find a seat to strap into, she was surprised
when Dante did the same. She'd already decided to stay
on the deck with the horses so she was ready to help the
grooms as soon as the plane landed. 'Why don't you strap
in upstairs?' she suggested to Dante. 'We can manage here,
and if you don't rest after treatment you'll never get better.'

'If you don't learn that I don't accept orders you and I
are in for a bumpy ride,' he shot back.

Pressing her lips together so she didn't say something
she might regret, Jess reflected tensely, *You don't frighten
me, Dante Acosta, and, whether you like it or not, for the
duration of your treatment I'm in charge.*

With the horses safely arrived in Spain and loaded into
transporters waiting on the tarmac, it was Jess's turn to
climb into Dante's flatbed alongside.

Flinging his cane into the back, Dante hauled himself into the driving seat beside her. 'You'll be in pain for some time yet,' she explained when he grimaced and paused to knead a cramped muscle. 'I dare say I've woken up nerve endings you'd forgotten about.'

'No chance of that now,' he agreed grimly. 'How long must I suffer cramp?'

'Until you're cured.'

'Then you'd better get on with it.'

'I intend to.'

As Dante shook his head with exasperation, Jess knew she was dealing with a warrior, a man who had thought himself invincible until the accident.

'You'd better make sure I'm ready for the new polo season,' he threatened, grimacing.

'I'd be lying if I said I could guarantee that. It's largely up to you, and how seriously you take my treatment plan.'

'Do you have to be so honest?'

'Always.'

'I can hire a therapist any day of the week.'

'Then go ahead and do so, though I can't imagine you'll have many takers if that expression settles on your face.'

'*Ha!* And what about the ponies? Or have you forgotten about them?'

'I've forgotten nothing,' she fired back. 'I'll stay on your *estancia* until they're settled, but that doesn't mean you have to keep me on as your therapist. Go ahead and hire someone else.' *At least I wouldn't have to tolerate you as a patient*, she thought, though deep down she knew it was the frustration of Dante's injury driving him to lash out at her. Better he did that than he took it out on someone who didn't understand him. 'I'm here to help and until you fire me that's what I'm going to do.'

'So you can put Acosta on your CV?' he suggested with an ugly snarl.

'So you can walk without a cane, and ride again, and maybe even play polo at international level again,' she argued calmly.

'Only maybe?' he said with a narrow-eyed look.

'There are no guarantees where the body is concerned,' she said honestly, 'but I've never shirked in my attempt to heal a patient yet, and I don't intend to start with you. I'm not a quitter, Dante.'

'Just my bad luck,' Dante murmured beneath his breath. Releasing the handbrake, he gunned the engine and they were off to a future even Skylar would find hard to predict.

While they were driving, Jess called her father to reassure him they'd landed safely and the horses had been loaded successfully without drama and were now on their way to Dante's ranch in Spain. It would have been a lie to add that things were going well, she reflected, and so she confined herself in a very British way to talking about the weather. 'It's warmer here in winter than Yorkshire in summer,' she told her father with a laugh.

'You enjoy yourself,' he said before cutting the line. 'All work and no play et cetera.'

'Thanks, Dad, I'll remember that.'

Dante glanced at her as they ended the conversation and she huffed a rueful laugh. 'Everything okay?' he asked.

'My father seems fine—on top of the world, in fact. I've never heard him sounding quite so optimistic.'

'Good. That's good.'

They both fell silent and she tried to relax, but it wasn't easy when she was trapped in the confines of a cab with so much man. Dante's lean tanned hands effortlessly tickling the wheel while his biceps bulged and his iron-hard thighs rested a hair's breadth away from hers would have tested the endurance of a saint. His machismo was like a living thing that sucked the air from her lungs, leaving her nothing to breathe but pure sex.

'I'm fast but safe,' he stated.

She laughed inside, wondering if she should feel quite so disappointed about the fast reference in that statement.

'You drive very well,' she said in an attempt to blank images of her life becoming fast and extremely unsafe. Her body wanted one thing, while common sense dictated caution. Twenty-seven years old and she couldn't boast a single successful sexual relationship, and that was all down to one man setting the bar at an unattainable height. Dante hadn't made things better with his most recent kiss. Even if it was just a token to say thank you, she was still buzzing with awareness and kept touching her lips with the tip of her tongue, as if to recreate the moment.

Okay, so she had been one hundred per cent guilty of sabotaging any potential love affair in the past by picking unworthy men. She didn't have time for love, she'd tell herself as she concentrated on her studies. Though she did have time to dream about Dante Acosta. And the failed love affairs? Were down to not wanting to tarnish that first romantic image of a memorable kiss in a stable. And who could blame her, when even a routine 'thank you' kiss from Dante Acosta set her heart pounding? He knocked the competition out of the park.

But there was no point in falling for a lost cause. She had to find a way to get him out of her system, or she'd never move forward and have the chance to love.

Not that she was in danger of falling in love with Dante Acosta. No way! Jess assured herself in the most forceful manner possible. Sucking in a deep breath, she made herself relax.

They'd been driving for around an hour when Dante announced, 'We're here.'

Anything Jess had imagined was obliterated by what

she saw in front of her. Having left the bustling coast behind, the peace of this much lusher, greener interior held immediate appeal for Jess. 'How lucky you are,' she murmured as high gates swung back to reveal a crown of snow-capped mountains circling Dante's land. Neatly fenced paddocks full of ponies stretched away as far as the eye could see.

'I can ski in the morning and swim in the sea in the afternoon,' he said as they passed through the gates and drove on down an immaculately maintained road.

Lush green was fed by a glittering river, while clusters of trees provided shelter for the ponies. Jess was rendered speechless, and wondered how Dante could ever bring himself to leave.

'I spoke with my brother while you were busy with Moon. He says they booked you for a month.'

'I can't predict how long your treatment will take, but I would expect a substantial improvement by then.'

Dante hummed, leaving Jess to wonder if, for him, a month was too long or not long enough. Either way, she must separate her personal feelings from what she'd been tasked to do.

Each bend in the road revealed a new vista of contented animals and tidily maintained land. 'I've never seen so many ponies in one place before,' Jess admitted on an incredulous laugh, 'but what about security?'

'High-tech.'

Like everything else in Dante's life, she imagined. 'You've got a lot of plates to keep spinning, and once you return to full fitness I suspect you'll want to spin even more. Do you ever take a break?'

'Do you?' he countered with a swift sideways glance.

They fell silent after that, which allowed Jess to appreciate how big his ranch was. It was like a small country within a country, and when she contrasted that with the small hill farm where she'd grown up she got an even greater sense of the yawning gulf between them.

'Do you like what you see?' Dante enquired.

'The more I see, the more I understand why you chose to come here to lick your wounds.'

'It's my home,' he said, as if this were obvious.

But it was more than that, Jess suspected. This was Dante's retreat from the world, where he could live free from comment or the cruel gossip that suggested he might never play again. That gossip made her doubly determined to heal him.

Though there might be more to heal than Dante's leg, she accepted. He was a complex man who had famously run wild in his youth, only to be drawn to a shuddering halt by the death of his parents. Since then, it was well documented that Dante had done everything he could to help his oldest brother take care of the family. That took its toll as well, she reflected, thinking of her father's distressing retreat from the world when he'd lost his wife. Nothing hurt more than seeing someone she loved suffering as much as her father had, and Dante had gone through that same torment with his brothers and sister, which made her wonder how much time he'd taken to grieve.

'Another couple of miles and you'll be able to see all the facilities, as well as the ranch house and the stables.'

Meanwhile, she would feast her eyes on Dante's hands, lightly controlling the wheel, and his powerful forearms, shaded with just the right amount of dark hair.

Another couple of miles?

Could she control her breathing for that long?

She must, and she would. It wasn't a gulf between them; it was an ocean. She had entered a kingdom for one, which would be forced in the short term to play host to an invader with a medical bag.

And a will every bit as strong as Dante Acosta's.

CHAPTER SEVEN

'MY FATHER TAUGHT me that the handing over process is as important as the sale, so I'll see the ponies settled in before I go to my accommodation, if that's okay with you?' Jess said as Dante drew into a courtyard the size of a couple of football pitches.

'Don't worry. Your father's ponies have come to the best home in Spain.'

'I can imagine,' she agreed, 'but I promised that I would see them settled, and then ring to reassure him. After that, I'll concentrate on you.'

'That sounds ominous,' Dante said as he rested his hands on the wheel.

'You're my patient, and that makes you my primary concern.'

'I'm very glad to hear it.'

The way he spoke, the way he looked at her, was going to make it hard to remain immune to the infamous Acosta charm.

Make that impossible, Jess thought as Dante climbed down from the driver's side and came around the vehicle to help her out.

'I can manage, thank you.'

Ignoring her comment, he lifted her down, leaving her with the overwhelming and inconvenient urge to be naked with him, skin to heated skin.

'When you've reassured yourself regarding the ponies, my housekeeper will show you around the ranch house. Or you can sit on the fence and watch as I allow the ponies to stretch their legs. They've been cooped up and will appreciate some carefully controlled freedom.'

'Sit on the fence?' she queried wryly. 'Does that sound like me?'

'No,' Dante admitted, 'but the sooner the ponies get used to new handlers, the happier they will be.'

For a moment Jess felt excluded, and had to remind herself that interaction with her father's ponies was to reassure him and that her main job was to treat Dante.

But she couldn't help herself, and when she noticed Moon playing up she walked over to the wrangler. 'Let me do this,' she insisted as the tricky mare reared. 'I know Moon. I understand her.'

'*Está bien*, Manuel. Back off,' Dante instructed as Jess took charge.

The ease with which she was able to calm Moon was almost embarrassing. Everyone stopped to watch as she brought the pony down the yard but, not wanting to start off on the wrong foot, she explained to the assembled wranglers, while Dante translated her words from English to Spanish, that the mare trusted her because she'd known Jess since the day she was born.

'They appreciated that,' Dante remarked as he led the way into the quarantine area where Moon would be allowed to roam.

'No problem. I know the ponies, and soon they will too. 'Treatment after supper,' she reminded him as they removed Moon's halter and set her free.

'I'm braced and ready,' Dante assured her dryly, 'but I'm handing you over to my housekeeper, Maria, while I catch up with what's been happening on the ranch.'

Maria gave Jess the warmest of welcomes, but even the

most informative tour of the spacious and luxuriously appointed ranch house, with its burnished wood and richly coloured furnishings, failed to distract Jess from thoughts of Dante. She had to find a way to put him out of her mind. At least until his next treatment when, for a short time only, he would be the focus of her mind and not her heart, she determined.

'I see you've made yourself at home,' Dante commented later at supper. He had lined up in the cookhouse with everyone else, while Jess was behind the counter, serving with Maria and Manuel, the wrangler she'd met earlier.

'And what a home,' Jess commented, smiling as she handed over Dante's loaded plate. 'Maria invited me to throw myself in at the deep end, which was exactly what I wanted to do. So here I am.'

Dante glanced around. 'You approve?'

'Who wouldn't?' she enthused. Dante's ranch had an air of purpose and everything was of the highest quality, including the delicious food.

'You don't have to do this,' he said bluntly.

'But I want to. I'm not used to idling my time away.'

His eyes took on a darkly amused glint. 'I'm not enough for you?'

'Even with two therapy sessions a day, that's only a few hours of my time.'

With a shrug, he moved on and she attended to the line behind him.

When it came to Jess's turn to eat, there was one space left and Dante was sitting at the same table. It was a table for two, and their knees brushed when she sat down. An attempt to tuck her legs away failed. There just wasn't enough room. 'Sorry,' she said wryly.

'Too close to the fire?' Dante suggested.

'I can handle it,' she assured him.

'I'm sure you can,' he agreed.

Brooding and aloof was easier to deal with than a decidedly relaxed man, Jess reflected as she got stuck in to the spicy paella.

'One last check on the ponies and then I'll be ready for my treatment,' he said, pushing his plate away and standing up.

'I'll come with you.'

'As you wish.'

Dante stabbed his cane impatiently against the cobbles as they crossed the yard. She guessed his leg was giving him hell, as she had predicted. Her treatment on the plane had been deep and thorough. The memory of her hands on Dante's body made a frisson of anticipation rip down her spine at the thought of doing it again. Could she resist him for an entire month? Would Jess, the coolly professional therapist, do her work and go home, or would all that longing locked inside her break free at some point?

She could do this, she told herself as she followed Dante into the isolation block where her ponies would be kept until they had been checked over and passed fit by his veterinarians. The past had formed her and made her strong. The present brought new challenges, but so far she'd seen them through. There was no reason to suppose she'd falter now.

The facility resembled a top-class equine hotel. She turned full circle to take it in. 'This is wonderful.' Spotless surroundings, spacious stalls and animals contentedly resting was Jess's idea of heaven. She told him so.

'You can move in,' he offered, lips tugging in the hint of a smile.

'If I liked hay for a bed and oats for supper, I might just do that.' But she was laughing and relaxed; they both were.

His libido shot through the roof at the sound of Jess laughing, but his leg let him down by yowling on cue. He couldn't wait long for that treatment.

They checked each pony in turn. When Jess ran capable hands over them, murmuring soft words of encouragement, he craved the same attention. When they walked out of the stable block even the resident cats in the yard came to wind themselves around her legs. 'Next time I'll come prepared with treats,' Jess promised her feline admirers, kneeling down to give them a fuss.

'You have quite a menagerie,' she commented, smiling in welcome as one of his older dogs heaved itself up from its vantage point in front of the kitchen door. Animals were the best judge of character, he knew, and from then on Bouncer stuck close to her side as they completed the tour.

Several members of staff greeted Jess as if she'd lived on the *estancia* all her life. Light spilled onto her auburn hair in the veterinary hospital, setting it on fire as she chatted easily with his veterinarians in the sick bay. When they left the facility she reminded him he was due a treatment. 'Another session tonight, and then I'll leave you alone until tomorrow morning,' she promised.

Drawing her into the safety of the shadows as a truck loaded with sacks of feed trundled past, it was Jess who broke free first. 'Sorry,' she said as if she'd done something wrong.

He gave a relaxed shrug. 'Don't apologise.' He could get used to the feel of Jess beneath his hands. 'See you in half an hour for my treatment? Ask Maria to show you the way to the sports complex. There are treatment rooms there we can use.'

'Fine,' Jess confirmed. 'I'll do that.' But her emerald eyes were as dark as night and her tone was breathy.

Had that just happened? Almost happened. She was still tingling with awareness where Dante had held her out of the way of the truck. She had wanted to stay in his arms but couldn't do that and remain professional. This was only the start of her contract and she was already in danger of melting.

Entering the empty kitchen, she leaned back against the door and closed her eyes briefly. These might be fabulous surroundings and Dante was definitely the most attractive man she'd ever come across, but that was no excuse for her to lose her grip on reality. She couldn't afford to do that, even for a moment. She was here to treat a patient, and though the urge to continue what they'd started ten years ago—what *she* had started ten years ago—was overwhelming, it must remain locked in her mind. Maybe she would have to remain unsatisfied for the rest of her life, but better that than throw away everything she'd worked for on a dream that could never come true.

'Can I get you something, Señorita Slatehome?'

She jumped guiltily as Maria entered the kitchen. 'Jess. Please call me Jess.'

Quickly reorganising her features into those of a woman who hadn't been thinking heated thoughts, she smiled at Maria. 'I'm sorry to invade your beautiful kitchen, but Señor Acosta said you would be able to tell me where to find the sports complex.'

'He didn't have the patience to tell you himself?'

Maria's raisin-black eyes twinkled with laughter, as if this was the Señor Acosta she knew. 'You are a very welcome invasion, Señorita Jess, and I'm happy to direct you.'

But it was a struggle to concentrate when Maria began to explain. Jess felt as if her life had taken on a new and rapid speed and she had no way of slowing it down.

'If I can do anything else for you…' she realised Maria was saying.

'No, no, that's fine—to the side of the stable block, behind the yard—'

Maria laughed and corrected her indulgently. 'Señor

Acosta is enough to make a saint lose concentration,' she reassured her.

'I'm hardly that,' Jess admitted.

'But you are a great improvement on previous visitors,' Maria told her with a significant look.

'Thank goodness for that.'

As they smiled at each other, Jess felt as if the bond that had formed the moment they met had tightened.

'Señorita Jess,' Maria added, catching hold of her before she left the kitchen, 'I would appreciate it if you could let me know if there's anything else you might need over the weekend, as I'm taking the day off on Saturday to start the preparations for my wedding.'

'Oh, how exciting!' And how good to have something to think about, apart from Dante. And a wedding was the best of all distractions.

'You're invited, of course,' Maria told her.

'Me?' Jess's hands flew to her chest.

'Of course you,' Maria confirmed. 'Everyone on the *estancia* is invited.'

Even Dante?

Jess's smile lost some of its sparkle. The less she saw of him in social situations, the better. Seeing him in the stable with horses was safe. Safe-ish, she amended. But weddings were emotionally charged affairs, infused with romantic overtones.

'Please say you'll accept,' Maria pressed. 'I think you'll enjoy it. I'm planning a traditional *gitanos* wedding with a Christmas theme. It will be held before Christmas in the marquee Señor Acosta has arranged here. He's so kind… so generous—'

So The Wolf had a heart after all, Jess reflected wryly as Maria continued to enthuse about Dante's many virtues. 'I'd be honoured to celebrate the day with you, Maria.' Whatever she thought of Dante, Jess wouldn't dream of offending her new friend, and the prospect of attending an authentic *gitanos* wedding was a bonus she had never expected. 'I'm really excited for you,' she admitted as she and Maria shared a hug. 'It's a privilege to be included in something so personal and romantic when I'm a newcomer to the ranch. Please let me know if I can do anything for you.'

'Just be happy here,' Maria implored her with a long thoughtful look as they released each other and stood back.

'Being welcomed like this, how could I not be happy?'

Dante. Wanting more than he could ever give her.

So, Jess reflected as she made her way to the sports building, twice daily physio sessions with Dante, and now a wedding. Was it even ethical to continue treating him, when all she could think about were the possibilities ahead?

These were early days, Jess reassured herself as the sports complex loomed in front of her. All stark steel and glass, it appeared more than fit for a billionaire's purpose. Which was more than could be said for her, Jess concluded with amusement when she caught sight of her reflection in a sheet of glass. She doubted many of Dante's companions went to meet him dressed in scrubs and clogs, carrying a medical bag—unless he had kinks she didn't know about. This thought made her smile, made her determined to get used to seeing him, touching him. She would rein in her feelings. She had to.

But could she?

CHAPTER EIGHT

DANTE PICKED UP some calls while he waited for Jess in the sports block. Each supplied another small piece of the jigsaw that was Jess. He already knew she was a complicated woman, driven, successful and determined. She was also beautiful and he wanted her, but these shreds of information supplied by his team fleshed out the back-story of who she was.

He should have known the bold teenager would rise above the tragedy of losing her mother and develop into someone whose only thought was helping others. Competent and organised, Jess's reputation in her profession was second to none. But did he want to get close to her? Did he want to get close to anyone? The loss of his parents had been unbearable. Grief had frozen his heart.

With nothing but his racing thoughts for company, he soon became impatient. Before the accident he'd had many outlets for his energy: riding horses, women, working out in the gym. That appetite was only slumbering. Flexing his muscles, he turned on his stomach to rest his face on folded arms. Closing his eyes, he breathed steadily and deeply in an attempt to block Jess out, and then flinched, feeling her cool hands on his skin.

'Apologies,' she said in her best no-nonsense voice. 'Are my hands too cold for you?'

'You'll soon warm up,' he predicted.

Telling his body to behave was unnecessary when she began work on his muscles. *'Infierno sangriento!* Hold off!' he warned as she delved into the site of his injury with all the finesse of a commando in the gym.

'I know what I'm doing.'

And with that she put the flat of her hands between his shoulder blades and shoved him down again. 'Don't worry,' she soothed. 'This will soon be over.'

More accustomed to caresses and hungry, urging grips, he growled a soft warning as she kneaded and probed his tender damaged leg.

'Try to relax,' she insisted.

'Are you enjoying this?'

'It's my job.'

'Then improve your bedside manner,' he rapped, 'and while you're at it refine your touch.'

'It's my intention to heal, not pleasure.'

He huffed a cynical believing laugh.

'Settle down,' she instructed.

'Don't tell me what to do.'

'Are you going to take over the session?' She stood back.

'Get on with it,' he growled ungraciously.

'No more talking. Or laughing,' she added as he shook his head and huffed with incredulity that he was still here, still tolerating her torture.

'You've got enough to think about,' Jess assured him. 'As I do, if these leg muscles are ever going to heal.' To prove her point, she applied even greater force to her pummelling and kneading.

'I'm not a lump of dough.'

'No. You're a lot noisier,' she observed. 'And far less pliable. So be quiet.'

'I could fire you.'

'Really?'

She sounded far too enthusiastic about that idea, so reluctantly he submitted, but not before he had acknowledged how quickly charming Jess could revert to Jess the therapist. That impressed him. In the ability to disconnect, she was very like him.

'If you don't obey my instructions,' she murmured as she worked, 'these sessions will be endless.'

'Really?'

'Stop that,' she warned in response to his amusement. 'Any slight improvement you've noticed after our session on the plane only signals the fact that certain muscles and nerve endings are being called into use again. That's a good sign, but it doesn't mean you're cured.'

He gritted his teeth as she gave him a good workout.

'Turn over. I need to work on the front of your leg,' she explained.

He couldn't turn over until his body took the hint. 'Give me a minute,' he ground out, before silently reciting the alphabet backwards.

'Maybe I can help you,' she suggested with concern.

She certainly could.

'Do you have cramp?'

He had something. The mother of all hard-ons meant taking longer than he'd thought. 'Don't touch me,' he warned when Jess attempted to turn him over. 'You might strain your back, and then what happens to my treatment?'

'I'm overwhelmed by your concern,' she murmured with a smile in her voice. 'But if you co-operate I won't need to strain my back.'

'Wait,' he insisted.

'As you please.'

She wouldn't sound so prim if she knew the extent of his problem. She was killing him in more ways than one.

At last he could turn over. 'Carry on.'

* * *

Dante had the most beautiful body she'd ever seen. How could she ignore that—ignore him? Patients were at their most vulnerable on the couch beneath her hands, and Dante was no exception. She wanted to heal him and she knew what to do. She also wanted to touch and pleasure him, but that was off the menu. Thankfully, he behaved himself for the rest of the session, which allowed her to concentrate on her work.

Most of the time.

'I'm done for today,' she announced as she satisfied herself that progress had been made.

'Exhausted?' Dante suggested, turning his head to look at her.

'It would take more than a single session with you to do that.'

'You sound very sure.'

His expression made her blush, made her smile...made her smile broaden. It was impossible not to find some humour in this situation, and it seemed the harder she tried to remain aloof from Dante, the harder fate worked to screw up her plan.

Trapped in the beam of very dangerous eyes, she said firmly, 'I'm done for today.'

'*Muchas gracias, señorita,*' Dante murmured as he rolled off the couch.

'Don't mention it,' Jess said politely as he straightened up and towered over her. 'It's what I do. First thing tomorrow morning, back here, around eight?'

'I'll be in town tomorrow,' Dante said flatly as he snatched up a robe.

'What about your treatment?'

'It will have to wait.'

'But I need to establish a routine.'

Dante grunted. Was this his way of dismissing her? Was

she going to be ditched like the doctors in the hospital? Was he really going to risk his future mobility?

'You can't afford to miss a treatment.'

'You decide this?' he asked with a narrowing of his night-black eyes.

'Yes,' Jess said bluntly. 'I decide your treatment programme. You're not cured yet. If you have to go into town, I can start earlier. Name your time.'

'Six o'clock.'

He made it sound like a challenge. 'Earlier, if you like,' she suggested mildly.

'The time suits me.'

'Then it suits me too,' she said pleasantly, as she seriously considered stamping on Dante's one good foot.

Rewarded by a grunt of assent, Jess had to admit the banter and contest of wills between them was arousing. Dante was a patient like no other. And there was no law against dreaming. No code of ethics could find fault with that.

'Excellent,' she confirmed, turning to go. 'I look forward to seeing you in the morning.'

Delay was the servant of pleasure, Dante reminded himself grimly as he took note of the resolve in Jess's expression. Next stop the pool. He glared at the loathed cane, hating that he needed it to balance as he thrust his feet into sliders.

'You won't need that soon,' Jess called across on her way out.

He hated that she witnessed his plight. But Jess of all people was bound to, he accepted reluctantly. That was why she was here. His siblings would hear more of this. Why had they chosen this disturbingly beautiful woman on a mission, when a troll would have suited him better? Were Jess's soft hands even capable of delivering pleasure? He was beginning to doubt he would ever find out. And that was a first for Dante Acosta.

So. That went well, Jess reflected grimly.

Instead of blanking Dante's brazen sexual appeal, she had thought of little else throughout that entire session. And now it was a struggle not to stare at him through the floor-to-ceiling windows as he sliced through the pool like the hottest thing in black swimming shorts. Even with one leg below par, Dante's body housed an immensely powerful engine. Massive shoulders, rippling muscles and those steel girder arms required supercharged apparatus to drive them on.

'Don't overdo it!' she yelled out as he performed a neat turn at speed. Maybe he heard, probably not, but she doubted he was in the mood to heed advice. There was only so much instruction Dante could take before needing to paddle his own canoe.

A wave of unaccustomed uncertainty washed over her. The prospect of curing him seemed more elusive than ever.

'On your head be it,' she muttered as she walked on. If this was the first day, it would be a long month.

A long month of reliving what had happened between them all those years ago, and wondering if it would ever happen again. She had never forgotten the feeling of his lips on hers at the farm and that brush of his mouth on the plane had only served to intensify her longing.

Get a hold of yourself, Jess; it's never going to happen. And you shouldn't want it to. The man is a nightmare. It would never work.

Look on the bright side, Jess decided as she headed to the kitchen for a snack. In just a few weeks' time there'd be a wedding and lots of new people to meet. She didn't have to spend time with Dante. She could skirt around him between treatments; she'd do it. There was no excuse not to work hard and enjoy herself while she was here.

He felt peckish after his swim. Having checked the new ponies for the last time that day, he headed back to the house to find Maria baking in the kitchen, with Jess clearing up. Jess tensed when he walked in.

Helping himself to a handful of Maria's delicious *churros,* he watched the two women, marvelling at the speed with which they'd formed an easy friendship. He took years to get the measure of a man, and had no reason to get to know women in any depth. Since being misled about his parents' condition at the hospital, he'd found it hard to trust anyone outside his immediate family and staff. Jess was in the group marked pending.

He still remembered the vultures swooping at his parents' funeral, and how he and his siblings had quite literally stood back to back to defend from their greedy demands. The general thought had been that young headstrong youths couldn't hope to take care of themselves, let alone handle a family fortune and land. The scavengers soon learned that the Acostas might have been headstrong at one time, but duty had changed them for good. Some, like Maria, said the change was for the better. Others said not. One thing was sure. No one crossed them.

'I'll miss this woman when she leaves,' Maria told him in Spanish, distracting him as she fondly squeezed Jess's arm.

He grunted a response. His leg twinged. He flexed it.

Jess noticed.

'Better or worse?' she enquired, brushing a loose strand of hair back from her face.

'I haven't decided yet.' If anyone could look sexier with flour on their nose he had yet to meet them.

'I think you're feeling an improvement.'

'Oh, do you?' he said, indicating her nose.

She swiped at it. 'Better?'

'I think I liked it better before.'

His reward was her paint-stripping look.

'Didn't I give you exercises to do?' she prompted. 'Why are you here?'

'I choose to be.'

Their eyes met in a combative glance, accompanied by a now familiar tug in his groin. Jess's eyes had darkened. She could act professional all she liked, but Jess was a woman too.

'If you will excuse me?' he said politely as he made for the door. There was no rush. She was here for a month, and it was no longer a question of *if* Jess would yield to the hunger inside her, but how long it would take.

Stabbing his cane into the long-suffering yard, he conceded that even after one day of treatment his leg was beginning to show faint signs of improvement. He'd probably be stiff tomorrow, as Jess had predicted, but as she was around to sort it he wasn't too concerned. Anticipating more banter between them, he smiled. There was only one problem. Celibacy didn't suit him.

He took out his frustration in the gym. Boxing shorts, boots, strapped wrists, bandaged knuckles and a bandana to keep the sweat out of his eyes. He gave the bag hell. Jess had stressed no violent exercise, but Jess wasn't here. to hell with the programme. She should have taken his frustration into account.

And now he was aroused. He stopped, swore and resumed his vicious pounding until the heavy bag almost swung off the hook. Pausing to stare in the mirror, a monster stared back: Dante Acosta in his most primal form. He checked his leg with a scowl. It was still attached to his body. That was good enough for him.

Muscles pumped, his body covered in ink, signalling his

allegiance to team Lobos; there was nothing genteel about men who played polo at his level. Or the level at which he'd played before the accident, he grimly amended with an explosive curse. Retrieving the hated cane, he swung around to find Jess watching him. 'Yes?'

'I thought I told you not to exercise, apart from the regime I gave you. Did you forget, or do you still imagine you can go your own way?'

'As I did when I left hospital?' he suggested, easing his neck.

'Look where that got you,' Jess countered, hands on hips. 'You shouldn't be standing without a cane so soon, and you certainly shouldn't be putting so much pressure on your leg.'

'You put unnecessary pressure on my patience,' he snarled.

'So, get out? Leave me alone?' she suggested with a lift of her brow.

'You put the words into my mouth.'

He glared down. Jess lifted her chin. Daggers drawn, they stared at each other until he murmured, 'Well? Are you going to punish me?'

She shrugged. 'If I must, I will.' Her words were casual, but the sexual tension between them had soared. This wasn't Jess the therapist but Jess the sexually aware woman. Smiling faintly, he raised a brow and waited. Her blush deepened, as he knew it would, but that didn't stop her mouthing off. 'So the great Dante Acosta knows better than a trained professional?'

'I stand by all my decisions.'

'Stubbornness doesn't seem to have worked for you,' she observed coolly with a pointed look at his leg. Then her gaze tracked up to his half-naked torso. She studied the snarling wolf tattooed in all its dramatic splendour across his heart. 'If you care about your team at all, you should listen.'

'And obey?' he suggested with a tug of his mouth.

'If you don't co-operate you won't progress and I can't extend my contract.'

'Did I ask you to?'

'No,' she admitted. 'But you should know I'm very busy.'

'And likely to be more so,' he observed shrewdly, 'if you succeed in curing me.'

'True,' she admitted. 'But I do have other successes.'

'Or you wouldn't be here,' he pointed out.

'Don't mess up, Dante,' she warned. 'I really think we're getting somewhere with your leg.'

It was good to see her tiger claws. To walk again without a limp, and play world class polo, was all he wanted, and Jess's expression was absolutely firm.

'What do you want from me, Jess?' he asked as he swung a towel around his neck. 'What do you really want? You could have refused to treat me—recommended someone else. I'm not easy, and that's putting it mildly. You must have known you were taking a chance on complications after our encounter all those years ago.'

'If by complications you mean that foolhardy kiss...'

He hadn't expected her to be so blunt.

'I've come a long way since then. I'm a lot older, and successful in my own right. I viewed the chance to work on your leg as an interesting and challenging opportunity. Curing you remains my aim. It's not such a coincidence that your family hired me, or that you saved my family farm by buying up the best of the breeding stock. The Acostas and Jim Slatehome have a history of trust that extends back a number of years. I'm part of that.'

'So your agreeing to treat me had nothing to do with money, publicity, sex or bragging rights?'

'Correct,' she said with a huff of disbelief. 'Wow,' she

added. 'You really do have a high opinion of yourself. You're not my only celebrity client. And if I wanted sex it wouldn't be here, and it wouldn't be with you.'

'You sure about that?'

'Let's get one thing straight. My focus remains returning you to full fitness. I don't accept *if*, only when you are cured. You may not like my regime. You may not like me, but that's irrelevant because if you do as I suggest you will be cured, if a cure is at all possible.'

Jess was all heat and anger as she stared into his eyes, but then, as if she'd been clinging to the edge of a cliff with her fingertips, she exhaled and closed her eyes. The result should be inevitable. It might have been, had he been a different man.

CHAPTER NINE

HAD SHE REALLY been that close to falling under the notorious Acosta spell? Her body confirmed the lapse by softening and yearning.

Dante made it easy to snap out of the slip when he murmured, 'You think I want to kiss you now?'

'I'm just hoping and praying that you see sense.' They had to work together, and it was crucial for Dante's injury that there were no more interruptions in his treatment.

His harsh laugh suggested there was no warmth inside him, but they had both suffered loss and unimaginable grief, and that could so often lead to closing down feelings. She wasn't exactly a dab hand at showing emotion herself. Since her mother's death it had been a relief to lose herself in work, where caring for the individual was paramount, and personal feelings had no place. Dante was challenging her isolation, making Jess want things she had never believed possible, like learning to love and daring to show it, and having the courage to lay her heart on the line.

Maybe they could help each other.

In another universe, she concluded. One where she wasn't a medical professional treating a patient, and Dante actually wanted to lower the barricade he'd built around his heart.

She jerked to attention when he spoke. 'Tired?' she queried. 'I guess I'm running on fumes too. Could I join you in town tomorrow, though, after our morning session?'

'So you do need something from me,' he remarked dryly.

'Yes, I could do with some advice on what to buy Maria for her wedding. She's invited me. I don't have anything to wear, or a gift to give the bride.'

'You don't have to give her anything. You weren't to know about this. You've just arrived from England. I'm sure Maria doesn't expect a gift.'

'That's not the point. I wouldn't dream of turning up without something nice after all her kindness to me. And I can't go dressed like this...' Jess ran a hand down her scrubs. 'This is all I've got with me, apart from spare uniforms and gear for riding.'

Dante dismissed her concerns with a shrug. 'Order what you like and I'll pay for it. The gift too.'

'That's not how it works,' she informed him bluntly. 'I set my own budget. The gift for Maria must come from my pocket, not yours.'

Dante's impatience showed itself again. 'You wouldn't be borrowing anything from me. Just think of it as a bonus on your charges.'

'Your brothers and sister have already paid me.' *But not danger money*, Jess thought as Dante speared her with an impatient stare. He was wealth-blind, and didn't have a clue how patronising he sounded sometimes. 'If it's not convenient to take me into town, just say so. Maybe I can borrow a car or a bike?'

'A bike?' he queried. 'Why not take a horse? You could tether it to the nearest lamppost while you shop.'

'Is there a bus?'

'No,' he said flatly. 'We're deep in the countryside and the nearest town is around twenty miles away. Why the rush? Must you go tomorrow?'

'It seems like a good opportunity. I'd like to start looking for a gift sooner rather than later, so if I don't find anything tomorrow I can always try again.'

'Nothing daunts you, does it?' he remarked.

'You'd better hope not,' she countered.

'I'll take you into town. Get some sleep. We leave first thing.'

'After your treatment,' she reminded him.

'At seven we leave.'

'Deal,' she said happily. It would be tight, but she'd make it work.

The next morning's physio went without a hitch—when you were on the clock there was no time for banter. There would be chance for plenty of that on their journey into town, Jess anticipated as they set off, but she would confine herself to bland remarks and try not to look too hard at Dante.

The sparring didn't take long to start.

'You shop, and then I'll take you to lunch,' he stated.

'There's no need. I imagined you'd drop me—'

'Over a cliff?' he suggested.

'In town, close to the shops,' she said evenly, refusing to rise to the bait. 'And don't worry. I'll make my own way back. A taxi or something.'

'Am I driving too fast? Are you frightened?'

Not of his driving, though Dante's skilful handling of the low-slung muscle car as it blazed a trail down the tarmac was surely at the limit of what was possible. 'I'm not frightened of anything.'

'Except yourself,' Dante suggested as she remembered to release her fingers from the edge of the seat. 'Don't worry. I won't hold you to my schedule.'

'I'm not worried, but you really don't have to buy lunch. I'm not dressed for somewhere fancy.'

'Am I?'

She had vowed not to look at him, study him, drink him

in, but Dante had just made that pledge impossible. Even in jeans and a form-fitting top, he could go anywhere and be treated royally. With a body made for sin and a face to launch a thousand fantasies, Dante's piratical good looks would open any door.

'Can I trust you not to get lost?' he said when they arrived in town. 'Or had I better show you around first?'

'I'm sure I can manage,' she said, holding up her phone. It was time to escape from temptation.

Unfolding his formidable frame with annoying ease from the confines of the vehicle, Dante swore, retrieved his cane and swore again. Then, with a jerk of his chin, he led the way. She maintained space between them, but the streets were crowded. There seemed to be some sort of festival going on.

'It's market day,' Dante explained. 'Anything goes. Any excuse for a party.'

Jess glanced down at herself self-consciously. She certainly wasn't dressed for a *fiesta*. She'd had a quick shower and changed her clothes after Dante's treatment session, but her hair remained tied back and she was still make-up-free. She yelped as he held her back as a motorbike with a youth on board roared past within inches of her toes. Dante's touch was like an incendiary device to her senses.

'Careful,' he advised. 'You must remember what it was like to be a teenager—wild, reckless, risk-taking?' Her cheeks burned up as he added, 'There'll be a lot of them around today.'

'They grow up,' she said tensely.

'Some of them very well,' he agreed with a long, steady look. 'What made you decide to be a physiotherapist?'

It was a relief to have a question to answer. 'I promised my mother I'd finish my studies, whatever happened. I always had an interest in sports-related injuries, and equine sports in particular. When she died it made sense to have regular money coming in. My father went to pieces. I could help him.'

'So you tore yourself in two, working in London and spending your spare time on the farm.'

'I was lucky to land such a prestigious job,' she argued. 'I didn't want to leave my father, but my friends in the village promised to keep an eye on him. We needed the money, and I'd promised my mother. We all do what we must.'

'Your father's very lucky.'

'And so am I,' Jess insisted. 'My father was the first to encourage me to take the post. He reminded me of my mother's wishes, saying they were as one in that, and he'd never forgive himself if I stayed in the village because of him.'

'He struggled that much alone that you would have needed to?'

Jess hesitated, but then drew herself up tall. She was so lovely, Dante reflected, and so very proud. 'He loved my mother very much. It was…hard. I guessed he was lonely, so I returned home permanently. If it hadn't been for the help of the local village, I don't know what we'd have done. While I was freelancing, one of our neighbours would make sure to keep him company, and somehow we made it work.'

'Did London fulfil your expectations? Do you want to go back?'

'To living in one room in someone else's house?' She laughed. 'Don't get me wrong—the job was brilliant. I learned so much and had the most wonderful colleagues. I made lots of friends…'

'I'm sure you did.' There was an edge to Dante's voice. What did he imagine she meant?

'The type of friends you share a pizza with, maybe pick up some restricted-view seats in the West End to see a show.'

'Sounds…'

'Interesting?' she suggested with a grin. 'You've got no idea. It was fun and it was formative. You don't need money to enjoy life. And I appreciate the quiet of Yorkshire and the peace of your *estancia* so much more now. The calm certainty and trust in the eyes of the animals we both love is enough for me. And yes, London's hectic and crowded, but it's fabulous too. There's so much to see, and not all of it has to be paid for. I always think that people like me with hardly any money can have the very best of London at their fingertips.'

Dante frowned. 'How's that?'

'There are so many opportunities available if you search them out. Loads of places are free to visit. There are beautiful parks and glorious buildings, and the river—' Was she boring him with her ultimate guide to the simple life? Dante's life was so very far removed from Jess's experience, it was hard to tell.

But his life on the ranch was low-key.

True, she conceded.

'Anyway, enough about me. Why don't we turn the spotlight on you?'

'I'd have to want you to do that,' Dante pointed out, 'and I don't.'

Undaunted, Jess pressed on. 'I don't imagine you have to hunt for parking spaces, catch a bus or miss the last Tube home.'

'I do have a house in London,' he revealed, 'but that doesn't mean I wouldn't like to see your side of London one day.'

'I'd be a flat-out liar if I didn't admit I'd like to see yours,' Jess admitted on a laugh.

'Are we talking compromise?' Dante enquired with a frown.

His expression was more amused than disapproving. 'We're talking,' she conceded with a smile.

Dante's sideways look made heat rush through her. 'It must have been hard for you.'

'No harder than it is for other people. What's hard about working alongside people I really liked and admired or being taught the skills that allow me to help people like you? I count that as a real privilege.'

'A vocation?'

'If you like.'

'You must miss your colleagues now you're self-employed.'

'We keep in touch, and I meet new people all the time. My life is rich and varied, so please don't feel sorry for me.' *It's one heck of a sight better than your life in your grass-fed ivory tower*, Jess concluded. Dante's inactivity was obviously eating away at him. She didn't need to be a medical professional to see that.

'So why physiotherapy?'

'Why specialise? It seemed an obvious choice. I grew up in the horse world where, like any extreme sport, there's always a need for medical professionals on standby. My skills allow me to work close to the animals I love, with the people surrounding them.'

'An introduction from me into the world of top-class polo wouldn't hurt your career,' Dante stated bluntly.

'No, it wouldn't,' she agreed, 'but that's a very cynical view. This isn't about me; it's about you, and returning you to fitness. I don't know who's used you in the past, but please don't tar me with the same brush. What you see is what you get with me. Take it or leave it.'

'But there's another side to your character.'

'Skylar?' she queried, cocking her head to one side to smile up. 'That's just a childhood nickname.'

'That suits you,' he said.

'Sometimes,' she agreed, 'but a name doesn't change me.'

'Just how you act,' he suggested.

'In a fortune-telling tent, maybe,' Jess conceded, 'but doesn't everyone have two sides to their character—private and public?'

He stared at her long and hard.

'There are a lot of genuine people out there,' she insisted, feeling she was being judged. 'You don't have to look any further than your ranch.'

'I hand-pick my staff.'

'While I was foisted on you?' Jess suggested lightly, but Dante didn't answer.

They had reached the main square. Guessing he must be desperate to break free, she suggested a plan. 'Leave me here. I'll take a cab back to the ranch.'

'I have something to drop off at my lawyer's office. You can shop while I do that, then we'll eat and I'll drive you back.'

A restaurant was a public place. There was no harm in eating with a patient and if he caught up with her shopping, Dante could advise on what Maria might like.

'Okay. I'll see you around here,' she agreed. 'But please, no swanky eateries. I'm not dressed for it; I'd feel uncomfortable.'

'I've got a restaurant in mind,' he informed her. 'Don't worry; it's casual. I think you'll like it.'

Nothing like her local greasy spoon, she guessed, but anything was fine by her.

She stood to watch as Dante made his way across the square. Taller than most, he was a standout figure. It was impossible for him to pass unnoticed. Plenty of people recognised him, and some asked for a photograph with the famous polo star. Not once did he swerve their attention or pretend not to see his fans. Dante behaved at all times with unfailing courtesy, as if he had all the time in the world to stand and chat. What she'd seen of him so far suggested Dante could be brooding and difficult, but who could blame him when he was reliant on a cane? This was the true side of him, she suspected, and it was a side she longed to see more of.

Caught out, she gasped when he swung around and pointed to her. The man he was talking to joined his hands together and shook them in the air, as if to praise and congratulate Jess. *We're not there yet*, she wanted to say. *We're a long way off.* But Dante telling people she was helping him gave her a thrill of pleasure that had nothing to do with boosting her CV.

Dante was back from his appointment before she knew it. She'd been so busy scouring the market stalls for likely gifts and trinkets she'd lost track of time. 'You haven't been away long.'

'Long enough to do what I needed to. That guy in the square,' he added, neatly side-stepping any potential questions, 'used to work for me before he retired. He asked how I was getting on, so I told him you'd get me back in the game.'

'That is my aim.'

'If I do as you say?' Dante suggested, dipping his head to direct a stare into her eyes.

'That will be the day,' she observed good-humouredly. 'But you will improve immeasurably. I'll make sure of it.'

'For some reason,' Dante confessed, 'I believe you.'

Having steered her towards a cobbled passageway leading off the square, Dante ushered her through a stone archway leading into a modest courtyard. Decorated with simple clay pots overflowing with flowers, the quaint wrought iron tables and chairs made eating outside a real treat for Jess at this time of year. But, to her disappointment, the restaurant was full. 'We can go somewhere else,' she suggested with a rueful shrug.

Dante's answer was to put his hand in the small of her

back and usher her forward to where a small, capable-looking woman, wearing a mob-cap-style chef's hat and a crisp white apron, was cooking up a storm on an outside grill.

Catching sight of them, she passed her dishes over to an assistant and bustled forward to greet them. 'Dante, *mi amor! Cómo estás?*'

Jess knew enough Spanish to understand that the chef was asking how Dante was getting on. Concern showed clearly in the woman's eyes. When she turned to shake hands with Jess, she clasped both of Jess's hands in hers when Dante explained that it was Jess who was treating his leg. 'Your poor leg,' she exclaimed in English for Jess's benefit. 'Still no improvement?'

'Some,' he said, 'according to Skylar here.'

'Skylar?' she queried, studying Jess. 'What an interesting name.'

'Chef Ana,' Dante explained, introducing them.

'It's more of a childhood nickname,' Jess explained to the cheery-faced older woman, 'but Señor Acosta likes to use it.'

'Does he now?' Chef Ana murmured. Her smile broadened as she glanced between them.

'We're hungry,' Dante stated, as if eager to break the spell.

'When are you not hungry?' Chef Ana commented with a shrug. 'It will take all your skills to heal him,' she added in a stage whisper to Jess, before adding in a far more discreet tone when Dante had turned away to greet the waiters he knew, 'Dante has wounds you cannot see.'

'I know,' Jess whispered back.

The two women exchanged a lingering glance as a table and chairs were hastily set up for Dante and Jess, and then, with a squeeze of Jess's shoulder, Chef Ana gave Jess one last smile and left them to it.

Chef Ana's food was absolutely delicious. Platters of

finger-food to share lightened the mood and made banter between Dante and Jess inevitable as they jousted for the last morsel of deliciousness. By the time the platters were empty all Jess's sensible resolutions had floated away. Was it even possible to sit across from Dante and not want their legs to touch or their fingers to brush, or their glances to meet and hold? With his hunger satisfied, Dante was a different man. Easy and charming, he made Jess relax to the point where she really believed they were beginning to know each other. She couldn't find much that was sensible in that, but if she were sensible what was she doing here?

Leaning back in his seat, Dante stared as he stretched out his legs. Part of her could have stayed like this all day, but her sensible head won through. 'What time does the market pack up?'

'Is that a hint?' he enquired.

'Yes,' Jess admitted, digging in her bag for some high value notes. It might be a small, modest-looking restaurant, but the food was top-class and the prices reflected this.

'Put your money away,' Dante insisted, but on this occasion she was too fast for him.

'I prefer to be independent,' she reminded him as she handed her money over to a waiter. 'You gave me a lift into town, so I pay for lunch. It's only fair.'

He seemed to find this amusing and exclaimed, '*Dios me salve de una mujer independiente!* God save me from an independent woman,' he translated when she gave him a look.

'You prefer a woman to be dependent?' It was a loaded question.

'Tell that to my sister and I'm a dead man,' he said. And Dante was smiling…laughing. 'I invited you to lunch, so I should pay.'

'Sounds to me as if you need more independent women in your life.'

'*Dios!* I have enough of them,' Dante exclaimed. Standing, he snatched up his cane. 'Okay, this is the deal. You pay for the meal, I pay for your dress.'

'Okay. But nothing fancy,' she insisted. 'And I buy Maria's wedding present with my own money. That's not up for discussion,' she added, 'though I would appreciate your advice as to what she might like.'

'We have a deal,' Dante confirmed.

This time Jess was sensible enough to nod rather than shake his hand and risk the consequences of touching him. 'I believe we do,' she agreed.

CHAPTER TEN

THE TOWN WAS more packed than ever by the time they left the restaurant. There were so many stalls she hadn't visited, Jess wasn't sure where to head first.

'Here,' Dante prompted, drawing her attention to a group of women on a stall full of beautifully crafted items.

She had set out to buy Maria's gift from what many would call a 'proper shop', but it soon became apparent that the items on the stall were unique. A tablecloth with drawn thread work was absolutely exquisite, but Jess doubted she could afford it. The cloth was so intricately worked the price would surely reflect the hours of dedication involved.

'Why don't we give it as a joint gift?' Dante suggested, seeing Jess's disappointment when she read the price tag.

'I couldn't do that,' she protested. Her mind raced as she considered how that might look.

'Why not?' he asked with a shrug.

She could give him a dozen good reasons. 'Don't worry; I'll find something else.'

'Here's another suggestion. Why don't I buy the cloth and you buy the napkins? You'd be helping me out,' Dante added. 'I don't have a clue what Maria might like, but I do know she loves to entertain, so this seems right to me.'

'And to me,' Jess agreed.

She loved the way Dante's mouth tugged up when he got his own way, but this suited her too, Jess reminded herself as they completed the transaction. She truly hoped Maria would love the tablecloth as much as Jess did.

More people recognised Dante as they left the stall. He stopped to chat, which gave Jess the chance to pick up some more things from neighbouring stalls.

'Have you found a dress?' he asked when the pack around him moved on.

'Not yet.'

'Follow me.'

How many times had he done this? she wondered before scolding herself for being so obviously jealous. Was it likely the type of glamorous women Dante was renowned for dating would pick out their clothes from a market stall?

He took her to what turned out to be the most popular outlet on the market. 'My sister loves this stall,' he explained, which put Jess firmly back in her box.

'Your sister has excellent taste.'

'Yes, she does. And I'm sure Skylar would approve.'

The clothes were certainly more colourful than Jess would usually choose, but no less attractive for that. There was no harm in combining Skylar and Jess for a harmless day out shopping, Jess decided. Her father sometimes accused her of not having a life outside work, and this was her chance to prove him wrong. She longed to try on something different, and Dante had predicted Skylar's taste to a tee. Her gaze did linger on a sensible mid-length tea dress, but that was definitely out of the running, she realised as Dante shook his head.

'You don't seriously expect me to wear one of these?' she protested when he handed over his selection. They were flirty and flimsy and quite definitely eye-catching, when Jess's preferred choice would suit a mouse.

His mother used to say he was an old soul, Dante remembered. He called it intuition. With no idea how he knew things in advance of them happening, he just accepted that he did. His gift was invaluable today when it came to choosing an outfit for Jess. 'We'll take the red dress,' he stated before Jess had chance to argue. That was the one she wanted. She could stare all she liked at the dull, sensible dress, but he wasn't buying it. As if to confirm his decision, her gaze strayed again to the racy red.

'Seriously?' she exclaimed. 'But that's the most expensive dress on the stall.'

'You want it, don't you?'

'What about this one?' she suggested, pointing to the dowdy offering she thought she should have.

'I'm not buying a dress for my grandmother.' And his decision was final.

The bright red dress with its spaghetti straps and a length barely south of decent was perfect for Jess, in his opinion. Handing over the cash, he ignored Jess's complaint that the dress was too short, too revealing, and that she'd probably catch a chill. 'This is the south of Spain, not the wild moors of Yorkshire,' he said as he pressed the package into her hands. 'And you want this one,' he pointed out with a shrug. 'Why pretend otherwise? We'll take the shawl too,' he told the stallholder, indicating an exquisitely worked length of smoke-grey lace. 'For decency's sake at the ceremony,' he explained to Jess. 'And for when it grows cool in the evening.'

'But the shawl's even more expensive than the dress,' she protested. 'I can't possibly accept these gifts when you've picked out the two priciest items on the stall.'

'You don't want them?' His expression remained deadpan.

'I can't accept them,' Jess insisted, tightening her lips.

'Hard luck. They're paid for. They're yours.'

'Ask for your money back,' she pleaded as he walked

away. 'Please, Dante,' she begged, chasing after him. 'Don't embarrass me like this.'

'The stallholder's packing up.'

'Then catch her before she leaves!'

'So she loses the last sale of the day? Is that what you want?'

Jess deflated in front of his eyes. She was far too considerate to allow that to happen. 'Well, you shouldn't have done this,' she said with a shake of her head.

'I can. I did. And I should,' he argued. 'After all, you have to put up with me.'

'There is that,' she murmured dryly, 'though I'm determined to pay you back.'

As they passed the impromptu dance floor in the middle of the square, one of the local bands struck up. 'If you insist on paying me back, do so with a dance. It would be a great boost to my self-esteem.'

Like that needed a boost, he reflected with irony. 'It would prove your therapy's working.' True. It would also ease the ache in his groin. He had to put his hands on her soon, or he'd go mad. Delay might be the servant of pleasure, but it was also an aching test of his endurance.

'I can't dance,' Jess protested. 'I've got two left feet.'

'What about my self-esteem?' He delivered the words deadpan, with just the right edge of vulnerability in his tone to appeal to Jess's generous nature.

Her cheeks flushed pink. 'Put like that...'

'You can't refuse,' he confirmed.

'But just one dance,' Jess insisted with a concerned look in her eyes. 'You've been on your feet a lot today.'

He'd settle for that. 'I'll put your parcels behind the bar, and then we'll dance. If I feel the strain, I'll lean on you.'

He'd gone too far and she laughed. 'That'll be the day!' she exploded. 'But I do owe you for steering me towards such beautiful gifts.'

'That's right,' he confirmed, 'you do.' *Now, let's get on with it*, he silently urged. But his attitude towards Jess soon mellowed when he reviewed the sincerity in her eyes when she thanked him. Was he the first man to treat Jess as a woman should be treated? She should be spoiled. Jess had been working her ass off for years. What was wrong with cutting loose now and then?

'The dress wasn't a gift; it was a necessity,' he insisted. 'I brought you here—I landed you in this—'

'Fabulous and unexpected wedding invitation with a lovely new friend,' Jess interjected.

'Agreed. But you have to wear something at the wedding, apart from jodhpurs or scrubs.'

'True,' she conceded, smiling. 'And I'm thrilled to have such a pretty dress to wear at Maria's wedding, and I'm very grateful—'

'You don't have to be grateful. You've earned it. If there's a shortfall…' he pretended to ponder this '… I'll make sure you earn it. Does that salve your delicate conscience, and soothe your touchy pride?'

She shrugged ruefully. 'Whether I'll have the courage on the day to wear that particular dress remains to be seen,' she admitted with a grin. 'And I can't see it coming in handy at the farm.'

'Skylar would wear it,' he remarked.

'Yes, but she's a shameless hussy whose only skill is telling fortunes,' she dismissed.

'Can she dance?'

Jess's kissable lips pressed down as she considered this. 'Skylar can dance,' she confirmed.

'Just to be clear, when we hit the dance floor, am I dancing with Skylar or Jess?'

'Which would you prefer?'

'A freestyle combination of the two.'

'I'll have to see what we can do,' Jess offered with a grin.

'Knock yourself out.'

'I'll try to make things interesting,' she promised.

His lips curved. 'That's what I expect.'

But the best laid plans, et cetera, et cetera...

They'd barely reached the dance floor when his leg cramped. Seeing his grimace, Jess quickly reverted to professional in a trice and found him a seat. Kneeling on the cobbles in front of him, completely unconcerned by the people who had gathered to watch, she worked on the spasm, oblivious to everything but easing his pain.

Hell. This was not how he'd planned the evening to end.

'Better?' she asked, gazing up at him with concern.

'Much better,' he admitted in an ungracious low growl.

'No dancing for you,' she told him. 'It's time to go. That cramp was a warning. I'll get the rest of our things—' She handed him the cane.

He had never hated it more. 'I can manage without your assistance.'

Jess opened her mouth to reply, then thought better of it and stood back while he levered himself up.

They didn't speak a word for the first part of the journey home. He was in a foul mood, thanks to the cramp in his leg, and Jess had more sense than to attempt conversation. At least she showed more sense to begin with...

'You have to accept that your leg will take time to heal,' she ventured after they'd covered a few tense blocks. 'There will be setbacks, sometimes when you least expect them.'

'Thanks for the advice. Can we leave it now?' To emphasise the point he played some music. Jess talked over it.

'You're not invincible, Dante. You're a man, you're injured and you hurt. That isn't something to be embarrassed about.'

'Embarrassed?' he spat out with affront.

'If you tell me as soon as you get these cramps, maybe I can help.'

'Like you have done so far?' he derided.

'You're in pain now,' she intuited, 'so, rather than take it out on me, stop the car and let me drive.'

A short incredulous laugh shot out of him 'Are you serious?'

'Never more so,' she stated bluntly. 'It isn't a weakness to admit you need help. Open up. Trust someone—'

'Trust you?'

She blushed, but that didn't stop her asking, 'Why not? You have to start somewhere.'

'That's rich, coming from you, Jess. And no, you can't change places with me, either to drive this vehicle or to see things the way I do. So let's just agree to disagree and restrict our comments in future to subjects connected to my treatment.'

'Fine by me,' she bit out.

'Good.'

'Good,' she echoed before sinking back in her seat.

His mood didn't improve. If anything, it grew worse. If it hadn't been for the setback with his leg, he would be planning to mark the successful business deal he'd signed off at his lawyers round about now.

With Jess?

The connection between them was undeniable, but they were worlds apart. She deserved more than he could give—more than he wanted to give. Casual relationships suited him. His siblings were the one constant in his life. He doubted he'd ever be tempted to extend his family. After the tragedy of his parents' death, he chose to fiercely protect what he had.

He glanced across at Jess. They couldn't avoid each other. He needed more treatment, and they'd meet socially at Maria's wedding, where he'd be polite, nothing more. His world was constructed around practicality with no space for pointless emotion. A good night's sleep should sort him out, he reasoned as they hit the highway and headed out of town. He'd attend Jess's therapy sessions religiously, and he'd be civil when they met away from the treatment couch, so when Jess's contract ended he'd say goodbye without regret.

Jess felt the need to beat herself up. How could a day that had started so well end so badly? She and Dante were further apart than they had ever been, which made it hard, if not impossible, to work with him. If she didn't have Dante's trust she had nothing, and right now the gulf between them felt wider than ever.

What more did she want?

To put it another way: what more could she expect? Try nothing and she'd be close. Dante had spelled out exactly what he wanted and expected of her, which was for Jess to heal him in the shortest time possible.

Frustrated by Dante's impatience, for which she had no answer, and by the black cloud surrounding them, Jess realised that she was gripping the packages they'd bought on the market as if they were comfort blankets. She desperately wanted Dante to be free from the shackles of his past. The loss of his parents was a scar he'd wear for ever, but would his parents have wanted him to pay a penance for their death every day of his life? She refused to believe it, but how could she help when Dante had shut her out? Perhaps he was right to do so and being professional from now on *was* the only way forward.

When Dante was under her hands on the treatment couch later that evening she marvelled at the miracle of healing. It had nothing to do with rich or poor, privileged or not, and had everything to do with training. Staring down at one of the most brutally physical men on the planet, currently resting on his stomach buck naked with the small exception of the towel she'd placed across his buttocks, she realised it was possible to separate her two selves and concentrate solely on healing. Manipulating his muscles until she felt the knots release was all the satisfaction she would ever need.

Was it? her cynical inner voice demanded.

It had to be.

'Well done,' she said, standing back when the session was over. 'That can't have been much fun.'

'Fun?' Turning over, he grimaced. 'If torture is fun, that was hilarious. You're a lot stronger than you look.'

Wasn't that the truth? Helping her father out of his financial difficulties was only half the story. When her mother died he took to drink, thinking this might numb the pain. But it was still there in the morning, only now he had a hangover to cope with, while Jess changed his sheets, washed his clothes and begged him to please take a shower. She suspected that these were secrets many other families were forced to keep.

As much as it had hurt like hell, the whole sorry experience had made her strong: physically strong as well as mentally robust. The first time she'd picked him up off the stairs, she'd strained her back. A refresher class in recovering unconscious patients from the floor had reminded her of techniques she should use to avoid injury. One step at a time, she'd told herself as she came to grips with caring for the broken man her father had become. 'One step at a time,' she'd whispered when he sobbed in her arms.

Now, thanks to the sale of the ponies, those dark nights were behind him and her father was back on top. He'd stopped drinking and took a shower every day. The washing machine went back to its regular cycle. Jess rejoiced to see him recover, but if she was totally honest she could see that being strong for her father had left her with no time to grieve. Just as well, she determined, firming her jaw. She had responsibilities, and a job to do, which she was good at.

What had caused the shadows in Jess's eyes? Dante reflected. Had someone hurt her?

Dante didn't invite questions into his life, and if Jess wanted to tell him she would. He wasn't used to dealing with women who had so many onion skins to peel away before their true self was revealed, or maybe he'd never had the time or the inclination to do so before. Compared to Jess, those other women seemed like mannequins to him now. Jess was real—so real he missed the rapport they'd shared before their spat in the car. Their banter enlivened him, lifted him, and the pointless argument had been largely down to him and his frustration at not snapping back to full fitness immediately. That wasn't Jess's fault. She was doing her best to help.

'Don't rush off,' he said as she packed up her kit. Swinging off the couch, he tested his leg…not too bad. 'A lot of water has passed beneath the bridge since that kitten peed down your front, and you've shared so little with me.'

'While you've been incredibly forthcoming,' Jess observed dryly.

'Touché,' he conceded with a shrug and a smile. Then, after another few moments, he added, 'I apologise.'

That stopped her dead in her tracks. 'I'm sorry?'

'I was unreasonable in the car.'

'You were in pain.'

He didn't want understanding; he wanted a return to the up and down relationship they'd shared before. That was never boring. Professional civility was borderline. 'We can continue to snipe at each other or—'

'I must have stank in that stable,' she said, softening into the woman he wanted to know better. 'Belated apologies,' she added.

'For caring for a kitten?' He grinned. 'Apology unnecessary.'

'They were cute, weren't they…?'

She looked wistful as she thought back, no doubt remembering her mother alongside her in the barn, introducing her to the miracle of birth and teaching her how to care for kittens. How lovely she was.

'I have to go,' she said, breaking the spell. 'Apologies again, but I can't stay to chat. I promised Maria I'd call by to see if there's anything I can do to help with the wedding.'

'That's very kind of you.'

'I am kind.'

Yes, she was, and he'd almost lost her. Even now it was as if the connection between them had been reduced to the slimmest of threads. He wanted to kiss her, reassure her, and banish that sad look in her eyes, but not yet. This was not the time.

'Dante?' she queried. 'What are you thinking? You look so far away, yet so intense.'

He snapped to immediately. 'Just thinking about your charity event.'

'It was a good day, wasn't it?'

'A very good day. Successful, I hope?'

'Massively,' she admitted. 'Mostly thanks to you.'

He shrugged this off. 'It was your day. You organised it.' Jess was always thinking up ways to help others. Why hadn't someone helped Jess?

'The main thing to me is that it lifted my father.'

He nodded in agreement. Everyone in the horse world knew the saga of Jim Slatehome, and how the great man had been devastated by the death of his childhood sweetheart. When his wife had died Jim had gone to ground and hadn't been seen for several seasons. Surely someone must have noticed that Jess was reeling too? He guessed she'd put on a brave face because that was who she was.

Her father had relied on her completely, and anything Jess had achieved personally, or for him, was a result of sheer willpower and grit. She didn't deserve to be abandoned now with no one to confide in.

'Three sessions tomorrow,' she reminded him brightly before she turned to go.

'Am I supposed to cheer?' he asked dryly.

'You're supposed to get up bright and early and set your mind to accepting three sessions a day from now on. If you attend each one and follow my exercise regime, I predict that in around a month you'll be back on your feet without that cane.'

His stare followed Jess as she walked away. There was such an air of purpose in her stride. He couldn't go right ahead and seduce her because Jess was special, unique, precious and oh, so tender beneath her onion skins of professionalism and grit. There weren't many he held in high regard outside his immediate family, but Jess Slatehome was right up there.

CHAPTER ELEVEN

A LOT COULD happen in a month. The run-up to Maria's wedding seemed to fly by. Jess had grown to feel at home on the ranch. In her free time she helped out wherever she could.

Dante had been as good as his word, attending each treatment session promptly, before fulfilling his quota of exercises as diligently as Jess could have wished for a patient.

She did a lot of wishing that month—that their banter could progress beyond amusing and superficial to something deeper, and that the man beneath her hands might somehow wake up one day to find her totally irresistible. This led to a lot of sleepless nights, but if she hoped for Dante to act on the ever-strengthening bond of friendship between them she was to be disappointed.

They learned more about each other for sure, but the facts remained these: Dante worked on his leg. She worked on him.

He rode more and more, which was amazing to see, while she made notes on his progress, revelled in his surprisingly wide-ranging library, walked the ranch, rode out on her own, which was what she was used to in Yorkshire, and spent time with Maria, who was the closest thing to a sister Jess had ever had.

And today was the morning of the wedding.

Jess stood, hand clasped to her mouth in shock, in the

middle of Maria's cosy sitting room. 'Me? Be your brides-maid? Are you serious?'

Jess was overwhelmed, while Maria was clearly em-barrassed at having to ask Jess at the last moment to stand in for her one and only bridesmaid, who had gone down with a bad cold. 'It's such an honour! I can't believe it. Of course I'll hold your flowers at the crucial moment. I'll do anything I can. Are you sure? Isn't there anyone else you'd like to ask?'

Maria bit down on her lip. 'Can I be completely honest?'

'Of course,' Jess said warmly.

Pulling a face, Maria laughed and blushed. 'You're the only one who'll fit into the dress.'

Jess's peal of laughter set Maria off. 'I can't think of a better reason,' Jess admitted as the two women hugged.

'But the best reason of all,' Maria said in all serious-ness when they parted, 'is that I like you and trust you to do this for me.'

'Then I'm honoured and thrilled to accept,' Jess con-firmed. 'Do you think I should try on the dress, just to be sure it fits?'

'Of course…'

Crossing the room, Maria returned with a dream of a gown.

'This is so beautiful,' Jess breathed in awe. The deli-cate confection comprised of lace and tulle and was lovely enough for any bride to wear on her wedding day.

'I hope you like it?' Maria asked with concern.

'I love it.' Jess sighed as she stroked the peach lace and chiffon. 'I've never had the chance to wear anything like this.'

'Wait until you see my wedding dress,' Maria exclaimed happily. 'Señor Acosta insisted that the gowns came from Paris, so he flew me and my mother there, saying she must have a special outfit too.'

'He's very generous,' Jess murmured thoughtfully.

'Oh, yes, he is,' Maria enthused. 'Everything was hand-made in the atelier of a very famous designer.'

'If only he weren't so obstinate and remote. If he just let people in and...' Her voice tailed away. Maria was looking at her as if she sympathised and yet wanted Jess to come to some conclusion by herself.

'I'm sorry,' Jess said gently. 'He's always been kind to both of us. I didn't mean to criticise him—especially not to you, and not on the morning of your wedding. How selfish you must think me.'

'Not at all.' Maria took Jess's hands in hers and held them tightly. 'Like you, he's hurt and scarred by loss and, like you, he says nothing. Both of you lose yourselves in work, and it's only this accident that forced Dante to pause and take a proper look around at things that matter. Like you—'

'Me?' Jess exclaimed incredulously.

'Can't you see it? Can't you see how much he needs you—how much you need him? You complete each other. You're the missing parts to each other's heart. Perhaps I can see it clearly because I have The Sight, but you do too, don't you... Skylar?'

Jess smiled crookedly as she stared into the eyes of a woman she trusted like no other. 'Who told you my mother's name for me?'

'Dante. He doesn't open up very often, but when he does and I see the man behind the scars I love him like a brother. Neither of you is looking for pity, Jess, I know that, but what you should be looking for is love to fill the hollow in your heart.'

They hugged and then Maria whispered, 'Okay now?'

'Okay,' Jess confirmed, burying her face in Maria's shoulder. 'And so honoured that you've asked me to be part of your special day. Are you sure you trust me to wear this?'

she asked as they broke apart and Maria took the beautiful gown she wanted Jess to wear off its hanger.

Jess viewed the intricately worked creation with awe. The beading was so delicate, and the cut of the gown so flattering it belonged in a costume museum rather than on the sturdy body of a hill farmer's daughter.

'Of course I'm sure,' Maria stated firmly. 'You'll look beautiful. Pale peach is the perfect foil for your fiery auburn hair.'

'I'll take good care of it,' Jess promised, vowing silently not to step on the hem and rip it, or snag the beading with her ragged nails.

As if reading her concerns, Maria added, 'Señor Acosta has arranged a beautician and a hairdresser to attend me, and I hope you'll join in the fun. I'm guessing you're not used to that sort of thing any more than I am. It would give me confidence,' she insisted. 'Señor Acosta has made the premier guest suite on his *estancia* available for our use.'

'I... Oh...'

What was wrong with getting changed into a bridal outfit in Dante's house, apart from the fact that it was a reminder that Jess had no happy occasion on the horizon, or anywhere close, for that matter?

'It would really help me,' Maria said, having no doubt interpreted Jess's expression as stage fright. 'Neither of us is used to dressing up in such finery, but I'd feel so much better if you'd share this experience with me. I'd really value your honest opinion.'

'You can be sure of it,' Jess promised warmly. This was Maria's day and she'd give her all to it.

Dante had offered to act as father of the bride and give Maria away, but Maria had refused, saying she would walk herself down the aisle. Maria's attitude reminded him why he had hired her. No-nonsense and capable in so many ways, Maria, in turn, reminded him of Jess, a woman he confidently expected to appear at any moment, dressed in a provocative slip of a bright red dress. It was too late to wonder why he hadn't agreed to purchase Jess's staid choice, which would at least have given him chance to relax.

As if by some silent signal the excited chatter surrounding him died down. There was a rustle of best clothes as everyone stood up. A few more tense seconds passed and then a guitar began to strum, announcing the arrival of the bride. A collective sigh went up, but Dante was facing forward. He was no romantic and was more concerned about Jess's absence. The seat he had saved for her was still empty. Was something wrong?

He focused his attention of Manuel, Maria's soon-to-be husband. The man appeared to be overwhelmed with emotion. He'd never seen Manuel cry. He might well cry with a lifetime of hen-pecking ahead of him, Dante reflected.

A waft of unbelievably agreeable perfume accompanied by the rustle of delicate fabric finally forced him to turn around. To say he was stunned by Maria's arrival would be seriously understating the case. But he was looking past Maria to her one and only bridesmaid, Señorita Jessica Slatehome.

This was Jess as he'd never seen her before. Dressed in a gown so ethereal and lovely it belonged in a painting rather than on a living, breathing woman—or it would have done, had that woman not been Jess. He was also struck by the fact that Jess had made no attempt to overshadow the bride. He'd seen that before, but Jess had chosen to wear very little make-up, and must have directed the hairdresser to draw her hair back demurely at the nape of her neck, rather than allow it to cascade down her back in all its fiery rippling glory. She wore no jewellery to catch the eye, though it occurred to him she might have none to wear...

Sensing his interest, she turned her head to look at him.

Her face was perfectly composed, though her emerald eyes held enough of Skylar to make him anticipate the rest of the day even more than he had expected.

And then she was gone.

Moving on down the aisle until she came to a halt behind the bride and groom, Jess shattered his honourable resolutions and left Dante counting the seconds until he could be with her again.

Jess hadn't been to many weddings, and though she had a few ideas about the high-octane atmosphere on such occasions she could never have anticipated the level of testosterone at this one. Dante's wranglers were young, tough and high-spirited, while Maria's relatives were *gitanos*, experts in the art of flamenco with their own customs and language.

Maria's people had enriched Spanish culture for centuries with their valuable contribution of music and dance and finely crafted wares, and many of the young women who had travelled down from their mountain villages were extremely beautiful. Safe to say, Dante's ranch hands were on full alert.

Dante had instructed his people to erect the marquee on the paddock closest to his ranch house. The path leading up to it was lined with candles and flowers while the inside of the tent was a riot of music, excited guests, colourful clothes and flashing jewellery. Blooms so perfect they hardly looked real filled the air with exotic scent, but what touched Jess the most was the sight of the toughest men with their recently smoothed-down hair and newly shaven faces. All except for Dante, who had gone for his customary rugged look, and who, apart from his dark, custommade suit, managed to look as swarthy and as dangerous as he ever had.

Concentrating fiercely on Maria so as not to be distracted by him, Jess found tears pricking the back of her eyes. Maria had never looked more beautiful in a wedding gown that gave more than a passing nod to the flamenco tradition of her kin. It would be no exaggeration to say that Maria had been transformed from diligent housekeeper to fairy tale bride.

Who didn't love a wedding? She couldn't help but glance at Dante, and there was her answer. Maria had already told her he'd refused a seat of honour at the front, as Dante believed that was where Maria's relatives should be seated. In a position halfway down the aisle, he was already restless. Dragging her attention away, she was just in time to take Maria's bridal bouquet as the ceremony began.

Incense swirled while soft words of praise were spoken, though through it all an underlying tension and discreet glances suggested the congregation's thoughts were already turning to more earthly pleasures.

When the ceremony ended Maria called out excitedly, 'I'm married! I'm married!'

To which her new husband replied in a rather different tone, '*Terminado! Ya he terminado!* I'm done for! I'm done for!' which set the entire place rolling with laughter.

'You may kiss the bride…'

The poor priest battled in vain to restore order to a congregation that was more interested in partying. Everyone was on their feet, cheering and applauding, while Maria, being tiny, disappeared completely behind a wall of guests. The first intimation Jess received that the bride was safe was when the bridal bouquet came sailing over the human barricade to land squarely in the centre of her chest. Cradling it close to keep it from being trampled, she backed straight into a roadblock that turned out to be Dante Acosta.

'I'm getting you out of here before you're squashed to a pulp,' he informed her.

'You're not using your stick.'

'Thanks for reminding me,' Dante growled as he forged a passage for them through the crowd. The throng parted like the Red Sea to allow him through, and it was only when he had her safe on the fringes that Dante relaxed and turned to face her. 'You sure you're okay?'

'Thanks to you, even Maria's bouquet made it through.'

'You know what this means, don't you?' Dante prompted as he stared at the lush arrangement Jess was holding close to her heart.

'Maria can dry the flowers and keep them?' Jess suggested, tongue in cheek.

Dante huffed at this. 'Trust you to strip the romance out of it.'

'Me?' Jess queried. 'Like you're so romantic?'

'I do have my moments, given half a chance.'

Excitement and jealousy roiled inside her. It was a flippant remark. Dante made it while they were eyeballing each other, but it was enough to rouse Jess. Neither emotion was appropriate, so she quickly moved on to professional concerns. 'Where's your cane?'

'Thanks to you, I don't need it so much.'

'You'll need it tonight. You'll be on your feet a lot.'

Dante speared her with a look. 'Okay, *señorita*, so I left it by the table. Is that good enough for you?'

'You're learning,' she approved, holding his fierce look steadily.

'I've got the best of teachers,' Dante conceded with a look that sizzled its way through her veins, leaving her breathless.

Approachable Dante was far more dangerous than grim Dante, Jess concluded. His smile and the way he dipped his head to whisper in her ear made all her good intentions turn bad.

'Aren't the decorations lovely?' she blurted in a lame attempt to distract them both from the sexual tension between them. The boisterous congregation had spilled out of the seating area in front of the altar, which meant the quiet place Dante had found for them would soon be swamped.

'These pine cones remind me of home at Christmas,' she admitted wistfully as they moved on to the shade of an awning decorated with swags and bows.

'Maria's people brought them from the mountains where they live. It was Maria's dream to have everything reflect her heritage today.'

'Which you've helped her achieve, and beautifully.'

'She's worth it. I'd trust Maria with my life.'

'What will you do for Christmas?' Maria had explained she was taking time off for a honeymoon, so there would be no one else living in the house, as far as she knew. 'Will you join family?'

'Why are you so interested?'

Jess shrugged. 'I'm not. I just don't like to think of people being alone at such a special time of year. I'd never leave my father at Christmas, but don't worry, your treatment can safely be handed over by then,' she hurried to reassure Dante. 'And if you stick to your regime you could be back on the polo field by New Year.'

Breath shot from her lungs as Dante lifted her up in his arms. Until she realised he was moving her out of the way of the wait staff.

'Don't squash the flowers!' she exclaimed to cover her breathless shock and excitement.

'I'll have them delivered to Maria,' Dante offered. 'Or do you want to hang on to them for some reason?'

'What reason?' Jess demanded. 'Do you think I'm going to take a turn around the marquee to try and drum up some interest?'

'Now I'm offended,' Dante protested, hand on heart.

She thought of the snarling wolf beneath. 'You?' she queried. 'The only certainty about you is that you enjoy teasing me. Would you care to accompany me so you can make a list of my potential suitors?'

He stared at her darkly for a moment, then laughed. They both laughed, and both relaxed. 'I think the bride's calling you,' Dante prompted. 'You'd better go and attend to your duties. How lucky am I,' he added as Jess turned to leave, 'to be spared the ordeal of trying to find you a mate?'

'A mate?' Jess queried, stopping to throw him a paint-stripping look. 'You should be so lucky.'

Dante's lips pressed down but his eyes were firing with laughter. 'When I lifted you, that was what your body told me you needed.'

'You and my body don't speak the same language,' she assured him in a flash. 'And now, if you'll excuse me—'

'And if I don't?'

She stared at Dante's hand on her arm.

'It would be my pleasure to escort you to Maria's table,' he murmured.

'There's no need. I can find my way.'

'As I'm sitting next to you and it's my table too, it would seem sensible for us to walk there together.'

There was nothing sensible about this, Jess reasoned as she paused. 'It seems I have no option,' she said at last.

'None at all,' Dante agreed.

Conversation between them and the other guests was lively at the top table, but on one of their many tours around the marquee to make sure everyone had everything they needed it was inevitable that Jess encountered Dante. What she hadn't expected was that he would catch her around the waist and whirl her on to the dance floor. 'You can enjoy yourself too,' he insisted when Jess protested that she had her duties to attend to.

'Your duty is to check on me and make sure I don't overdo it,' he informed her.

'And how am I supposed to do that when you never listen to a word I say?'

'My recovery would argue otherwise. You can gauge the extent of my recovery as we dance.'

And a number of other things, she thought hotly as Dante drew her close. 'I'm not sure it's appropriate.'

'Uncertainty doesn't become you, Señorita Slatehome. Should I doubt your prowess now?'

'Not where my therapy's concerned.'

'What else should I doubt?'

Jess's cheeks burned.

'If you don't want to dance with me, that's another matter,' Dante told her with a relaxed shrug of his powerful shoulders, 'but this is our promised dance—to celebrate my recovery,' he reminded her.

'I don't remember promising that.'

'Amnesia can be a terrible thing.'

'Don't make jokes. I know you're teasing me again.'

'Am I?'

Dante's voice was so warm and coaxing, and his body so hot and strong, that just for a moment she allowed herself to relax.

Of course she should have known better.

'I won't allow you to play the professional card at a wedding,' Dante warned, 'or assume the role of Cinderella. You can't run out on me at midnight.'

'So you're Prince Charming now?'

'I have a white horse.'

'And an answer for everything.'

'I do my best,' Dante agreed.

'If I agree to dance, it's only on the condition that you sit down and rest afterwards.'

'Rest?' Dante's lips tugged up at one corner in a smile. 'Not a chance,' he murmured dangerously close to her ear.

'A resting wolf is still a dangerous animal. Your treatment worked, and now you must take the consequences.'

Why did she choose that moment to stare up into Dante's laughing eyes?

'That's better,' he whispered, drawing her attention to his mouth. 'Relax. You have permission to enjoy yourself without feeling guilty.'

She drew in a shaking breath while Dante continued in the same soothing tone, 'You look beautiful tonight and, as Maria is happily entwined around her new husband, you're free of your duties, and free to dance with me.'

Oh, but this was dangerous. And irresistible. Wearing such a fabulous gown made Jess feel different, as if anything might be possible for the woman who wore the gown. When morning came she'd be a farmer's daughter again and see things differently, but for now...

Something fundamental had changed between them, Dante reflected as Jess quite clearly debated whether or not to move into his arms. She knew what that entailed as much as he did. It was line crossed that could never be redrawn. The tension between them was too much for that to happen. They knew each other better, and yet in some ways not at all. There were still too many pieces of the jigsaw missing. He had pledged to keep everything professional, and so had Jess. He wasn't satisfied with that. Was she?

What did she think about while he lay on the treatment couch beneath her hands? He had to try very hard not to think. Thinking was dangerous because the sight of her was enough to arouse him. Even the pain he suffered beneath her probing fingers aroused him. Everything about Jess was arousing, but the stakes were high because slaking his lust would never be enough where Jess was concerned. She was a special woman who demanded more of him emotionally than he had ever been prepared to give.

* * *

Banked-up feelings exploded inside her as Dante drew her into his arms. There was something so compelling and right about it, and that in itself made her wary. This wasn't just a dance; it was a barrier crashing down. It was permission to feel, to respond, to hope for something more. She'd been so careful around him up to now, not just because of professionalism. Natural caution played its part. Dante was a player in every sense of the word. His relationships were famously many and short-lived, though at the moment he was making her feel as if she was the only woman capable of reaching him. How many others had he made feel that way?

He knew how to tease. Dante's grip was frustratingly light and stirred a primal need inside her. *Leave it at dancing or regret it in the morning*, were inner words of caution she ignored. Dancing like this was a prelude to sex. Every inch of her body was moulded to his. Dante was exerting no pressure, but Jess's body had its own ideas. His thigh was threaded through hers, bringing them into the closest contact possible outside of sex. But how—*how*—was she supposed to resist him? And did she want to?

'You seem distracted,' Dante commented when the first dance ended.

'Nothing could be further from the truth,' she assured him. 'I'm wide awake.'

'And firing on all cylinders,' he observed, bringing her with him as the band started playing again.

She should have stopped at that point, excused herself politely and left the floor. Instead, she warned, 'Behave yourself or I'll make you sit down to rest that leg.'

'I love that you're so masterful,' Dante mocked in a husky whisper, bringing his mouth very close to hers.

'And I love that you accept my authority,' Jess countered with a half teasing smile. She couldn't be serious all the time. 'At one point I thought I'd have trouble with you.'

'You will,' Dante promised, drawing her closer still.

Dancing with Jess was like seizing hold of a red-hot brand and asking to be consumed by it. Any lingering thought he might have had that they could rewind to achieve their previously careful and polite relationship was now implausible, impossible; it just couldn't happen. It only took millimetres of subtle shift in their bodies to tell him Jess felt the same. There was no need for grandiose gestures or unnecessary words between them. Coming together like this was enough. No woman had ever felt so right in his arms or been so receptive. There were a lot of beautiful women at the wedding but there was only one Jess. Who made him laugh as she did? Who had the wit to exchange banter that could be funny but was never cruel?

'This is better than I thought,' she whispered, surprising him with her boldness, and yet not really surprising him at all.

'Better still,' she murmured when he drew her close.

Jess's duties as bridesmaid were the only obstacles he faced. She had a keen eye for detail and noticed everything, which meant leaving his side on a number of occasions to help the wait staff or to answer a guest's query. Nothing was too much trouble for Jess. Apart from dancing with him, apparently. By now they should be somewhere else, but he hadn't bargained on dancing with a Girl Scout.

God bless the Scouts, he reflected, shaking his head with amusement as Jess embarked on yet another mission. He might as well go rest his leg.

The party went on late into the night. When Maria teased Jess into joining her in dancing on the table, Jess laughed. 'I hope you know I've got two left feet.'

'Too late now,' Maria told her as the bridegroom, Manuel, lifted Jess and deposited her next to his bride. Guests had gathered to watch the spectacle, which meant Jess couldn't let her new friend down.

'Lift your gown like this,' Maria instructed as she picked up the hem of her wedding dress to strut a few dramatic flamenco steps. 'Arch your back and stamp your feet in time to the music. Clap your hands like this.'

Having been forced to borrow shoes that were becoming increasingly uncomfortable, Jess confined herself to a series of poses and enthusiastic shouts of *'Olé!'* Carried away by the excellence of Maria's dancing, she acted on a wave of enthusiasm, so when the music ended and Maria jumped into her bridegroom's arms, Jess jumped too—straight into the arms of Dante Acosta, who'd been standing watching with a look she found impossible to interpret. Catching her with no effort at all, he carried her away through the crowd.

So much for her resolve to keep Dante at arm's length, Jess mused, excitement mounting. This was a night to remember, and whatever came next she was more than ready for it.

CHAPTER TWELVE

THE HUNGER TO be alone with Jess had been burning a hole through his head throughout the entire wedding. He could think of nothing else but being alone with her, but once they were inside the ranch house he reined in the wolf. Lowering Jess to her feet, he stood in the shadows staring down. 'Another drink?'

'I haven't had a drink yet. Bridesmaid duties,' she reminded him. 'Clear head and all that?'

'Keeping a clear head is always wise.'

'With you around,' she agreed cheekily.

Angling her chin to stare up at him with that same playful, challenging look in her eyes, she plumbed some deep, untapped well inside him. This couldn't end here. It wouldn't end here. They continued to stare at each other until the tension snapped, he seized her hand and they headed for the stairs—ran, rushed, with no sign of his injury now. Jess was the woman who'd broken through his reserve, and they were both laughing. It felt good after so long of having nothing to laugh about. Humour was a healing balm, and it was a glorious irony to want Jess so badly and yet be laughing so much that they couldn't get there fast enough. Tears of laughter were streaming down Jess's face as she finally dropped down on the stairs. He joined her and when eventually she fell silent that silence was charged with sexual energy. Who needed a bed?

'May I?' she asked, her voice hoarse with laughter.

'Do I have a choice, *señorita*?' he asked as she reached for his belt.

'None at all.'

Those were the last few moments of calm. The next saw them tearing at each other's clothes. Several of the tiny buttons down the back of the bridesmaid's dress bounced down the stairs and skittered across the floor in the hallway.

To hell with this! He had no intention of making love to Jess on a staircase.

'Dante! Give your leg a break,' she protested as he swung her into his arms.

'Why? If I injure it again, you'll have to stay on.'

'Dante, I can't do that. You know I can't—'

That was the last sensible conversation they had. It was as if an atomic force had consumed them both. Crashing into his room, he rocked back against the door, slamming it behind them. Lowering Jess to her feet, he wrenched off his jacket and tossed it on a chair as Jess slipped off her dress with catlike grace. Tugging his shirt free, Jess started work on his zip. At the same time they were kissing wildly, lips, teeth clashing in a dance as old as time. Animal sounds of need escaped their throats until finally he cupped Jess's face in his hands and silenced her with kisses that were deep and long.

'You're overdressed,' she complained when they came up for air.

'So are you,' he growled as he viewed her flimsy thong.

Cocking her head to one side, Jess smiled a witchy smile. 'Do you like it?'

His groin tightened to the point of pain. 'Depends on how easily it rips.'

'Why don't you try it and see?' she suggested.

It ripped.

* * *

When Dante touched her she was his—right away, no hesitation. Fears and consequences were instantly banished to a place so deep in her mind she doubted they'd ever break free. This was right. This was how it should be. Falling back on the bed, she pulled him down on top of her. Guiding his hand, she directed him shamelessly. Not that Dante needed much direction. Moving her hand away, he continued to pleasure her in more ways than she knew existed.

'Don't,' she begged when he pulled away. She needed this—needed Dante. The world she had previously inhabited made no sense now. Without emotion, sensation or risk, it was empty, as everything else was without Dante.

'There are rules,' he informed her in a husky whisper.

'What? Like you make me wait? You leave me frustrated?'

'I make you show me what you want,' he added to her list.

'I can't do that.'

'Why not?' Dante enquired with his mouth very close to hers.

Jess's heart thumped wildly. Surely Dante couldn't mean she should touch herself in front of him?

'You're not shy,' he observed in a clinical tone, 'and we both know how hungry you are.'

'Just as I know you're teasing me.'

'Am I?'

Emotion churned wildly inside her. All her adult life she'd had disappointing sexual encounters, and these had left Jess with the firm belief that the pleasure everyone talked about must be overrated. So what did she want Dante to do about it? Prove her wrong? Prove her so wrong she'd be in a worse state than before—wanting him with no possibility of ever having him? She'd end up as chaste as a nun.

'I feel as if I've lost you,' he remarked, staring down. 'If you've changed your mind—'

'I haven't changed my mind.' This was what she wanted. At least she'd have something to think back on.

She shivered with pleasure as Dante ran one slightly roughened palm down the length of her back. 'You're beautiful. Why make such a deal out of denying yourself pleasure?'

She was wedded to her career? That was a flimsy excuse. She wouldn't be the first professional to cross the line, nor would she be the last.

Dante had spoiled her for all other men when she was just seventeen. Being older made the risk greater. Making love with Dante would reopen that wound and leave her worse off than before. So she was a coward, Jess concluded, destined to live out her life without knowing if sexual pleasure was even possible.

'I get that you need time,' Dante murmured, but that didn't stop him continuing to waken her body until she doubted it would ever sleep again.

'Not too much time,' she admitted dryly.

'What are you doing?' he asked as she moved down the bed.

Putting off the moment? Pleasing Dante? Both of those things.

What she discovered slowed her right down.

Were all men this...built exactly to scale?

'You'd better stop,' he advised.

'I've no intention of stopping.' Brave words, but was this even possible when it took both her hands to encompass him?

Jess won and for the first time ever he was glad to be on the losing side. Tangling his fingers in Jess's hair, he urged her on. Beyond intuitive, she knew everything about pleasure.

Exploring with her lips, her hands and dangerously thrilling passes of her tongue, she cupped him with exquisite sensitivity, and then she teased him with the lightest flicks of her tongue. The instant she took him firmly in both hands, moving them steadily up and down the length of his shaft, she brought him to the edge in seconds.

Sucking the tip brought his hips off the bed. The master of control was finding it hard to hold on. Pleasure built until it refused to be contained and with a roar of relief he claimed his release. What he hadn't expected was that Jess would scramble off the bed.

'I shouldn't be here,' she blurted out.

'Why not?' Catching her close, he searched her eyes. 'Jess, what's wrong?'

'You know this is wrong. I know it's wrong—'

'I know nothing of the sort,' he assured her. But the mood had changed and couldn't be recovered.

Swinging off the bed, he crossed the room naked. Jess was right to call a halt. What could he offer her? Very soon he'd be back on top, with a fast-paced life that demanded selfish focus. Polo took him around the world, as did his business. Jess deserved a man who'd be there for her, someone kind and steady who would treasure her as she deserved. He was not that man, though the thought of some unknown goon pawing her made him sick. That didn't change the facts. He had no right to hold her back from the happiness she deserved.

Bringing a robe from the adjoining bathroom, he wrapped it around her shoulders. He couldn't bear seeing her looking so vulnerable. He'd secured a towel around his waist, for her sake rather than his.

'I'm sorry if I led you on,' she blurted as she moved about the room, gathering up her belongings.

'What are you talking about?'

'You must know,' she insisted, halting with clothes bundled in her arms to turn and stare at him.

'I'm afraid I don't. You didn't lead me anywhere I didn't want to go. I thought that applied to both of us.'

'I should go,' she declared, scouring the room to make sure she hadn't left anything behind.

'Go,' he invited, spreading his arms wide.

He frowned as he watched her leave. Jess was a sensualist, and beautiful, and he had thought her eager to be with him. What on earth was going on in her head? Yes, she was a professional woman with a successful career, but why was she denying herself a life?

Why couldn't she accept pleasure for pleasure's sake? Jess reasoned as she rushed to her room in the guest wing of the *estancia*. Wasn't that what other people did? Where was it written that every relationship must be everlasting? Why couldn't she accept a night of passion with Dante and leave it at that? Was she really bound by duty, or by fear that her teenage dreams could be dust by the morning? Would any man succeed in challenging her belief that she was better on her own, to sort out her life, care for her father, progress her career—

And still be lonely?

Well done, Jess. Everything and nothing has changed.

After a sleepless night she went to the stables to check on the horses. It was early and the yard was mostly silent. The *estancia* had that morning-after feeling that so often hung over a venue after a big event like a soothing web of remembered music and laughter. The door to the facility slid open on well-oiled hinges, and it didn't take long for Jess to satisfy herself that her father's ponies were still happy and contented. Dragging deep on the familiar scent of warm horse and clean hay, she went to take up her usual perch on a hay bale. Tucked away in the shadows of a stable had always been Jess's safe place of choice. It gave her chance to think, to plan, to reflect, and thankfully not regret too much this morning. Life could continue as it always had, a Dante-free zone with no more wild thoughts at a wedding or anywhere else.

With a sigh, she rested back. Going without sleep had left her exhausted. The sound was a cue for Dante's big old dog Bouncer to come and nuzzle her leg. As if he understood the turmoil inside her and was determined to soothe her troubled mind, he settled himself down beside her. Resting his head on her lap, Bouncer exhaled heavily, which made tears sting Jess's eyes at the thought of leaving the *estancia*, and all the many things she would miss. When she should be thrilled that Dante was cured...

'Stealing my dog now?'

Breath shot out of her lungs, with surprise at seeing him and the horrified response to the film reel playing behind her eyes of their aborted love scene last night. 'Dante? What are you doing here?'

'Checking on the animals, like you. I didn't expect to find you here. But then again...'

'What?'

'This is exactly where I should expect to find you.'

'You know me so well,' she teased, trying to keep things light.

'Hardly at all,' he argued. Staring down with concern, he added, 'Are you okay?'

'Of course,' she blustered, stroking Bouncer's ears furiously.

'Hey, leave some of that for me,' Dante insisted as he hunkered down beside her. 'You're spoiling him.'

'And so are you,' she remarked with a smile as Dante fed his old dog some treats. How did anyone manage to look so laid-back and gorgeous so early in the morning—after everything that had happened last night? She felt like a failure, like a ragbag in banged-up jeans and a faded top. It didn't help that Dante was wearing exactly the same sort of clothes, because they only made him seem more tantalisingly attractive and out of reach than ever.

'I'm glad I caught you,' he said in the most relaxed tone ever. 'I have to cancel my eight o'clock therapy session because of some pressing business.'

Her face was burning red with thoughts of last night, and it was a relief to have this shift of focus forced on her. 'No problem,' she blurted on a tight throat. 'We can change the time.' Gently moving Bouncer's head from her knee, she stood up. Dante stood too. 'Any time to suit you,' she offered.

'Hey, you've fulfilled your contract, remember?'

Dante was smiling down as warmly as ever, so why was ice flooding her veins?

'Have this one on me?' she offered awkwardly.

'I would never take advantage of you.'

'Even if I want you to?' So now she sounded desperate. The humiliation of last night put another thought in her mind: Dante was done with amateur hour.

'I've arranged your flight home,' he said as if confirming this.

Yes, she'd half expected it, but still she was stunned into silence. It was as if the floor was dropping away beneath her feet, and she was dropping away with it.

'Thank you. That's very kind of you. I appreciate it' She spoke all the expected words on autopilot. Her lips felt numb, and she had to remind herself that she had always intended to be home in time for Christmas. 'Time flies,' she murmured distractedly.

'When you're enjoying yourself?' Dante suggested wryly.

'I enjoy seeing you without a cane,' she said honestly.

'My PA will be able to tell you all the details. You'll be escorted every step of the way—taxi home, et cetera.'

'Thank you,' she said again as Dante pulled away from the wall. He was clearly in a hurry to leave. 'Don't let me keep you.'

Instead of leaving, he took hold of her hands. 'Jess, this isn't over. I really do have business to attend to.'

'You don't have to explain to me.'

'I think I do. I'm not punishing you or sending you away. Last night was a learning experience for both of us.'

When he learned how unsophisticated she truly was and she learned that Dante was way out of her league.

'It's time for you to get on with your life,' he continued gently. 'You can't be on call here for ever. I don't want to restrict you, but I don't want to lose what we've got either.'

What had they got? What had she allowed them to have? She'd gone into something without thinking it through. Dante wasn't a half-measures man and she had tried to short-change him. And now she could do no more than stand rigidly to attention, not trusting herself to say anything more than, 'Thank you again. It's very kind of you to see to the arrangements.'

'It's not kind,' Dante argued. 'It's in your contract. You'll leave tomorrow morning. The car will collect you prompt at six. That should still give you time to pack your things and say your goodbyes today.'

How could she have forgotten that this was Dante Acosta, a member of the famous Acosta family, tech billionaire and world class polo player? Having recovered full use of his leg, Dante was no longer dependent on anyone, and he was obviously keen to move on—especially from an ingénue who knew next to nothing about sex.

'I thought you'd want the first available flight back, so you can prepare for Christmas at home with your father.'

'That's right. That's so thoughtful of you.'

'Will you need an extra suitcase?'

For two outfits and some knick-knacks she'd bought on the market? 'That won't be necessary, but thank you again.'

'Flight time okay for you?' Dante prompted.

Jess could only hope she didn't look the mess she felt inside. 'Perfect,' she lied. 'The flight's perfect.' Even Bouncer was looking at her with concern. Trust a dog to sense trouble. You couldn't fool an animal. 'I'll be ready to leave at six.'

'Good. Please don't worry about my ongoing treatment. I've already hired someone else to carry on where you left off.'

'Good idea,' she confirmed mechanically. Dante hadn't wasted any time, but when did he ever?

'I won't be slacking,' he promised with a smile.

'I would never think that of you.' To her horror a tear stole down her cheek.

'It's a big, burly man, in case you were wondering,' Dante informed her with a grin.

Try as she might, she couldn't feel light-hearted. She had to get away before a complete meltdown happened and she betrayed her true feelings with huge racking sobs. 'Physios come in all shapes and sizes,' she agreed with a tight smile. 'And I'm sure that whoever you've chosen will be very good.'

'He'd better be,' Dante agreed with a crooked smile. 'You set the bar pretty high.'

But her contract had ended. *Deal with it.* 'I'll leave my notes, though doubtless your new therapist will have his own ideas.'

'Jess—'

'That's okay. I always intended to be back home for Christmas.'

Extricating herself gently from Bouncer, who had wound

himself around her like a comfort blanket, she dipped down to give the big yellow dog one last hug.

Dante blocked her way as she stood up to go. 'Your father will be pleased to see you.'

'I'll be pleased to see him,' she said on a throat turned to ash.

'I'd fly you back myself,' Dante explained as he held the door for her when they left the stables, 'but I have this business deal, and then my first team practice the day after tomorrow and I want to get some training in before then.'

'That's wonderful news,' she said truthfully.

'I know what you're going to say—don't overdo it,' Dante supplied. 'I promise I won't. I owe my recovery to you, and I'll never underestimate what you've done for me.'

And you for me, Jess thought as the curve of Dante's lips twisted her heart until she wanted to cry out in pain. *You've taught me never to be naïve again*, she concluded with her usual sensible self back in charge.

'It's my job,' she said, pinning a smile to dry lips as she shrugged.

How much more of this could she take? She was breaking up inside and desperate to put space between them. The last thing she wanted was to break down in front of Dante. What good would it do, other than make her look even more pathetic than she felt?

She was halfway across the yard when Dante caught hold of her arm. 'Was this just another job for you, Jess?'

There was no chance to hide the tears in her eyes, nor did she even try. 'I'll miss you,' she blurted. To hell with pride! What did pride count for in the end? What did she stand to lose when there was nothing left to lose?

'I'll miss you too,' Dante admitted.

'Just take care of those ponies—and yourself,' she insisted. 'Take care of Moon for me in particular. She needs a lot of attention.' Unlike her human counterpart, thankfully, Jess thought as she firmed her jaw.

'How can you doubt it?' Dante queried.

'I don't,' she said honestly. When it came to his animals, Dante's love and desire to care for them was as acutely honed as her own. It was just human beings outside his family and staff he had a problem with.

'We won't forget you on the *estancia*, Skylar,' he said dryly, standing back.

An ugly swearword came to mind when Dante mentioned Skylar. Sadly, her mother had been wrong. There was no magic in the name. There was just Jess. Hurting like hell.

CHAPTER THIRTEEN

SHE WOULDN'T CRY, Jess determined as she stood at the kitchen sink on Christmas Eve in Yorkshire. This wasn't about her, or missing Dante so much it made her heart drum a lament in her chest. This was about the village where she lived, and about her father and the wonderful pals who had kept him afloat while she was working. This year, thanks to the sale of the ponies, they could afford a real Yorkshire Christmas, which meant she could thank everyone by holding open house as her mother used to do.

The scene beyond the steamed-up window would be perfect for a Christmas card. The snow fairies had arrived early this year, frosting the paddocks with pristine white, capping the fences with sparkling meringue peaks of snow. Her father had been out most of the day with the other local farmers, scouring the moors for stranded animals. They deserved a good feed when they got back.

No longer a lonely widower crushed by grief, Jim Slatehome was part of the village again, and part of the horse world too, just as her mother would have wanted. Of course he felt sad and still missed his wife, but now, thanks to all his friends and the medical help he had finally agreed to accept, he had strategies to deal with black moments, which was the most anyone could hope for.

Everything was right with the world, Jess told herself firmly as she put the finishing touches to the feast she'd prepared. Everything apart from one notable thing, she accepted with a pang. Where was Dante? What was he doing this Christmas? It made her unhappy to think of him alone. Surely he'd be with his family? It was such a big family.

Dante playing gooseberry? Did that seem likely?

If only he lived closer, she would have swallowed her pride and invited him over. *If only.* What an overworked phrase. It was no use to anyone, because it spoke of regret and things left undone.

So where was he?

According to her most reliable informant, the *Polo Times*, Dante Acosta had already whupped three types of hell out of his arch rival, Nero Caracas.

He'd better not have damaged that leg.

She'd researched the man who had taken over Dante's treatment and, to be fair, his reputation was impeccable. Trust Dante to choose the best.

It was the most frustrating thing on earth to care as deeply as she cared for Dante, Jess reflected as she pulled away from the sink, and yet be prevented from caring *for* him. He'd never played so well, according to *Polo Times.* And in a direct quote from Dante, that was all thanks to his physiotherapist, Jess Slatehome, who, together with her close associate Skylar Slates, had raised him up when he'd been down.

Dante had more than kept his promise to let the polo world know that Jess was good at her job. The phone had been ringing off the hook since the article was printed. Admittedly, most of the calls had been from reporters wanting to know what the 'real' Dante Acosta was like.

'He's such a loner and an enigma,' they'd prompted, 'while you were a young woman on her own.'

'I'm a medical professional with a job to do,' she had reminded them, remembering to add, 'Happy Christmas,' genuinely and warmly—because, like her, they were only doing their job.

Happy Christmas.

Jess's mouth twisted with the pain. She missed Dante so much the words meant nothing. Swiping tears away, she cleaned down the kitchen until it gleamed like never before. Checking the fire, she hung up her apron. With a shake of her head, as if that might knock some sense into it, she thought through the rest of the day. The food was ready. There was nothing more to do, and she longed to get outside. There could be more sheep to find.

He could go anywhere for Christmas. Invitations were stacked up in a pile on his desk at the *estancia*. Those from his family had received polite refusals. Those who craved Acosta glitter to brag about went in the bin.

He checked again. Nothing from Jess.

Why should there be?

Shifting position impatiently, he picked up a call from his sister, Sofia. 'Yes?'

'Compliments of the season to you too,' she said dryly. 'I gather you're in a good mood.'

'What do you want?'

Accustomed to his stormy moods since the injury, Sofia gave his bad manners a bye. 'I'm ringing to tell you not to buy so many presents. A truckload arrived today, when all we want is you.'

'Another year, perhaps,' he promised gruffly.

The Acostas always gathered at Christmas to remember their parents, though all five of them under one roof for any length of time could be a recipe for disaster. To put it mildly, they could be fiery. Dante's eldest brother always referred them to the Argentinian branch of the family which, he insisted, was far better balanced since all the brothers had married. He tried this same lecture each year but, as he remained unattached, it lacked bite.

The problem, Dante reflected, was that none of them was prepared to risk their heart after the crushing grief of losing their parents.

Even him?

Why couldn't he date Jess in a way she'd find acceptable? What was stopping him giving her the future she deserved?

Only his stubbornness. And possibly Jess's too.

Glancing at the phone, he felt a stab of regret. He loved his sister, and would miss catching up with Sofia and his brothers at the annual get-together, but this year there was only one place to be.

Why the change of heart?

Try living anything approaching a normal life with one exceptional woman, with whom he had unfinished business, permanently lodged in his mind.

Everything was ready for whoever dropped by, Jess reassured herself as she left the farm. Gifts for her father were wrapped and ready, together with the 'little somethings', as her mother used to call them, for his pals, and for any surprise visitors. She'd brought in extra folding chairs from the barn, so all that remained was to tempt her father back to the house with the promise of a delicious feast.

Financially, the year had ended on a high, mainly thanks to Dante's purchase of their ponies. It was a real treat to have enough money to buy her father things he'd denied himself for far too long. There would be a satisfyingly large heap of gifts beneath a tree laden with baubles that carried memories. Everything was warm and welcoming, just as her mother would have wanted it to be. The tradition of open house at Bell Farm would continue.

She paused at the top of a rise to stare out over the winter wonderland with its coating of snow and inevitably her thoughts turned to Dante.

Where was he? Who was he with? What was he doing? Would he be lonely? Was his leg still okay?

'Stop it,' she said out loud. This was going to be a wonderful Christmas, to which her broken heart was most definitely not invited.

Dante's flight through thunderclouds on his way from Spain to England was, to put it mildly, interesting, even in the luxurious surroundings of his private jet. The drive to the farm was even more so. No one was prepared to release a helicopter in such uncertain weather, so he hired a big workhorse-style SUV, but even that was brought to a sliding halt by snowdrifts on the exposed Yorkshire moors.

Grinding his jaw, he grabbed some belongings and set off to walk to the farm. According to the satnav on his phone, he was close to his destination. This wasn't the way he'd planned to arrive, but Jess wouldn't care less if he arrived in a helicopter or on foot. Unimpressed by shows of wealth, she was the most down-to-earth woman he'd ever met. She demanded an entirely new rulebook. He was still finessing the detail as he ploughed on through the snow.

He thought about Jess with each step, and what he owed her for restoring the strength in his leg. Most of all he thought about holding her. Maybe that was a stretch. There were no guarantees where Jess was concerned. She'd pick her own route through life.

Pausing to look around and get his bearings, he was grateful for the map on his phone. There were no recognisable landmarks. Everything was covered in a blanket of snow. Even the road had become one with the field. Jess's home turf seemed determined to show him an increasingly hostile face. If Jess did the same, he was wasting his time.

Pulling up his jacket collar, he pushed on. There was an

occasional flicker of light and a glimpse of colour down the hill, where a cluster of homesteads sat squat in the snow. He exhaled on a cloud of humourless laughter. Why was he surprised that a woman from such a bleak and forbidding landscape would be anything but strong and self-determining?

It had occurred to him that Jess might refuse to see him. Who rocked up unannounced on Christmas Eve? It couldn't be helped. He wasn't going anywhere until they met up face to face. Jess had rocked his world on its axis and there was no way he'd let this go. If he reached the village—*when* he reached the village, Dante amended—he'd surely find lodgings for the night. The roads were impassable, so he was stuck here whether Jess agreed to see him or not.

After another half a mile or so, he stopped to blink and rub snow from his eyes, seeing shadows moving in the distance. As he drew closer, he realised the shadows were men working in the field. Driven almost sideways by gusting wind, they were attempting to heave sheep out of a ditch. Several more animals were stranded, and he didn't hesitate before pitching in.

Fate had dealt him a kindness, Dante concluded as he worked with the other men. Rescuing the terrified animals built an instant camaraderie that allowed him to ask the way, enquire about lodgings and even learn something about Jess.

The moors had a peculiar stillness that only descended after a recent fall of snow. It was like being alone on the planet, without even birdsong to keep her company, Jess mused as she trudged on. She was keeping a lookout for her father and for his friends, as well as any stranded animals she might find along the way. She'd come prepared, with a snow shovel strung across her shoulder on a strap.

She paused for a moment when she got to the brow of

the hill. The view was immense. Now the snow flurries had died down she could see right across the moors to Derbyshire. But it was only a temporary respite because snow had started falling again.

Bringing her muffler over her mouth, she prepared to slither down what was now a treacherous slope. Halfway down, she dug in her heels and skidded to a halt. An SUV was stuck in a snowdrift and tilted on its side. Thoughts flashed through her head. Uppermost was saving whoever was in the vehicle before they froze to death. Hurtling down the bank regardless of safety, she sucked in great lungsful of air. She had to conquer that panic. She'd be no use to anyone like this.

Once she'd gathered herself, another question occurred: who drove a flashy SUV in the village?

Could it be Dante?

Don't be ridiculous, she railed at her inner voice. Why would Dante come here on Christmas Eve? There were no ponies to buy. He'd bought them all. And would a billionaire's Christmas include the simple pleasures of a small isolated village on top of the Yorkshire moors? He had absolutely no reason to come here.

That didn't stop her wading through the sometimes thigh-high snow. She had to reach the SUV. Not only would the driver and any passengers be in danger of freezing inside the vehicle; if they left it they could quickly become disorientated, and the result would be the same. Wind chill was deadly, and it was vital they reached safety and warmth soon.

Fast progress was impossible, which gave Jess's thoughts the chance to run free. Maybe Dante had somehow heard that Bell Farm was throwing its doors open to all-comers at Christmas. It wasn't beyond the bounds of reason that he'd spoken to her dad but, whoever was in that vehicle, or maybe wandering around lost on the moors, she had to do her best to find them.

There were times when Jess thought her feet would freeze into icicles and break off. This wasn't helped by the local brook being covered by a thin layer of ice beneath a concealing carpet of snow. She yelped as her feet sank beneath the surface yet again, but now she was within touching distance of the vehicle and she pressed on.

Swinging the snow shovel off her shoulder, she braced herself for whatever, or whoever, she might find inside. Was she too late? What if Dante had driven up to the moors? Why hadn't she had the courage to tell him how she felt before now? It wasn't as if she was shy or retiring. Tears froze on her face as she frantically dug out the snow. Why had she never told him she loved him? Why had she held back?

Why had they both held back?

It wasn't as if Dante had plied her with words of love and reassurance, any more than Jess had unleashed her true feelings for him.

Straightening up, she eased her aching back. It wasn't as if they hadn't talked, but neither of them was comfortable talking about feelings. They'd both built grief-driven barricades. Was that what those they'd lost would want for them?

Please, please, please! Don't let it end like this, she begged the fates and anyone else who was listening. *Please let me have one last chance to tell Dante how I feel. I promise I won't shy away from it.*

There was no way of predicting, of course, how Dante might respond to that, but as he was hardly likely to be the driver of the vehicle that hardly mattered.

But there was no one in the SUV, and fresh snow had covered any footprints around it. Planting her shovel, Jess flopped down in the snow. Exhausted and dispirited she might be, but she couldn't spare the time to catch her breath. Getting up again, she resolved to solve the mystery of the abandoned SUV because whoever had been driving was still in danger.

She'd search the whole damn moor if she had to, Jess determined as she stumbled on. Thank goodness she knew the terrain.

CHAPTER FOURTEEN

'JESS?'

'*Dante!*'

Out of the blizzard came a shape: a man—the only
man—a powerful, healthy, vigorous life force in a world
grown so bleak and frightening even Jess had begun to
doubt that it would ever be summer again.

She went rigid at first and then started laughing and crying at the same time, before launching herself at Dante. 'I
can't believe you're here! I'm so glad you're safe!' Pulling
back, she searched his eyes with relief.

'Believe,' he said dryly, gently disentangling himself.

'Were you in the SUV?' she demanded, swinging around
to look over her shoulder.

'I had that pleasure.'

'Of landing in a ditch?' she suggested, laughing with
happiness now.

'That was somewhat unexpected,' he conceded.

'So why are you here?' She was breathless with excitement.

'I keep asking myself that same question.'

Her eyes narrowed with suspicion. 'No one arrives on
top of the Yorkshire moors in a blizzard without a very
good reason. And it's Christmas Eve,' she pointed out, 'so
it must have been something big to bring you here.'

Something small, he thought, measuring her fragility

against the frozen landscape, but if you added spirit into the mix Jess was a match for any and all conditions.

'Are you saying I've got no excuse to be here?'

'Not unless you're hiding the reindeer.'

His lips tugged with the urge to laugh. Suddenly the trip was more than worthwhile. But there was something he had to know. 'Good surprise, or bad?'

'Lucky for you that you're in time to eat with us,' Jess exclaimed happily without attempting to answer his question.

'I wouldn't dream of putting you to that trouble.'

'No trouble,' she said, cocking her head to one side to bait him with a grin. 'We've got enough food for an army, so I could do with another mouth.'

'*Dios*, no!' he murmured dryly. 'I can't imagine you with another mouth. One is enough to contend with.'

She smiled and relaxed at this. 'But you will come and join us?' she pressed.

'I'd be delighted to join you. Solely in the interest of helping you out on the food front, of course.'

'Of course,' she teased back. 'Great!' Biting down on her bottom lip, Jess shook her head as she smiled up at him, as if she couldn't believe the evidence of her own eyes.

The force of Dante's personality alone was like a blaze of fire in a frozen monochrome landscape. Jess's feelings were in danger of overflowing. It was as if her world had exploded into a blizzard of happiness. Beyond relieved to have solved the mystery of the missing driver in the stranded SUV, she knew now that nothing could be better than discovering the driver was Dante.

'You're safe,' she marvelled as they walked along.

'That I am,' Dante confirmed while she imprinted every rugged detail of his face on her mind.

Of course he was safe. Dante Acosta would never set out on a mission without proper planning first. Hence the backpack and the storm-proof clothing and the tough workmanlike boots. The question was: what was his mission this time? Jess wondered.

Meeting up with her father and his friends a little way closer to the farm was such a happy reunion. 'So you found her!' Jess's father enthused, slapping Dante on the back as if he'd known him all his life.

'Have you two met already today?' Jess asked, cocking her head to one side to study both men.

'We met in the field where your father was rescuing sheep,' Dante revealed.

'And you joined in,' Jess guessed. Her father confirmed this with his customary grunt that reminded her so much of Dante.

Dipping his head, Dante whispered in her ear, 'We have to stop meeting like this.'

You have to stop sending shivers spinning down my spine when my father is watching, Jess thought. 'Suits me,' she said coolly.

Meaningful glances exchanged between Dante and her father made Jess instantly suspicious. 'What's going on?' she prompted. 'What aren't you telling me?'

'This is no place to linger for a chat,' her father scolded gruffly.

There was nothing underhand about Jess's father. If he knew something he spat it out. This behaviour wasn't like him. She frowned. Her father wasn't frowning. A smile had spread across his face as he walked along with Dante. It was almost as if he had expected their visitor—if not today, then at some point soon. What weren't they sharing? Why had Dante come to Yorkshire?

'We'll take these sheep back to the barn,' her father was telling Dante. 'And then I hope you'll join us for our first Christmas feast.'

'I'd love to,' Dante confirmed.

'Excellent,' her father exclaimed, slapping his hands together to keep them warm. 'With Jess's cooking I can confidently guarantee you a very happy Christmas!'

'Happy Christmas to you too,' Dante echoed with an unreadable glance at Jess. 'And the best of everything in the New Year.'

'The New Year's going to be so much better for us,' her father enthused. 'You made sure of it,' he told Dante.

How had Dante made sure of it? The sale of the ponies would only take them so far. Jess didn't have chance to think it over as the group of men with her father chorused in a shout, 'Happy Christmas!'

Having seen the sheep safely gathered in, they ended up at the packed pub where, as Jess might have expected, her father invited everyone back to the farm. Steam rose from their clothes as the roaring log fire did its work. While the general air of celebration and good-humoured complaints about the weather rang out around her, Jess's focus was all on Dante. He bought a round of drinks for everyone and was soon swapping stories with the best. Not once did he let on that his life was extraordinary, and though the locals might have known he was a polo-playing billionaire, as far as they were concerned he'd helped them save the sheep, and that made him one of them.

It was wonderful to have Dante here in the place she loved best. And at Christmas, Jess's favourite time of year. Most important of all, he was safe. Why he'd come to the village didn't matter. All she cared about was that they were together. Dante was the best Christmas gift of all.

The farmhouse kitchen was almost as crowded as the pub and definitely as noisy, and in all the right ways. He was instantly struck by the warm and homely atmosphere Jess had created. She was special. This was special. With enough delicious food to feed an army and an assortment of chairs and stools gathered from who knew where, she soon had her visitors munching happily.

'I'm sorry,' she said as she squeezed past with yet another oven dish brimming with crunchy golden roast potatoes. 'This can't be what you're used to.'

She was gone before he had chance to tell her that this was so much better than anything he had, and that he envied everything about it. No Michelin starred restaurant could better the happy family atmosphere Jess had created here.

He'd never eaten food like it, and he prided himself on his chefs. If the way to a man's heart was through his stomach Jess had the route map down. They didn't have chance to speak as Jess was so busy, but he pounced on the cue when a rather attractive widow from a neighbouring farm invited her father over. 'I've got a room at the pub,' he told Jess, 'if you'd care to join me for a nightcap?'

'Why, Señor Acosta,' Jess challenged with a smile, turning her bright eyes up to his, 'are you propositioning me?'

'I'm offering to buy you a drink to thank you for the meal. Then I'll walk you home.'

And I'm supposed to believe it's as simple as that, her narrowed eyes clearly told him. Who could blame her when testosterone was firing off him in spears of hot light?

'Do you have people to look after the animals?' he asked.

'We drafted in some extra help over Christmas. They'll take it in turns to keep a watch through the night.'

'Then you have no excuse.' His lips pressed down as he shrugged.

'Apart from natural caution, do you mean?'

'What would Skylar say?' he challenged.

She laughed. 'I'm not sure I want to know.'

'You need a break so you can enjoy Christmas too,' he pointed out.

'You think?' Jess laughed as she wiped a forearm across her glowing face.

'I know it,' he stated firmly.

Her cheeks pinked up even more but she was in no hurry to give him her answer. *Brava*, Jess. This woman was exactly the challenge he wanted.

Should she go with Dante? Life was complicated, and he had made it even more so because she wanted to go with him, more than she'd ever wanted anything before.

There were so many reasons not to go. The kitchen was a mess—inevitable after a successful party—and she would have liked to stay and clear up.

'You go,' her father's friend Ella told her, having intuited Jess's dilemma. 'I'll handle this first thing tomorrow morning—and I'll handle your dad too.'

Jess could believe it as she exchanged a smile with the older woman. Ella coped with a farm on her own so there was no reason why she couldn't take on Jess's dad. 'If you're sure?'

'I'm positive. You've more than put the effort in to making today a great success, and if you can't go and have a quiet drink down the local pub I don't know what's wrong with the world.'

But would it be a quiet drink down the local pub? 'Thank you. You're very kind—'

Before Jess had chance to continue, her father interrupted with the surprising news that she shouldn't wait up for him.

'I don't know what time I'll be back,' he explained.

'Oh.' Jess's jaw must have dropped. She quickly pinned on a smile. Yes, she was surprised. Things seemed to be moving quickly between her father and Ella, though she'd been away in Spain and, with work and the animals, maybe it was Jess who was guilty for being out of the loop. She had never asked the relevant questions. Her father had been lost and lonely without her mother; why shouldn't he be happy now?

'See you, Dad,' she called out as he left with Ella. With all her heart, she wished them well, and her father a much better future.

They'd all come a long way, Jess reflected as the rest of their guests left for home. Dante was waiting by the door with her coat. So what was she going to do? Turn him down? She could stay here and nothing would change. He'd probably be gone by the morning. And what would she have missed?

That remained to be seen, she concluded, firming her jaw.

Glancing around the familiar kitchen, she couldn't help feeling that, whatever happened next, her life would never be the same again.

When he planned something, he planned down to the last detail. He'd taken the top floor of the pub in advance and had Christmas gifts for Jess and her father in his emergency backpack. He would arrange the recovery of the SUV as and when; meanwhile, champagne was on ice and, as he'd also requested, tasty snacks were in the icebox he'd had installed in one of the rooms. This wouldn't be his only visit to the village, so home comforts were essential. As for him and Jess? It was crucial they had a chance to talk in private.

Inviting her into the cosy sitting room, where the landlord had the good sense to light the log fire, he took her coat and then they stared at each other in silence.

Jess made the first move. Moving closer, she stood on tiptoe to brush her lips against his. 'That wasn't a mistake,' she informed him. With a shrug she added, 'Maybe it was as reckless as when I was seventeen, but I think I'm old enough to handle the consequences now.'

'You expect consequences?' He smiled and shook his head.

'You'd better not disappoint,' she warned cheekily.

'What's been holding you back?'

Jess's mouth twisted as she turned serious to think about this. 'Duty—like you? Career—like you?'

'Disappointments in the past?'

'If you think you can do better…'

She was only half joking, he suspected. 'Try me and find out.'

'I intend to.'

'Do you think you should take your boots off first?'

'My boots?' she echoed with surprise, glancing down.

'Your feet must be frozen.'

She stared at him and laughed. They both laughed, and were still laughing when he brought Jess into his arms to kiss her—gently at first, and then as if he would never let her go. Whatever doubts had been in Jess's mind, it soon became clear she'd given them the night off. Having left her boots by the door, she informed him, 'My heart is set on undressing you.'

He held his arms out. 'Be my guest.'

She did this slowly and deliberately, as if every button took her closer to a personal goal that had less to do with sex and more to do with establishing trust between them. His urges were far less worthy. He wanted to strip her naked, throw her on the bed and make love to Jess until she was too tired to move, but this was such a pivotal moment for both of them he decided to run with Jess's approach. Until she sank to her knees in front of him.

'Did I do something wrong?' she asked, wounded eyes fixed on his as he brought her to her feet.

'You've done nothing wrong,' he said gently. Now he understood why Jess's sex life had been so disappointing. If she'd had to do all the work, what pleasure was there in that for Jess? Sex should be a shared experience with mutual pleasure.

Swinging her into his arms, he carried her into the bedroom. 'Now it's my turn,' he warned as he peeled off the heavy socks she was wearing beneath her boots. 'These are disgusting.' He tossed them aside as she laughed, and then she took turns smiling and groaning with pleasure as he warmed her feet in his hands.

'You know all the best routes to a girl's heart.'

'Dealing with frozen feet is my speciality,' he conceded as he bathed her tiny feet in kisses and hot breath.

'How many hearts have you broken with that technique?'

'I've never been much interested in finding my way to anyone's heart,' he admitted.

She seemed surprised so he asked, 'Why do you find that so hard to believe?'

'Your reputation precedes you?' she suggested.

'Do you believe everything you read?' When she shrugged, he explained, 'I love my brothers and my sister, Sofia. And, before you ask—no, I have never put their feet near my mouth.'

Everything changed in that moment. Jess's smile broadened until it lit up her face, and he knew that the biggest hurdle had been crossed. Before sex came trust, and he had won Jess's trust.

CHAPTER FIFTEEN

DANTE UNDRESSED HER with as much care as he might have shown a skittish pony—if that pony had been wearing ten layers of Arctic gear. And with each item of clothing he removed, he kissed her. When she was naked the room seemed to grow very still. The only sound was their breathing—Dante's steady and Jess's interrupted by short gasps of pleasure when Dante found some new place to kiss.

It was possible to soothe and arouse at the same time, she was fast discovering, and Dante was a master of the art. Long, soothing strokes down her back quietened her, but made her want so much more. He gave her chance to feel her body waking to his touch, but his restraint was a torment. The urge to take the lead began to overwhelm her, but each time she tried to make a move Dante dissuaded her with kisses, telling her to concentrate on sensation and nothing else.

She hadn't just stepped over that line; she'd leapt over it, Jess concluded as a soft moan of pleasure escaped her throat. They could never be close enough and when Dante's hand found her she cried out loud with excitement. He'd made her wait so long she was right on the edge. 'Please don't stop,' she begged when he moved his hand. His answer was to kiss her neck, her lips, her cheeks and her eyes, while she trembled with anticipation beneath him like a greyhound in the traps. Then he turned her and, holding her hands in one giant fist above her head, he made control impossible. As she bucked uncontrollably beneath him Dante released her pinned hands and captured her thrusting buttocks in one hand while he helped her to extract every last pulse of pleasure with his other hand. Having found her slick warmth, he made her take the short journey again, until she found herself right on the edge.

'Again?' he suggested in a low growl.

She had no chance to do anything but cry out, 'Yes!' Dante's fingers were magic and he knew just what to do. Grinding her body frantically against the heel of his hand, she claimed her second powerful release. He silenced her panting and groaning with a kiss that was as deep as it was tender.

She loved the way he held her buttocks firmly in place with one hand as he pleasured her with the other. 'Are you going to be as greedy as this all night?' he teased in a deep, husky tone as he loomed over her, swarthy and dangerous, and so impossibly sexy.

'You made me insatiable,' she said, marvelling at how gentle he could be, how persuasive. She was half his size and Dante treated her as if she were made of rice paper, which was frustrating but also reassuring.

'I want to taste you,' he growled, moving down the bed.

She laughed softly. 'Do I have a say in this?'

'No.' Lifting her legs onto his shoulders, Dante dipped his head.

She thought she knew pleasure? She was wrong. *This* was pleasure. This was something beyond anything else.

'I can't,' she protested, speaking her thoughts out loud. 'Not again.'

'Is that a fact?' Dante queried with a wicked look, pausing.

His tongue, his mouth and fingers continued to work their magic. This time the pleasure waves were so strong she was tossed about on a wild tide of sensation that stole away every thought except one: could she remain suspended in Dante's erotic net for ever?

Jess...

Holding himself back was the biggest test he'd ever faced. Jess took even longer to recover and when she did her eyes were heavy. She wasn't just tired; she was exhausted. It had been a long day, with the shock of seeing him and the rescue of the sheep. Then she'd gone on to cater a meal for who knew how many before allowing herself downtime. Who wouldn't be exhausted? Taking her now would be taking advantage. She was sleepily sexy but her conscious mind was taking a well-earned breath. He'd waited a long time to make love to Jess and when it happened he aimed for special, not something to tag to a long, draining day.

'You're smiling,' she commented drowsily.

Because he wasn't used to waiting, but Jess was different.

'Well?' she prompted softly, reaching out. 'Are you going to explain?'

Turning off the light, he drew her into his arms.

'Are you asleep?' she asked when some quiet time had passed. 'Do you regret this?'

'No.'

'Then...?'

'You're tired,' he murmured.

'I'm not,' Jess protested.

'Exhausted, then.'

'I do need a hug,' she admitted.

To reassure her, he tightened his grip.

'I don't want you to think I'm having second thoughts,' she whispered.

It was obvious she wanted to talk. Releasing her, he sat up beside her. 'Talk to me,' he encouraged her gently.

'About loss and grief and duty, and how there's never enough time to mull over those things?'

'There hasn't been a right time for either of us, I'm guessing,' he admitted, raking his hair.

'Stop distracting me,' she scolded, smiling, 'or we're wasting another chance to talk it out.'

'I'm not even sure we should be talking about it now, when you so clearly need to sleep.'

Searching his eyes, she explained, 'I need to talk first and then sleep.'

'Go ahead,' he said softly, waiting.

'I didn't cry when my mother died,' Jess eventually revealed in a small voice, as if she still felt guilty about it. But then, remembering his loss, she reverted to her customary warm, concerned self. 'I don't expect you showed any emotion either when you lost your parents.'

'Oh, I was angry,' he confessed, thinking back. 'When I arrived at the hospital one of the doctors told me, "Where there's life there's hope."'

'And of course you desperately hoped he was right and believed him.' Her eyes were in that moment as she stared into his.

'There was no hope,' he confirmed flatly. 'My parents were already dead, as I discovered when I barged into the room where they had been treated.'

'You were how old?'

'Old enough to know better—seventeen or eighteen. I've found it hard to trust anyone outside my inner circle since that day.'

'And who could blame you?'

'Not you, apparently,' he remarked as he stared into Jess's eyes. 'So, what's your excuse for being so bottled-up?'

'Events,' she said succinctly in the way people did when there was a world of trouble hidden behind a single word.

'Tell me about those events,' he said gently. 'The grief you hid I know about, so I'm guessing we're talking about your father.'

She was silent for a while and then confessed, 'He was such a proud man...'

'Was?' he prompted.

'You must remember...' Her eyes were big and wounded.

'I do. Everyone's brought low by grief, so I'm guessing your father took some time to pull through.'

'It wasn't easy for him.'

'Or for you,' he observed quietly.

'Don't they say love makes anything possible?'

She looked so sad as she asked the question. His imagination could fill in the blanks for now. Jess wasn't ready to tell him the detail. Maybe she never would be. She was right about her father being a proud man, and Jess was as protective of family as he was. It was up to her to decide if and when and how much she told him.

'I trust you,' she admitted before falling into a thoughtful silence. 'I know you won't say anything to harm my father's reputation,' she added at last, staring into his eyes, unblinking.

'Never,' he pledged.

He let the silence hang until Jess was ready to continue. 'I built my adult life on the promises I made to my mother, which were to continue my education and to qualify so I could earn a living and look after my father and the farm. That didn't leave much time to mourn my mother's loss, but it was a relief to be busy because the alternative was to sink into grief and achieve nothing, which would have betrayed her trust.'

'We all need time to mourn.'

'Says you,' she rebuked him with a sad smile.

'Let's build on the past and remember those we loved

happily, positively, knowing that's what they'd want us to do.'

'You always find a way to make me smile,' she observed thoughtfully.

'Do you want to punish me for that?'

'Do you want to be punished?'

His smile darkened. 'Not for that.'

Her gaze flew to the rumpled bed. 'You spoiled me for other men ten years ago.'

'That kiss in your father's stable?'

'That was just the start,' she admitted. 'And now you've spoiled me all over again.'

'Don't expect me to apologise.'

When he fell silent she asked, 'Dante, is something wrong?'

This was not the right time to explain what was happening with the farm. 'No. There's nothing wrong. We'll talk again in the morning.'

'Promise?' she asked softly.

'I promise.' Drawing Jess into his arms, he settled down on the bed. Feeling her tears wet his chest, he turned to look at her. 'Why are you crying?'

'I'm happy,' she confessed.

Cradling her in his arms, he kissed the top of her head. 'Sleep now. I'm not going anywhere.' She was possibly already asleep, he thought as Jess's breathing steadied, and he was surprised by the deep sense of satisfaction that stole over him at the thought that she could relax in his arms.

Was this love?

Deep trust was love. Unpacking memories that had wounded them both and entrusting them to each other was closer to love than anything else he could think of. The warm contentment inside him felt like love. How else could he be lying here, wanting this woman as he did, without the slightest intention of disturbing her?

Had there ever been a better way to start Christmas Day than this? Jess woke slowly to find she was naked in bed with Dante in the dark quiet hours of early morning. Naked and contented, she amended, though not for long. It was a small step from lazy contentment to making her wishes clear, and Dante was as eager as she was. With a soft growl of cooperation, he shifted position to make things easier for her.

Guiding him, she used Dante's body to rouse a place that could never get enough of him, and now badly needed more.

'Hey,' Dante whispered, 'take it easy.' Moving over her, he whispered, 'There's no hurry.'

She was way past listening to advice, but when he allowed her the smooth tip of his erection she was more than ready to bow to his greater knowledge, especially as he had moved her hands by this time and taken over.

'When I say and not before,' he instructed.

How could she answer when all her concentration was focused on getting him to probe a little deeper? Dante's jaw was set, she noticed, glancing up. He was suffering too. So much restraint had to be torture for him. Damping down the urge to thrust forward and bring their torture to an end, she settled for doing as he suggested, which was to let everything go and allow Dante to set the pace.

'That's right... Relax,' he encouraged. 'Sensation will be so much greater if you allow me to pleasure you, while you do absolutely nothing.'

Heaving a shaking sigh, she knew at once he was right. Each touch was amplified by her stillness. She could concentrate on every feeling as Dante pleasured her at his own pace. She tensed momentarily as he sank a little deeper, stretching her beyond belief. They weren't even past the smooth, domed head of his erection yet but, feeling her concern, he stopped to allow her to become used to the new sensation. When she was ready to move on, he cupped her buttocks and took her a little deeper still. There was no pain. He'd prepared her too well. There was only pleasure—wave after wave of incredible pleasure, fired by the overwhelming need to be one with him.

Sinking deeper still, he took her to the hilt in one slow, firm thrust. She couldn't help but gasp, but Dante had an answer for the shock of his invasion. Massaging her with rotating movements of his hips, he brought her swiftly to the point of no return and then he commanded in a low voice, 'Now.'

She didn't need any encouragement and plunged into pleasure with repeated cries of relief. Even when the waves crashing down on her eased off, Dante was still moving. He took her steadily and gently until her hunger built again, when she grasped his buttocks to work him faster and harder, and he pounded into her as if they would never ever stop.

Now the dam had burst their lovemaking was fierce. They enjoyed each other in as many ways as they could, gorging on pleasure, sometimes on the bed and sometimes not. A shared shower to cool down after more heated activity proved another excuse for lovemaking, only this time she scrambled up him and Dante slammed her against the wall to take her deep. Towelling dry was another opportunity to test the resilience of the black marble countertop, and when they returned to bed they didn't quite make it.

'Not so fast,' he said, dragging her close. Bending her over where she was standing at the side of the bed, he encouraged her to brace her hands against the mattress so he could take her from behind, while using his hand to encourage somewhere that needed no encouragement. He allowed her cries of release to subside before turning her so she was sitting on the edge of the bed, facing him. Moving between her legs, he pressed her back. Grabbing a pillow, he placed it beneath her buttocks.

There was no end to pleasure with your soulmate, Jess reflected some considerable time later when she sank back, gasping, on the bed.

What else could she call Dante? Could fate be so cruel that it had thrown them together again for no reason? The gulf between them remained wide in terms of financial success and lifestyle, but were these the most important measures? Wasn't the way they played off each other, and improved each other, far more important than that? Would this feeling of euphoria last? she wondered as she stared at Dante. Why not, she reasoned, when his care of her, and his sheer damn sexy self, was so different to the grim face he showed the world? Was that a coincidence too? Couples could destroy each other, while others were improved in every way just by being together. She wanted to believe that she and Dante were builders not destroyers, and that they would be stronger together than they were apart.

'It's your turn now?' she teased as Dante joined her on the bed.

She reached for him. They reached for each other. Dante took them both to the edge, and over it.

They slept for what must have been hours. When she woke the light was filtering through the curtains. Could it really be Christmas morning? Tiptoeing across the room, she tweaked back the edge of the curtain.

'Hey,' Dante complained huskily as light poured into the room. 'Don't you ever need to rest?'

Bouncing back on to the bed, she threw her head back with sheer happiness. 'Says the man who keeps more plates spinning than anyone I know?

'Happy Christmas! The best Christmas ever!' Tossing her hair back, she laughed with sheer happiness at the dawning of this special new day.

'Ah,' Dante said, sitting up. 'Thanks for reminding me—'

'You needed reminding? You are a lost cause.'

'Not quite,' he assured her. 'Let me grab a robe.'

'Wow. This sounds serious,' she said as Dante rolled out of bed. Her spirits took a dive when he didn't answer. 'While you do that, I'm going to take a quick shower.'

Freshen up, think, organise her brain cells. Last night had been spectacular, but now it was another day. And she was determined to remain optimistic.

One of the advantages of Dante taking the entire top floor of the pub was that they didn't have to share a bathroom, so she luxuriated for quite a while before dressing and returning to the bedroom to find Dante seated at the desk. He'd showered too, and was dressed in jeans and a form-fitting top—a pairing that pointed up his spectacular physique. She didn't have long to dwell on that. There were some documents on the desk that somehow made her nerves twang. And Dante was looking serious. This wasn't good.

'Why are you frowning?' he asked.

'Am I?'

He gave her one of his amused, forbearing looks. 'I'm not allowed to give you a Christmas present?' he queried.

'Depends what it is. And I feel terrible,' she added.

'Oh?'

'I don't have anything for you,' she explained.

'But I'm not expecting anything,' Dante told her with a shrug. 'You didn't know I was coming.'

'I could have sent a card.'

'Write one now,' he suggested with a casual jerk of his chin in the direction of the pub's info pack, which would almost certainly contain some of the striking postcards they sold at the bar.

'I wouldn't know what to say,' she admitted honestly.

'Really?' Dante barked a short laugh. 'You being short of words must be a first.'

She hummed while her heart raced. What was Dante hiding in that case?

'Well?' he prompted as she hovered by the door. 'Are you coming in properly, or are you going out again?'

She shut the door, but stayed where she was.

'Don't you want to know what your gift is?' he coaxed.

'A halter and a bag of pony nuts?' she ventured, unable to rip her gaze from the official-looking papers.

Dante pulled a mock-disappointed look. 'Is that your best guess?'

'It's my only guess.'

'How would you feel if I said that this document is my way of gifting you the farm?'

As Dante held out an official-looking envelope time stood still. Jess didn't speak or move a muscle, and was completely incapable of rational thought.

'Well?' he prompted.

She attempted to moisten her lips so she could reply, but her mouth had turned as dry as dust. 'I'd say you were teasing me,' she said at last. 'But it isn't a very funny joke.'

'I'm not joking, Jess,' Dante assured her with a long steady look. 'That's why I've come here. Well, partly, anyway. I guess I could have sent the contract, but I wanted to hand it to you in person.'

'Why?' she demanded faintly. 'Why have you done this?'

'Your father needed help. He asked me for help.'

She was confused. 'You mean more help after the sale of the ponies?'

'You must have known that buying his stock would only temporarily bail him out of trouble. He needed more. The bank needed more.'

'So what are you saying?' She shook her head as if none of this made sense.

'I'm saying I bought the farm, paid off your father's debts and cleared his overdraft at the bank. He's a wealthy man now, so he can breed and train ponies to his heart's content. That's what he's good at, Jess. It's what he should be allowed to do. Business isn't his thing. And you need a life too.'

She frowned. 'And you decided this?'

'It was the best way to help your father and help you too.'

'Help yourself, don't you mean?' she flared. 'My father owns the best pasture in Yorkshire, the best gallops, the best ponies—or he will once the new foals are born and brought on. Anyone would want to buy Bell Farm.'

'Then why haven't they?' Dante asked bluntly. Jess blanched as he went on, 'According to your father, there hasn't been a single offer. He explained that not everyone has the appetite to live up here and cope with the climate and unrelenting work involved.'

'So what will be his position?' she demanded. 'Lackey to you?'

'He will do the job that suits him best, leaving my professional team to handle the business side of things. It's time to face facts. Your father needs more help than you can give him. You can't go on like this, working on the farm, caring for your father, maintaining a practice—you're running yourself ragged. And you would still have the bank hounding you.'

'It's not up to you to decide how I handle this, or what I need,' she gritted out, filled with fury that any and all decisions had been made, irrespective of her opinion.

'So you don't want this?' Dante held out the document.

She waited for the red mist to clear before trusting herself to speak. What he said made a certain amount of sense. It was the way Dante was looking at her now that chilled her. So many people must have seen that same stare—in Dante's office, his boardroom or in his lawyer's office. It was a cool and decisive look that contained no emotion. Dante had struck a deal and that was that. Even half an hour ago she would have said it was impossible for him to treat her like this.

'It's a done deal,' he said as if to confirm her thoughts. 'It's what your father wanted, so there's no going back. You might as well accept—'

'I don't have to accept anything,' she interrupted. 'And I'm not prepared to say anything more to you until I've spoken to my father.'

'Be my guest,' Dante invited, glancing at the phone. 'I'll leave you to it,' he added, standing up. 'But I can assure you that your father is extremely happy with our deal. He sees it as a great way forward—for both of you.'

'So the two of you have decided my future without discussing it with me?'

'Your father didn't want to give you anything more to worry about. He wanted to present it to you as a *fait accompli*. It's his farm to sell, Jess. He thought you'd be pleased. His knowledge and experience is invaluable to me, and now he'll have a wider role as advisor to all my equine facilities.'

'I can't deal with this right now.' She held up her hands, palms flat. 'I can't believe you've done this. I trusted you.'

'I'm not the enemy here, Jess.'

How could she deny her father what would be the most wonderful opportunity? She couldn't. She loved him too much. Protecting him was her mother's last wish, and this was a chance beyond their wildest dreams. But there was one thing she could refuse. 'You can take that contract with you. I don't want the farm. I haven't earned it.'

'You don't want your family farm, free from debt and with money in the bank?' Dante asked, frowning.

'If you're such a philanthropist, why didn't you give the farm to my father?'

'Because this was what he wanted, what he asked for. And this is what I want to do for you.'

'Seriously?' Jess shook her head. 'How do you think that makes me feel? Will you call by each time you're in Yorkshire to accept payment in kind?'

'*Dios*, Jess! Is that how little you think of me?'

'I don't know what to think,' she admitted, grabbing her coat. 'I'll speak to my father face to face, and then I'll decide what to do.'

CHAPTER SIXTEEN

IT TOOK JESS a while to catch her breath as she rushed down the lane leading home. Dante's offer was too much to take in. *He* was too much. She should have known better than to give way to feelings that had been ten long years in the making. Dante wanted more than she could give.

Huge sums of money passed through his hands on a regular basis, but his offer of the farm was incredible to Jess. It didn't seem right. She had to hear directly from her father that it was his wish too. Maybe he'd been blinded by the fact that Dante's offer put him back on top and hadn't thought things through.

She would do anything not to spoil his chances, but pride alone would stop her accepting Dante's gift. In monetary terms, she accepted that it was probably equal to Jess shaking out a few coins from her piggy bank, but that didn't make it right.

What made Dante's offer sting the most was that all she wanted was him, but Dante hadn't put that on the table. That wasn't part of his deal.

Jess marched towards the farmhouse entrance before suddenly hesitating. It was Christmas morning. Was she really going to ruin it with a blazing row with her father? Was that really what she wanted after all they'd been through? Changing course, she headed for the stables, made for it like a homing pigeon flying back to its roost. She had some serious thinking to do.

Diplomacy had never been his strong point, but he would not allow things between him and Jess to end like this. Tugging on his jacket, he headed out. It was a straight road to the farm and the directions were imprinted on his memory. He guessed he'd find Jess in the stable with the animals, where their company would warm her better than any brazier.

As he had expected, he found her hunched up in the bleak grey light on a hay bale. 'Hey…'

'Dante!' Jess didn't appear to breathe, and then noisily dragged in a huge gulp of air. 'I told you I needed time to think. Don't do this. You stunned me. I need space.'

'I'm here to make sure you got home safely.'

'I do know the way.'

'It can still be dangerous in this weather.'

'You're concerned about me now?' she challenged with a sceptical sideways look.

'Always.'

'Then why drop the bombshell about the farm as you did? Why cut me out of the discussions in the first place?'

'I could have led up to telling you with more grace,' he conceded, 'but I was impatient for you to know. As for cutting you out? I did what your father asked, but keeping you in the dark didn't sit well with me—hence my impatience to make things right.'

'It's all a mix-up,' she flared with a shake of her head. 'The only thing not in doubt is that you're an impatient man. Leaving hospital too soon. Riding before you could walk.'

He conceded all these comments with a shrug—all except one. 'I'm not always impatient. Not when it comes to you.'

She blushed at the reminder.

'You must see me as overbearing,' he confirmed with a shrug.

'You think?' she fired back.

'This was something I had to do for you, Jess.'

'I haven't had chance to speak to my father yet,' she admitted in an attempt to close the conversation down.

'What are you waiting for?' he challenged.

'You are overbearing, and you should have run this past me,' she stated hotly, 'but I won't disturb my father when he might have a second shot at happiness.'

'He's not here?'

'He's with Ella.'

He let that hang for a while and then remarked, 'It's good he's finally got his life back.'

'Meaning I haven't?' Jess suggested with an accusing look.

'You can do anything you choose to,' he said evenly. 'In the words of the cliché, the world is your oyster.'

'You mean, if I sell the farm back to you?'

'That's a novel idea.'

'I'm full of them.'

'I'd prefer you to keep the farm as your security going forward,' he said honestly. 'You don't have to live here. You can live anywhere you like.'

'Your people will move in to help out,' she intuited.

'If you want them to—they're waiting for your instructions.'

'You've thought of everything, haven't you, Dante?'

He remained silent.

Averting her face, Jess chewed her thumb before turning back to face him. 'This is all about trust,' she said.

'Without it we're going nowhere,' he agreed.

'*We?*' she queried.

There was a long silence, and then she said, 'Isn't time supposed to heal all wounds?'

'Some cut deeper than others and leave scars we have to deal with, but they do get better over time.'

She looked at him as if she wanted to believe him. 'I didn't mean to make this about me. I just wish I had my mother to confide in sometimes.'

'I understand that. It's as if we've both been set adrift. I was without an anchor for years until I got my head together and knew we must pull together as a family. You've changed and grown too,' he reminded Jess. 'You completed your training, as you promised your mother you would, and now you're an excellent physiotherapist. Here's the living proof,' he added with a flourish as he spread his hands wide.

'No cane,' Jess agreed with the glimmer of a smile. 'Your return to polo's been well documented, though playing like the devil on horseback so soon after your recovery is asking for trouble.'

He seized on her cue. 'That's why I need you. See what happens when you leave me to my own devices?'

'As I remember it, my contract ended and you appointed someone else in my place.'

'To take over your good work,' he pointed out.

'Yet now you risk that good work by launching yourself like an avenging angel on Nero Caracas and his team.'

'The important thing is, my team won.'

'Of course it did,' Jess agreed with the lift of a brow. 'And by some miracle you survived.'

'No miracle,' he argued. 'My recovery is thanks to extremely effective therapy from a certain Señorita Slate-home.' He didn't want to talk about that. He wanted to talk about Jess. She was all that mattered. He wanted her to trust him and relax in his company. He'd handled things badly when he told her about the farm, but his remorse was genuine and he wanted her to have security in the future, whatever choice she made next.

'Just don't take too many chances in the future,' she warned.

He shrugged. 'See what happens when you cut me loose? There's only one way to sort this. The next time I play polo you'd better be there.'

'What are you saying, Dante?'

'I'm admitting I need you,' he confessed.

'As a therapist?'

'What do you think?'

'I think it makes sense from that point of view to keep me on speed dial.'

'Speed dial?' His lips pressed down as he considered this for all of a split second. 'I'm not sure that would suit either of us.'

Even in the dim light he saw her blush at this reminder of their inexhaustible appetite for each other.

'Will you be heading home now?' she asked on the way to recovering her composure.

'Not until I know you've spoken to your father, and I feel confident you're reassured about what's happening with the farm.'

Then he would leave, with or without Jess. If he'd been in doubt about the nature of love, he understood now that it sometimes involved sacrifice, and if staying here was what Jess wanted he had no option but to let her go. He had been overbearing with his purchase of her family's farm and in trying to help her father he'd only succeeded in railroading Jess. She couldn't fight him. The sale was a done deal, and she wouldn't do anything to upset her father's future.

'Dante—'

'Yes?' He hardly knew what to expect. Jess's face was tight with tension.

'I can't let you go without telling you I love you.'

Her eyes snapped shut after this statement. She didn't move. She didn't breathe and then, with a ragged exhalation of air, she opened her eyes and zoned in on his. 'I love you,' she repeated with fiery emphasis.

His entire body thrilled. Jess's words were a statement, a challenge, a baring of her soul that rang in his head like a carillon of happy Christmas bells.

'I'm not going anywhere.' Closing the distance between them in a couple of strides, he lifted Jess into his arms. Sacrifice was one thing, but he was the kind of man who always had to fight tooth and nail for what he believed in. He should have known that all along.

Urgency consumed them both. Jess met him with matching fire. She was already reaching for him. They didn't trouble to undress completely. Just enough to fall back on the hay and mate like wild animals. It was a wordless, mindless coupling that said everything about how far they'd come, and how deep was their trust.

'It feels as if we've come full circle,' Jess murmured as they put their clothes back in order.

'This is where we first met,' he agreed with a grin. 'And things get more interesting each time.'

'There's a new litter of kittens,' she warned, 'so watch out.'

She smiled. So did he, and as they stared into each other's eyes he knew the situation could be rescued, but lovemaking wasn't enough. He had to prove to Jess that when it came to business he might be brusque, brisk and to the point, but he hadn't meant to hurt her over the farm, as he so obviously had.

Stable cats and dogs stood by, ready to assist him. Jess's motley assortment of strays and beloved pets had sensed they were needed and had gathered around them to provide a welcome distraction. Neither Jess nor he could remain immune to them for long, or remain tense, not with animals around.

When she'd fed them some treats Jess held up her grimy

fingernails and grimaced. 'I'll never make it in your world. I'm just too down-homey and—'

'Chilled out?' he suggested. 'Don't you think that's what I need?'

'Just as well,' she commented, grimacing as she took in the damage to her sweater from a new naughty kitten.

'I still love you,' he said as she pulled a face.

Her gaze flashed up to his. 'Please don't say that unless you mean it.'

'I love you,' he said again, his eye-line steady on Jess's.

'Don't make this any harder than it has to be,' she said firmly. 'especially when I know you're about to leave.'

He shrugged. 'What's so hard about leaving with me? Or are you more concerned about dealing with the damage from a leaking kitten?'

'Don't make a joke of this,' she said softly.

'Because…?'

'Because I love you too much for that.'

'Then be with me always.'

'Always? As in for ever?' she exclaimed, incredulous. 'As your therapist?'

'As my wife. I can't think of anyone else who'd have you,' he teased with a pointed look at the stain on Jess's sweater. 'Let me love you as you deserve. Let me spoil you. Let me lavish things on you.'

'You should know by now that's not me. I don't need any of those things.'

'But you'll grow to love being spoiled, I promise,' he insisted.

'I love *you*,' she stated firmly, 'not what you can give me.'

'As I love you,' he said, 'but you must allow me to have the pleasure of giving you things. Love, and gifts like the farm are not mutually exclusive, so get used to it because there's a lot more coming your way. The farm is just the beginning.'

'But I haven't given you my answer yet,' she pointed out.

'I'm not a patient man,' he warned.

'So I shouldn't push you too hard?' she suggested.

'Unless it's in bed.'

'Do you take anything seriously?' she scolded.

'I'm extremely serious when I take you.' And when she shook her head, he added, 'I love you for everything you are, and everything you will be in the future. So what's your answer?'

Jess gasped as he dragged her close. 'My answer's yes. I'll come with you wherever you go.'

'You can depend on it,' he promised.

A few potent seconds ticked by while they laughed and took in the trust that was the bedrock of their decision to be together for ever, but then, as might have been expected, their control snapped at exactly the same moment and as Jess reached for him he drove his mouth down on hers.

It was a long time later when Jess fell back, exhausted. They could never get enough of each other and had made love fiercely, tenderly and, last of all, and most affecting of all, they had made love slowly and deliberately, with love and trust in their eyes, while Dante told Jess she was the only woman he could ever love and that he would be proud to have her at his side for the rest of his life.

'There's so much we don't know about each other,' she whispered, frowning as she turned languidly in his arms.

'Great,' Dante approved. 'So much to learn about each other. New surprises each day.'

She had to be certain. 'Are you sure I'm enough for you? I'm not fancy. I live a plain life in plain clothes, surrounded by plain-speaking people.'

'Enough for me?' he exclaimed softly. 'You're perfect for me. And to prove I'm serious I've got something for you.'

'Nothing expensive, I hope?' Laughter pealed out of her as Dante produced a wisp of hay.

'Jessica Slatehome, sometimes known as Skylar... I'm prepared to be adaptable when it comes to you, so I'm asking again, formally this time, will you marry me?'

'You know my answer, but I'll happily give it again *formally*,' she teased, knowing her face must betray her feelings. 'My answer's yes.'

'Now, I've just got to get this to stay on,' Dante said, frowning as he secured the hay ring around her marriage finger with a few well-judged twists.

Jess stared at her hay ring. She loved it as much as any diamond a fashionable jeweller.

'This is just a start,' Dante insisted, 'We can't change who we are, and it would be wrong to try and change each other.'

'But how will I fit in to your glamorous life?'

'You'll fit in perfectly. We fit together perfectly,' he added, though as he'd moved over her to prove his point, Jess kept her opinion to herself. Providing therapy for injured athletes was her life's work. Riding the horses she loved was her passion. That was the world where she belonged.

Was it? Was it really?

How could she live without Dante? How would she feel if she saw him with other women, knowing she hadn't even put up a fight for the best thing in her life? Were her dreams dust? Was it even possible to hold on to her familiar world while sharing his? 'You're at the top of your field in the tech world, and on the polo circuit,' she mused when they were quiet again. 'And although I could happily fit into your equine world, I belong backstage, not out front with the beautiful people.'

'Is that a fact?' Dante queried with a long sideways look as he set about repeating what he did so very well.

'In my opinion,' he added much much later, 'you outshine anyone I've ever met. When men on the polo circuit are as dazzled by your beauty as I am I'll have to flatten them. Is that good enough for you? There's no question of you being backstage. You'll be at my side and for ever, I hope.'

'Dante—'

'What?'

She gave a long sigh of pleasure.

'I hear you,' he reassured as he brushed her mouth with lingering kisses. 'You don't want to talk now. You want this, you need this, so please don't ever stop?'

'For ever is a long time,' she reminded him in between hectic gasps of breath.

Dante shrugged as he moved firmly towards the inevitable conclusion. 'That's one thing over which we'll have to agree to disagree. For ever with you can never be long enough for me. Merry Christmas, Jess.'

CHAPTER SEVENTEEN

MORE THAN A week later, when Jess had spent quality time with her father and Dante had spent earthy, intimate, getting to know her every which-way time with Jess, they boarded his private jet to return to Spain. He was happy to think Jess was doubly reassured—not just by the news that the arrangement for the farm suited her father, but by something even better than that.

'It's never too late to fall in love,' Jim Slatehome had explained to both of them, saying he'd been struck by lightning when he had the opportunity to get to know his neighbour Ella again.

Confident that her father was not only financially secure but was happy and well looked after, Jess was ready to embark on her new life. Everyone, including the animals, was on tenterhooks at the thought of her return to what Maria described as Jess's home.

Dante owned numerous properties across the world. Jess could take her pick. He imagined she might choose his simple shack on a Pacific island, judging by the way she'd held on to the wisp of hay he'd tied around her wedding finger.

That was Jess. That was the Jess he loved. The woman who had insisted she needed no other ring. He'd taken her at her word. For now.

It had taken him a short time or a little over ten years, depending on how he looked at it, to win Jess's trust and now she could have whatever she wanted. Nothing could corrupt her moral compass and, with their lives ahead of them, she'd have plenty of opportunity to counter his riches with hay bales and sound common sense. They were like two pieces of a jigsaw that fitted together perfectly and he could never repay her for what she'd given him.

They'd slept at the pub each night after Christmas, and each night before she slept he told Jess how much he loved her, and how much he owed her, not just for healing him but for teaching him how to trust, and to give his heart deeply and completely. Those quiet times alone had allowed him to reassure her that she would never have to give up her career. His proposal was that Jess headed up a travelling clinic, so they could be together wherever he played polo. She had instantly approved the idea and was excited to make a start. He was confident she'd soon build up a regular practice, especially with him around as visible proof of Jess's excellence as a therapist.

She was playing with the hay wisp, he noticed, turning it round and round her finger. 'I can't believe you managed to hold on to that,' he admitted. 'You can have a ring of your choice as soon as we land in Spain. You can design your own, if you like.'

She gave him a teasing smile. 'It would have to look exactly like this one.'

'I'm sure that can be arranged.'

She remained silent for a while and then she said, 'Could we have a Christmas wedding?'

'You can have a wedding whenever and wherever you like. We don't have to get married at all.'

'Is that your get-out?' she half scolded, half teased him. 'Are you tired of me already?'

'I will never tire of you.' His heart had found its home and wanted no other.

'Then next Christmas it is,' she declared happily, clearly

brim-full of excitement. 'There's something special about the holiday season, don't you think?'

'It won't be snowing in Spain,' he cautioned.

'Not where you live,' she agreed.

He thought of his ski chalet, high in the Sierra Nevada, and conceded, 'Snow can be arranged.'

Jess laughed. 'Is there anything you can't do?'

He huffed a sigh as he thought about this for the time it took to kiss her neck and then her lips. 'Resist you?' he suggested. 'But remember, if you're set on this idea of a Christmas wedding, there's almost a year to wait.'

'For the veil and the dress,' she pointed out.

He laughed as he got the picture. 'You are a shameless hussy.'

'You made me so.'

'I plead innocent,' he fired back with amusement. 'It must have been Skylar who led me astray.'

'Can she do so again?' Jess suggested as the aircraft levelled off.

'There are several bedrooms in the back—take your pick.'

'Lead the way,' she whispered.

A little less than one year later

Christmas Day was approaching fast. Since moving to Spain to live on Dante's *estancia*, Jess had travelled the world. Watching Dante play polo and dispensing necessary therapy, both to his polo-playing associates and to Dante under rather more intimate circumstances, had given her a new insight into the lives of the super-rich.

They had the same worries and the same ailments as everyone else, but some were so remote and removed from the realities of everyday life she felt sorry for them. Rather than envy their so-called gilded existence, she thought of them, locked in their ivory towers with their sights set on some far-off horizon, missing the little things down on the ground that, in Jess's opinion, made life worth living.

Dante's sister Sofia was a glaring exception. They thought alike, and Sofia had become Jess closest friend. Sofia had persuaded Jess that she could navigate the role of star player's wife, and billionaire's soulmate, with the same grace with which Jess handled her job at the mobile clinic. 'You love him. That's all that matters,' Sofia had pointed out. 'And my brother adores you. I love you because you brought him back to us. I've never seen Dante like this before. He wants to be with his family. He wants to share us with you. You've healed him in more ways than one.'

Both Jess and Sofia were excited that Maria and her relatives had agreed to play a major role in Jess's wedding ceremony, providing music and dance. Jess wanted a real party and for everyone to join in. As Dante had promised, their marriage would be celebrated high on the Sierra Nevada mountain range, where snow and fiery passion went hand in hand.

Sofia's wedding gift for Jess couldn't have pleased her more. It was a new horse blanket for Moon. The mare had fretted for Jess, Dante had explained, and so the pony she'd loved since the day Moon was born was his wedding gift to Jess.

Sofia had insisted on giving Jess a few more small presents—or 'thingamajigs' as Sofia liked to call them.

'I want to spoil you with bits of nonsense,' she'd said.

'Not nonsense,' Jess had protested as she opened the boxes of accessories—hairbands, bracelets that jingled and Spanish mantilla combs with filmy, lacy veils. 'These are lovely, thoughtful gifts.'

She only wished Sofia could find the same happiness she had.

'Here comes the groom. He's going to be late,' Sofia announced tensely.

Looking out of the window, Jess saw Dante and his brothers skiing up to the door of his magnificent chalet. Her heart sang at the sight of Dante, as skilful on snow as he was on Zeus, his mighty black stallion. He had to do something first thing in the morning, Dante had told her last night, or he wouldn't be capable of staying away from his bride before their wedding.

The year leading up to this moment had been packed full of polo and patients and horses and Dante, which was pretty much everything Jess could ask of life. Dante hadn't forced the issue when he asked her to marry him and, predictably, that had made her want him all the more. The ring she would wear when they were married remained the only bone of contention between them.

'A plain gold band will do me,' she'd insisted, while Dante had countered by assuring her that the first time they made love as man and wife Jess would be wearing nothing but diamonds.

'The first time?' Jess had queried with amusement.

'The first time as husband and wife,' Dante had countered before taking her in the most delicious way.

Would she ever get enough of him? Not a chance, Jess concluded as she watched him shoulder his skis. There was a sense of purpose and a particular speed to his actions she recognised. Dante wouldn't be late for his wedding, because he was already thinking about taking her to bed.

'Jess? Your gown,' Sofia prompted.

Jess turned to see the sparkling lace and chiffon dream of a dress Dante had insisted must come from Paris. It was a restrained and beautiful creation, a fairy tale dress, as Sofia described it, and one that made dreams come true.

Arranging the gown reverently on the bed, Sofia stood

back. 'I can't wait to have you as a sister,' she admitted, glowing with pent-up excitement.

'I'm already your sister,' Jess insisted as they exchanged the warmest of hugs. 'Skylar too?' Sofia teased as they broke apart.

'Of course. We can't leave her out, can we?'

'And now this dream of a dress,' Sofia said as she lifted it carefully from the bed.

Jess had dreamed of this moment since that first encounter with Dante in her father's stable ten years ago and now, quite incredibly, those dreams were about to come true.

'Not incredible,' Sofia argued when Jess voiced these thoughts. 'My brother is lucky to have found you. A woman less likely to be cast about by the winds of fate, I have yet to meet. You are a strong, determined woman who will bloom wherever you're planted, and I'm proud to be your friend.'

Jess was so popular on the *estancia* everyone had made a special effort to travel to the mountains to attend her wedding ceremony, which was as relaxed and authentic as Jess had always dreamed it would be. to make things easier for their guests, Dante had laid on two of his aircraft to bring them in from far and wide. Sofia had dipped into her billions too, to ensure the most magical scene.

A huge pavilion had been erected in the deep snow in the garden of Dante's chalet overlooking the dramatic mountain range. Fairy lights were strung lavishly around, while a pathway of pink rose petals, edged by sweet-smelling country flowers flown in from Yorkshire, filled the air with delicate scent. The ambient temperature inside the pavilion was cosy, thanks to heaters hidden in the roof, and the guests agreed they had never been more comfortable at a wedding than they were on the deeply upholstered white seats. Haunting music from a single acoustic guitar set the romantic mood, while candles glowed on the altar and jewel-coloured lanterns cast a magical glow across the excited congregation.

Peeping through the entrance, Jess saw her father seated with Ella on the front row. They looked so happy together and, never one to miss a business trick, her father had flown in from England on one of Dante's specially adapted jets accompanied by not just his lively and down-to-earth partner but by several promising ponies as well.

There was a Christmas tree in the entrance covered with small gifts for their guests. Dante had told Jess that her gift was the small brown paper-covered box at the top of the tree and that she must claim it and open it before she came down the aisle.

One of the taller attendants got it down for her, and when she opened it she gasped. It was a perfect replica of Jess's hay twist ring, but crafted in pure rose gold.

Her wedding ring was perfect and so was the groom, Jess thought when Dante turned at the moment she appeared and their eyes met.

Every seat was taken by Dante's family and staff, and by a select number of guests. Maria had settled into the chalet weeks ago to prepare food and the mix of delicious cooking smells had stayed with him, making him hungry, and hungry for Jess. *Dios*, where was she? When could they get away from here?

At last!

His heart filled with love as he caught sight of his bride, who looked beyond ravishingly beautiful as she walked up the petal-strewn aisle.

'Thank you for my ring,' Jess whispered when she reached his side. 'It's absolutely perfect. I have something for you...'

'What?' he demanded as Jess turned to hand over her bouquet to Sofia, thinking of all the small, thoughtful gifts

Jess had bought him in the lead up to the wedding. Her answer was to take hold of his hand and rest it gently against her stomach. A lightning bolt of excitement struck him as Jess stared up with eyes full of trust.

'You…?' He was stunned into silence, and not just because the celebrant had indicated that the ceremony was about to begin.

'Yes,' Jess confirmed. 'We're having a baby. We're going to be adding to the Acosta clan soon.'

'Oh, *Dios*!' he exclaimed on a hectic rush of breath. 'Thank you! Thank you!'

'You may *not* yet kiss your bride,' the priest scolded them with a twinkle in his eyes.

But Dante Acosta had always broken the rules, as had Skylar, so they kissed passionately and everyone applauded until at last, with love surrounding them on every side, Jess and Dante were married.

* * * * *

MILLS & BOON

Coming next month

CLAIMING HIS BOLLYWOOD CINDERELLA
Tara Pammi

The scent of her hit him first. A subtle blend of jasmine and her that he'd remember for the rest of his life. And equate with honesty and irreverence and passion and laughter. There was a joy about this woman, despite her insecurities and vulnerabilities, that he found almost magical.

The mask she wore was black satin with elaborate gold threading at the edges and was woven tightly into her hair, leaving just enough of her beautiful dark brown eyes visible. The bridge of her small nose was revealed as was the slice of her cheekbones. For a few seconds, Vikram had the overwhelming urge to tear it off. He wanted to see her face. Not because he wanted to find out her identity.

He wanted to see her face because he wanted to know this woman. He wanted to know everything about her. He wanted… With a rueful shake of his head, he pushed away the urge. It was more than clear that men had only ever disappointed her. He was damned if he was going to be counted as one of them. He wanted to be different in her memory.

When she remembered him after tonight, he wanted her to smile. He wanted her to crave more of him. Just as he would crave more of her. He knew this before their lips even touched. And he would find a way to discover her identity. He was just as sure of that too.

Her mouth was completely uncovered. Her lipstick was

mostly gone leaving a faint pink smudge that he wanted to lick away with his tongue.

She held the edge of her silk dress with one hand and as she'd lifted it to move, he got a flash of a thigh. Soft and smooth and silky. It was like receiving a jolt of electricity, with every inch he discovered of this woman. The dress swooped low in the front, baring the upper curves of her breasts in a tantalizing display.

And then there she was, within touching distance. Sitting with her legs folded beneath her, looking straight into his eyes. One arm held the sofa while the other smoothed repeatedly over the slight curve of her belly. She was nervous and he found it both endearing and incredibly arousing. She wanted to please herself. And him. And he'd never wanted more for a woman to discover pleasure with him.

Her warm breath hit him somewhere between his mouth and jaw in silky strokes that resonated with his heartbeat. This close, he could see the tiny scar on the other corner of her mouth.

"Are you going to do anything?" she asked after a couple of seconds, sounding completely put out.

He wanted to laugh and tug that pouty lower lip with his teeth. Instead he forced himself to take a breath. He was never going to smell jasmine and not think of her ever again. "It's your kiss, darling. You take it."

Continue reading
CLAIMING HIS BOLLYWOOD CINDERELLA
Tara Pammi

Available next month
www.millsandboon.co.uk

COMING SOON!

We really hope you enjoyed reading this book.
If you're looking for more romance, be sure to
head to the shops when new books are
available on

Thursday 15th October

To see which titles are coming soon, please visit

millsandboon.co.uk/nextmonth

LET'S TALK
Romance

For exclusive extracts, competitions
and special offers, find us online:

 facebook.com/millsandboon

@MillsandBoon

@MillsandBoonUK

Get in touch on 01413 063232

For all the latest titles coming soon, visit
millsandboon.co.uk/nextmonth

MILLS & BOON

THE HEART OF ROMANCE

A ROMANCE FOR EVERY KIND OF READER

MODERN

Prepare to be swept off your feet by sophisticated, sexy and seductive heroes, in some of the world's most glamourous and romantic locations, where power and passion collide.
8 stories per month.

HISTORICAL

Escape with historical heroes from time gone by. Whether your passion is for wicked Regency Rakes, muscled Vikings or rugged Highlanders, awaken the romance of the past.
6 stories per month.

MEDICAL

Set your pulse racing with dedicated, delectable doctors in the high-pressure world of medicine, where emotions run high and passion, comfort and love are the best medicine.
6 stories per month.

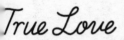

Celebrate true love with tender stories of heartfelt romance, from the rush of falling in love to the joy a new baby can bring, and a focus on the emotional heart of a relationship.
8 stories per month.

Indulge in secrets and scandal, intense drama and plenty of sizzling hot action with powerful and passionate heroes who have it all: wealth, status, good looks…everything but the right woman.
6 stories per month.

HEROES

Experience all the excitement of a gripping thriller, with an intense romance at its heart. Resourceful, true-to-life women and strong, fearless men face danger and desire - a killer combination!
8 stories per month.

Sensual love stories featuring smart, sassy heroines you'd want as a best friend, and compelling intense heroes who are worthy of them.
4 stories per month.

To see which titles are coming soon, please visit

millsandboon.co.uk/nextmonth

JOIN US ON SOCIAL MEDIA!

Stay up to date with our latest releases, author news and gossip, special offers and discounts, and all the behind-the-scenes action from Mills & Boon...

 millsandboon

 millsandboonuk

 millsandboon

It might just be true love...

MILLS & BOON

HEROES

At Your Service

Experience all the excitement of a gripping thriller, with an intense romance at its heart. Resourceful, true-to-life women and strong, fearless men face danger and desire - a killer combination!

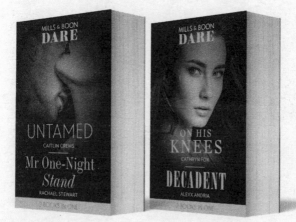